PRAISE FOR FAR ON THE RINGING PLAINS

Two guys writing, seamlessly blending the lives of three guys in WW 2 at Guadalcanal. Real people all—gritty and honest. Real life—not glossed over, not ignoring weakness and uncertainties. Real questions—the kind we all ask, whether we're in war, in school, on the job or in the family. Real faith—expressed in that real world amidst the questions. Real change—these three warriors develop during the book, sometimes in surprising ways.

Men will love this, they can visualize the descriptions, can see themselves there, and can identify with the three-dimensional characters. And the quality of the story and the writing will grab them up to the last page. Five out of five stars.

Whether military vets or not, whether male or female, all readers will appreciate how two writers seamlessly open up the lives of three WW 2 soldiers on Guadalcanal. Real, gritty, more questions than easy answers.

— TIM RITER, AUTHOR OF GOD, A
MOTORCYCLE, AND THE OPEN ROAD AND
NOT A SAFE GOD.

This is a book about war, about three Mennonite boys (for they truly were boys) who, for different reasons felt the need to join the Marines during WWII and quickly become men as they struggle through boot camp and head into battle. This is not a love story. "War isn't supposed to be a love story." (Billy Martens). This story is well written. It was hard to put down. The characters are real and believable. I can't believe I am saying this, but I am eager to read the next book in this series.

— MARIA WEEKS

"Far on the Ringing Plains," is an excellent coming of age tale that reads fast—a real action thriller set in World War II in the Pacific Ocean during the bloody island hopping campaign. Authors Pura and Craig have fashioned settings that continuously form and shape the main characters from boys into men. The constant action, battle and danger build the characters from their first day on Guadalcanal.

The challenges life and war throw at these young US Marines propel them towards their unknowable wartime fates. How they confront that fate and who they become when they do gives us a very accessible novel full of reader surprises.

— SPEC4 REB BLAKE II FIRE CRASH RESCUE
1ST INFANTRY DIV PHI LOI ARMY AIR BASE
REPUBLIC OF SOUTH VIETNAM 1967—1968

Five Stars out of 5 stars—If you like history, learning about WW II and really getting to know what happened during the war time, this is a great book to read. It has action, love for the fellow men who served our country and what they had to miss in their lives. And also the voice of a mother and of God during battle... even my husband enjoyed this book..

When I read it I felt like I was the one in the foxhole, while the snipers were shooting. Craig and Pura did a great job making it so real...

— BARB BEECHY

Captivating, each chapter reaches deeper into the WWII military experience of three very different young Mennonite men. Truly an excellent reading experience by authors who have completed their research in history and life in WWII military.

— CONNIE SPRADLING LYNCH

"Far on the Ringing Plains" is a historical fiction. It tells the compelling story of three young men of Mennonite faith as they grow from their neighborhoods into U.S. Marines fighting on far off Islands in the Pacific theater. It is accurately told in its detail of the time period and point of view of its characters.

— WILLARD CARPENTER SSG U.S. ARMY STAFF
SERGEANT RET.

The first book in The Islands Series will keep you gripping your seat. Fast-paced and gritty, this well scripted book puts you right in the characters' minds and hearts as they grapple with what it means to be a warrior and a Mennonite Christian. It kept me interested through the entire, often violent and bloody tale. By the end, I cared so much about Billy, Bud, and Johnny, that I keep wondering how after the hell these men endured, they could return stateside to apple pie and Pepsi Cola? Would love to read that story, too! Kudos to Patrick E. Craig and Murray Pura for a stellar, gutsy tale.

— JEANNE DICKSON

FAR ON THE RINGING PLAINS

MURRAY PURA

PATRICK E. CRAIG

To the Veterans of WW II, the Greatest Generation.

ISLANDS

A series by Murray A. Pura & Patrick E. Craig

Three friends, three years, six islands and a war that demanded from all three the ultimate in faith, courage, honor & sacrifice.

THE ISLAND SERIES

Book 1: Far On The Ringing Plains
—Guadalcanal—

CONTENTS

PREAMBLE: THE CORPSMAN

GUADALCANAL 1942

When I first saw the Islands, it was August 7, 1942, at 0400 hours...

The sky was still dark, but from the deck of the ship I could see the dark mass of the mountains of Guadalcanal standing in sharp relief against the lighter sky. As the first glow of a golden dawn touched the mountaintops and flowed down their jagged sides, I thought this place must be heaven. Palm trees waved their fronds in the soft breeze. Off the bow, a school of dolphins cast luminescent rainbows into the air as they played in the blue Solomon Sea.

But then I remembered—waiting for us in that beautiful jungle, just over there, was the enemy. An enemy as determined to kill us, as we were to kill them. And it occurred to me that perhaps we should be the most careful in the beautiful places of this world. For in these places we often let down our guard. The beauty surrounds us and numbs us to danger. We don't pay attention, and that could kill us.

I am preparing to go ashore with the boys of the U.S. Marines 2nd Division. We have trained and practiced; we are in shape and tough. But that's only on the outside. Inside we are still boys. We shout and strut in front of our leaders, but we do not know how we will behave when hell comes looking for us.

War is the great separator. It separates heroes from cowards, the noble from ignoble, men from boys. There is no second chance and no going back. War is the great decider, the last chance café, the non-refundable offer. Beside me are my friends and on that soon-invaded shore, the enemy. I pray that the story we write here will be one of men who discover the greatest that lives within them, and the God that is all around them.

Corpsman

1

THE DOGS OF WAR—DECEMBER 1941

JOHNNY STRANGE

Johnny Strange put the paper down in front of his father. The headlines screamed at the old man.

1500 Dead in Hawaii—Congress Votes War.

Peter Strange pushed the paper aside and continued eating his oatmeal. "What does that have to do with me, Johnny?"

"What does that have to do with you? The country that gives you the freedom to be a pacifist is in a war. Thousands, maybe millions of young men will die to protect your right to sit here and ask, 'What has that to do with me.' Are you blind? Can't you see what's going on?"

"This war is the fruit of godless men who do not obey the teachings of Jesus Christ. I cannot help them have right thinking. I can only live my life as I believe I must live it and do what I must do."

Johnny picked up the paper and folded it. "And just what will you do?"

"Nothing."

"Nothing? That's what I thought, Dad. Doing nothing is how you live your life. Even if it comes to the well-being of your own children."

Peter scowled at his son. "Let's not bring that up again. You're like a broken record. Harold Jenkins paid his penalty and repented. We could do nothing more than welcome him back to fellowship."

"Right, welcome him back. Meanwhile I live every day and every night with the reality of what that jerk did." He put his face down close to Peter's. "Jenkins messed me up, he hurt me." Johnny's voice took on an edge. "He tried to rape me and you did nothing. He's a lowlife scumbag."

"You will not talk that way about an elder of the church."

"Elder? The man is a sicko who does it with young boys. He lied to you. He's still doing the same thing—he's just being sneakier about it. He should be in jail—on death row."

"Do not accuse if you have no proof."

"Proof? I have proof. Ask Kenny, ask Bob, they'll tell you. He went after them, too."

"Harold swears that he has repented of the devil's work in his life and is righteous before God."

"Hogwash, Dad, pure hogwash. The man is a snake."

"It's your word against his."

Johnny Strange looked at his father's face, set in that hard, unyielding look he knew so well.

"So you would believe Jenkins over your own son, just because he's an elder in your stinking church? You would sit and do nothing, again! You make me sick!"

Peter Strange's mouth opened in surprise and a rebuke started on his lips, but Johnny slammed the paper down on the table.

"Don't say a word, Dad," he shouted. "Just shut your mouth. I'm eighteen and I'm done with you and this town and your BS bunch of hypocrites that call themselves Christians." Johnny grabbed up the paper and pointed at the headline. "You and the rest of the church can stay here and let that pervert loose in your flock, but not me." He leaned over his father and put his finger in Peter's face. "You won't do anything about him, but I will, Dad."

Peter Strange looked up at his son and his face was pale. "What are you going to do?"

"I'm joining the Marines. I'm going away to war. My bag is packed and I'm outta here. Tomorrow I'm getting on the bus down to the Recruiting Station in Idaho Falls and signing up. And you know what, Dad? I want them to teach me to kill. I want them to make me love it. And when they finish with me, I hope they send me to the worst battles where there are thousands of Japs because when I get there, I will shoot and stab and blow up every Jap I see. And when I've killed enough, and cut enough and blown enough Japs up and I'm hard inside, and unfeeling, I will come back to Bonners Ferry and find Harold Jenkins and beat him and cut him and stab him until he's just a rotting piece of meat. So help me, God."

THE 1939 CHRIS-CRAFT CUSTOM CRUISER ROARED ACROSS LAKE Pend Oreille. Johnny Strange was pushing it as hard as it would go. The rebuilt Ford Flathead V8 was thundering, driving the wooden racer headlong. The bow crashed through the waves and the spray blew up and then back into Johnny's face, washing the thoughts from his mind, cleansing the memory of the groping hands, the leering face.

Everyone on the lake knew Johnny was a pounder. When boaters saw him coming, they tried to get out of his way. One old guy in a Boston Whaler yelled at him and shook a fist as Johnny roared by, nearly swamping him, but Johnny was away and gone long before the man's outraged screech could catch up to him.

Most days Johnny ran the boat up and down the lake until he was exhausted, but somehow that never flushed out the demons

in his head. Today was different. He felt empty, purified somehow. Maybe it was because for once in his life Johnny Strange
had gotten his father's attention. He laughed out loud.

"The look on his face..."

Johnny made a sweeping turn as he pointed the boat back
toward the far side of the lake. In ten minutes he was nosing into
a quiet cove. At the end of the quiet inlet he could see the King
cabin and the boathouse where Gerald King let him dock the
cruiser. The Chris-Craft purred as he slid into the darkness and
brought the boat up against the bumpers. There was nobody
around, so he climbed out on the dock and walked past the King's
boats and up the stairs toward his Chevy. As he came around the
corner of the house, he saw someone standing at the front door. It
was a girl, a very nice-looking girl. She had corn silk hair that
peeked out from underneath a ski cap, framing an oval face, full
lips and startling green eyes. The winter coat and long pants did
little to conceal her shape. She looked up, startled.

"Oh! Hi... I was waiting for the Kings. I..." She stopped in
confusion, uncertainty on her face.

Johnny smiled. "Don't be afraid. I'm Johnny Strange. Gerald
lets me dock my boat here. Friend of the family and all that."

A tiny look of relief passed over her face. "Oh, Johnny
Strange. Yes, Gerald told me about you."

"I hope he said good things."

"He said you're his best friend and you're a nice guy, but sometimes you drive your boat too fast. Oh, I..." The girl's face
turned red.

"Telling secrets out of school, Miss..."

"Marjean. I'm Marjean Langston."

"Dr. Langston's daughter?"

"Yes, that Marjean."

"I thought you lived back east?"

The girl paled. "I lived in Rhode Island with my mom..."—a

little quiver in her voice— "...but she died, and I came to live with Dad."

"I'm sorry, I didn't mean to pry. Say would you like to go for a ride in my boat? She's a beauty."

"What about the Kings?"

"What time is it?"

The girl looked at the watch on her wrist. It was expensive looking and set with diamonds. "It's two o'clock."

She looked up and smiled, and Johnny Strange realized that Marjean Langston was the most beautiful girl he had ever seen. It flustered him.

"The Kings rarely get here until around three on Friday. They drive over from Sandpoint after Gerald's dad gets off work." He pointed toward the dock. "We still have time for a little cruise."

She hesitated. The sunlight through the pines speckled her face, and for a moment she reminded him of a fawn, poised for flight. He wondered if he frightened her. Then she smiled again, and the thought passed.

"Yes, I'd like to."

There was an expensive-looking roadster parked in the driveway.

"You should put your things in your car, especially the watch."

"Am I dressed warm enough?"

"You won't freeze to death."

"Will we be going fast?"

"As fast as you want."

MARJEAN LANGSTON SAT NEXT TO JOHNNY AS THE BOAT RIPPED through the water. He looked over at her. There was a look on her face he had never seen on a girl. She looked like a wild animal. Her lips were parted, and she bared her eyeteeth like a wolf. Her hands were clenching and unclenching, and her face was alive. She threw back her head and laughed, and the sound was bells and ice.

Johnny looked up. A flock of geese made its way across the Idaho sky. The wind cut his face, and he felt more alive than he had in a long time. He laughed with her and she looked at him, held his eyes, her little wolf teeth exposed beneath her parted lips. Something in him rose, an animal gut feeling that rocketed through him, and he wondered if he could love someone in a day, in a moment.

———————

THE BOAT SLID INTO THE QUIET AND DARKNESS OF THE BOATHOUSE. He clambered out and then reached down to pull her out. He lifted her easily and then they were standing face-to-face, his arms still around her, and she looked straight into his eyes and the little wolf teeth showed. Her arms went around him.

"That was wonderful, Johnny."

"Marjean... I'm going away... to the Marines, tomorrow."

"Tomorrow?"

"Yes, I'm taking a bus to Idaho Falls and I won't be back."

"Johnny..."

Her face had the same look on it he had seen on the boat, wild and alive, and then she put her face up and he was kissing her, kissing her with all the passion in his young, strong body. Her lips parted, and she kissed him back, and then it was like she caught on fire and she was holding him so tight he couldn't breathe. He pulled away.

"Marjean, what's happening?"

"Nothing I don't want to happen."

He felt the press of her firm body against his and he pulled her back into his arms.

"You sure?"

She answered him by pulling his face down and kissing him, not just a kiss though, but a volcano of heat and passion and desire, and the strength in her arms locked him to her. They broke the kiss, and she was panting deep gasping breaths like a dog that has run too far. "Johnny, Johnny... I..."

"There's a room at the back of the boathouse with a bed. Do you..."

Marjean blushed, but the fire was still in her breath. "Yes, Johnny, oh yes..."

WIND WHIPPED HIS HAIR, THE ASPHALT ROARING UNDER THE wheels of his Chevy as it rushed past his open window. It was freezing outside, but he didn't care. His suitcase was on the backseat. His birth certificate, ID and a folded piece of paper with a note from Marjean lay in a bundle on the seat beside him. He had left early in the morning, headed for Sandpoint. Johnny had not wakened his father, and he didn't look back. He just walked out the door, down the path to the street, climbed in his car and left.

When he got to Sandpoint, he drove to Carrabello's garage. Danny Carrabello was just opening the shop.

"Hey, Johnny, what's up?"

"I'm joining up, Danny. I need a place to store my car."

"Room in the back, always, my friend. Drive it in."

He pulled in and drove to the back of the big Quonset hut. Danny walked up beside the car.

"Sure is a beauty, Johnny. Can I take her out once in a while?"

"Any time. And Danny... if I don't come back, she's yours."

"So you're joining up. What about your dad, Johnny, what about the church?"

"My dad left me a long time ago, Danny. I got no regrets—and the church?" He shook his head and laughed. "Suckers, hypocrites—I don't give a damn about them and their phony religion."

A picture came into his mind—corn silk hair, deep green eyes, little wolf-teeth.

"There's only one thing I regret, Danny. It's the one thing about Idaho I won't forget."

2

THE HUNTER

BILLY MARTENS

T he little church was crammed with less than three weeks left until Christmas. Since it was the first Sunday in December, they had begun to sing the carols. Billy Martens liked the carols more than anything else they sang at the Mennonite church his father pastored, so he put a lot of strength into *O Come All Ye Faithful* and *Joy to the World.* He was restless to be on his way by the time his father had finished his sermon though, most of which Billy hadn't really heard. When he was impatient, he would run his hand through his sandy brown hair repeatedly, and that's what he was doing during the final prayer which, to the eighteen-year-old, seemed to drone on forever. His mother, eyes still closed for the *amen,* smiled and grasped his hand to keep it still. Finally, they were dismissed, and she said softly, still smiling, "All the elk in Montana will not have fled to Idaho or North Dakota while we sat in church, dear."

He grinned. "I know, mom. I'm just eager to get out into the mountains and the woods."

"I see that. Remember. No hunting till Monday morning. Just set up your camp this afternoon."

"I will not dishonor the Lord's Day, mom."

"Good."

His father approached and shook his son's hand. "Are you heading out right after lunch, Billy?"

"Yes, Sir."

"Well, I hope I gave you something to think about. *The mountains shall bring peace to the people.* Hold on to that when you look up at the stars tonight. Peace in our world, peace in our hearts, eternal peace—it's all so very important."

"Yes, Sir, it is."

His two younger brothers, one a redhead, thanks to a relative who had died during the Civil War eighty years before, both pulled long faces.

"We should be able to go with you," complained Jake, the redhead. "I'm sixteen in January."

"And I'm fifteen in March," argued Mike. "I'll be taller than you, Billy."

"You think so?" laughed Billy, messing Mike's hair.

"I know so." Mike jerked his head away. "And don't do that. I'm not a kid."

Two girls crowded around Billy.

"Why do boys get to do everything?" whined a tall, skinny blonde with her hair in one long braid down her back. "I'm bigger than other twelve-year-old girls. I'm bigger than all the boys my age, too."

"I want to learn to hunt," argued the girl at her side. "I should be able to do anything I want now that I'm ten. That's what Aunt Mercy said."

"Hmm," responded her mother, looking down at the nut-brown girl. "Aunt Mercy would say that, wouldn't she?"

"When she visits at Christmas, she'll say it again, you'll see."

Her mother laughed. "I am sure she will. But ten-year-old girls do not prance about in the Rocky Mountains in winter, Bekka. And they certainly don't prance about with guns."

Bekka frowned and crossed her arms over her chest. "Who says so?"

"I do, for one. Now, let's get over to the house and have some stew. It will have simmered to perfection. Just like you and Nancy."

The house was only about one hundred feet from the log church, and it also was made of peeled logs. *Rock solid*, thought Billy, as he placed his hand on the doorframe, though he would need to repair some chinking in the spring. He glanced up at the moose antlers over the door as he went into their two-story home —what he really wanted to see nailed there were huge elk antlers. Maybe tomorrow he'd be lucky. Or blessed.

———

IT WAS EASY TO FIND A GOOD CAMPSITE ON THE WESTERN SLOPES OF the Montana Rockies. He and his father had used at least a dozen different sites since Billy had turned sixteen. The one he liked best was a cave with a stream nearby. The stream was frozen, but he intended to chop through to the water. That afternoon he made his way up a steep slope far from the house, found the cave, and checked it carefully, trudging through the snow to its entrance. Thank goodness, no bear had discovered it or made use of it. Billy had been unpleasantly surprised before.

He took the wooden-framed pack off his back, cut some poles from the trees with a large Bowie knife, and set up a small canvas tent. No stove for this one; he'd use a sleeping bag that weighed a ton but never failed to keep him warm. Soon he had a fire going. He was wearing two woolen shirts and a thick woolen jacket of red and black checks, buffalo plaid, but the early winter chill still bit into his bones. His mother had packed some bratwurst. He roasted three of the sausages on a branch he sharpened with his pocket knife, washing the bratwurst down with hot chocolate he brought to a boil. Before he turned in, he read some of Robert

Service's poetry by the firelight. Then he put out the flames and sat in complete darkness. The Milky Way was as white as a water-fall. He thought about what his father had said about peace.

———

HE WAS UP BEFORE DAWN AND HAD A COLD BREAKFAST OF DEER jerky he had smoked himself, black bread Bekka and Nancy had baked for him that was like stone, and hot chocolate from the night before that was partially frozen and cold as snow. There had been a light dusting overnight for which he was grateful as it would make tracking much easier. His Model 1903 bolt-action Springfield was in his hands, its stock and barrel smooth and well-oiled, passed down to him from his grandfather in Missoula. He checked the iron sights as a silver line of light rimmed the mountain peaks at his back—it fired a clip of five cartridges in thirty caliber which could handle anything in the mountains, even grizzlies, elk, and moose. He set off downslope and soon cut the hoof prints of a large elk. Perfect.

But the elk led him on a merry chase. Billy kept expecting to catch sight of it over another rise or on a nearby slope. He never did, and he tracked it all day. Refusing to return to camp, he ate raisins and peanuts he'd stuffed in his pants pockets, and filled his mouth with snow when he was thirsty. Nevertheless, as the sun began to set far off over Idaho and Washington and the Pacific, in a color like wet blood and shining brass, he cursed a bit and admitted defeat. It took him an hour to reach his camp, and by then the sky was part black and part scarlet. Then he saw the bull.

It had emerged just ahead of him. He was downwind of the large elk and it had not scented him or seen his slow movement. Its rack was enormous, its head proud and beautifully chiseled, and it was standing as still as a statue. He put the Springfield to his shoulder. There was already a round in the chamber. The distance was about 200 yards, an easy shot for him, especially with sunset setting the bull and his coat on fire. Every hair glistened. No detail was lost. Billy slowly exhaled and began to squeeze the trigger.

The bull threw back his head and trumpeted.

Billy froze at the sound.

Then aimed again.

But the bull trumpeted a second time, that wild grunting and screeching wail that sent electricity through Billy and made him think of peaks and fast rivers and cliffs and tall pines. And freedom. Always of freedom. He aimed a third time. Saw the scars of battle on the bull's antlers and flanks. And lowered his rifle.

"You had something worth fighting for," he whispered. "I'll let you enjoy that. I'll let you have your lifetime."

Billy stood and watched the bull another half hour. The fire in the sky dimmed and became coals. Then the coals were gone too, and it was just him, a white moon dropping back from being full four days before, the Milky Way and the elk. The bull finally moved on just as the moon slipped from east to west, disappearing behind the mountain peaks. Billy walked to his campsite and sat by the ashes of his fire. He could not explain why he had not fired. He did not care to explain. He had simply felt what he felt. Finally, he coaxed flames to life with twigs and matches and cooked a small steak along with potatoes and onions. He decided to stay up, so he made the blackest coffee he had ever brewed.

———

HE COULD NOT EXPLAIN WHY HE STAYED UP TILL DAWN ANY MORE than he could explain why he had not shot the trophy elk. It was Tuesday, December 9th, about eight-thirty, when he dozed in the bright winter light, hunched up by the fire. Cold, he woke at noon and broke camp under a sky as blue and shimmering as the sea. It took him three hours to reach the house. It surprised him to see

cars and wagons parked at the church. The windows were gold
with lamplight and he could see people standing, hear hymn
singing, and make out Deacon Reimer praying loudly in a voice
that never softened.

"What is going on, father?" he murmured to himself, leaning
his rifle and pack against the wall outside. "What?"

The church was warm from the number of bodies. The cold
immediately fled from Billy's arms and legs. There were no
women or children in the church, only the men of the Mennonite
congregation. They were all standing for prayer. So Billy
remained standing just inside the door. Deacon Reimer went on
and on—"We ask for peace, Lord; deliver us from war, Lord;
deliver us from evil; spare America; spare the world; let hostilities
end as swiftly as they have begun; let us eat the bread of reconcili-
ation and forgiveness; let America turn the other cheek; let all
world leaders lay down their swords; let there be no further shedding of blood; we are mindful of your eternal words, oh Lord, that
we must not kill; we are mindful of your eternal words, oh Lord,
that blessed are the peacemakers, for they shall be called the children of God; we are mindful of your eternal words, oh Lord, that
we ought to beat our swords into plowshares and our spears into
pruning hooks—"

Deacon Reimer paused, as if uncertain what to pray next.

Billy's father suddenly quoted Scripture: "*Nation shall not lift
up sword against nation, neither shall they learn war any more.* The
Word of God. Amen and amen."

"Amen," came the rumbled response from dozens of male
throats.

Eyes opened.

And Billy's father gazed straight at his bewildered son in his
woolen hunting jacket.

"What is going on?" Billy demanded. "Why are you all gathered here on a Tuesday night praying about war and peace?"

At first, the church was silent. The men remained on their

feet. It was Deacon Reimer who spoke up. "So, we found out on Sunday night that the Empire of Japan had attacked our naval base in Hawaii. Thousands of sailors were killed. President Roosevelt has declared war. Of course, this is not something we want. We are a people of peace."

Billy stared at their backs. "You mean the Empire of Japan that has been devastating China and murdering her women and children for years while we did nothing? That Empire of Japan?"

His father looked away but replied, "Yes."

"So now they have come after us?"

No one in the church responded.

Billy sat in a pew. "The Nazis attacked Poland, and we said it wasn't our fight."

"And so it wasn't," his father said.

"They invaded Holland and Belgium and France, and we said it wasn't our fight. They have been bombing Britain for over a year, and we said that wasn't our fight either. Greece, Crete, Russia... it was never our fight. And now they're at the door. And it's still not our fight."

"We do not fight as others fight," his father argued. "We do not use guns and bombs. We fight our battles with prayer and worship and the Word of God."

"That did not save the missionaries in Nanking. It did not save the people they ministered to."

"There are different ways of being saved. The body is nothing. The soul is everything."

Billy ran a hand through his brown hair. "The body is the house of the soul. If the body is gone, the soul is gone too."

"If the body is destroyed, the soul is set free."

Billy thought of the bull elk and its battle scars.

He remembered how the sun had set over its beauty and power in a kind of divine magnificence.

"Murder and slaughter are not freedom." Billy's eyes locked

with his father's. "Freedom is the freedom to live. Not having no other choice but to die."

His father shook his head, clutching his black leather Bible more tightly in his hands. "Fighting is not love, my son."

"It is if you are defending those you care about. Even a whole country you care about. *Greater love hath no man than this but that he lays down his life for his friends.*" Billy stood up, walked to the front of the church and looked around at the faces. "It's not as if I haven't thought about these things or prayed about these things. War and peace have been tangled up in my mind since Japan invaded China in 1937 when I was fourteen. Then Germany attacked Poland two years later and I thought even harder and prayed even harder. I even fasted for three days, I wanted so badly to hear from God about all this. Listen. Here is where I am now— I am fond of you all. Very fond. If you will not protect yourselves, then I must protect you. I'm sure it's God's will that you men and your families and your way of life are delivered from harm."

His father shook his head. "The Japanese will never come to Montana, my son."

"No? And what if the Nazis come?"

"The Nazis will not come. We are not at war with Germany."

"Neither was Poland. Neither was Russia."

Two days later, Germany declared war on the United States and, in response, the United States declared war on Germany. News articles appeared about German submarines off the coasts of New York and Massachusetts and Florida. Billy had packed a suitcase the night he returned from hunting. He brought the case downstairs on Friday the 12th, had a final breakfast with his family, cried a bit when his mother and siblings cried, and then shook his father's hand, explaining he was driving down to Missoula to enlist.

"I cannot spare our truck for this foolishness," his father told him. "I cannot spare our precious gasoline to aid and abet the sin of warfare and killing."

"I respect that, father." Billy nodded. "And I cannot sit by and sin by watching people lose their lives and their freedoms and tell God the lie that I cannot do anything about it. I want you to respect that. I've made arrangements to go down to Missoula with our neighbor Hank Finch. His son Thomas is enlisting too."

"And what about our ranch here, Billy? What about our 200 head? Have you given a thought to that?"

"I haven't forgotten, father. You have your hired hands, Zeke and Clay. I was always just an extra, the rancher's son, not a necessity. Nevertheless, I've spoken with Dutch Van Brewer. I've helped him out at the Bar Six more than once. If the war lasts, he will be there for you at the spring and fall roundups. Him and his four boys." Billy smiled at his brothers and sisters, but they were too upset to smile back. "And here you have another four sturdy cowpokes who will be ready to go by May."

"May?" His mother looked as if Billy had stabbed her. "How long do you think this war will go on?"

Looking at her, Billy saw how frail she was, and how small. Against his will, his eyes filled. "We are fighting two great nations, mother. Two great powerful nations that are armed to the teeth. It will take years to set things right."

His mother's eyes were streaming, and Billy could not fight his pain back any longer either.

"God has given us a great ocean to protect us, William," she groaned, hugging him. "A great and large ocean."

Billy gently folded his strong arms around her. "No ocean is so large it cannot be crossed, mother. By friend or foe."

3

BASIC TRAINING 1942

THE CORPSMAN

I am a Hambo. At least that's what the rest of the boots at Camp Elliot call me. That's because I'm a CO, a conscientious objector. I joined the Marines because I have a responsibility to help defend the country that keeps me free to believe what I want. But my faith tells me it is wrong to kill other men. So I told them that when I signed up.

They tried everything they could to shake me—stood me up in front of the boots and called me a coward, a sissy and a homo. One noncom even bloodied my nose when he tried to get me to fight.

Every time the DI pushes me, I quote the Marine regs back at him at the top of my voice. "The person seeking conscientious objector status bears the initial responsibility of presenting evidence which shows a sincere opposition to war in any form based upon religious training and belief, Sir! Once an objector meets this responsibility, the U.S. Marine Corps will grant conscientious objector status unless the Government can establish a rational basis in fact for denying the application, Sir!"

My DI, Sergeant Orval Butterworth, doesn't like that too

much. He's a fourth generation Marine from Providence, Rhode
Island. I hear when he's ashore he is a quiet guy, but you couldn't
prove it by me. When he gets in my face because I'm a CO, he
puts his nose about an inch from my nose and screams, "Well you
little candyass, are you going to pick up your rifle and kill Japs
when we go ashore?"

I always say, "Sir, no Sir."

He doesn't like that either, so I always get a reward. "Okay
pogey bait, drop and give me one hundred and fifty of your
finest."

"Sir, yes Sir."

I never fight with Butterworth, I never get mad. I do what he
says. When I joined up, I told them I would learn how to use my
M1, take it apart, put it back together, and load it. I learned it fast
and I'm the best fieldstripper in my squad. But that doesn't help
much. Most of the guys avoid me or try to rile me.

There are two guys, though, that I get along with okay. That's
because they are both Mennonite kids from the Pacific Northwest. I'm a Mennonite, too, and I'm also from the great PNW.
That's why we hit it off. I grew up in a little town in Washington
called Ritzville. Ritzville is one of those thin places you pass
through when you're driving from Seattle to Spokane—nothing
there but horizon. Dry wheat, dry heat and no girls. Well, some
girls, but they all look like the country around town—dry, brown,
angular, gritty. The large empty sky above Ritzville is a good place
for a guy to learn astronomy, though, which got me into studying
Greek mythology, so I guess good came out of something in
Ritzville.

I'm a CO by birth. We didn't do a lot of things in our church,
but the main thing we didn't do was get in a fight. When I was
growing up, I wondered about that when the bullies in school
picked on me, and my dad told me to just ignore them. It's kind of
hard to ignore some big jerk that is giving you a wedgie and slapping you around. But when I got bigger than most, I found out

that a quiet demeanor puts bullies on guard. If you're a big guy but you're not strutting around and bragging about it, most guys wise up and leave you alone because they don't know if you're crazy, and you are too big for them to want to chance it.

Oh, I guess I'll tell you my name. Philo Parmalee. How's that for a chancre of a name? My dad was one of those guys who subscribed to *Popular Mechanics* magazine. We had stacks of them around our house. That's where he found out about Philo Farnsworth, the guy who invented television. Dad used to tell me that television was the greatest invention in the history of the world. He read everything he could about it, and one time he even went to Seattle just to see a television set in a store there. He was so struck by it he named me Philo. My mom didn't like it much, but I guess Dad thought it would give me brainpower or something. He would say, "One day, Philo, there will be a television set in every home. Wouldn't it be great if you could invent something like that?"

Well, I thought my dad was a little crazy, wanting me to be an inventor and all, but who was I to piss on his fire? Sadly, things just didn't go that way for me. By the time I was twelve he and I both knew I would never invent anything—I bet that's when he wished he had called me Joe or Pete. Anyway, I carried that Philo moniker around and took a lot of crap because of it. You can't guess how grateful I was when one of my Junior High friends started calling me Bud. He'd seen me go red in the face when some jerk of a teacher stretched it out and called me "File-Ohhh," or when the girls would giggle and say, "Hey Philo, wadda ya know? Just get back from a Broadway show?" So I was Bud from then on, and things got a little easier. Now I'm in the Marines and we are going into battle; I imagine the only thing they will call me once we get to wrestling with the Imperial Japanese army is Corpsman. And they won't be saying it to themselves—they will scream it.

Anyway, the two guys I was telling you about: One is Billy

Martens. He's from Montana. He's a hunter and a fisherman, and he's a crack shot. I've never seen a guy who can handle a rifle better. They issued him a 1903 Garand Rifle, and he worked on it until he zeroed it in. He's got 20/20 vision and on Record Day he walked away with an expert rifleman qualification. Besides being an incredible rifleman, Billy's a real nice guy, but he struggles with the thought of killing someone. He shared that with me when we were on watch one night. He's been in the Mennonite church for so long that "Thou shalt not kill" is part of his makeup. So, I think he wonders if he will measure up when we are in battle.

Then there's Johnny Strange. He's a real quiet type, but if you get him going, he'll tell you he came to the Marines to learn to kill. He's a real handsome guy, and one day when we were on latrine duty, this guy put his hand on Johnny's shoulder and called him "Pretty Boy." Big mistake. Johnny took that guy up against the wall and was looking to kill him before we got him off. When the guy said he meant nothing by it, Johnny tells him that if he ever did it again, he'd kill him. There is something twisting Johnny Strange up inside, but he doesn't talk about it.

When I grew up, I was a picky eater, but I have to tell you that since I've been in Boot Camp, I eat everything that's put in front of me. Some of it is more than foul; the guys call it SOS, shit-on-a-shingle, but after you've been out doing marching drills, two-hour exercise drills and such, you can build up an appetite, so I just hold my nose and eat it. Here at Elliot, we run everywhere, we get called 'maggot' a lot, and I found out there's three ways to do everything: the right way, the wrong way and the Marine way.

Now about my status—I don't consider myself one of those religious nuts, but I have a grip on the fact that God is real, and I believe the Bible from front to back. If you ask me, I'll tell you Jesus is coming back to this world to straighten everything out... someday. I'm a short-shot prayer guy because I used to watch these evangelists that would come to our church, ranting and raving and putting out long-winded prayers that just were a lot of hooey. After a while you figured out the guy just liked to hear himself talk. One time one of those evangelists came to our house for dinner after church. You know the type. Longish hair swept back like the wind's blowing all the time, green safari suit and saddle shoes. When he said the word God, he put an "uh" on the end so it sounds like "God-uh." My dad asked him to pray over the meal, and he takes off praying for all the missionaries in the world and all the churches in the world and he's going on and on "in His Name" and "for His sake," and I got in big trouble when I interrupted him and asked him if we could eat "for Christ's sake." Ooh-whee—that was very dumb. No supper that day, and for dessert I got a hiding out in the shed.

When I pray, I try to make it to the point. I figure God has enough incoming he doesn't want to wade through all the pontifications, so he's happy when somebody makes it short and sweet. I figure to pray a lot when we hit the islands. That's the scuttlebutt, anyway, that we're headed for the Pacific, and we will take back every island that the Japs have conquered.

So here I am at Camp Elliot training to be a corpsman. I think it's a great solution to my problem with the Marines. When I first signed up, I told them I would go anywhere the riflemen go and I would help any guy that gets shot I can, and I won't let them down, and after a while they believed me and so, I'm in good standing with the brass. I don't mind risking my neck with the other guys because I know there's a better life waiting anyway— lots of guys haven't figured that out yet. Besides that, I'm a tough guy as far as keeping up with everything they throw at me. I run fast, I can do lots of pushups, I don't complain when I pull head duty, so even though the other boots aren't friendly, they still respect me—I can tell.

What I know is a lot of these boots don't want to die in battle, and they cover it up with macho talk, but I see through it. They are tinhorns, and most of them are scared stiff. It's easy to tell when somebody's got faith for the next life—they rest easy in the saddle. Billy Martens, he's like that. He brought enough of his faith with him from Montana to keep him through the bad stuff. He's got a real faith he doesn't shove down your throat. But Johnny, he lost his faith a long time ago. He doesn't talk about it, but I think when he left Idaho, he left everything. Well, not everything, because there's a girl he talks about a little—a gal named Marjean. He writes to her and I think he got one letter back so far. I don't know if it was a good one or a bad one because he didn't talk about her for a week after he got it.

Anyway, when I was on the train coming down to California, I prayed a lot. I asked God to make me faithful, to give me courage in battle, and to let me be a good comrade to my buddies. By the time I got to Camp Elliot, he had given me a settled assurance he would be with me through all this. I knew his promise already, but sometimes you have to wrestle things out with God, just to make sure.

I don't get a lot of free time, but when I do, I pray for all the guys, but more for Billy and Johnny. Johnny needs a lot of prayer because he's got something inside that eats at him. He tries to prove himself a man at everything he does here, and he doesn't take guff from anyone, so he gets in fights and he's been on report three times. But he does a lot of things well. We were on the Crucible, our toughest training test; we're out in the field, and the General's jeep breaks down as he's headed by. Johnny jumps out smart and in an instant he's got the hood open and his head inside. In a minute he tells the General exactly how to fix it and how long it will take. Well, the general thinks he's just a smartass, so he tells him to be at the motor pool at 0700 to fix that jeep or wash out. It's midnight, and we still got a 20-mile hike to get home. Well, Johnny does it. The general was pretty impressed, and the next thing I know Johnny's running the motor pool.

I'm pretty sure that praying helped get Johnny over the hump, so I will keep praying for both of them and hoping we all make it through what's coming because I'd hate to make good friends and then lose them. I ask God to help me on that score a lot.

4

PRETTY BOY

JOHNNY STRANGE

J ohnny Strange didn't like boot camp. In fact he hated it, everything about it. He especially hated the DI, Sergeant Orval Butterworth. Butterworth was an eastern Yankee, born and raised in Providence, Rhode Island. He was a fourth generation Marine, and his face looked like someone had set fire to it and then put it out with a track shoe. This combination of physical and locational limitations made Butterworth hate three kinds of people—Johnny Rebs, Cowboys, and Pretty Boys. He called everyone from the West "Sissy Gene," a reference to Gene Autry. Given that the preponderance of boots from the fertile fields of the Southland east of the Mississippi went to Parris Island, South Carolina, that left Butterworth free to expel his hatred on westerners, and more often on handsome westerners. And that put Johnny Strange in Butterworth's sights from the get-go. But that all fell into place when he arrived at Camp Elliot.

On the train down to Dago, which he found out from the Corporal in charge of the trainload of boots was "San Diego, numb nuts," Johnny hooked up with Billy Martens, a kid he met at a Pacific Northwest Mennonite youth camp a few years before and liked. They made it a habit to hang out together when they went to camp the next couple of years, and so they knew each other pretty well. Still, it was strange to see Billy on the train. They shared a seat and beat their gums for a while.

"How did you get into this, Billy? I thought your dad locked you up tight in church."

"I don't know, except that I've been watching the Japanese army march through China since 1937, and to tell you the truth, what they did in Nanking made me sick. The way I figure it, these guys need a good old-fashioned American butt kicking. My dad didn't want me to go, but what was I supposed to do, sit around and watch every able-bodied man leave town while I stayed home with the girls and the babies?"

"I see your point."

"What about you, Johnny? You're Mennonite, too."

Johnny shook his head with a wry grin. "I haven't really been a Mennonite for a long time, Billy. Oh, yeah, I went to church and all, but just to keep my dad's yap shut. Now I'm getting about as far away from that pack of gumbars as the sun is from the moon."

"So were you feeling patriotic or something?"

"Nope, I got my own reasons for joining up."

"Like...?"

"I want to learn to kill, Billy. That may sound strange, but I have my reasons. A lot of it is about getting as far away from the pacifist mentality as I can, but there's other stuff, too."

"Like what?"

Johnny smiled a strange smile at Billy. "You got a girl friend, Billy?"

And that was that.

AFTER BILLY WENT TO SLEEP IN THE SEAT ACROSS FROM HIM, Johnny got out the note from Marjean. She had written it when he asked for her address after they... after they were together. She had asked him not to read it before he got on the train, so he waited. His time with Marjean had been a big surprise. She had been responsive and...well, wonderful, but afterwards she seemed to retreat into herself and barely spoke before he left.

When he asked her for her address, she walked down to her car to get a pen and paper. Gerald and his family showed up.

Gerald climbed out of the car and waved. "Hey, Johnny, what's up?"

He told Gerald he was enlisting the next day.

"Enlisting? A bit sudden isn't it?"

"There's a war on, Gerald."

Gerald turned to his dad.

"See, Dad? Johnny's enlisting. Why can't I go?"

Gerald's dad gave Johnny a sidelong look and then addressed his son's question. "I need you at the mill, Gerald. The country will want lots of wood products, and we supply them. I want you to stay here and help me run the place. I'll make sure you get a deferment."

"But I don't want a deferment. I want to go fight."

Gerald's dad put his hand on Johnny's shoulder. "I'm sure Johnny will do enough fighting for both of you. Now the discussion is over. And here's Marjean! How long have you been here?"

Johnny didn't like the hand on his shoulder—it creeped him out. Johnny wanted no one to touch him... well, he had liked it when Marjean touched him. She walked up the path.

"Long enough for Johnny to take me for a ride in his boat." He looked over at her. She blushed. No one noticed but him.

She was standing with Gerald's mom. The blush faded, and now her face was pale. Her corn silk hair was peeking out from under the cap. She looked beautiful but distant, like an ice queen on a far-away throne. At that moment Johnny realized that something had happened that he didn't want to happen. She had gotten to him, and she was in his head. He tried to catch her eye, but she was talking to Mrs. King.

Shit! I don't need the distraction.

He moved out from under Mr. King's hand.

"Can I take out the boat while you're gone, Johnny?"

"Sure, Gerald, but you got to keep her serviced and covered in between."

"Great, but who's gonna fix our boats if they break down?"

"Call Danny Carrabello over in Sandpoint. He'll come out. Gotta go."

He shook hands with Gerald and Mr. King and then climbed into his Chevy. He wanted to leave quickly, leave her behind, forget about what happened, but she came over and stood by the window until he rolled it down. She reached in and shook his hand.

"It was so nice to meet you, Johnny. Thank you for the wonderful ride in your boat."

He felt the paper in her hand. She lowered her voice.

"Don't read it until you're on the train. Goodbye."

She turned and walked away.

JOHNNY SAT IN THE DARKENED TRAIN LISTENING TO BILLY SNORE softly from the other seat. His head was full of whirling stuff.

Dear Johnny,

I am sorry and glad about what happened. Sorry because I've never done that before and I feel a little dirty. I always dreamed that it would happen on my wedding night. But I'm glad because you made me feel something I've never felt before. Do you believe in love at first sight? Anyway, I don't know how you feel. You may go away and never think of me again. But here's how I feel. I'm yours forever. I will wait for you, no matter what. Please write.

Marjean

He folded up the note and then unfolded it and read it again.

I don't want to love anyone, Marjean. There's only room in my heart for hate.

But then it occurred to him he wanted her to be his girl, more than anything. He wanted nobody else to ever touch her. And that was a pain in the butt he didn't need.

"WELL, WHADDA WE GOT HERE? A BUNCH OF SISSY GENE AUTRYS from way out west. You boys think you will ride in here on your white horses and save the day, right? Well, you slime bags are WRONG! You are stupid homo slackers who couldn't find your ass with both hands. The only thing you will ride is the train outta here after I hammer you so hard you die."

The DI walked along the line of boots. "I am your Drill Instructor. My name is Sergeant Orval H. Butterworth. The H stands for Hammer and I will hammer you. You will not call me Sergeant; nor will you call me Mr. Butterworth, because if you do I will disable your masculinity. You will call me Sir! You will preface everything you say with the word, Sir, and you will answer every question with three words and three words only. They are 'Sir, yes Sir!' Am I understood?"

Eighty voices responded. "Sir, yes Sir!"

"And since you are the most stupid maggots on the face of God's green earth, I will make it simple for you. I will never ask you a question you can't answer with my favorite three words. Is that understood?"

"Sir, yes Sir!"

"I am here to teach you putrid maggots to hate; hate Japs, hate every other service except the Marines and hate me. It is that hate that will allow you to look into the eyes of that little yellow Tojo boy and shove your bayonet down his throat without batting an eye. When you are crawling through the mud of some godforsaken island, you will think back on me with a fondness that outshines the love you have for your mother. You will thank me for the hate I instilled in you. You will weep with joy as you remember me. That's because we are not sending you over there to love your enemy. We are sending you to kill them, brutally, horribly and without remorse. And that reminds me."

Butterworth stopped in front of a big, strong looking kid on the front row. "This maggot is what we call a Hambo. That's because he's a CO, a conscientious objector. He doesn't believe in killing, do you, maggot?"

"Sir, no Sir!"

"Wrong answer, Maggot. What's your name, Hambo?"

"Sir, Philo Parmalee, Sir, but everyone calls me Bud."

Butterworth got right into the boot's face. "I don't give a rat's ass what everyone calls you. I and I alone will decide what to call you, maggot. And I have a brand new name for you. From hence-forth you are Maggot Hambo. Is that clear?"

"Sir, yes, Sir!"

"Good answer, Maggot Hambo. Now you little homo, are you going to pick up your rifle and kill Japs when we go ashore?"

"Sir, no Sir."

"And just why are you not going to kill Japs, Maggot Hambo?"

The tall kid looked the DI right in the eye. There was no backing down in him. "The person seeking conscientious objector status bears the initial responsibility of presenting evidence which shows a sincere opposition to war in any form based upon religious training and belief, Sir! Once the objector meets this responsibility, the Marine Corps will grant conscientious objector status unless the Government can establish a rational basis in fact for denying the application, Sir!"

"Quite a speech, Maggot Faggot. Okay, you pogey bait homo, drop and give me one hundred and fifty of your finest."

"Sir, yes, Sir."

The big boy dropped and did the pushups with ease. He was

strong, and Johnny could see the muscles at work as he polished them off. The big guy had a good attitude and Johnny smiled. This gave Butterworth the opportunity to focus on him.

"So, we got all you sissy Gene Autry pretty boys, but you, maggot, are the prettiest. Are you smiling, Pretty Boy?"

Johnny felt the heat gather in his stomach and start upwards.

"Sir, yes Sir."

"Do you think I'm funny, Pretty Boy?"

"Sir, no Sir!"

"Do you think I'm attractive, Pretty Boy?"

The heat was Johnny's face.

"Sir, no Sir!"

Butterworth smiled. "Oh, look everyone, maggot Pretty Boy doesn't like his new name, do you Pretty Boy?"

"Sir, no Sir!"

"So what are you going to do about it?"

"Sir, kill you, Sir!"

Instantly Butterworth grabbed Johnny, and with a twist he threw him over his shoulder. Johnny landed flat on his back with the wind knocked out of him. The DI was on him like a cat, with his knife out of its sheath and pressed against Johnny's neck.

"Kill me? Kill me? You couldn't kill a fly, you little maggot. But I will teach you to kill. Would you like that, Pretty Boy?"

"Sir, yes Sir."

"Good. Now are you going to thank me for your first lesson in combat readiness?"

"Sir, thank you, Sir."

"Good boy. Now get your sorry ass up and get back in line."

He turned to the rest of the boots. "Just like Pretty Boy here, you pieces of human feces think you are men. But you are not. You are mewling, puking maggots that still nursed on your mama yesterday afternoon. But I will make you men. You will leave this training one of two ways—as a Marine or dead. Do you understand?"

"Sir, yes Sir!"

"Remember this day and remember that you are mine. Do I make myself clear, Maggot Hambo?"

"Sir, yes Sir!"

"And do I make myself clear, Maggot Pretty Boy?"

"Sir, yes Sir!"

And that was why Johnny hated his DI.

5

UNITED STATES RIFLE MODEL 1903

BILLY MARTENS

It could be John Strange. Or Bud, the conscientious objector. Today it was Billy Martens. It didn't matter to Drill Instructor Butterworth. Anytime he got to hammer one of the three Mennonites in his company, he saw the opportunity as a gift from God—and his God was not a Mennonite God.

"Are you going to fight, Mennonite?" hissed the Drill Instructor, his nose inches from Billy Martens' face, his voice like steam erupting from a cast-iron kettle.

"Sir, yes, Sir!" Martens roared back, standing at attention outside his barracks.

"I'm having trouble hearing you. Do I need a corpsman to check my ears out?"

"Sir, no, Sir!"

"NO? You mean you're not going to fight for your country, Mennonite?"

"Sir, yes, Sir, I'll fight!"

"What am I hearing? That the Mennonite will fight?"

"Yes, Sir!"

"What will you fight for?"

"My country, Sir!"

"Is that all? What about your God?"

"Sir, I will fight for God and country, Sir!"

"Is that all? What about your girl?"

"I don't have a girl, Sir!"

"WHAT?"

"Sir, I will fight for God and country and my girl, Sir!"

"I have my doubts, I truly have my doubts, Martinez. The only thing I see you fighting for is your place in line when the cook serves up hot chow."

"Sir, it's Martens, Sir!"

"WHAT?"

"Sir, my name is Martens, Sir!"

"The hell it is! You're Martinez! Got it? Martinez!"

"Sir, yes, Sir, Martinez, Sir!"

"Bulls in the corn! You got no backbone, Martinez, no backbone at all! Your name is Martens!"

"Martens, yes, Sir!"

"WHAT?"

"My name is Martens, Sir!"

"The hell it is! You're Martinez! Martens is a Mennonite, and Mennonites don't fight! Do you fight?"

"Sir, yes, Sir, I fight!"

"Then you're Martinez, not Martens! MARTINEZ!"

"Sir, I'm Martinez, yes, Sir!"

"You're yellow, Martens! Hit the deck and give me fifty!"

"Sir, yes, Sir!"

"Shut up and do it, you Mennonite shit! And when you're done that, you can clean out the officers' head, and I want it so clean it smells like a rose garden. And then you can hit my favorite three hills. You know my favorite three hills, Martinez?"

"Sir, I do, Sir!"

"I'll be there in thirty, Martinez, I'll be there to watch you run them. Have you finished those pushups yet?"

"Sir, no, Sir!"

"WHAT?"

"Almost there, Sir!"

"Almost doesn't win wars, Martinez. Almost doesn't stop the Empire of Japan from landing troops in California. Almost doesn't keep America free."

"Done, Sir, I'm done!"

"Give me 50 more!"

"Sir, yes, Sir!"

"And get that head clean! I need to use it! Get it clean and stop your pathetic Mennonite goldbricking, Martinez!"

"Yes, Sir!"

"Be at my hills in twenty-five. Twenty-five, Martinez!"

"On my way to the officers' head, Sir!"

"I'm just getting warmed up, Martinez. I'll make a Marine out of you even if it kills you, even if it kills you stone dead."

Billy thought it might. Butterworth rode him day after day. The few friends he'd made avoided him—no one wanted to get in the DI's line of fire more than they already were. If they did 20 pushups, Billy did forty. If they ran ten miles, he ran twenty-five. If they hiked two hills, he hiked four. If the DI woke them at four, he woke Billy at two. It never ended.

Billy came close to quitting or going AWOL. It was Johnny Strange, one of the other two Mennonites he knew about at Boot Camp, who began to eat with him when others wouldn't, and sit down and talk when others wouldn't come near. He refused to allow Billy to wash out of basic training.

"It's what Nimrods like the DI want," Strange argued with Billy behind the barracks one evening when they had a few minutes peace. "He thinks all Mennonites and Quakers are conscientious objectors because they're gutless, too yellow to fight, so they hide behind God and their religion. You and I have to show him otherwise."

"He's wearing me down, Johnny. I'm lucky if I get three hours of sleep at a time."

"Nah. You're wearing him down. I'm wearing him down too. I'll bet he thought you and I would fold in a week. Two weeks later, we're still here. So, he's losing sleep too. Billy, look, you can't go back to mommy and daddy with your tail between your legs. The cowboys would never respect you. Billy Martens, the man who let down his country and the state of Montana and the United States Marine Corps—you wouldn't be allowed to run a soup kitchen, never mind a roundup, and you can be darn sure no one would listen to one word of any sermon you preached either."

"So, what do I do, Johnny?"

"Well... you hunt?"

"Yeah."

"Go out for days at a time? Set up a tent? Live off beans and sourdough? Hump it through the mountains tracking deer and elk?"

"Yeah."

"So, this here is your hunting camp. This Camp Elliott. Every day you are stalking your prey... maybe it's latrine duty. Maybe running a hill in full pack. Maybe doing 200 pushups. Maybe cleaning your rifle a thousand times. It doesn't matter. Do it. Do it all. Then move on to the next day. And the next. Tough it out like you do in the mountains. In seven weeks, you'll bring home the bacon—you'll be a Marine."

"You make it sound easy."

"It is easy. Easier than scrambling after a white-tail at 10,000 feet with a north wind freezing your butt off. Look, I got a hunch you're a good shot."

Billy shrugged. "I can hold my own."

"We're going to shoot for keeps. Record Day is coming up. Drive Butterworth crazy, Billy. Drill the targets. Knock out bullseye after bullseye. Frustrate him. Annoy him. You shoot like a sniper and pretty soon you won't belong to the DI anymore. The CO will hear about it. The Corps will hear about it. San Diego will hear about it. They'll turn you into a darn hero if you keep shooting like Sergeant York. He came from a pacifist church. He could've claimed conscientious objector status. But he fought like a lion, and he won the Medal of Honor." Strange grinned and extended a pack of Player's cigarettes. "Let's see if we Mennonite boys can't do the same."

Billy took one cigarette from the pack. "I've never done this before."

"All part of basic training. Light it up and breathe it in. The tobacco will settle your nerves. We want you steady as a rock on that rifle range." Strange shrugged and blew out a stream of white smoke. "I'm partial to Camels, but all I could get my hands on this week were Player's and Wings. No filters on any of them. We need the nicotine kick, Billy. We Mennonites have to be the best fighters in the Corps."

"WHAT HAVE YOU GOT IN YOUR HANDS, MENNONITE?" STEAM-kettle hissed the DI the next morning at the firing range.

"United States Rifle, Caliber Thirty-Aught-Six, Model 1903, Sir!" Billy snapped back. "Bolt action, five round stripper clip, muzzle velocity 28 hundred feet per second, rate of fire ten to 15 rounds per minute, effective firing range 1000 yards, Sir!"

"Aren't you the smartass this morning, Mennonite? I intend to wash you out of Camp Elliott before the day's over. If you can't shoot, you can't be a Marine. Put five in the bull's eye at 200 yards. Prone position."

"Sir, yes, Sir."

The rifle was exactly like the one his grandfather had given him. Billy didn't even take his time. He squeezed off five shots. At the all clear, the recruits working the butts where the targets were located, well out of harm's way below ground once the firing began, used shot spotters to indicate where bullets had struck. Billy had five bull's eyes.

Butterworth spat. "Montana luck. Let's see how you do kneeling."

"Sir, yes, Sir."

Billy repeated his performance.

"Even dumber luck," snarled the DI. "Three hundred will cook you."

But when the company set up for 300 yards, and commenced firing, Billy was still putting the bullets dead center—prone, kneeling, standing, sitting, it made no difference. Recruits from one end of the line to the other could hear Butterworth bawling his frustration: "You screwing me around, you low life? No Mennonite shoots like that!"

"I hunt, Sir."

"WHAT?"

"I hunt elk and moose, Sir. With a Model 1903 just like this, Sir. My father's father used it in The Great War, Sir."

"WHAT?"

"He was at Chateau-Thierry, Sir. He was a Marine, Sir."

"Bullshit, Mennonite. Your grandpa was a Mennonite Marine? He was with the American Expeditionary Force?"

"Yes, Sir. He won the Silver Star."

"Bulls in the corn, Mennonite. Big bulls in the corn, Martinez. You screwing me around again? I'll check the official records. If you're lying to me, I'll string you up with the Stars and Stripes and let you flap in the wind till we win the war without you."

"No need to check, Sir."

"WHAT?"

"I carry it in my pocket, Sir. For good luck, Sir. And maybe a blessing, Sir."

"Martinez! Empty your pockets and show me!"

Billy got to his feet and gave Butterworth the star with its red, white and blue ribbon. A few spots were tarnished after 20-odd years, but most of the silver still shone true.

"Buy this fake at a pawnbroker's in Missoula, did you, you little lying shit? It couldn't be this shiny all the way from 1918."

"I polish it, Sir. Every night, Sir."

"Bullshit, Martinez. You some kind of patriot or something?"

"Sir, yes, Sir."

"Shut your face, Martinez. I'll decide what you are. You're nothing but a low-life puke liar with a faked-up medal from a low-life puke pawnbroker."

"May I see that, sergeant?"

It was the company CO, Rudebaker. The DI saluted and handed him the medal. "Of course, Sir."

Rudebaker, a tall, gangly Coloradan with pitch-black hair, turned the medal over in his palm. "For gallantry in action," he said, reading the inscription. "David J. Martens." Rudebaker glanced at the DI with sharp blue eyes. "It's the real thing, sergeant."

"Yes, Sir."

"Chateau-Thierry, I believe I overheard, recruit?" Rudebaker asked Billy.

"Yes, Sir. He was wounded, Sir. At Mont Blanc Ridge."

"So, there's a Purple Heart, as well?"

"Yes, Sir."

"Where is it? In the other pocket?"

Billy smiled and Rudebaker smiled in return.

"Yes, Sir," Billy replied.

"May I?"

Billy produced the medal. It was in immaculate condition. "For military merit," Rudebaker read on the back. "David J. Martens. Well, recruit. Quite a family history, especially when that family has Mennonite roots."

"Yes, Sir."

"How badly do you want to be a Marine, recruit?"

"I can taste it, Sir."

"What?"

"It's my food, Sir. It's my drink. When I bleed, I taste it in my blood, Sir."

"Do you?" Rudebaker handed him back both medals. "Word in the company is you haven't missed a bull's eye yet, recruit." He looked downrange. "Let's move on to the 500-yard line, sergeant."

"Yes, Sir."

"We'll see how our Mennonite fares."

"Yes, Sir."

Billy had hunted with iron sights well beyond 500 yards. He held his breath, then exhaled slowly, working the bolt of the Model 1903 smoothly and rapidly. He fired five times from a prone position. He and Rudebaker and Butterworth waited, staring downrange. Two in the middle. Three just outside the bull's eye. Butterworth heard Billy curse under his breath and arched an eyebrow.

"Think you can do better than that, Martinez?" he demanded.

"Yes, Sir, I know so, Sir."

"Go again."

Billy put three in the bull's eye.

"Stand and fire, recruit," ordered Butterworth.

Billy placed two shots dead center.

"Sit," said Butterworth.

Three hit home.

"Kneel, Martinez."

All five shots hit dead center.

"Again."

Five more bull's eyes.

"Prepare four stripper clips, Martinez," ordered Butterworth.

"Yes, Sir."

"You seem to do best kneeling before God. The maximum rate of fire is considered 15 rounds per minute with this rifle. I want twenty. Twenty, Martinez. Can you give me that?"

"Yes, Sir, I can, Sir."

"You're confident of that?"

"Yes, Sir, I am, Sir, confident, Sir."

"Fire at will, recruit. I'll start my stopwatch the moment you work the bolt."

Billy closed his eyes and prayed. He never could recall what it was he said or asked. He was conscious that firing had stopped up and down the line. The entire company was watching him. Then he heard a soft voice behind him.

"Blessed be the Lord my strength, which teacheth my hands to war and my fingers to fight."

It was Captain Rudebaker.

Billy felt that a kind of strength went through him.

He aimed.

His gaze was rock solid. So was his rifle.

He worked the bolt quickly and put a cartridge in the chamber.

And fired.

Again and again and again.

Slapped home a second stripper clip of five rounds.

Worked the bolt. And fired them off in the blink of an eye.

Put in the third stripper clip. And the fourth.

And stopped.

"Fifty-seven seconds." Butterworth sounded as if he were in pain. "Fifty-seven seconds. Great balls of fire, Martinez."

Billy stared downrange along with everyone else on the line.

Fast was fine. But not if you missed every shot.

His grandfather had pounded Wyatt Earp's words into his head when he had taught Billy to shoot at 13: *Fast is fine, but accuracy is everything. In a gun fight, you need to take your time in a hurry.*

The shot spotters indicated fourteen bull's eyes and six in the first ring outside the bull's eye.

Billy cursed again.

But Butterworth gave him a look of death. "Shut your face, Martinez. Twenty shots in less than one minute and 14 of them are dead center and the other six near misses that would kill any Jap or Kraut. And at five hundred yards. A third of a mile. With iron sights. You don't cuss shooting like that. Do you hear me? No low-life recruit like you cusses shooting like that."

"No, Sir, sorry, Sir."

"Great Balls of Fire, Martinez! Nobody shoots like that, nobody on God's green earth. Do you hear me, Martinez? Nobody."

"Sir, yes, Sir, nobody, Sir."

"I brought you here today to wash you out of the Corps. How the hell am I going to do that now, Mennonite? Tell me!"

"Sir, I don't know, Sir."

"It's not good news, Mennonite! None of this is good for the Corps or the war!"

"No, Sir."

Rudebaker was smiling at Butterworth's flushed face and at Billy's pale cheeks.

"Was it your grandfather who taught you how to shoot, recruit?" Rudebaker asked. "The Marine who won the Silver Star at Chateau-Thierry?"

"Yes, Sir."

"Did the rest of the family know?"

"They knew he was teaching me to hunt."

"Did they tell you he had fought in the war?"

"No, Sir. I never knew he had served, Sir. They never mentioned it. He told me himself when I turned sixteen."

"Is that when he trained you to be a marksman?"

"He did that from the start, Sir. He taught me to shoot on target with iron sights up to seven hundred and fifty yards."

"And no one in the family knew?"

"Not about that kind of shooting, no, Sir. It was just between the two of us."

Rudebaker smiled at him. "Just between the two of you. And Almighty God."

"And Almighty God, yes, Sir."

"This is nuts, Mennonite, frigging nuts," fumed Butterworth. "You're going to make a religious man out of me if you keep up with this kind of shooting. You've got too much spunk to be anything less than a Marine. Too much. Balls of fire, Mennonite. Great thundering balls of fire."

"Yes, Sir, understood, Sir, great thundering balls of fire, Sir."

6

MAKING THE GRADE

THE CORPSMAN

I ran the same hills as everyone else, did the beach slogs in full pack, hauled myself through the obstacle courses, and crawled under sharp wire with guns blasting over my head. I marched, I drilled with an empty rifle, yes, I even fired one on the range, but I was no Billy Martens. I was bad. But they didn't wash me out. I surpassed everyone with my first aid skills in the field. So much so, "Rudy" Rudebaker called me into his office and said they'd like to ship me out with the Division as a corpsman. I said yes. When basic was over, and I graduated with the others, my medical training began, and it was as intense in its own way as anything the DI had dished out on the hills of San Diego.

Butterworth bet on Billy on Record Day and made a bundle of greenbacks. Billy was firing the M1 Garand, the new semi-auto rifles they were issuing us that had eight rounds in the stripper clips, and he aced the course. Until then, I'd kind of thought young Billy would be the first of the three Mennonites to fold. But after he shot the targets to pieces from every position and every distance, Butterworth treated Billy like gold. He even ignored me, but for a few choice curses on the parade ground every morning, probably because he knew Rudebaker had given me the go ahead for corpsman. No, now it was John Strange he wanted more than anyone else, and he pushed him triply hard the sixth week, hoping to wash him out before graduation. It looked to me as if he wanted to provoke Johnny into a full-blown fistfight.

That would have been it for John if he'd hit a non-commissioned officer. In my gut, I knew Johnny could lose it and deck Butterworth. Then they'd put him in those weird bright-colored civvies we'd seen them dress other washouts in and toss him on a train back to Podunk, Idaho, or wherever it was he'd come from, and that would be it. Mister Tower of Fury would have to join the police and crack skulls with a billy club to work the demons out of his system. But they might not even ship Johnny out if he hit Butterworth. They could just as easily stick him behind bars.

So, I prayed for John in a new way. I'd already been praying for him every morning before reveille. Heck, I was praying for Billy Martens and Butterworth and Rudebaker and the entire company, I was even praying for the Corps. But for John it was prayer morning, noon, and night now. I even fasted once, and it nearly killed me to hump the hills on an empty stomach. Five days before grad, with Butterworth riding him so hard I knew a left hook was on its way to the DI's square jaw, I volunteered to help hand out Bibles and I got Johnny alone for a few minutes.

There were three chaplains—Protestant, Catholic, and Jewish —and each one distributed a different pocket Bible. Often enough, the men just lined up and picked out the version they wanted, but sometimes the recruits had to be hunted down. The Protestant Bible was a brown Gideon New Testament with a message from President Roosevelt in the front. I found Johnny cussing and cleaning out the officers' head, a job that used to belong to Billy, and told him we needed to talk. His hands were filthy, so I took a Camel out of a pack in his shirt pocket for him, lit it with his USMC Zippo, and placed it between his lips.

"What's up, Doc?" he asked, imitating the voice of Bugs

Bunny in the cartoon *A Wild Hare,* which most of us had seen more than once.

"I'm not a Doc yet, Johnny," I replied. "I've got a Gideon for you from Chaplain Jackson."

"A Gideon? You mean, like a Bible or something? Are you kidding me, Doc? What am I going to do with that? Use the pages to roll my own?"

"I thought you might read it."

"Read it? Are you kidding?"

"In Ecclesiastes, it says there's a time for war and a time for peace. What time do you think it is now?"

Johnny sucked on his cigarette and made a face. "What kind of dumb question is that? The country's at war. And I'm going to war with it."

"Maybe."

"Whaddya mean, maybe?"

"You slug Butterworth and you'll wind up in the brig. Slug him hard enough and they'll send you to Leavenworth. Kill him and you'll hang."

"I don't care. I frigging hate him."

"Hard to fight a war in prison, Johnny. Unless you'd rather fight criminals than help win the war against Japan."

"The guy's asking for it. You know the guy's asking for it. And I'm more than happy to oblige."

"So, he wins and you lose."

"Oh, he won't win, Doc. I'll pound seven kinds of pork out of him. Before I'm done, he'll be crying and begging and licking my boots."

"Before you're done, he'll be laughing his can off as the MPs drag you to your cell, knowing he outwitted the pretty Mennonite boy, and loving that you'll spend the war behind bars. He will come by, still laughing, when the Division sails for the South Pacific and combat, just to let you know the Corps is off to cover itself in glory. Great balls of fire, Johnny. Great thundering balls of fire."

"Shut up."

"It's a monster war, Johnny. You know that. The kind of war that creates legends and heroes. No one will ever forget those of us who won it, Johnny, they won't even forget the medics and corpsmen who patched the boys up and got them home alive. They'll pin medals on our chests. Billy will probably win a Silver Star just like his grandfather. Or maybe even the Medal of Honor. You can see he's got it in him. You can see he's got the fire. It'll be Belleau Wood for him. But you? You, Johnny? You'll be in Leavenworth, Kansas still cleaning toilets like you are here."

"Don't push me, Doc, I've got just as much frigging fight in me as that Montana Mennonite."

"Maybe. But no one will ever know. The Japs sure won't know. It's a long way from Kansas to Tokyo."

"What do you expect me to do? Keep eating Butterworth's crap?"

"Yes," I replied, lighting another Camel, taking a draw on it, and shoving it between his lips. "I do."

He puffed furiously. "Hell. I won't do it. I'll deck him first. Then I'll deck the MPs too."

"And then they'll lock you up so tight you'll never see the light of day again."

Johnny closed his eyes and shook his head angrily. "I can't back down. I've got these crazy demons kicking around inside my head. What do you expect me to do with them?"

"Take them to Japan."

"What about Butterworth?"

"Leave him here to rot. You go win the Navy Cross."

John finally smiled. "Yeah? The Navy Cross? I'd like that. The Navy Cross'd be a big deal back in Podunk, Idaho. I know a young lady who might look favorably upon the young man who wore it on his chest."

"A lot more favorably than visiting you in prison in Kansas."

"Ha. That's for sure." He shook his head. "I won't hit him. I won't touch him. He's not worth it. He's not worth my girl. He's not worth missing the war. But it won't be easy, Doc."

"Only a few days left. Suck it up, Marine."

"I'm not a Marine yet."

"You will be if you don't throw it all away on Butterworth." I got up to go. "And I'll be praying for you."

"Hey."

"What?"

"You said you had a Bible for me."

"I do."

"Put it in my other shirt pocket."

I tucked it in and punched it. "God be with you. Get past Butterworth and you'll be a Marine."

"I'll do it. For me. For the Corps. For my girl. Even for God."

"But especially for your girl."

He grinned. "Especially for my girl, Doc."

I don't tell people I'll pray and then not do it. I prayed hard for Johnny all right. He was still like a grenade about to go off. I was there the afternoon Butterworth kicked out the pin. Literally. By booting Johnny in the can and sending him sprawling in Camp Elliott dirt and gravel. Johnny turned himself over, his face cut with blood, gritting his perfect pretty boy teeth, clenching his big strong Idaho fists. Butterworth taunted him and cussed him and egged him on, daring him, praying Johnny'd throw a right or a left.

But I was praying too. Praying like an army of angels. A Marine Corps of the most raggedy butt ones. And whatever angels Butterworth had backing him up, they weren't enough. Johnny smiled: "Want 50 of my best, Sir?" And he began to do pushups, never letting up until he had the 50 count. Then he cranked his head up and around and grinned at Butterworth again: "Fifty more, Sir?"

"Great balls of fire!" Butterworth flared, his face scarlet: "Give me a hundred, you low-life shit!"

"Sir, yes, Sir!"

I watched John do another hundred. The whole platoon watched, Billy included.

"Not enough!" roared Butterworth, stomping down on Johnny's back with his size thirteen boot and grinding him into the dirt. "A hundred more, you Mennonite scum, you yellow-bellied pacifist swine!"

"Sir, yes, Sir!"

Johnny was strong, but he wasn't a machine. At one hundred and ninety-five, his arms gave out, and he collapsed. Butterworth howled: "Great balls of fire! You're gutless, Pretty Boy, gutless and weak. Not fit for the war or the Corps. Do your legs still work, you pacifist swine? Run my hills. Run them, you shit. I'll be there to watch. Run all three. After that, get your rifle and report for guard duty. You've pulled an all-nighter."

Johnny climbed to his feet and saluted. "Sir, thank you, Sir, pleasure to serve my country, Sir!"

Butterworth gave a shout like a peal of thunder. "Get out of my face, you scum! You won't be wearing dress blues this weekend! You'll be on a fast train back to Idaho in an ugly yellow civvies' suit with green checks! You're done, Pretty Boy! You're a washout!"

I suppose if Butterworth had the final say then Johnny Strange would have been tossed on a train heading north to Idaho. But Johnny made the grade with the rest of us. All of us had filled out in our arms and chests and narrowed out at our waists after seven weeks of basic and we looked fine in our dress blues doing close quarter drill on the parade ground that Saturday at the beginning of February 1942. We were Marines, even I was a Marine, and we held our heads high as we filed past the company and regimental and battalion commanders. And past Charles Price, our cool-headed and strong-hearted Major

General who ran the Second Marine Division. Major General
Clayton Vogel had reactivated the division on February Ist, 1941,
almost a year before Pearl Harbor; Price had taken over on
November Ist, and they had attached us to the 2nd when we
arrived mid-December, '41. "You are going to war, Marines," Price
told us as we stood at attention under the California winter sun.
"You will become legends and you will make America proud."

So, now we had new lives. All of us did. I think there was a
day or maybe two at the beginning of Boot Camp where we all
thought: *what are we doing here, why did I sign up, what if they ship
me somewhere and I get shot?* But then the grueling routine they
put us through, day after day, night after night, soon drove away
all thoughts of the future and meeting death at the end of a
Japanese bayonet—or, in my case, fears of being forced to bear
arms or fight in a combat zone. I felt obliterated by the end of the
seventh week, non-existent, unknown, a cipher to myself. I only
knew I would be a corpsman, and I wanted that.

Others took advanced weapons training—some learned how
to handle the Browning Automatic Rifle or BAR and the
Browning 50 caliber heavy machine gun, others were given
Thompson submachine guns like the gangsters used in Chicago
and New York, and still others learned to use bazookas or how to
handle high explosives, satchel charges and Bangalore torpedoes.
Some took communications and radio training. But I got into
bandages, into dressing wounds, dealing with burns and shock,
extracting bullets, giving blood plasma, and injecting ampoules
or syrettes of morphine, and it was a miracle; I had a knack for it.
Billy was the talk of the rifle range, but I was the talk of the
corpsmen and doctors and nurses who were training me.

It was like I was born to it. I'd never even thought of being
involved medically with the war, I'd just been concerned with
avoiding the killing of other human beings. It overwhelmed me.
It's kind of stunning when you discover you're an exact fit for
something. Especially when two months before you weren't a fit

for anything. I was so caught up in a crazy kind of happiness at stumbling into this surprise niche in the Corps, I hardly gave a thought to where being a corpsman would take me on the battle-field. For whatever reason, I blanked out there. I was ecstatic over the idea that I could save lives. That's all I could see.

I would save lives. That's what medics and corpsmen do. They send guys back to their mothers breathing. The jungle would teach me the truth of that. But it would teach me the truth of other things as well. The hard truths that stripped war down to the bone, down to its naked bones and its blood.

7

LETTERS

JOHNNY STRANGE

D ear John,
That's a funny way to start, because this is not a 'Dear John' letter, not by a long shot. I hope you remember me and are thinking of me even a little. I told you how I feel and so I won't make it a federal case. When a girl gives her heart the first time, she wants it to be the last time she ever does. I love you and am waiting for you. You may come home and walk right by me at the station, but I don't care. I have this big love for you inside me and it's what is making my world real. I hope you write back soon. Please take care of yourself and be careful. I'll be waiting.

Marjean

Johnny read the letter until the folds were tearing. He thought about Marjean a lot when Butterworth pushed him. When Bud pulled his head out of the crapper that day and told him to hang in for America, God and his girl, he had realized right then, maybe for the first time, that Marjean was his girl and he didn't want it to be any other way. The thought made him feel good in a strange way but uncomfortable, too.

I don't wanna be thinking about some damn dame out there. But I don't want to not be thinking about her either. Shit!

So he decided that he would make it through Boot Camp because of her. Not for America, not for God, but for his girl.

The final two weeks had been hell. No matter what he did, he never made the grade in Butterworth's eyes. Every night he lay awake thinking about Butterworth standing over him—Butterworth with his finger in his face, Butterworth shoving him down or stepping on his back as he did countless pushups, Butterworth screaming at him.

"You're a scumbag, you Mennonite piece of shit. When push comes to shove and the chips are down, you'll just piss yourself. You won't fight and you won't kill Japs. I guarantee you will freeze like a deer in the headlights, Pretty Boy. The first time a bullet whips past your head, you'll crap your pants. You, my Pretty Boy Maggot, are a guaranteed washout. You will never be a Marine."

He was exhausted, worn down, and every minute he had to fight the rage. Every time Butterworth called him Pretty Boy he thought of Jenkins, the homo back home who tried to get him to... It made him puke. Once one guy called him Pretty Boy and touched him. He only remembered Bud and Billy holding him down as he came to. The guy was crumpled against the wall rubbing his throat, his nose a bloody mess. He kept apologizing but Bud was signaling for him to beat it.

"Whoa, Johnny boy, you nearly killed that guy. Good thing me and Sniper got here in time. What's the deal, anyway?"

Johnny stood up. "I don't want to talk about it. It's none of your damn business."

Johnny knew Bud was a good guy, but sometimes he talked too much. "Come on, Johnny. We're your buddies. Us Mennos got to stick together, right? Why don't you tell us what's got you wound up so tight? Be a man about it."

Johnny turned on Bud and grabbed him by the shirt front. "I should belt you, Bud. I am already a man, and I will prove it—to you, to Butterworth, to my dad, to... to everyone back home. Never say it again."

Bud took hold of Johnny's wrists and pried his hands away. "Okay, Johnny, okay. Whatever. I'm your pal, just remember that."

DEAR MARJEAN,

I got your letter. Why don't you start the next ones off with Dear Johnny, so I know you're not dumping me for some civilian? Does that sound like I don't want you to dump me? Because that's what I want you to know. I don't want you to dump me, or be with anybody else. I thought maybe what happened between us was just something that happened, you know, like we got carried away and went too far. But something happened out in that boathouse, and it was you. You touched me in a big way, bigger than I ever knew could happen. I dream about you—your eyes, your hair, your face and your funny little sharp teeth. I'm in love with you, Marjean. And that's what's keeping me going. And you know what? I never loved any girl before.

They say war is hell, but I wouldn't know about that. Whoever said it never went through boot camp because Boot is triple-dog hell. Fighting Japs will be a walk in the park compared to this. My DI, that's my Drill Instructor, he has it in for me because I come from a Mennonite church. It's funny because the other two Mennonite guys here are doing well, and they both still believe. I'm the least believing Mennonite of the bunch, I'm not even sure if there is a God, and yet the guy has singled me out. He says I don't have what it takes. But I will prove him wrong. I've got one thing going for me—that you're my girl. I will make it, I will be a Marine and I will do it because you have faith in me.

So as we say in the Marines, Semper Fi, always faithful, and that's you. I don't know why you love me, but it gives me the will to go on. Don't stop.

Johnny

P.S. I'll add more to this letter after I get back from the Crucible.

ONE OF THE FRUSTRATING THINGS WAS THAT BILLY AND BUD seemed to have found a niche they fit into. Billy was the best man with a rifle Johnny had ever seen. The guy was incredible. One hundred, two hundred, five hundred, even seven hundred yards, Billy Martens had it locked in. And Bud was training to be a corpsman. Scuttlebutt was that the guy was a natural.

Watching his buddies do so well made Johnny chafe under the weight of feeling useless. Until one day when he got his chance. They were in the middle of their forty-mile march during the Crucible, the last big test in their training. With Marjean always in his thoughts, Johnny had overcome Butterworth's constant riding and had made it this far. But he was still feeling useless until the Commanding Officer, Major General C. F. B. Price, drove by in a jeep. As the General went by, Johnny could see the vehicle was in trouble. The front end was vibrating and swinging back and forth. The General yelled at his driver and they pulled over.

"What the hell is going on, Corporal?"

"I don't know, Sir. Maybe the steering's bad."

Johnny saw his chance. He stepped up to the Jeep and saluted. "May I help, Sir?"

"You know anything about Jeeps, Recruit?"

"Sir, yes, Sir."

"What's going on here?"

"It's a death wobble, Sir."

The driver spoke up. "Yeah, maybe bad stabilizers."

"If I may, Sir, it's not just that."

The General was interested now. "Then what is it, uhh...?"

"Strange, Sir, Recruit John Strange."

"Well, Recruit Strange, tell me what's going on here?"

"Sir, the death wobble is not caused by one component, is it the total amount of play in all the steering components. Worn tie rods, idler arm, track bar, wheel bearings, pitman arm, steering center link and shaft, ball joints, alignment and even tire pressure can combine to cause the death wobble. This makes diagnosing the problem difficult and leads inexperienced mechanics..." he nodded at the Corporal... "leads inexperienced mechanics to blame the steering stabilizer when no other obvious cause presents itself. You must inspect each individual component for signs of wear. Any play in any component of the steering system warrants replacement, Sir."

General Price grinned. "Well, well, a friggin' walking encyclopedia. Okay, here's the question, Recruit Strange. This is my personal Jeep. Can you fix it?"

"Sir, give me four hours in the motor pool and parts for anything that's worn out and I'll have it ship-shape for you, Sir."

General Price looked around and saw the DI coming up at the tail of the column. "Sergeant Butterworth!"

Butterworth trotted up and then saw Johnny. "Say, Pretty Boy, what are you doing bothering the General? Get back in formation!"

"Just a minute, Sergeant. Did you know Recruit Strange is a mechanic?"

"No, Sir, I did not. What I know is that he will wash out of the Crucible tonight, and after that it won't make a dang bit of difference if he's Superman."

The General turned to Johnny. "Are you going to wash out, Recruit Strange?"

"Sir, no, Sir!"

General Price looked at Butterworth. "If this man makes it through tonight, I want him sent to the motor pool tomorrow. He's got four hours to fix my Jeep. If he doesn't do it, you can do what you want with him. If he's not just a braggin' son of a bitch and he can do it, assign him to the pool until we ship out. We will need good mechanics out there in the field."

"But, Sir?"

"Yes, Recruit?"

"I joined up to kill Japs."

"Pretty gung ho, eh?"

"Sir, yes, Sir!"

"If you make it through tonight, and fix this Jeep, believe me, you'll be killing all the Japs you want. Sergeant!"

Butterworth saluted. "I will see to it this little homo gets his shot, Sir."

Johnny ventured one more thing. "Sir, if I may?"

"What is it, Recruit?"

"If you don't go over twenty, you will make it back to camp. And stay out of the ruts."

"You hear what Recruit Strange said, Corporal?"

"Yes, Sir!"

"Good. All right, Sergeant, carry on. And Strange..."

"Sir?"

"Do your best tonight, boy. I'm dying to see if you're a friggin' miracle worker or just a damn liar."

He nodded to the driver. "Turn it around, Corporal. I need another Jeep."

As they drove off, the General was laughing.

Butterworth turned to Johnny. "What is it about you Menno's? God seems to smile on you in a big way. Now get your raggedy ass back in line. You got a Crucible to make it through. And if you make it, and that's a huge if, Pretty Boy, I will send you right on over to the Motor Pool with no sleep. We'll see how damn tough you are."

———

So that's how I made it through, Marjean. The Crucible was

everything they said it would be. They marched us forty miles on minimum food and no sleep. We got two C-rations to eat. We ended late and had to clean our weapons. Two hours after we hit the sack, they woke us up. Then we did night movement and then they hiked us back another forty for the Eagle Globe and Anchor event. But I didn't get to sleep. I went straight to the Motor Pool. The General was there with two colonels and Butterworth. I guess he wanted to see if I was the real deal. Didn't bother me though. That pool had everything I needed and, just as I suspected, it was only a few of the parts that needed replacing. I had that baby out of there in three hours. Boy, was Butterworth mad. But I got through.

So I'm a Marine, Marjean. And it's because of you. You kept me going. And I want to ask one more thing. Can you send me a picture so I can carry you close? I've never said this to anyone Marjean. I love you. And maybe Butterworth was right. Maybe God is smiling on me.

Johnny

Johnny stared down at the letter. He felt weird, strange, and he didn't know why. He sat there for a long time with the letter in his hand. That's when Bud walked in.

"Got a letter for Marjean, Johnny? I'm going to the PO, I'd be glad to mail it."

Johnny said nothing.

"What's up, Strange?"

Suddenly Johnny knew why he felt weird. He stood up. "I don't want to send it, Bud."

"Why not, kid?"

"Marjean says she loves me. That part makes me feel good. But I told her I loved her too and that sticks in my craw."

"What's wrong with that?"

Johnny crumpled up the letter and threw it against the wall. "Damn it, Bud, I don't want to love anybody. I can't love anybody. Don't you get it? There's no room in me for love, just hate. I can feel good in my head, but in my heart it just hurts. I don't need this shit."

"Why can't you love anyone?"

Johnny turned away. "None of your damn business, Bud."

Bud walked over and picked up the letter. He didn't say a word, he just smoothed it out over the rail of Johnny's bunk until it was almost flat. Then he folded it into thirds. "Got an envelope, Johnny?"

"I told you I don't want to mail the friggin' letter!"

Bud looked at Johnny and there was sadness in his eyes. "Mail it Johnny. You got a disease down inside you and you need to shine some light on it. The only way to do that is by letting yourself love someone. You're my friend and I want the best for you. And mailing this letter is the best thing you will ever do in your life. Now damn it, Johnny, get me an envelope and address it."

Johnny's eyes popped at the unaccustomed swear word from straight-laced Bud. Then he picked up an envelope. "It's already addressed, Bud."

Bud took it and put the letter inside. "You're pissed now, Johnny, but you will thank me later." And he turned and walked out.

8

ULYSSES

BILLY MARTENS

T he Corps had Billy Martens help train recruits in shooting skills after they had developed his proficiency as a sniper and BAR gunner. Thousands of recruits were pouring into Elliott, inspired by the heroic Marine defense of Wake Island that had gone on for weeks before they were overwhelmed by the Japanese. There was talk of keeping Billy behind when the 2nd Division deployed so he could work with several more Boot Camps of recruits. He argued against this not only with Captain "Rudy" Rudebaker, but also the regimental commander and even appealed to Major General Price. The new Marines had less and less use for the brass that strutted around Camp Elliott, but they respected two senior officers: their Commander-in-Chief in Washington and Major General Price.

Price listened to Billy's complaint without interrupting, delivered while the young Marine stood flagpole stiff in the Major General's office. Once Billy had finished, the General asked him to stand easy and then lifted a newspaper from his large desk. He tapped it with a finger.

"We're losing the war, Private Martens," Price rumbled. "This winter has been an unholy mess for American arms. And for the

Brits too. They lost Singapore on February 15th. And now they're
in trouble in Burma. MacArthur fled Corregidor on March 11th...
we've pretty much surrendered the Philippines, in my opinion,
even though I know our boys and the Filipino troops will fight on
as long as they can. When Jap planes bombed Darwin on
February 19 they sank thirteen or fourteen ships—it was an
Aussie Pearl Harbor. And the United States Navy has already lost
the carrier 'Langley' and the largest warship we had in the South
Pacific, the 'Houston.' Private Martens, the Japs trounced us at the
Battle of the Java Sea on March 1st."

"Yes, Sir."

"We need good Marines, well-trained Marines, if we can ever
hope to stem the tide in the Pacific War. I've been informed you
turn raw recruits into crackerjack riflemen in half the time other
trainers do."

"Yes, Sir, but I'm one of my men now, Sir, not just a trainer,
Sir."

"Explain yourself, Marine."

"Training here is one thing, Sir. Helping my men shoot
straighter in a combat area is something else. It makes all the
difference. I can't do that from California, Sir. They're my men,
Sir. My buddies. I need to be with them. All of us who went
through Boot together. We need to be there for each other, Sir. I
need to help them out. I have to be there when they fight, Sir. I
have to. I can't let them down."

Billy saw the small smile that came and went on the General's
face, but he did not understand it.

"Captain Rudebaker tells me your grandfather fought with
the American Expeditionary Force in 1918," Price said.

"Yes, Sir."

"That he taught you how to hunt and shoot."

"Yes, Sir."

"That you carry his medals with you for good luck."

"For good luck and God's blessing, yes, Sir."

"May I?"

"Of course, General."

Billy handed over the medals. The General examined them minutely. Then he left them on his desktop a moment and stared at Billy without saying a word. Finally, he broke the silence with two words: "Chateau-Thierry."

Billy blinked. "Yes, Sir."

"Do you know what General Pershing said about us?"

"No, Sir."

"He said, and I quote, 'The deadliest weapon in the world is a United States Marine and his rifle.' We need topnotch riflemen in the Pacific, Private Martens. If we have them, we whip the Empire of Japan. Whatever our flyboys and sailors think, the war will be won on the ground and they can't win that war for us. The Marines have to do it. With their BARS and Thompsons and Browning Fifties. And M1 Garands and 1903s. Understood?"

"Understood, Sir."

"Having said that, I acknowledge the value of placing a Marine in the field to help others hone their shooting skills in a combat engagement. Conditions on a battlefield are not the conditions recruits find themselves in at Camp Elliott, no matter how difficult we try to make it for you. It would be a pity if our men forgot more than they had learned once the first shot was fired. Having a marksman or two in the thick of it with our boys might prove useful. Certainly, we can't leave all our best shooters in the States."

"No, Sir."

General Price reached across his desk and handed the medals back to Billy, along with a booklet. "Give me another Château-Thierry, Marine. Give me a dozen Château-Thierrys and we'll win this war. You will be deployed with the 2nd Regiment of the 2nd Division."

"Sir! Yes, Sir!"

"You are dismissed, Marine. Godspeed."

They both saluted.

Outside, Billy took a moment to light up a cigarette, a bright happiness rippling all through him at knowing he would be shipped out with the rest of the boys. He had a pack of Chesterfields he'd been issued and he flipped through the booklet the General had given him while he smoked one through. There were only a few pages. It was a poem. One part of it had been underlined in black ink.

That which we are, we are;
One equal temper of heroic hearts.

Billy thought about this and began to read the poem which was entitled *Ulysses*. Poetry was not something he was used to, so he took his time. Members of his platoon began to drift by. His reputation as a marksman had made him popular, and everyone had something to say.

Tommy Earp, who always called himself "Tommy Earp Not Related," a Browning Fifty gunner, and Sid Greene, who fed the ammo belt into the big machine gun, were both sure he was reading a Superman comic and wanted to see the pictures.

"Poetry?" Earp was astonished. "Are you frigging kidding me?"

"Price gave it to me," explained Billy.

"What's he trying to do? Civilize you?"

"Me?" Greene filched one of Billy's Chesterfields. "I'd have asked for a beer instead."

"I didn't ask for anything, Sid."

"That's your problem. If you'd have asked, the General would have known what you really wanted. You sniper types are too damn quiet."

Sam Kane, a redhead whose nickname in the company was Raising Kane, and who played around with satchel charges and other explosives, was sure Billy had a copy of the latest Batman.

He confessed he had a thing for Catwoman and that he intended to find her and marry her after the war. She was in New York, he knew that, because Batman's Gotham and New York City were one and the same.

Frank Harte, who joked that he was "Not Related to Bret Harte the Writer" whenever Tommy Earp made an appearance, and who was being trained on the BAR and the 30-caliber water-cooled machine gun, was convinced the booklet on poetry camouflaged a comic on Captain America beating the snot out of the Nazis. What "Sniper," Billy's nickname in the platoon, was doing holding a poem and a cigarette at the same time, was a mystery greater than the mystery of Captain America's super-human strength and cunning. He told Billy that if he was a DI, he'd have made him hit the deck and deliver 175 pushups with one arm. Or maybe one thumb.

"Teacher," on the other hand, Mike "Hot Kiss" Hotchkiss, who looked more like a football lineman than a Math wizard, declared his love for the intricacies and precision of fine poetry. So, he read the poem in the booklet out loud, gathering a small audience while he did so, enjoying the smattering of applause and catcalls when he finished with a melodramatic flourish:

> *It may be that the gulfs will wash us down:*
> *It may be we shall touch the Happy Isles,*
> *And see the great Achilles, whom we knew.*
> *Tho' much is taken, much abides; and tho'*
> *We are not now that strength which in old days*
> *Moved earth and heaven, that which we are, we are;*
> *One equal temper of heroic hearts,*
> *Made weak by time and fate, but strong in will*
> *To strive, to seek, to find, and not to yield.*

THE RABBI, THE JEWISH CHAPLAIN SOL DAVIDS, ALSO READ THE poem out loud, but so quietly no one but Billy heard him and no one stopped to listen. Except Father McKean, the Catholic chaplain, who said he'd never heard anything by Tennyson, or any British poet or author, delivered in a Bronx accent. The Rabbi shrugged, running his fingers through his long black beard in an imitation of a wise Hasidic Rebbe from the Old Country: "Such an accent unlocks hidden truths, Padre. Which is why you have never gotten the Torah right in any of your homilies."

McKean laughed. "Care to enlighten me, Rabbi?"

"It depends where and when and what."

"Officer's Mess, now, I have two rare bottles of Guinness on ice."

Sol Davids' eyes lit up and he handed the poem back to Billy. "I'm the rabbi for the job. I hope there are more than two bottles."

"I suppose it depends on how lengthy your instruction is."

"Oh, very lengthy. You know so very little, Erik."

Billy had actually smoked three Chesterfields before the impromptu poetry reading played itself out. He was on his way to help recruits at the range alongside Butterworth and the other DIs when he bumped into Bud who wanted to know what he was reading—"Is it the Green Lantern, Sniper? Because the Lantern is my favorite superhero. Well, him or Flash."

Billy laughed. "What a crazy platoon. Batman, Superman, Catwoman, Captain America, and now the Green Lantern and Flash. I don't know any of these people."

"What? You've never read a comic book?"

"No."

"I'm Mennonite too, Billy Boy, but that doesn't mean I didn't have a few stashed by the outhouse. You need to read a couple of them. They never kill the bad guys, you know. Just beat them up and throw them in jail."

"This isn't a comic book. It's a poem. *Ulysses*. By a writer named Tennyson."

"*Ulysses*? Let me see."

"I suppose you had a copy of it by the outhouse too?"

"I wasn't that fancy. But I did read *The Red Badge of Courage* about five times. *War and Peace* once. And *All Quiet on the Western Front* two times that I remember. The Nazis burned that one, you know."

"I didn't know."

"And Helen Keller. And *Bambi*. They tried to burn Zane Grey too, but the Germans raised such a hue and cry they left *Riders of the Purple Sage* alone."

"You're a walking encyclopedia."

"I can be." Bud read the poem over quickly. "I think I've heard parts of this before. I know this Tennyson. He wrote a war poem, *The Charge of the Light Brigade*."

"I thought you didn't like war."

"I don't. Neither do veterans. The only ones who get excited about war are politicians who use it and raw recruits who've never seen it. Still, I love the excitement of the galloping horses in the poem. But, *theirs not to reason why, theirs but to do and die*? That's stupid." Billy watched Bud's lips move as he read *Ulysses* over a second time. "The story in this poem is taken from a Greek myth. About a hero named Ulysses or Odysseus who is trying to make his way home after a long war against the city of Troy."

"Yeah?" Billy started what he called his fourth "poetry cigarette" and inhaled deeply. "Learn all this in Mennonite Sunday School?"

"Ha. Hardly."

"Had a book on Greek myths stashed with the comic books?"

"I think it was there, yeah. Listen to this."

> *Come, my friends, 'tis not too late to seek a newer world.*
> *Push off, and sitting well in order smite*
> *The sounding furrows; for my purpose holds*
> *To sail beyond the sunset, and the baths*

Of all the western stars, until I die.

"Kind of sad," Billy responded.

"Kind of brave. Where did you get this?"

"General Price gave it to me."

"Why?"

"I don't know why. All I know is he cleared the deck for me to ship out with all of you to the South Pacific. And for that, I thank God—whatever God is really out there."

Bud grinned and slapped him on the back. "That's good news. Look out, Tokyo."

"Look out, Tokyo."

"Hey, can I borrow this? I'd like to spend some time with it."

Billy shrugged. "Keep it as long as you want. Just don't lose it. I want to take it home as a souvenir. The General's signature is at the front."

"Thanks. It could be our story too, you know. We're going out to fight our battle against Troy. And then we're going to have to make our way home again. It might take us a while. Just like it did Ulysses."

"Did he have a long journey, Bud?"

Bud nodded. "Oh, yeah. A long journey, Billy. And a hard one."

9

DEPARTING FROM ITHACA

THE CORPSMAN

I always loved the story of Ulysses the Wanderer. I told you about studying the constellations when I was a kid, lying out in the yard on a horizon-less night in Ritzville. One night my dad was with me and he pointed out a group of stars and said, "That's Aquarius, Philo." I didn't mind being called Philo by my dad.

All I could see was stars, but I asked anyway. "What's Aquarius, Dad?"

"It's a constellation, Philo. It's a group of stars that reminded the ancient Greeks of characters from their stories. They believed you could find all their main heroes and gods right up there in the stars. That one there is Aquarius, the Water Bearer. He's most often associated with Ganymede, the cup-carrier to the Olympian gods. In the story, Ganymede was the son of King Tros. He's the king they named Troy after. Ganymede was the most beautiful boy alive and Zeus was so infatuated with him he took the form of an eagle and abducted the boy."

"Wow, that's neat, Dad. What else is up there?"

"Well, there's Cancer, the Crab, and Canis Major, the big dog, and over there is Orion the Hunter. That one over there, the double star, is Gemini, the Twins, and that big one is Hercules."

"And all these characters are in their stories?"

"Sure and a lot more, Son."

"Wow, that's interesting, Dad."

That was a special night because my dad and I got on the same track for once. It surprised me he knew so much about the Greeks, being a Mennonite and all. What I found out that night is that faith and knowledge can live in the same head. My dad is a real smart guy, and he knows about a lot of things. Lots of Amish and Mennonite folks think if you even get close to the world, it will taint you and mess you up. But my dad believes the Bible, especially that verse that says "*All things were made by him; and without him was not anything made that was made.*" Dad is wise enough to know God made everything, and the only reason it's messed up is because the Devil put his oar in. He always told me, "Just stay on God's side and do what he says and you'll be okay." So we are Mennonites that fit in a little more with the world. No buggies for us, we're just farmers that believe you shouldn't kill each other. We have a telephone and an old Ford truck and we even have a radio.

My dad, being so smart and all, he always wanted me to be a brain. I mean, he named me after the guy who invented the television, so he was pleased as punch when I followed through on our conversation that night and went to the library and found out all this keen stuff. But I got the most excited when I read *The Iliad* and *The Odyssey*, two books by Homer. I didn't read them in the Greek, I didn't even read the poems, but I read the books that some modern guys had written retelling all the stories. The one I liked best was Odysseus The Wanderer. It's all about this guy Odysseus, or Ulysses as the twentieth century guys call him. Ulysses is this guy who gets caught up in the Trojan War. He's the King of a little Island called Ithaca that's out in the middle of the Aegean Sea. It's a gorgeous place, all mountains and clouds and the beautiful blue sea all around. He's happy living there with his wife Penelope and their son

Telemachus. He loves his son and the poet Tennyson wrote this about him:

This is my son, mine own Telemachus,
To whom I leave the sceptre and the isle,—
Well-loved of me, discerning to fulfil
This labour, by slow prudence to make mild

Kind of made me think about how our CO and most of the brass and even Butterworth really love us. It's the love that men feel for other men they know they will share a great adventure with and maybe even die beside. And it's the love I feel for the guys sacked out all around me while I'm writing this under my blanket. It's not a sissy thing—it's a strong, real, powerful kind of love that means you would go the distance to protect your buddies and even die for them if need be.

To go on with my story, Ulysses has to join the Greek army because of an oath he took and leave his wife and son behind. He goes to Troy and the Greeks are getting their rears kicked—it's been ten years and they still can't get into the city. So Ulysses comes up with a plan. They build a big old wooden horse and then leave it on the beach as an offering to the Trojan gods and the army sails away. What the Trojans don't know is that Ulysses and fifty Greeks are inside the horse and when the Trojans roll it inside the walls in celebration, they wait until dark and then open the gates and let in the Greek army that has snuck back. Well, there is hell to pay and all the Trojans get killed.

Ulysses sails for home, but on the way he gets captured by this giant one-eyed guy named Polyphemos. Polyphemos is a cannibal, what the Greeks called a Cyclops, and the first night he cooks two of Ulysses' crew up for dinner. Each day the Cyclops goes off to tend his sheep and locks Ulysses and his crew in the cave by rolling a big stone in front of the door. One day when he's gone they sharpen a big stake in the fire. Then when Polyphemus gets home they get him drunk and shove the stake in his eye and blind him. They escape because Polyphemos can't see them riding out of his cave under the sheep. Well, it turns out that the Cyclops is the son of Poseidon, the god of the sea, and when Ulysses blinds his son, it ticks Poseidon off. Ulysses keeps sailing from island to island, but Poseidon won't let him get home. He sends winds and storms and all kinds of stuff that blows him off course—it takes him twenty more years before he gets back to Ithaca. But Poseidon can't kill him because the main Greek god, a guy named Zeus, is on Ulysses' side. He tries to keep Poseidon off Ulysses' back so he can get home.

Now a few days ago Billy Martens brings in this poem he got from General Price. It's the poem I mentioned, *Ulysses*, by Alfred Lord Tennyson, and when Billy reads it I get chills. It makes me think about how Ulysses sailed from island to island, and that's what the 2nd Division will do.

So why all this rambling about Ulysses? Well Ulysses had this band of guys with him and some were brave and some were cowards and some were just plain stupid. Boy, that's a lot like our bunch. We're shipping out tomorrow for the South Pacific and who knows how long we'll be out there. Some of us will be heroes and some will run away and a lot of us will die on some island we never ever heard about. Billy let me borrow the poem, and I've been reading it. I really like this part:

> *Death closes all: but something ere the end,*
> *Some work of noble note, may yet be done,*
> *Not unbecoming men that strove with Gods.*
> *The lights begin to twinkle from the rocks:*
> *The long day wanes: the slow moon climbs: the deep*
> *Moans round with many voices. Come, my friends,*
> *'Tis not too late to seek a newer world.*
> *Push off and sitting well in order smite*
> *The sounding furrows; for my purpose holds*

To sail beyond the sunset, and the baths
Of all the western stars until I die.

See, on the one hand we have our own Poseidon—that's the Japs and they are against us. They're mad at us because we cut off their oil and natural resources. It's kind of like we blind Polyphemos. But we have the main God on our side. He will be with us the whole trip and what he decides will be, that's what will be.

Now Ulysses, he met all these strange people, witches and stuff. One time they met these guys called the Lotus Eaters. They land on this island after Poseidon has been blowing them off course for days. While most of the crew gathers provisions, Ulysses sent three men to explore the island. Lotus Eaters were not dangerous in the usual sense, but they ate the lotus plant every day and it made them lethargic and simpleminded. These Lotus Eaters offered the scouting party the sweet fruit of the lotus. It was delicious, and when the men ate it they forgot their mission and did not return to the ship.

After a search of the island, Ulysses found them, but they loved the way the Lotus made them feel so much they didn't want to leave. He had to drag the weeping men back to the ships where he tied them to the rowing benches to prevent their escape. Then Ulysses ordered his ships to sea so they could escape the island of the Lotus Eaters.

We will run into places like that—places that seem so beautiful, but like I always say, the beautiful places are where the enemy can hide the easiest. Some of us have to stay on guard, and if we see our guys getting simple-minded and forgetful of their mission, why, we will have to smack some sense into them.

I think the worst thing that happened to Ulysses was when this gal named Circe lured Ulysses' crew to her house with sweet singing. They drank these potions and passed out, and then Circe turned them all into pigs. One guy got away and wanted Ulysses to sail away and leave his crew behind—a real coward. Ulysses almost killed the guy. Then he ran back to Circe's house and rescued his men. Circe warned Ulysses that before he got home, he would have to sail to the gates of the underworld.

And there it is. We are going out and Circe will be waiting for us. I've heard men in battle turn into beasts and I believe it, but like Ulysses we will keep our guys on the straight and narrow. We may see some inhuman things, but we have to behave like men and not animals. Even though the Japs are against us, our God is fighting for us and he'll either see us through or take us home, to the real Ithaca, with him.

Tomorrow we are all going to sail beyond the sunset. What's out there? Thunder and sunshine. There lies the port down on San Diego Bay. The vessel puffs her sails. Here lie my shipmates all around me—their breath sounding quiet and muffled in the long dark of this last night ashore. Maybe this is the last time they will ever sleep peacefully in a bed. How many of these guys will ever see Ithaca again? The mumbling Cyclops of war will eat many of them. The Sirens will lure many to their deaths and terrible Scylla, the seven-headed monster, will snatch many of them off the decks.

Charybdis, the whirlpool that sucks down ships and spits them back out, is lurking out there somewhere, and before we get home we are going to the gates of hell. I told Billy we're going out to fight our battle against Troy. And then we will have to make our way home again. It might take us a while. Just like it did Ulysses. But most of his crew died on the way.

Billy asked me, "Did Ulysses make it home, Bud?"

And I told him as clearly as I could—"Ulysses did, but some of us ain't coming back to Ithaca."

10

SECRETS

JOHNNY STRANGE

M arjean Langston stood in front of the mirror. She pulled
on her Alpaca sweater and stood sideways in the light.
There it was, the little bump.

Oh, my gosh. Am I...

She had been irregular in her cycle since her mom died, but
she thought it was just her body dealing with the grief and loss.
But now a terrible certainty came over her.

I'm pregnant!

She had never considered the consequences when she had
given herself to Johnny that day at the King's cabin. Now the
chickens had come home to roost. She put her hands to her hair
and paced around the room.

I can't tell Dad, it will kill him.

She thought of Johnny, so far away, getting ready to ship out
to who knew where.

I can't tell Johnny, either. He's got so much to worry about already.

Marjean sat down on the edge of her bed and thought about
what this meant. She would have to leave, go to an unwed mother's home and then give the baby up for adoption.

Oh, I couldn't give up my baby!

She thought of the alternative—stay home and have the baby and hope Johnny would marry her when he got home... if he got home. And what if he didn't want her, what if he didn't want the baby?

No, it would be better if she went away and gave the baby up.

But if I leave, what will I tell Dad?

Then everything flooded in on her, her mother dying, moving home from New York, and now this. She collapsed on her bed and wept.

After a while there was a quiet knock on the door. "Jean, are you okay?"

She struggled to control her emotions. "No, Dad. I'm not."

"Can I come in?"

She didn't want to see him, but right now she needed him. "Come in, Dad."

She pulled herself up and tried to compose herself. Her dad came in. Dr. Langston was a doctor that looked the part—tall, handsome, just a touch of gray around the temples, great bedside manner—If you saw him walking down the street you would say, "That guy's a doctor." Most days he had a smile and a twinkle in his eye. But today he had a worried look. He walked to the bed and put his hand on her shoulder.

"What's wrong, Honey?"

And then without even thinking, she said it.

"I'm pregnant, Dad."

Dr. Langston nodded. "I know, Honey."

"You know? But how..."

Her dad sat down beside her. "Jean, I'm a woman's doctor, remember. I notice things. Over the last three weeks your skin has taken on a rosy glow, and when you were in your pajamas last night, I saw that your bosom is bigger. That doesn't happen overnight unless... And the little tummy bump. It's fairly obvious."

"Oh, Dad!" Marjean burst into tears again. "What am I going to do, Dad?"

"Does Johnny know?"

She looked up, her eyes wide.

"Dad, how did you know it was Johnny?"

Her dad's face cracked a big smile. "Come on, Honey. You've been sending letters every week to Johnny Strange. I take them to the post office, remember?"

Marjean wiped away tears with the back of her hand. "Are you mad at me, Dad?"

Dr. Langston took his daughter into his arms. "Mad? No, Honey. You're my little girl. You are all I have left. When you said you wanted to come home after Janine died, it was the best day of my life... well, unless it was the day I married your mom, and the day you were born."

"Why did you let us go, Dad?"

Dr. Langston sighed. "Your mom didn't trust me. You know, the handsome gynecologist with all the lovely patients. She thought I was having affairs."

"Were you, Dad?"

There was a long silence in the room. Dr. Langston looked away. Marjean could barely hear his response.

"Yes, I am ashamed to say."

"So Mom left?"

"Yes. At first I thought it would be great to be free again, to do what I wanted to do. But after you both left, I realized what a big hole I had in my life."

"But mom loved you, and you loved her. Why didn't you guys try to work it out?"

"I don't know, Jean—my pride, her stubbornness and hurt I guess. After a while I asked her to come back, but she said she could never trust me again, and I didn't blame her. I messed everything good in my life up. But it's too late to make it right, so let's deal with the present. You have decisions to make."

"Dad, I'm ruined. I'm pregnant and I'm not married.

Dr. Langston pulled Marjean closer.

"Let me tell you a secret, Jean. It may help."

"A secret, Dad."

"Your mother was pregnant with you when we got married."

"What?"

"That's right, Honey. We fell in love the first time we met. We couldn't keep our hands off each other, and it was the roaring twenties. When she found out, Janine wanted to go away to have you, but I told her no. I wanted to get married. That surprised her because she thought I looked down on her for sleeping with me. I was an up-and-coming young Doctor with my whole life in front of me, and she was just some girl who got pregnant. But I didn't feel that way. I loved her with all my heart."

"I know she only loved you, Dad."

They sat together for a long time, not saying anything. At last Dr. Langston spoke. "What are you going to tell Johnny?"

"Nothing, Dad. I know he's going into battle soon, and I..." Marjean broke into tears again.

"You don't want to put too much pressure on him?"

"Yes, Dad."

"Can I give you some advice, Jean?" He handed her a hanky out of his coat pocket.

She took the hanky and nodded as she blew her nose.

"Tell Johnny. He deserves to know."

Her eyes got big, and she started to protest.

He put up his hand. "No, Jean. He has a right to know. He's going to war. Maybe he'll come back, maybe not. But he's got to know what he's fighting for. Knowing he has a woman who loves him and a baby coming will give him something bigger to fight for than the reason he's got now."

"What do you mean, Dad?"

Dr. Langston went to the window and looked out at the city of Sandpoint. He was quiet for a moment, and then he turned to

Marjean. "I've lived around here for a long time. It's a small community and everybody knows everybody's business. The Mennonite Church where Johnny's dad is an elder—they have had problems."

"Problems, Dad?"

"Yes." He paused and then went on. "There was a man on their Elder Board a few years ago who the church forced to step down and excommunicated. They are a tight bunch up there and they said nothing, but the word got around he was a molester; that he abused young boys in the church."

"Dad, that's awful."

"Yes, and the word was that Johnny Strange was one boy he abused."

"Oh, Dad! Did the man get arrested?"

"No. The church kept a lid on the whole thing. It got out that this guy, Harold Jenkins, had repented and promised he would never do it again so they let him back in the church. They didn't want the scandal, so they hushed it all up."

Marjean looked at her dad. "Oh, my poor Johnny."

"I've known Johnny for a long time, Jean. I like him. He's a good kid and a great mechanic. Gerald's dad can't say enough about him. But he's wound up tight. I suspect he joined up because he has a lot of hate—hate for Jenkins, hate for the church, hate for his dad for the cover-up."

Marjean sat in shocked silence.

"Does this change anything for you Jean?"

She looked up at him. "No, Dad, it doesn't."

"Good. That's what I thought you'd say. And that's why you need to tell him."

"I don't get you, Dad."

"Johnny Strange went to war because of all the hate he's carrying. Maybe you can give him a different reason for fighting."

"What reason, Dad?"

"Love, Honey, love."

JOHNNY LOOKED DOWN AT THE LETTER AND READ IT AGAIN. HIS hands were shaking.

A baby! Marjean's having my baby.

He put the letter down on his bunk and stared at the wall.

I'm going to be a dad.

Then a rush of shame and guilt washed over him. He put his head down. Tears dripped from his eyes.

There was a quiet sound of steps, and then Bud was standing next to his bunk.

"What's the skinny, Marine?"

Johnny didn't look up. He just handed Bud the letter.

Bud read it and then looked at Johnny. "That's just great, Johnny."

"No, Bud, it's not great."

"But Johnny, why not?"

"It's not great because, because I'm not... I mean..."

Bud sat on the bunk. "Spill it, Pal."

Johnny was quiet for a long time. Then he sighed. His voice was low. "Okay, I'm telling you because I trust you more than anyone. But this is where it stops, Bud. You got to promise me it doesn't leave this room or I clam up right now and screw you."

Bud nodded his agreement.

"There was a guy in my church, an elder. He was a great guy and all the guys liked him. He took us fishing and hunting, he led the Cub Scouts and the Boy Scout troop. He organized these great camp-outs, and we all wanted to go with him."

Bud listened.

"One time, when I was about thirteen, we went on a camping trip. It rained hard the first night and my tent was leaking, so he said I could sleep in his. No big deal, the guys always slept in each other's tents. I mean we were guys."

"What happened Johnny?"

"In the middle of the night I woke up. He'd lit a candle and he was sitting by my bedroll. He was rubbing my back and calling me 'Pretty Boy.' He pulled down the covers and started massaging me on my back and my legs... and my butt. At first I liked it because it felt good. Then he reached his hand under me and..."

"He touched you?"

"Yeah. For a few minutes I let him do it. It felt good. Then he rolled over on top of me." He was excited, rubbing his body against me, and suddenly I realized what it meant. He wanted to... well, you know..."

"Yeah, I kinda got it figured out, Johnny."

"He was a homo, a queer, and he wanted to do his homo stuff to me and I almost puked. I shoved him off me and jumped up. I had my hunting knife on the belt of my pants so I grabbed it up and told him to get away from me, that if he came any closer I would gut him from his crotch to his gullet. He turned white and backed off. I told him if he ever tried that again, if he ever even touched me, I would kill him."

"What happened?"

"He begged me not to tell anyone, that it would ruin him. I told him to go screw himself, I was going to tell what he did and I hoped he went to prison. He cried like a baby, but he stayed away because I had my knife. I got dressed and went back to my tent. When I got home, I told my dad. He told the Elder Board, and they excommunicated the guy."

"Did they tell the police?"

"No, they said it wasn't such a big deal. I mean, he didn't rape me or anything. After ten days, he repented, and they let him back in the church, even let him be back on the Elder Board."

"What a SNAFU, Johnny."

"Yeah, but that's not the worst part. They let him keep leading the scouts and doing the camp trips and everything. When he knew no one was looking, he would grin at me in this sick way and call me Pretty Boy. I knew he was still doing it to other kids, and I could see the guys he was playing up to. I told my dad, but he said I was lying. He said it was my word against Jenkins. He said the guy had repented before God and that was that."

"So what has that to do with Marjean?"

"Don't you see, Bud. When he did that to me, I liked it. That makes me a homo too. That's why I can't love Marjean, why I can't love any girl. I'm a queer."

Bud stared at Johnny for a long time. Then to Johnny's surprise, he laughed.

"What are you laughing for, Bud? I just told you I'm a queer, a homo. What's so friggin' funny about that?"

Bud shook his head and smiled his sad smile at Johnny. "You, Johnny Strange, are the least likely homo I ever met."

Johnny looked up. "What do you mean, Bud?"

"So you were thirteen and just starting to get, well those urges. You were young and full of vinegar and someone touched you and it felt good. So what? You bailed out and told him you'd kill him if he tried it again, and that's what a man would do. That means you aren't like him; you're a real man and a good friend. So you need to put all this aside and look at that letter again. Don't you get it?"

"Get what Bud?"

"You are one lucky guy. You've got a beautiful girl back home who loves you and is going to have your baby and you've got that to live for."

"But, I can't really love Marjean or my baby. I don't know how. I have too much hate in me, Bud. You know what I'm going to do when I get home, Bud? I want to kill Jenkins. I'm so full of hate for him, sometimes I can't see straight."

"Yeah, well you will have plenty of chances to work that out where we are going, my friend. In the meantime you need to let God get a hold of you and help you see what's good in your life."

"I don't believe in God, Bud."

Bud just smiled. "Oh you will, Johnny, believe me, you will."

11

BENEATH THE SOUTHERN CROSS

BILLY MARTENS

The 2nd Marine Division, the "Silent Second," slipped anchor and left America and San Diego astern on July 6th. Billy had never been out of the United States before, and he'd never been out on the open sea either. The vastness made mountain meadows seem small by comparison, and the waves were like castles. Others experienced sea sickness and home sickness. He didn't experience either. The sky was too big, and the ocean beneath it too deep, and the air too rich and alive for him to do anything but marvel. The combination made him feel better than he'd felt in weeks.

He'd written his family a letter the day before, and the Marine Corps and the US Postal Service would make sure it got to Montana. Whether or not his father read it didn't matter anymore. Billy was doing what he was doing and he was on his voyage and on his way. Bud, the corpsman, had read him a few lines from *Ulysses* as they left port with their destroyer escort: *There lies the port; the vessel puffs her sail: There gloom the dark, broad seas.* At church parade on deck, Ty Jackson, the Protestant chaplain, had talked about fear, and quoted Jesus—*Peace I leave with you, my peace I give unto you: not as the world giveth, give I unto you. Let not your heart be troubled, neither let it be afraid.* Billy could honestly say he didn't feel a lot of fear. But he could honestly say he didn't feel a lot of peace either. Prayers seemed to stick in his throat.

Yet he felt good, if restless. He hadn't been sure he would like sailing on a ship. He found out he did. He spent part of his time leaning over the rail to watch the stream of water rippling back from the bow, part of the time letting dolphins make him smile, part of the time cleaning his Model 1903, part of the time doing pushups with Johnny Strange, and part of the time on his hammock, listening to others in his platoon gripe and curse and play poker or tell what he called "brag stories." Brag stories could be about anything—hunting, a car, a woman, playing football or baseball, who you knew—but ultimately what they were really about was the person doing the talking and how important they were in the eyes of women, the world and God. Marines seemed to excel at such stories. They made Billy want to lean out of his hammock and laugh in their faces.

There were a lot of briefings, but no one told them where they were going. Sinking four Jap carriers at the Battle of Midway in June was a huge victory for American arms, but it hadn't ended the war. The Philippines had surrendered to the Empire of Japan, so had Burma, and Tokyo had landed troops on the Aleutian Islands, right by Alaska. Scuttlebutt had the 2nd Division heading to Australia for jungle training or to China where they'd clash with Japanese troops that had been ravaging the nation for years, as Billy knew better than anyone. Some said they would retake Wake Island, retake Bataan, retake Guam, and fortify Anchorage and Nome. A few even had them invading Japan and taking Tokyo before Christmas. But company, platoon and squad briefings didn't waste time on where. Just how.

King Company was going to take on a "shock troops" role,

Captain Rudebaker explained, using a chalkboard set up in a corner of the foredeck. More often than not, it would spearhead operations for the regiment and division, along with several other companies. So, General Price would make sure they got the gear and ammo they needed to fulfill that role. They were now part of the 2/2, 2nd Battalion, 2nd Marine Regiment, a unit that had been around since 1925 when they'd fought in Haiti and Cuba. Rudebaker reckoned they'd be a good crew to go into battle with.

Lt. Crandall's platoon would spearhead King Company once the ball was rolling. Crandall talked to his platoon about fighting Franco in Spain during their Civil War and the krauts in France when they launched their Blitzkrieg in May 1940. He said what gave a military man the most bang for his buck was firepower. For that reason, he was fighting like crazy to get everyone MI Garands or Thompsons. And plenty of BARs. And a Ma Deuce, the Browning M2 50-caliber machine gun, as well as a 30-caliber water-cooled machine gun, both of which he wanted permanently attached to his platoon.

"The krauts had it all," Crandall explained, smoking one of the Cuban cigars he favored. "In Spain and in Europe. We'd be shooting single shot rifles and they're using submachine guns. Guess who won? I was with the XV International Brigade in Spain, fighting with the Lincoln Battalion, all of 17 years old, not even a high school graduate in Rawlins, Wyoming, and we got hammered at the Battle of Jarama. We were defending Madrid and okay, we gave as good as we got, and yeah, we bloodied the Nationalists' noses—but we lost so many men! I remember a German heavy machine-gun battalion from the Condor Legion really working us over. Our casualties were so high, some of our Republican troops mutinied. I won't go into any more detail. Bravery is no match for tanks and machine guns when all you have is a bolt-action rifle. You get cut to pieces. You must possess firepower equal to or greater than the enemies'. Now I don't know what kind of air support or artillery support we can rely on out here in the South Pacific, but I don't think any of that will help us when it comes to jungle warfare. That kind of fighting is right in your face. We need firepower on the ground to win among the coconut trees, bamboo and the tall grass. Firepower that's in our hands and can move with us."

Crandall wanted Billy's squad to be the tip of the spear. He assigned a friend who'd fought beside him in Spain and France, a Basque from Mesquite, Nevada, to be the squad leader, Sergeant Bakar Zarate. Zarate requested that Corporal Jesus Navarro, from Rodeo, New Mexico, who Zarate knew from working cattle in the high desert, be his assistant squad leader. Crandall got the twelve-man squad in a circle on the deck after a week at sea, what he called a pow-wow, and made sure every one of them knew what was what and who was who.

"You'll be my heavy hitters," he said, passing out cigars and insisting every man take one. "If King Company goes in first, then our platoon is going in first and this squad is going in first. I was with the shock troops in Spain, the International Brigade shouldered that burden, and you heard Rudebaker. He wants King to fulfill that role with the 2/2, 2nd Battalion, 2nd Marines. You're gonna make Tojo wish he'd stayed home with his *katana* and *saki*. I want you guys to be slammers, absolute slammers. Remember Babe Ruth? The Big Bam? That's you." Crandall smacked his fist into his palm. "Rip a hole into the frigging enemy the rest of the platoon and company and 2nd Division can pour into. Hell, the whole Corps."

Crandall had scrounged Thompson submachine guns, 45-caliber, for Sergeant Zarate and Corporal Navarro, the weapon Crandall also used. In addition, like all squad leaders and officers, they had 1911 pistols as side arms. Zarate and Navarro turned over their M1s to Ricky Garowski, Seattle, and Eddie Kramer, Pagosa Springs, Colorado. Crandall, at 24, a full seven years older than he had been in Spain at the Battle of Jarama, cussed a streak that would have made Butterworth cringe when he confessed he hadn't been able to get his hands on any more M1 Garands. He blamed the 1st Marine Division, he blamed the State of Massachusetts where the armory that made the Garands was located, and he blamed Zeus and Thor and the man in the moon before he was done with his rant. The others in the squad would have to use the old Model 1903 with the bolt action and the five-round stripper clip—"Not an issue for Sniper here," he laughed, slapping Billy on the back, smoke pouring from his mouth as he burned through his third cigar of the pow-wow, "but the rest of you will have to kill Japs with it and win the war too. So, whatever you shot on Record Day, I want you to do a heck of a lot better in combat using the Old Girl. Understood? Become amazing and astonish me."

Teacher, Mike "Hot Kiss" Hotchkiss, Green River, Utah, was stuck with the Model 1903. So were Jimmy McKeever, LA; Leon Levy, San Francisco; Jake Sharples, Ketchum, Idaho; and Tony Malena, Yuma, Arizona. And Billy, who didn't mind at all, because the 1903 was his favorite firearm in the world. He'd been tagged as squad sniper and offered a scope which he refused —"It'll just throw me off."

"The added benefit of a 1903," puffed Crandall, "is it can launch grenades. The M1 can't. So, you Old Girl Guys will be holy terrors with the Japs. Why use a stripper clip of eight bullets with the M1 when you can blow the heads off a whole squad of Tokyo Joes with one shot from a 1903? Hey?"

Johnny Strange raised his hand. "Skipper?"

Crandall enjoyed being called that. "Yo, Marine."

"Uh, you want me to throw coconuts? Me and Julio gave up our M1s when we boarded. By your order."

Crandall grinned. "I did give that order. I had you two picked out for something different. Big band and swing. Ya know?"

"No, Sir, I don't get it."

"I'll come by with your new toys when you're bunked down tonight below decks. You and Julio are on the BAR."

"What?"

Billy could see that Johnny was genuinely excited, and excited in a good way, something that didn't happen often.

Crandall blew out a gray cloud that had the whole squad coughing. "Think you can handle the *boom boom*, Johnny? Julio?" He drew out the 'h' sound of *Hoo-leo*.

"I can, Skipper," Johnny responded, grinning to split his face wide open. "I like the power."

"I'm your man." Julio was grinning too. "I'm the *hombre*." Like Jesus Navarro, he was from New Mexico, a place called Las Cruces.

"We'll all be carrying extra ammo for you two," Crandall explained, "in addition to our own cartridges. And here's the deal —we split the squad into two fire teams. All my squads will use this set up. Sergeant Zarate will lead one team with a BAR gunner, Strange; an M1 rifleman, Garwoski; and three Model 1903 riflemen including our sniper: Hotchkiss, McKeever, Martens. Corporal Navarro will lead the second fire team with BAR gunner Hernandez; M1 rifleman Kramer; and three Model 1903 riflemen: Malena, Sharples, Levy. The two teams will always have one another's backs, and will spell each other, and move forward against the enemy together. Grasp the concept. It's how we'll face the Japanese in a few weeks. Don't worry. We'll drill using the two teams until you eat it, drink it and breathe it. Any questions?"

"Skipper." It was Garowski with what Billy called his "Downtown Seattle Accent," using the phrase only because Johnny had told him.

"Yo, Marine."

"Weren't you talking about getting a 50 and a 30 attached to our squad?"

"Yeah. But frigging Regiment is hanging onto all those frigging boys and their toys. They'll embed them where they see fit.

Rudy—Captain Rudebaker—is raising all kinds of Cain about it. Saying: 'You can't make King shock troops and not give 'em weapons that shock.'" Crandall laughed. "He was an attorney in Denver. I think he'll make an argument that will persuade Regiment and Division to give us "Big Bang for the Buck Boys." You all know Frank Harte, Captain America? Sam Kane, our Batman? Tommy Earp and Sid Greene, the Supermen? Those are the boys I want. Tell you one thing I made damn sure of. I got one of the company corpsmen embedded with our platoon and the squad here. Bud. The Corpsman. Whaddya think of that?"

The men clapped and cheered.

Crandall nodded. "He'll be serving all the platoons. But he sticks with you." He lit a fourth cigar from the tip of his third. "Final thing for today. Rudy wants to name the platoons instead of just calling them Crandall's platoon or Hawken's platoon. So, my platoon is now X-Ray. The other three in the company are Fox, Victor and Mike. Remember that. Don't let me hear you hollering for backup from Second Lieutenant Pincher's platoon. I don't want the Japs knowing our officers' names. Understood, Marines?"

As if it were still Boot Camp, all twelve men responded with, "Sir, yes, Sir!"

"We name the platoons in this company, we name the squads in each platoon. I don't want the Empire of Japan to know who our non-coms are either. No, 'Hey, Sergeant Garrity, bring up your BAR gunners, or, hey, Corporal Crook, we need covering fire.' I don't know, maybe the corpsman got to me, Bud, he's been running around with this poem *Ulysses* he claims he got from you, Sniper, and that Sniper got from no less a deity than Major General Price, our divisional commander. Anyway, it brings back good memories of reading about the warriors of Ancient Greece, you know, *Go tell the Spartans, stranger passing by, that here, obedient to their laws, we lie,* that big Greek fight at Thermopylae against the Persian Empire. Inspired and fortified by reading about Ulysses, a true Marine if ever there was one, who criss-crossed the ocean to fight his war, I'm naming my squads Zeus, Titan and Hades. I've already told the others what they are: Garrity's squad is Zeus, Brown's is Titan, Shanks' is Hades. You twelve? You're Achilles. The tip of the spear. Now get lost. That's enough of me beating my gums. Meet me back here at 2200 hours. No slackers. No goldbricking. I want to show you something, but it needs to be dark as a coal mine."

The entire platoon assembled on the deck with Crandall at the appointed hour. He pointed at a vivid configuration of stars glittering in the smooth black sky.

"It's the Southern Cross. They call it Crux too. I'm not sure if any of you noticed it last night. Most of you were below decks. I'm not a religious guy, but I kinda like a Jesus Cross being over my head as we go into battle. It's like a prayer or a blessing."

Billy noticed that Sergeant Zarate crossed himself and kissed a small crucifix that was hanging around his neck.

"They say the Emperor Constantine saw a vision of a cross," Crandall continued. "Just before a big fight. That's what turned him from Jupiter and Neptune and the other Roman gods and took him to Christianity." Crandall lit one of his ever-present cigars. The flare of the match transformed his face into a death mask. "Some of you believe, some of you don't. That's not my concern. I just need you to get what war is. The only ones who have combat experience in this platoon are myself and Sergeant Zarate. We've seen it for what it is. How would you describe it, Bakar?"

"It is an unholy mess, Sir," Bakar Zarate responded. "Yes, brave men do brave things. Good battles fought set good people free. But it is not an adventure, *hombres*. Just nasty work that has to be done. And your friends die. Your best friends bleed out and die. That's war."

Crandall nodded, the tip of his cigar glowing red. "I have to add this—some of you here will be the ones dying. Some of you will not make it. Yes, you can get hit. Yes, you can get killed. Sometimes in a finger snap. You won't even see it coming. And you won't have time for a long goodbye speech before you croak. War isn't a John Wayne movie like *Flying Tigers*. Death is a surprise. So is getting wounded. You never think it will happen to you. So, if you've been putting off writing home, get it done. The swabbies will make sure your letters get back to the States. Do it. You owe it to your family. To the people that love you." Crandall puffed out yet another cloud of smoke. "That's enough tear jerking from me. In a couple of days, we'll be off an island I've never seen, but they swear it has tall coconut trees and white sand beaches. You'll get shore leave there. Suck up the sunshine. Strip and swim in the sea. Listen to me: forget where you're going afterwards and forget why the heck you're in the South Pacific to begin with. Turn off your frigging mind completely and just drink up some of the good life. Now and then the Corps gives you a gift. The island of Tonga is it."

Billy lingered after most of the platoon had returned below decks. It gave him a lot of peace to stare at the stars and the Cross. He even felt a prayer form on his lips.

A few days later he was standing on a white beach, wading through surf as warm as bath water, watching a humpback whale leap from the sea, flip its huge magnificent body over, and then crash back into the sapphire waters again. Johnny Strange was standing beside him, except Johnny was in the water up to his chest.

"What do you think?" Billy asked him.

"This place is eggs in my beer." Johnny had his eyes closed. He grinned. "I think we should stay here until Japan surrenders. Then bring everyone we love to Tonga to live with us till we die in our sleep."

"That is the best plan I've heard since I enlisted."

"But either we have a fast war or I figure out some way to get my girl over here. A tropical paradise will always be more of a paradise when you're in love. Speaking of which, cowboy."

Billy shook his head. "Not me. I've never had a girl and I don't want one."

"Everybody needs love, Billy."

"Not that kind." He stared out over the water at another whale breaching. "War isn't supposed to be a love story."

TONGA

THE CORPSMAN

I couldn't have been farther away from a war I'd never seen than drifting along the white beaches of Tongatapu, the main island of Tonga where the 2nd Marine Division had dropped anchor. It brought back all kinds of memories of reading *Treasure Island, Kidnapped, The Coral Island, Swiss Family Robinson, Pitcairn's Island, Robinson Crusoe...* In my boy's mind, I had imagined tropical rainforests, coral reefs, fish in rainbow colors, water like glass, waves breaking and foaming like milk, sand like white coconut meat... I had even crayoned my childhood images onto paper... But now I was walking in my dreams... And because I had been one of the lucky ones who secured a two-day pass, I never returned to the ship at night... I slept in my dreams, on the beach and under the palms... It was never less than 70 from dusk to dawn, and I didn't experience any discomfort from bugs or mosquitoes... It was my paradise, and I often fantasized that the places where we would face the Japanese would be as perfect as Tonga... There would be no fighting... Tokyo and Washington would secure a peace treaty before a shot would be fired... Once our fleet arrived off shore an enemy stronghold, the Japs would emerge from the jungle and surrender... We would eat rice and tuna and drink *saki* on the beach...

Another part of my mind yelled at me like Butterworth: *Shots have already been fired, bombs dropped, ships sunk, Americans killed, Great Balls of Fire, do you really think you've arrived at the land of Happily Ever After, Marine? The trees here on Tongatapu might be soft and at peace, but where you are going, they are hard-edged, and when their fronds move in the night, they will whisper death, death...* But I refused to let Drill Instructor Butterworth take over my mind. Or an island I did not know where I would see war for the first time become another Battle of Bataan in my head. No. I would drink a beer or two and watch waves crack open and spray silver over the backs of coral reefs. I was in the Kingdom of Tonga and despite the presence of the US Army—and now the United States Marines—bullets and blood and rifles and bayonets were not only on a different island, but on a different planet. This Kingdom was at peace. This island had no quarrel with anyone. My beach was about sun and sleep and sparkling blue water. Sea birds swooping low and hump-back whales breaching with laughter—I swore I could hear them.

Platoon commander Crandall had fought in Spain with units that were not only international, but made up of different races too. He detested the US military policy of segregating blacks from whites, and he saw it happening on Tongatapu as well, not so much with US forces, truth be told, but because of the Brits and Aussies and Kiwis. So, I was not surprised to see him set up his own club on the beach. It was open to all, regardless of race or gender or rank. He and others, including many Tongans, men and women both, joined Marines and soldiers and put bamboo and coconut fronds together to create open huts with thatched roofs and bamboo chairs. There was plenty of American beer in buckets of cool water he claimed they'd hauled in a tanker truck from a waterfall—they must have done because the sea was almost 80° Fahrenheit. Once he spotted me he waved me over and laughed and said it was an order.

"Just remember," he warned me once I'd dropped into a bamboo chair, my feet burrowing under the warm sand, "there's no frigging war here and I don't tell war stories at this Clubhouse, Tonga America, okay? I only tell love stories. And that's all you can tell, too. No yap about plasma or morphine or compound fractures. Deal?"

"Deal, Sir."

"And don't get carried away with the 'Sir' thing either. For a few days, the war is in another universe. We don't know about it here in Club Tonga America. We've never heard about it. We're not interested. Okay?"

"Okay."

"Just love stories, Doc."

"I don't have any love stories."

"We here at Tonga America can help you with that. Never fear."

"Honestly, Sir, I'm fine."

"Dammit, no one is fine without love, Doc."

He forgot about his threat for a while, thank goodness. I'd have sooner dealt with a bull shark than attempted to make conversation with a woman. I had no experience at all, and females scared me to death.

Sergeant Bakar Zarate, my squad leader, and the squad assistant leader, Corporal Jesus Navarro, pulled me aside, plied me with coconut milk—some of which was fresh and some of which was fermented—planted me in a group of Aussies and Kiwis and Tongan men, and began to regal everyone with tales of Crandall's romances overseas and in the States. Zarate knew about Crandall's Spanish loves and, for some reason, Jesus—*Hey Zeus*—knew a lot about San Diego. I feigned interest, but quickly let my mind wander. In fact, I dozed. Until an Aussie soldier dug into my ribs with his elbow and hissed: "War stories now, mate."

And they were. Crandall had strolled far down the beach with a cluster of Tongan men and women, apparently looking for sea shells, and now Sergeant Zarate was free to talk about what had happened during the Spanish Civil War. I could not keep track of the dates and places and Spanish names, but it had clearly been a nasty war, the fascists had had better guns and equipment thanks to the Germans, and Zarate said it always felt like the forces against Franco were fighting with one hand tied behind their backs.

"Crandall was crazy brave, *loco* brave," Zarate grinned, swigging his coconut milk. "Wounded, hmm, maybe three times? If he goes for a swim, yeah? And pulls his shirt off, yeah? You will see." Zarate pointed to his own shoulder. "Like melted candle wax, the scar tissue. You will see."

Another quick swig and a wipe of his mouth and Zarate was off about France. "Crandall dragged me to Paris after Poland fell. In '39. He had friends there from the war in Spain. Well, we both did. But, you remember, nothing happened in 1939. Still, we stayed on with our comrades that rainy winter and drank Bordeaux and ate cheese and those long loaves of bread— so what, I tell our Frenchies, we have the long loaves in the Basque cities too, in Bilbao and Donostia, you know, all of them, and our sausage is better. Ahhh, so what, Bakar Zarate, bread has nothing to do with the story."

Another swig, a longer one, his mouth was dry from talking. "So, you know, the Germans come in May, yeah? You remember. BOOM! Blitzkrieg. Suddenly the sky is falling. The whole roof of Europe has caved in. What a mess! The fighting was brutal. Worse than Spain. Killing, dying, killing, dying, Stuka dive bombers that screamed with those crazy sirens they put on them, Panzers that crushed everything and blew holes through brick and stone."

He crossed himself, shrugged, laughed, and carried on. Street fighting. Hitching rides on lorries with the Brits and Canadians.

Stuck on the beach at Dunkirk. Finally getting away on a sailing
sloop, a family from Dover had crewed across the Channel. In
London during the Blitz. Helping fight the fires and haul bodies
out of the rubble—some breathing, most not. Finally getting on a
boat to the US in the winter of 1941 and one of the ships gets
torpedoed just outside New York harbor. Crandall champing at
the bit for America to get into the fight. Zarate certain Crandall
would have crossed the border and enlisted in the Canadian
Army except his plan was to do that December 15th. By
December 15th, Pearl Harbor had already happened, and Crandall was at Camp Elliott, both of them were, but their Boot Camp
experience had not been what the others had gone through. With
their time in the Spanish War and the fighting in France, the
Corps had thrown Crandall into officers' training right off and
Zarate into the course for non-commissioned officers.

Sergeant Zarate had more to say, and so did the fermented
coconut milk he'd been consuming, but Crandall and his beach-
combers returned, so the war stories were over. Which was fine
with me. I wanted to leave Spain and France and the shattered
bodies of the Blitz and return to the Kingdom of Tonga.

Which is what Crandall brought back with him along with
the seashells and a beautiful Tongan woman named Kalasia
whom he made me converse with. He pretty much blocked my
way out of Tonga America to be sure I did not run, and, I have to
confess, after an hour with Kalasia and the Polynesian tattoos on
her arms (and what I could see of her legs), I didn't want to be
anywhere else. Her sunset eyes and soft waves of words and
South Pacific smiles had a hypnotic effect. As if I were becoming
not only an islander, but part of the island itself—its shadows, its
green stalks of bamboo, its warm white sands, its tall brown
coconut trees, and its lapping, laughing waters. I fell asleep in my
chair while Kalasia was saying something about swimming
underwater.

I had slid out of the bamboo chair and was sleeping on the

beach when I woke up, well above the tide line, and so were Crandall and Sergeant Zarate and Corporal Navarro and a lot of others from the platoon. In fact, Crandall had declared that the final day of leave, which was today, would be Platoon Day at Tonga America, and we would get to know each other better. I didn't know how he planned to accomplish this because of the 48 or 50 in the platoon, and some 200 in King Company, I knew hardly anyone, hey, I hardly knew the 12 men in the squad I'd be tagging along with. I was assigned to the 2nd Regiment, 2nd Marine Division, but my niche was in King Company, and Captain Rudebaker had told me to embed myself in Lieutenant Crandall's platoon, and Crandall had placed me with Sergeant Zarate and Corporal Navarro's squad, Achilles. I knew that Billy Martens and Johnny Strange were in the same squad, but that's about all I knew. Maybe I hadn't been paying attention.

I doubted I'd pay attention during Platoon Day either. I was marooned on a remote tropical island, so far as I was concerned, and I intended to remain isolated and marooned at least one more day. The Corpsman, as the boys called me, was ship-wrecked and Crusoed and had no intention of asking the US Navy to rescue him. I slipped into the warm sea and began to swim around. *Dear mom, it turns out I am spending the war working at an army hospital on the island of ------. Don't worry about me. Pray, but don't worry. They have good Wesleyan churches here. Love, Philo.*

I'll admit I hadn't stopped thinking about the Polynesian beauty that Lt. Crandall had maneuvered me into a bamboo and coconut frond corner with. But I'll also admit I was so dreamed out on Tongan sunlight, and 80-degree-Fahrenheit Tongan waves, and white Tongan beaches, I half-believed I had imagined her. Crandall and Navarro and Zarate were soon stroking through the water nearby—I saw Crandall's scar tissue on his left shoulder and it was nasty—and I thought it was one of them when a brown shape darted past underneath me. Except none of us were that brown. Or that fast. Or, well, built that way.

Her head popped up next to mine, saltwater streaming from her face and dark hair. She grinned. "Good morning, Corpsman. How are you?"

I stumbled over my words—no man on earth knows how to chat with mermaids. "I'm fine... fine... I'm fine..."

"Must I always call you Corpsman?" Kalasia teased, her teeth as white as the sand.

No way was she going to hear about Philo. "Bud... I'm Bud," I managed to respond.

"Yes? So how is it some Marines call you Doc?"

"Because I... because..." I almost forgot what I was. "I am a corpsman. What the army calls a medic."

"Ah. So that's why they use that name for you, Corpsman guy. You are like a doctor or a nurse?"

I grinned. "Except better." I'd found my sense of humor.

She laughed and splashed me. "Truly?"

I tried to splash her back, but she was gone. It wasn't hard to track her through the crystal-clear ocean water though. She was wearing a sarong swimsuit, one piece, modest, but as bright yellow as the Tongan sun. I was a decent swimmer, and I went after her.

Yeah, for sure, a decent swimmer. But she was like something from *The Odyssey*, a sea nymph. I never caught her. She finally had mercy on me and slipped out of the water to sit on the beach and wait. I dragged my butt out after her and collapsed on the sand. She giggled.

"You don't swim much where you are from... Bud?" she asked, grinning.

"Not really." I was catching my breath. "I have a good bathtub though."

"A bathtub? Oh, ha ha. Funny guy, my American friend. Tell me, funny guy American friend, what do you think of my island? Tongatapu?"

"I'm in love."

"Yes? Truly?"

"Truly. I've been on shore two days now and I want to spend the rest of the war here."

"Oh. Can you? We have a soldier hospital that could use you, I'm sure."

"I saw it. Nice set up. I haven't thought about it much, to tell you the truth. One, because I'm a Marine and the Marines won't let me be a US Army soldier. And two? Because I've been too busy pretending there isn't a war to think about giving plasma if there is one. Mostly, I've been thinking about being stranded here forever. My boat sank and I'm the only human being on this island. Just me and the coconuts."

"Oh. Just you. What about me?"

"Do you want to be on this deserted island?"

"Very much."

"With a crazy American guy?"

"My funny guy American friend? Very much."

"Is this a *Treasure Island*?"

"Like in the book by Stevenson? Yes."

"Do you know where the treasure is?"

"I do."

"Where?" I asked.

"All around you."

"All around me?" I repeated.

"Of course. It's the island itself."

"Ah, okay."

"The island and its people." She tugged a chunk of coconut meat from a pocket in her sarong and began gnawing on it. "And me."

No one I knew in the Marine Corps or my hometown of Ritzville could look good chewing what she was chewing. But Kalasia was neither a Marine nor from Ritzville. So, she was kind of mesmerizing.

"Are you hungry?" she asked.

"Uh, no."

"You look hungry."

"Maybe a little."

She tossed me a piece of coconut meat. "Chew it well."

"Promise."

She flashed an incredible smile, the biggest and brightest smile I'd seen on her face. "Don't be afraid of me, American guy." She patted my knee. "I don't eat men. Just coconut and fish."

I smiled back. "Good to know."

"I wish you were stranded on a deserted island with me, Bud. Well, not too deserted. Let's say I wish you were stranded on my island of Tongatapu with me. It would be wonderful. Yes, it would. Don't be so shy about yourself, Corpsman. But," she paused. "I know your ship takes you away in the morning. I asked my army friends if your ship would bring you back. They didn't know. They only know you are going far. Very far." She suddenly grinned and patted my knee again. "Too far for me to swim."

"Why is your English so good?"

"British teachers. Our schools are run by the Wesleyan Church."

"Are you a Wesleyan? Like a Christian?"

"Of course. What about you?"

"Yes," I told her. "I'm a Christian. You won't have heard of Mennonites, but that's the church I'm part of."

"Are they good people, your Mennonites?"

"Very good. They don't believe in war or killing."

"No? Then how can you be here?"

"I heal. I save. At least, that's what I'm supposed to do. Run out on to the battlefield and pull men off it and bind up their wounds. I hope I'm brave enough."

She stared at me for several long moments. "Certainly, you are brave enough."

"Am I an open book?"

She did a one-shouldered shrug. "I see some things in people."

"Well, I'm a mystery to me. I don't even know where we're going."

"Wherever you are going, you are going to fight. But that's okay because Tongans are afraid of the Empire of Japan." She shrugged again with one bare brown shoulder, still nibbling on her coconut meat. "But also, it's not okay. I don't even know you, Corpsman, but I know enough to know I don't want you to be hurt. Or worse."

"Which is why I've spent the past two days hallucinating. And you're part of my hallucinations now."

"Am I? What part?"

"The best part."

That was me, flirting. With what I thought was delicacy and finesse. I knew my face had gone red from the burst of heat I felt go across it.

"Ah." She looked away to spare me. "Make this your Happy Isles."

"My what?"

"I knew you wouldn't remember. You were half asleep when you told me you were Ulysses. On a voyage to Troy to fight a war. A long war. So, I went to my old school, which has a good library, and found the book. By Homer. I read most of it. And the poem by Tennyson. *It may be we shall touch the Happy Isles, and see the great Achilles, whom we knew.* Make this your Happy Isles, Corpsman. Make this your Heaven." She looked at me again. "Forgive me for being so bold. I suppose I am by nature. But if you can make your ship steer this way after your war, after your battle *on the ringing plains of windy Troy*, do it. Take hold of the rudder and do it." Her eyes went as dark as the tropical night. "Do you think I'm fine?"

A Mennonite boy doesn't lie. "Yes."

"Then come back. Come back and be marooned here." She got up and brushed the sand off her sarong. "Walk with me?"

"Is this going to be a kind of hallucinations walk?"

"It can be."

"Count me in."

She laughed, held out her hand and hauled me to my feet. "My funny guy American friend. There is a strongbox buried not far from here. Shall I lead you there?"

"I'm pirate enough to fancy that."

"I thought you might be."

We walked a long time. Never held hands. Never kissed. Never cuddled. Never did any movie things lovers are supposed to do before the guy heads off to war. For one thing, we weren't lovers. For another thing, she spent half the time talking about God and Jesus and the spiritual journey she had been on since she was sixteen. I didn't mind that at all, but other Marines would have thought she was weird. And I did see other Marines walking with Tongan women. Or army nurses from the hospital on the island... I was wondering how that would go over with the soldiers based on Tongaputu and in the city of Nuku'alofa. Well, the Marines aren't here for long, boys. Lighten up. The nurses will be staying behind.

We made our way back to Club Tonga America. It was pretty noisy, and not a few of Crandall's platoon were plastered. A bunch of them were singing *Don't Sit Under the Apple Tree with Anyone Else but Me* in one hut, and another bunch were singing *Praise the Lord and Pass the Ammunition* in another. I found it embarrassing, but Kalasia shook her head at my concern and took my hand while she smiled at the singing. Crandall stayed sober. Him and his cigars and his impromptu speeches about every subject under the sun—one was about Captain Cook's first visit to Tonga in 1773—were the life of the party. At sunset, MPs began coaxing Marines and sailors back on board the ship.

Kalasia led me down to the water's edge. Her face was purple and gold, the colors of the sun that was sinking into the sea.

"Thank you for the day, Bud," she said. "I enjoyed it very much."

"I feel the same way."

"I know you have no control over if and when you can return to Tonga. I know we are just friends, no more than that. I will not walk the shoreline praying to see an American ship and hoping you will be on it. I do not pray you will write me. But I am going to pray you will survive the war, Bud. And I am going to pray that if you can, if there is an opportunity, you will return to Tonga. Even if I am married by then, even if I have a hundred children and a hundred hundred grandchildren, I will still welcome you back to our deserted island and invite you to stay at my home. I will never leave Tonga. I will never leave Tongatapu. So, you will always find me here."

It was quite a lot to say. I didn't have anything fancy to say in return. She was still holding my hand.

"Thank you, Kalasia," I replied. Her eyes had taken on the sunset too. "I... I don't think there's any Marine on this ship that wouldn't want to return here and even bring his family with him if he could. No one's going to forget this place. And I'm not going to forget you."

"Are you sure?"

"I'm sure."

"Let me make you more sure."

Her kiss was unexpected. I'd never been kissed on the lips and her mouth on mine sent rockets through me. Warm sea water splashed over my bare feet. She held one of my hands in two of hers and then she leaned into me. The scent of her hair and her skin was beautiful and overpowering. My arms went around her. I thought she would shrug them off. She didn't. The kiss continued, and now it wasn't just the war that no longer existed. Tonga and the South Pacific had ceased to exist as well. There was just us. And a setting sun.

ON THE 26TH OF JULY, WE RENDEZVOUSED WITH THE TASK FORCE carrying the 1st Marine Division off the coast of Fiji. We did not leave the ship except to practice climbing down cargo nets that had been slung from the deck to the waterline. We worked on dropping into Higgins boats that were bobbing on the ocean swells. I almost fell in the drink once or twice. Then we practiced amphibious landings on the Higgins or LCVP (landing craft, vehicle, personnel). No time on shore. No passes. Soon enough, we left Fiji behind just as we had left Tonga behind.

Years later, I would remember those two islands as my final experience of the tropics as paradise. I would never see the islands of the South Pacific in that way again. I sensed it too. When our ship had stood offshore from Tonga, I felt beauty and mystery and peace reach out to me from its beaches and palms. Offshore of Guadalcanal, and the smaller islands nearby, I felt danger and fear reach out and touch me from its jungles and hills. Not even the memory of Kalasia's kiss could extinguish my feelings of darkness and malevolence. Dawn was coming, the east was lined with bright silver, Marines were soon going to debark using the cargo nets, the ocean was quiet, the coconut fronds barely moving in the tropical air, but I knew I was going to a place where men and dreams would die and never rise again.

"Kinda pretty," said a young Marine next to me at the ship's side as he waited to climb down the nets. He was chewing gum rapidly and loudly. "Can't be too bad if it's that pretty, hey, Corpsman?"

I didn't respond. The task force had split into two, with one group heading to Guadalcanal and the other to a series of islands about 20 miles away—Florida, Tugali, Gavutu and Tanambogo.

We were with the second group. The weather had been crappy as we approached our war zone, big waves that pushed and shoved, and a lot of guys had been sea sick. Now hundreds of them were on deck as the Navy opened up with its big guns and plastered Florida Island and Tulagi for starters. The Japs had sea planes anchored by these islands and fortified positions on shore.

Friday, August 7ᵗʰ, 1942, I wrote in my diary, *was the most noise I'd heard in my life.* Huge explosions rocked the four small islands and big gouts of dirt and smoke and yellow flame soared into the tropical dawn. I looked over my shoulder at the warships, their barrels flickering and flashing, the roar reaching me seconds after I saw the spears of orange and amber stab from the guns. Then aircraft from the *USS Wasp* streaked over our heads and began dive bombing and strafing the islands, hitting military installations and blasting the sea planes. Balls of fire rolled over the jungle.

The gum chewer began to climb down the cargo nets along with swarms of other Marines. It was 1/2, 1ˢᵗ Battalion, 2ⁿᵈ Marines heading to Florida Island. They landed unopposed at 0740 hours. Then it was the turn of Edson's Raiders, the 1ˢᵗ Raider Battalion under Lt. Col. Merritt Edson's command, to clamber down the nets into the Higgins boats, followed by 2/5, 2ⁿᵈ Battalion, 5ᵗʰ Marines under Lt. Col. Harold Rosecrans. They splashed out into the waters off Tulagi, also unopposed, at 0800 hours. Those of us who watched and waited heard nothing from Tulagi. For hours. Then there'd be a smattering of firing. And silence. Another smattering of firing. And silence.

It was in the darkness that firing exploded on Tulagi and reached a fever pitch. I was in my bunk below decks, but Johnny Strange shook me awake: "Shit going down on shore, Doc." I stood with him and Billy and others from our company and saw the flashes of rifles and machine guns, the sounds reaching us after we saw the bursts of flame. It never ended. The fighting went on all night. I finally turned in, but Johnny was still staring at the island and the bright slashes that ripped up the blackness. For all I know, he never got back to his bunk. Sooner than I expected or wanted, I was being shaken awake again, this time by Crandall: "Let's go, Corpsman. Let's go Platoon X-Ray. The 2/2 is going in to reinforce. It's a hell of a mess on Tulagi. The Japs are holed up in caves and ravines and dug in on a hilltop. It's a frigging can of worms and we're gonna open the can. Grab some chow and you'll be briefed after you fill your bellies."

I was hoping I wouldn't feel anything. Just follow orders and move from one task to another. I got through the chow line okay even though I hardly ate a bite. But when I got on deck, ice cut all through me. There were already dead Marines on those islands in front of us. I couldn't do anything for them, God rest their souls. But there were lots of wounded, too. It was up to me and other corpsmen to give them a chance to live again. Maybe I couldn't do it. Maybe I couldn't stop the bleeding. Maybe I couldn't prevent the shock. Maybe I couldn't set splintered bones. Maybe I'd kill someone a better man could have saved.

And maybe, in the end, I was a coward.

I wouldn't run into the thick of the fighting and pull out the wounded.

I'd freeze up and hang back.

I'd watch men die that I'd killed by not helping as much as if I'd had a rifle in my hands and shot them.

WELCOME TO HELL

JOHNNY STRANGE

J ohnny Strange's first impression of Guadalcanal was the smell. It drifted across the dark water from the even darker blackness of the island—an island squatting among the waves, a monster waiting to swoop down out of the darkness, pluck him off the deck of the ship and gnash his bones into pulp. The nightmare smell slipped in on a tiny breeze as he stood sleepless on the deck of his transport. Dank, sick, rotten—a death bouquet oozing from the primordial swamp that was Guadalcanal. It was a stinking miasma whose foulness stirred up in Johnny's soul the archetypal fear of every man since hunter-gatherers roamed the vastness of the primitive wilderness—the fear of being killed and eaten by some prehistoric beast in a godforsaken waste. The smell came first and then, as the light grew, the vision—a green fastness, humped and desolate, broken only by small streams that flowed from inside the vast length of the island to empty into the sea.

Sergeant Zarate pointed to the distant end of the island, lost in the darkness to their right. "The bugger is as big as Long Island. That's a hundred miles, Strange. And we will walk every foot."

As the mist cleared, Johnny could see the hump that rose from the middle of the island. "That's Mount Austen," Zarate said. "The maps said it was only a mile from the beach, but our flyboys told us it's more like four or five. They want us to walk up that baby in a day—more like two weeks."

Lieutenant Crandall came out on the deck. He saw Zarate and Strange standing at the rail and ambled over. His nose picked up the smell, and he nodded to Johnny. "Ever been in the jungle, Strange?"

"No, Sir."

"It's no picnic. I've been there. That green you see over there? Those are hundred foot tall trees and they look grand from here, but underneath them are stinking matted cassia or lianas vines, or bamboo forest, or mangos. And underneath it all is the foulest ooze—a three-foot deep rotten sludge full of dead and dying and decomposing garbage. That's the smell you're getting. Pure evil. Pray that you're in good shape, Strange, because you will carry an 80-pound pack and a sixteen pound BAR through the rottenest part. You up for that?"

"Yes Sir. That's why I came."

IN THE HOURS BEFORE D-DAY, JOHNNY'S SQUAD HAD PREPPED THEIR packs below decks. Zarate came by to check each guy and recited the litany they would come to know well in the coming months and years. "Extra socks, underwear, toilet articles, mess gear. By the time you get back to a ship, your undies will be stiff as a board. Keep your socks changed if you don't want to watch the creeping crud eat your feet off. Mosquito nets—half of you will die from malaria. Bud! Roll that blanket inside your poncho."

Zarate stopped by Johnny. "What's that wad of paper, Strange?"

"Extra toilet paper, Sarge. Stole it from the head."

"That's my boy. The rest of you get that? Smart thinking. You will need extra toilet paper because the first time a Jap shell goes off above your head, you will crap your pants. And everybody take a shower. It may be the last you get for a long time."

And then sleep. "To sleep perchance to dream... there's the rub." He'd read that somewhere. And he didn't want to dream. Didn't want to dream and see Marjear's face or think about her growing belly or his baby because he didn't need the distraction. He didn't want to dream about Jenkins either, the man's nakedness against his back, his sweating flesh and his whispered requests, because it made him sick and angry. So he stayed awake and thought about Japs—dead Japs, dying Japs, screaming Japs. And in his thoughts every Jap was thrashing in the mud as he chopped them in half with his BAR or cut their throat with his Bowie knife, and each one wore the face of Harold Jenkins, and that was something that made life real and worthwhile.

He lay on his bunk, his thoughts tumbling round and round in his head, polishing each other to clarity until at last the growing excitement overpowered his need for sleep and he got up and went topside. And that's when he smelled the stinking island for the first time, and he knew over there, across that silent dark water, death waited, crouched on terrible legs and hiding in that jungle, waiting to spring on anyone who was fool enough to enter its domain.

THE CALL TO QUARTERS CAME AT 0300 HOURS. THE MARINES ROSE from their sacks and pulled on the fresh green jungle uniforms that had been waiting for this day. They moved into the long chow lines, filling their kits with breakfast beans. Then up to the decks where the rest of them smelled the death smell that had greeted Johnny hours before—carried on a sweat-wet breeze across the waiting channel. The night was still, as though all creation was holding its breath and waiting for the first salvo of the battle of the Titans to begin.

And then, just before dawn, the Navy ships opened with a thundering barrage. Shells sailed with horrible screams across the space between the two waiting armies and crashed into the oozing jungle. The island rocked with vast explosions and monstrous death-dealing detonations. Johnny spotted Lieutenant Crandall summoning his men aft. They gathered together as Crandall gave them the news. "We are not going ashore with the first wave." He lifted his hand to still the protests. "We are staying on board in a reinforcement capacity." He pointed toward the four smaller islands that had appeared out of the darkness between them and the main island of Guadalcanal. "That's Florida, Tulagi, Gavutu and Tanambogo. We don't know what the deal is with the Japs over there. Our info dates from somewhere around the Spanish American War. So Captain Crane is taking his boys to Florida, and Edson's Raiders are going in first on the other three. If they run into trouble, they will need tough guys to be a hammer—that would be us. So sit back and watch the show. More later. Squad leaders with me." Crandall and the four squad leaders left the group and gathered together, going over again the details of the King company involvement in this tussle.

AND SO THEY WATCHED AND WAITED. WAITED AS THE 1ST MARINES went over the side. Waited with clenched fists as the comments came. "Keep the coffee warm, Priscilla." "Don't go visiting my girlfriend while I'm gone." "Hey Gyrene, can you mail these for me?" They watched while the thunder of the naval barrage hid the shoreline in a dense pall of smoke. They watched while the First Battalion of their own division went over the side. King company raised a cheer as Colonel R. E. Hill stepped onto the cargo net, saluted the boys from King, and led the first members of the 2nd

Division to go ashore into battle against the Imperial Japanese Army down over the side. The waiting boats were bobbing on the waves below like small mouths ready to gobble the Marines up. "Give 'em hell, 2nd!"

AROUND NOON THE WORD CAME THAT ALTHOUGH THE FIGHTING HAD been light on Guadalcanal itself and on Florida Island, "Red Mike" Edson and his Raiders had run into hell on wheels on Gavutu and Tulagi. Word came back to the men waiting on the transport that Edson had discovered that cornered Japs were full of fight. Lieutenant Crandall called his squad leaders together to brief them, and Zarate rounded up Achilles squad and gave them the skinny.

"Our boys are catching hell over on those little islands, particularly Gavutu. They are getting heavy flank fire from that little piece of shit right there." He pointed. "That's Tanambogo. Brass is sending B Company over to clean it out." Johnny could see the Higgins boats that had been getting ready to disembark men on Gavutu swinging off and heading toward Tanambogo. The boats were about halfway across the channel when air raid Sirens went off on their ship. The surrounding ships took up the clamor. Ricky Garowski yelled and pointed toward the north. A wave of enemy aircraft appeared out of the clouds heading straight toward the transports. Johnny could see bursts going up from the 30 caliber Brownings mounted on the craft. Sailors on board their own ship manned the anti-aircraft guns and white and black puffs of smoke soon filled the sky, but the Jap planes kept boring in.

They all watched as one plane took a hit and trailed smoke. The plane banked and turned toward them. Another plane above and ahead of the crippled bomber turned and headed toward them. Johnny heard someone yell, "He's dropping bombs!" Two heavy bombs released from under the bomber's wings and sailed toward them. Everyone dived for cover... except Johnny. A huge explosion and then another shook their ship as the bombs bracketed them on both sides. Johnny watched the crippled fighter. Still trailing smoke, the pilot dropped his plane to just above the waves and headed straight toward them.

He's trying to crash into the ship!

Johnny looked around. There was a 50-caliber machine gun emplacement above him on the bridge, but the sailors manning it had disappeared when the bombs exploded. Johnny ran to the ladder and went up it like a cat. The plane was boring in, flying right at them. Johnny checked the belt—it was in. He pulled the bolt latch release and put the gun on automatic, then jerked the slide handle to the rear and released it. He swung the gun around, took aim at the incoming plane and fired a short burst to check his range. The heavy bullets whipped out and splashed up water ahead of the plane. Realizing someone was shooting at him, the Japanese pilot returned fire with his machine guns. Johnny saw the tracers cutting a path toward him and then felt them slamming into the bulkhead next to him. He elevated his muzzle and fired an extended burst straight at the incoming plane. Sparks flew from the nose of the fighter, and the prop broke up and whirled away. The plane's nose went down and the fighter crashed into the sea not a hundred yards from the ship. A great cheer went up from the deck below.

The plane was bobbing in the waves. Johnny saw the pilot climb out and stand on the wing. A red mist came over his eyes and then he was firing, firing and screaming at the man. He could see the pilot's face. Then the heavy fifty slugs caught the Jap in the middle of his chest and he blew apart. Johnny kept firing. The slugs tore into the fuel tank and the plane exploded with a terrific roar.

"I killed you, you bastard, I killed you." He screamed again, and then Johnny felt a hand on his shoulder. He whirled around. Sergeant Zarate was beside him.

"Easy Johnny, easy. He's dead, boy. You got him."

"I killed him, Sarge, I killed him."

"Yeah, you did, Johnny, and you saved the ship. Good going, Marine."

Then Johnny was shaking like a leaf. He dropped to his knees and threw up. He remembered the last look on the pilot's face when the fifty slugs tore into him—a look of hate and despair at the same time. But the face was not the face of Harold Jenkins. It was the face of the enemy, and Johnny knew he had looked into the eyes of death.

"I killed him, Sarge."

He smelled the smell again, the smell of death, and he remembered the beast waiting for him on that green mound across the water. A joy rose in him and a rage. He wanted to kill, kill them all, kill every stinking Jap on that island. And Johnny Strange took the long first step into hell.

HILL 281

BILLY MARTENS

B illy had watched Johnny take the big machine gun and hose the Jap fighter and its pilot as if he were looking at a movie on the silver screen.

He hadn't felt a thing.

He was flat.

But when King Company crawled down the nets, he thought he'd lose his breakfast, not because of the ocean swells, but because fear had knotted its fingers around his throat. He could hardly breathe. He tried to time his drop into the Higgins boat with it bobbing up with the roll of the sea, but he waited too long and fell farther than was good for him, banging up his knee bad enough to make him limp once he waded into the surf around Tulagi.

Sergeant Zarate quickly had his squad take the point for the platoon and the company, setting them up in the two fire teams, and Bud the Corpsman attached himself to the first one, trudging along through the jungle behind Johnny Strange, "Downtown Seattle" Garowski, "Hot Kiss" Hotchkiss, Jimmy "Mac" McKeever and Billy "Sniper" Martens. All the Mennonites were in one cozy little group, like a Bible study on a Sunday night, thought Billy. Except it was Saturday morning and maybe they were part of a Men's Breakfast. He should have laughed, but his guts were locked up like cement. He heard gunfire, a BAR with its rapid and loud single shots, different from a Garand or a machine gun, and it was close. His mind went cold and blank. Johnny glanced back at him from his position near the front of the squad.

"You okay, Sniper?" he asked.

"Never better," Billy lied. "It's just like heading to church."

Johnny snorted. "It's gonna be a hell of a service. I'm preaching the sermon."

"Yeah? That oughta be something. What's it on?"

A wild shine came into Johnny's eyes. "Ecclesiastes. A time to die, a time to pluck up that which is planted, a time to kill, a time to break down, a time to rend, a time to hate, a time for war." He laughed. "Yeah. It's that season, Sniper. The frigging season of destruction. And I'm thanking God for it."

Billy did not respond. His whole body was tightening up and his mind shutting down. He thought of his father getting ready for the fall roundup in another month. Saw him on his dapple gray. Saw him smile: "The good life, Billy. God, and family, and heartland, and love thy neighbor. It's peace, son. It's blessed peace."

"Sniper! Yo! Sniper!" Sergeant Zarate pumped his fist up and down. "Up front!"

Billy ran, his mind still elsewhere, his insides still locked in snow and ice.

"We got a runner. Jap machine-gun nests on a spur of Hill 281. Maybe 100 yards from us, no more. Have Edson's Raiders and 2nd Battalion, 5th Marines, 2/5, pinned down. They are taking casualties. Pick your spot, climb your tree, whatever. Get them. Drill them."

"Yes, Sir."

"Go." Zarate turned to Johnny Strange and to Ricky Garowski.

"Stay on his tail. Give him cover with the BAR and the M1.
Go, go."

Billy crept from the jungle to a spot where he could view the
hill. He saw Marines dug in all around it. Firing was constant
from one slope to the next. He concentrated on the side of the hill
closest to him. It was as if he were watching another person scan
the rocks and boulders. Then he saw the lemon flash. And
another not far from it. The machine gunners were in a cave.
How the heck was he supposed to get a shot?

Johnny was at his elbow. "Whaddya gonna do?"

Billy shrugged, feeling himself getting back into his own body
and his own skin. *I know how to hunt and how to stalk and how to
shoot.* "What any Mennonite farm boy'd do. Climb something."
He glanced into Johnny's eyes. "You with me? Menno Simons
with a BAR?"

"I'm here. Yes, Sir. With prayer and a BAR."

"I'll get those I can. I'm going to use ricochets too because I
can hardly see them. They're bound to start hopping and leaping.
Like deer. They'll expose themselves. Even if you only see an arm
or a leg, figure out where their stomachs and ribs are and hose
them. Hose them, Johnny. Heck of a thing we have to take life to
save life."

"Hell of a thing."

Billy stared at Garowski. "You with me, Seattle?"

"Yes, Sniper, I am."

"How'd you get that accent?"

Garowski grinned through his freckles even though Billy
could see his whole body was as rigid as a steel cable. "Fishing off
the downtown pier."

"You score good on Record Day?"

"Good enough."

"We're here to save American lives. When I make them jump,
get those sights on them and fire as fast as you can."

"I will, Sniper."

Billy slung his 1903 and climbed a tree thick with vines, using them for footholds and handholds. A pine would have more branches. So would a cottonwood. But he'd have to make this work. Heat and humidity had sweat pouring into his eyes, burning them. Halfway up, he stopped, yanked his helmet from his head, tore the left sleeve off his uniform, wrapped it around his skull like a bandana, replaced his helmet, and continued to climb. The wrap was soaked in no time. But his eyes were clear.

The tree had been a lucky choice. Or a God-given choice. He wasn't sure which. His church would say it was the devil's hand that gave him a perch that allowed him to see right into the cave and make out at least three Jap soldiers. But he was on a hunt. His mind filtered out unnecessary thoughts as if it were a steel colander. He used the sling to tighten his rifle against his body as he nestled the stock into his shoulder. He got the blade of his front sight on one gunner just as the Jap cut down a Marine on the move from one hole to the next. Then he moved the back sight into alignment with the blade. Exhaled. Squeezed, both eyes open. The shot took the Jap machine gunner off his seat and into the air and hurled him back into the dark of the cave. Billy fired again. He was high. The bullet took the top of the ammo feeder's head off. The third and fourth shot went into the second machine gunner's heart. Billy saw how red the blood was. The fifth shot he turned into a ricochet he was certain would make someone in the cave scramble.

It did. He was loading another five-round stripper clip when Johnny's BAR erupted. Two Japs near the mouth of the cave went sprawling. When his BAR went silent, Garowski's M1 barked and another Jap came tumbling out of the cave. Billy had his sights on two more soldiers jumping in to fire the machine guns. He squeezed off three rounds. They both collapsed over the guns, knocking the barrels skywards. Billy let off two more shots as ricochets. The cave boiled with bodies as Japs emerged shooting and yelling and attacking the Marine lines.

"Get "em, get 'em!" Johnny was hollering at the base of the tree. "We've flushed 'em out into the open! Frigging cream 'em!"

He charged towards the Japanese, firing his BAR from the hip, screaming his head off. Garowski was right beside him, M1 Garand blazing. Then the whole squad was there—Julio Hernandez leap frogging up to join Johnny, his BAR blasting into dozens of Japanese soldiers, Eddie Kramer emptying M1 stripper clip after stripper clip into the Japanese ranks, "Hot Kiss" Hotchkiss the "Teacher" banging away with his 1903 bolt action, Tony Malena, Jake Sharples, Leon Levy and Jimmy "Mac" McKeever running up the hill and not even shooting, two of them with bayonets fixed.

Looking down, Billy was shocked to see the squad piling into the Jap platoon that had exploded from the cave bent on taking as many Marines with them as they could. Sergeant Zarate and Corporal Navarro had to run like crazy men to keep up. Billy laughed. It was a nutty time to laugh, but the two non-coms looked ludicrous trying to catch up with their men. Achilles burned through the enemy platoon, using bullets and Bowies and bayonets and rifle butts and fists, then continued to brawl their way up the slope. Machine guns sighted in on them but Billy, aware like a cat is aware of a bird, sighted in on the Japanese machine guns so much faster. Two gunners got off a burst and then Billy silenced them—one, two, three, four shots.

"Malena! McKeever!" Zarate couldn't reach them on his legs, so he used his bawling voice. "The satchel charges I gave you! Those caves in front of the squad! Prime and toss! Do it, dammit!"

Billy watched the satchels sail through the air. One went into the black hole of a cave, the second landed on the lip of another. Both exploded in spears of orange fire and gray smoke. Japanese came flying like dolls from the one cave, twisting and spinning and crying through the air, while they burst out of the other firing their rifles and hurling grenades and brandishing swords and bayonets. Achilles crashed into them and Billy heard both

BARs banging like hammers on oil drums. Then the other squads were there—Hades, Titan, Zeus—and on the heels of Platoon X-Ray came the rest of the platoons of King Company—Fox, Victor and Mike—and behind them roared the rest of 2/2. Hill 281 was crawling with Marines... 1st Raider Battalion; 2nd Battalion, 5th Marines; and now, the reinforcements, 2nd Battalion, 2nd Marines. To Billy, it looked like an ant hill had been overturned by a grizzly. The ants were angry, but the grizzly was howling with hunger and savage for food, and he swept the ants up and devoured them between his monstrous snapping fangs.

How can men who have never fought be so fearless? How can they get past a terror of death that capable of paralyzing them to a place where they are attacking the enemy with raw courage? Is it that they just face their fears and overcome them by charging straight ahead? Or is it the yelling and running and shooting that blasts away the anxiety they feel and wipes away all possibility of cowardice or the reluctance to kill another human being?

Grenades and satchel charges were flung into caves and the ravine that cleft the hill. BARs kept thumping. Now and then a 30-caliber medium machine gun rattled. Bomb blast followed bomb blast. Billy saw stretcher bearers moving down the slope, but he couldn't spot Bud anywhere. From a sniper's point of view, he wondered how useful the red cross armbands and helmet markings were—to him, they made the corpsmen targets. In fact, he saw that three corpsmen were down, their heads twisted at impossible angles, proof that the red cross did not protect them from enemy fire. Each corpsman had fallen in such a way that Billy could see his face and he thanked God none were Bud. Then felt ashamed because he knew those men had mothers and families who would be stunned by grief when the bad news came two or three weeks later.

He kept firing. At machine gunners that he spotted. At Japanese priming grenades by slamming them against their boots or helmets. At sword-waving officers. At snipers he saw crouching in caves or crawling among the rocks. He fired till he ran out of cartridges. By then the fighting on the hill had sputtered to a stop. Now and then a single shot rang out. He distinctly saw Johnny standing over a wounded Japanese soldier near the hilltop. The Jap was trying to stab Johnny with a knife. Johnny emptied the rest of his clip into the man, about seven shots. Then he spat in the dead man's face.

Billy sank his head against his warm rifle barrel, too warm. He would never have used or abused a firearm like that on a hunt in Montana. Johnny killed with a brutality that made Billy uncomfortable. But what was the difference? Billy slew with single shots to the head or heart or lungs or guts. Johnny with multiple shots that cratered an entire body. Men were shattered and destroyed either way. If it was a sin to kill, as Billy's father and church would have it, and Johnny's too, then Billy was as much a sinner with his Model 1903 as his friend was with the Browning Automatic Rifle.

Somehow, inexplicably, Billy began to whisper Psalm 23—*The Lord is my Shepherd, I shall not want.* It felt like a blasphemy to him that those holy words should pass through his lips now. *He maketh me to lie down in green pastures. He leadeth me beside the still waters. He restoreth my soul.* Smashed bodies were strewn over the hill like piles of ripped and filthy clothes and boots. Faces were gone. Arms were gone. Legs were crushed as if by tractors. *He leadeth me in the paths of righteousness for his name's sake.* Flames crackled in caves and human bodies crackled and blackened with them. *Yea, though I walk through the valley of the shadow of death, I will fear no evil, for thou art with me. Thy rod and thy staff, they comfort me.* Smoke drifted over the hill and clung to burning bushes and hung like a haze over the ravine. It seemed to spurt and puff from a thousand different holes in an endless supply that had its source deep in the bowels of the island and the earth. *Thou preparest a table before me in the presence of my enemies. Thou anointest my head with oil. My cup runneth over.* He saw one corpsman giving a wounded Marine plasma, using his 1903 bayoneted into the ground to hang the bag. Another corpsman was pulling a rain poncho over a Marine's broken face. *Surely goodness and mercy shall follow me all the days of my life.* Billy's body began to shake with tremors he could not control. He clutched his rifle and the palm tree even more tightly, his knuckles white. Huge sobs made his chest heave. Tears slashed across his face. "Oh, my Father, my God," he groaned, "have mercy. Oh, Christ, have mercy." *And I will dwell in the house of the Lord forever.*

15

IN THE CAVE OF THE CYCLOPS

THE CORPSMAN

S aturday, August 8, 1943 was the day my squad went crazy. One minute they were hunkered down pouring concentrated fire into a bunch of caves on a ridge and the next minute my guys are cutting up a bunch of Japs with their bare hands while I'm standing there with my mouth open.

We were on Tulagi, one of those little islands right off the coast of Guadalcanal. It was August 8, the day after we watched while the 1st Division guys and the Raiders went over the side on D-Day, Guadalcanal. There was grumbling as they sailed off in the Higgins boats, but Lieutenant Crandall told us that the brass were saving "the hammer,"—that's us—to bail out the other guys when they get into tight spots. So we waited all day and all night for something to happen. Then first thing in the morning the word comes down. It was our turn to jump in, and like I said, I had my doubts. I mean, what am I doing here? Living out a stupid poem? I'm a Mennonite. I don't believe in war. My dad raised me to love life and help people, not kill them.

I'm watching Billy Martens and he keeps rubbing his hands together. Billy set his face like stone, but I can see his jaw working. And Johnny has a weird look on his face. It's as though his first taste of blood, when he shot that Jap out of the sky and then gunned him down when he crawled out of his plane, pushed him into another place, and not a good one. And then we go down the nets and into the boats, and the next thing I know I'm wading ashore onto a little piece of dirt smack in the middle of the wide Pacific Ocean.

Lieutenant Crandall pulled us in tight and briefed us as we stood on the beach. We were there to back up "Red Mike" Edson and his Raiders. They had gone ashore before us and run into some real crap. The word had been floating around that cornered Japs are nasty little critters, and now we were seeing it firsthand. When we got over to help, it was a hornet's nest. The Japs had holed up on a ridge—Hill 281, someone said—and we had them surrounded. Sergeant Zarate sent Garowski, Sniper and Johnny off to find a tree for Billy where he could get good shots down into the Jap emplacements. I was over to the right watching the squad and hoping I didn't have to jump into the mess, hoping that none of my guys would get killed or even worse, shot to pieces by one of those 30-caliber machine guns that were pouring fire down the hill.

The Japs hid in caves, behind trees, in bunkers, under rocks—and it pissed them off that we had the balls to come and kick them off their brand-new empire. In a few minutes I heard the pop of Billy's 1903 from up the hill—he had a way of firing in quick bursts. He had found a spot, and the Japs were in for it. Bam, bam, bam, bam. I knew he was killing Japs because he never missed. Then, right behind Billy's rifle came the heavier bark of Johnny's BAR. Up the hill I saw action around a cave mouth. A Jap soldier lurched out of the hole onto his face—I knew it was Sniper at work. I heard a weird scream, and another Jap rolled out of the cave mouth. Johnny's BAR was hammering now, a steady, pounding rhythm, like a Gene Krupa drum solo. Heavy fire was pouring into the Jap positions and then, like a horde of hornets that had its nest poked one too many times, the

Japs came pouring out of their holes. They were screaming,
running down the hill straight at the Marines.

That's when Achilles squad went into action. Like I said, my
guys went crazy. They jumped up and ran straight at the Japs,
firing and screaming just as loud as the Japs were. The raiders
and Parachutists were right behind. They crashed together like
waves coming from both sides of the ocean. I saw the mass of
men separate into little struggling groups. Here and there were
two soldiers, one Marine, one Jap, one-on-one and this was the
moment. All that training, all that prep boiled down to this—do
you live or do you die? I thought of Achilles and Hector, fighting
it out on the beach in front of the walls of Troy. This was no
different. Men had been doing this for thousands of years—I live
and you die. It came into my mind that Christ wanted us to live
another way. He wanted us to die so others could live. And just to
show us how that worked, he went first. It was an odd thing to
happen in the middle of a battle, but I heard my dad reading his
favorite Scripture. It was as clear as if I was sitting beside him at
the table during morning devotions... *"greater love hath no man
than that he lay down his life for a friend."* But that was then, and
today Achilles was laying down the lives of their enemies.

Sergeant Zarate was calling for satchel charges. I was
standing there like a deer in the headlights. I hadn't moved a
muscle, frozen up just like I thought I might, and then the call
came, "Corpsman! Corpsman!" This was it, what they had trained
me for, the reason I was here. I turned to see where the call came
from. One of our guys went running by, I think it was Hot Kiss,
maybe Eddie Kramer, but I couldn't tell. He had a satchel charge,
and it was smoking. He heaved it toward a gun emplacement, but
he had pulled the igniter too soon and it blew in mid-air. The
blast knocked me butt-over-teakettle—down an embankment,
over an edge and then a four-foot drop into a hole. I think I was
unconscious from the blast for a few seconds, maybe a minute.
When I came to, my head was still ringing. I couldn't hear. The

battle above sounded far away, like when you're two blocks away from a tight football game.

I was lying on my back in a small cave. The charge had blown the roof of the cave open and daylight was streaming in. There was someone lying on the floor, face down. I crawled over and turned him over. It was a Jap! He was an officer, because his fancy uniform had red bars on the lapels of his jacket. The blast that had torn open the cave had also torn half of this guy's face off, including his right eye. I was staring down at this one-eyed apparition when the remaining eye opened. And the poem came back. I'm in the cave of the Cyclops. Polyphemus is lying on the floor with blood running down his face just like it did when Ulysses stuck him with the sharpened stake.

Polyphemus looks up at me and tries to smile. But it was only half a smile because there was no skin where the other half should have been, and the effect almost made me puke. He plucked at my sleeve and spoke, a horrible gurgling squeak I could just make out.

"Maline, Maline, I surrender."

He must have seen the Red Cross on my arm because he motioned and gurgled again.

"You help, you help."

Without thinking, I pulled out my kit and opened his shirt. The shrapnel that had taken his face off had also riddled him from gullet to crotch so that his chest looked like a piece of Swiss cheese. Bright red blood was pumping out. This guy was a goner, but I would do what I could. I turned just for a second to get morphine, and out of the corner of my eye I saw him move. I turned back just in time to see the knife in his hand coming at my side. I don't know how I did it, sheer gut reaction I guess, but I grabbed his wrist just as I felt the point of the knife cut my side and heard it tear my shirt. And then I'm struggling for my life.

I don't know where this guy got his strength, but he came up off the floor and rolled me over on my back. I'm lying there on the floor of the cave with Polyphemus on top of me and I'm doing everything I can to keep that knife from going into my neck. Bright red blood is pumping down on me and Polyphemus is squeaking that horrible squeak through those missing lips.

"Maline, you die. Maline you die."

But I don't want to die. And then I don't see Polyphemus anymore, it's not a Cyclops bending over me, it's Kalasia, her dark hair drifting down and touching my face like angel hands and she's whispering, "*It may be we shall touch the Happy Isles, and see the great Achilles, whom we knew.* Make this your Happy Isles, Corpsman. Make this your Heaven." And right then I want nothing more in my life than to be back on Tonga with my beautiful Kalasia. I want to live. And I scream.

"God, help me. Father in heaven, help me!"

And the knife point is pressing into my neck and I'm holding it back with all my strength but my hands are slick with the Jap's blood and my arms are trembling and I know it will happen—a one-eyed monster in a stinking cave on some God-forsaken pus pocket that no one ever heard of will kill me and what will they tell my dad, and then there's a thump and Lieutenant Crandall drops into the cave. In an instant he sees what's happening, pulls out his 45 and puts two quick ones right into Polyphemus's remaining eye. The Jap jerks off me backwards, like he hit the end of a rope going forty miles an hour and then I'm lying there gasping for breath saying, "Thank you, God, thank you" over and over.

The Lieutenant sees the blood all over me and kneels down. "Are you hit, Bud?"

I do a quick inventory and find out that except for the gash in my side and the trickle of blood down my neck where the knife almost got buried, I'm in one piece and alive. "No, Sir, I'm good."

Crandall stands up. "Then why don't you quit screwing around down here and get your ass upstairs. We got men who need looking after. Oh, and one more thing—never turn your back on these little yellow pricks. They go by the code of Bushido. That means they'll do anything to kill you, son."

He turns, grabs the edge of the hole and pulls himself out. I grab my kit, take one last look, send one more fervent "Thank you," toward heaven, and then I'm up and out of the Cyclops' cave. The action had died down and I see my squad gathered around someone.

"Corpsman! Corpsman!"

I head over on the double. It's Eddie Kramer. He's lying on his back and the sleeve where his right arm should be is empty. I tear open his shirt. All that's left is a stub. Someone has tied it off, but the artery is still pumping blood out and I can tell by his face he's lost a lot of blood.

"What can we do, Bud?"

"Can we get a stretcher over here? I can't do any more for him. Just keep the tourniquet tight while you get him to the field hospital."

Eddie's eyes flutter open. "Damn it, Bud. Am I gonna die because I'm stupid?"

"Stupid, Eddie?"

"Yeah, frickin stupid. I pulled the igniter too soon, and it blew my arm off. What a dope."

And that was the last thing Eddie said. I stared down at my squad-mate and I felt that piercing blow to my spirit I would come to know so well in the months to come. My friend was lying there, blown apart, and there was nothing I could do. I thought of Polyphemus back in the cave and I looked at Eddie and I realized that though the guts, and the blood and the body parts all might be the same, the spirit behind each man on this island was different. And I knew I wouldn't worry about saving Japs anymore even though somewhere in me a voice was asking why...

16

THE SIREN SONG

JOHNNY STRANGE

The jungle was alive—horrible smells, strange sounds, creaking, rustling... Johnny Strange lay in the foxhole he and Sniper had pounded out of the sandy rock that comprised Hill 281 and listened. Billy lay next to him and Bud was in the next foxhole over. Johnny could hear a squadron of mosquitos right by his face, testing the netting they had spread over the hole. A few of the voracious buggers had gotten through, and he could feel them biting at any exposed parts. He remembered a story one of the Aussie coast-watchers that came on board told the believing kids below decks on the transport—about the two huge mosquitos who fought over a wounded soldier, trying to decide whether to eat him on the spot or carry him back to the jungle. The argument was decided when one reminded the other that if they took the soldier back to the jungle, their big brother mosquitos would take him away from them. He chuckled, remembering the wide eyes of the more gullible Gyrenes.

Billy stirred next to him. "What?"

"Nothing, just something I remembered about mosquitos."

Further away from him were other sounds. Johnny jerked as a

shriek came from nearby. It wasn't loud enough to be a man, but it was something in extremis. "What the hell…"

Now it was Billy's turn to laugh. "Something just got caught by something else out there, maybe a big snake catching one of those little rat things."

Above them a night bird passed with a rustle of wings, settling on a nearby limb. A hammering sound grew around them, blending in with the incessant buzz of the mosquitos—cicadas joining in the infernal symphony. The bird on the branch near them began a song, weird, discordant—three raucous notes in a weird chromatic scale and then four notes and then five. Then starting over—three notes, four, five.

"Can you see that thing Billy, because if you can would you shoot its head off please."

Again Billy chuckled. "That's a fever-bird. Lieutenant Crandall told me about them. He said if you listen long enough you'll count the notes and then you'll go crazy."

"Well, put it out of its misery then."

"Go to sleep, Johnny."

But Johnny couldn't sleep. Scenes from the day's battle came to him like a Movietone Newsreel. The Jap he shot and then spit on, the look on Billy Martens' face when he climbed down out of his sniper perch, Bud crawling up out of a hole covered in blood and the sad, resigned look on Eddie Kramer's face when he died, his arm blown away by a satchel charge.

There was a scuttling in the undergrowth a few feet in front of their hole. Johnny came fully awake. It sounded like someone was sneaking up on them.

"Billy wake up! I think there's a Jap out there."

Billy came up beside him. Johnny's eyes, adjusted to the dark, could just make out the leaves and branches of the brush moving. Then the moon came out from behind the scudding clouds, bathing the clearing in an eerie light. The bushes that Johnny was looking at parted and a huge, hideous crab emerged, its eyeballs waving on long stalks and its claws waving, opening and closing with audible clicks.

Billy whispered. "Land crab."

"Crap, look at that thing. It's uglier than Wilma Shottmeir."

"Wilma Shottmeir?"

"Yeah, she's a girl back in Bonner's Ferry. She was what we called coyote ugly."

"What's that?"

"Well she was so ugly the only way she could get a guy to like her was by sleeping with him. But I heard one guy woke up the next day and there she was, cuddled under his arm. And when he saw how ugly she was, he chewed his arm off so he wouldn't wake her up."

Billy made a choking sound, trying to keep from laughing. "Oh my stinking gosh, Johnny."

"Keep it down over there, you morons!" It was Corporal Navarro. His whisper cut through the night. "You want the Japs to spot you?"

Johnny and Billy looked at each other and struggled to keep from laughing. At last they settled down. Soon Johnny could hear Billy's regular breathing.

That guy can sleep anywhere.

The jungle noises took over again. Buzzing, creaking, scuttling, the fever-bird. Then like someone had flicked a switch, the jungle went silent.

In the jungle over to his right maybe twenty feet away, he heard a tiny scraping sound, like metal on a rock. Then he heard a voice. It was calling in English.

"Help me, help me. Johnny, help me."

Johnny whispered Billy awake.

"Wake up, there's somebody out there. He's calling me. It's one of our guys. We gotta help him."

"Everybody stay put. It's a Jap." Crandall's voice.

"But he knows my name, Lieutenant."

"That's cause he's close enough to hear you talking."

"It's one of our guys, lying out there wounded."

"Strange, shut up and keep your head down."

The voice came again. "Johnny, help me, I'm dying Johnny."

Then Bud chimed in. "Don't listen, Johnny, it's the Siren call."

"What the hell is that, Bud?"

"It's from our poem, *Ulysses*, remember?"

"What's it got to do with us?"

"The Sirens were women who lured sailors with their music and singing to shipwreck on the coast of their island. That guy out there is luring you. Put wax in your ears."

"Awww, Bud, I don't believe in that junk."

"Yeah, well I had a wrestling match with a Cyclops today so, I'm a believer in more ways than one."

Johnny shook his head. "It's one of our guys, Bud."

"No, Johnny, listen up. It's the Siren call."

It's not a Jap. He's speaking English—good English. One of our guys...

"If you want to live, stay down." Crandall again.

"Johnny, help me Johnny. Come get me before the Japs do."

Johnny was tensing to leap out of the foxhole when he felt a hand on his back. "Don't try it, Johnny. It's Japs and they're waiting." Billy jerked Johnny back down in the hole. "I'll prove it." Billy pried a big chunk of rock out of the side of the foxhole and looked at Johnny. "Stay down, Gyrene." They both ducked lower in the hole and Billy tossed the rock out and away from their lines. It crashed into the brush and a 30-caliber cut loose, the tracers zeroing right in on where the rock landed. Then the jungle seemed to erupt with light as gunfire from four or five different spots lined in on the foxholes. A scream cut the darkness like a knife. "Johnny, you die!"

Billy and Johnny got their backsides down as far as they could go while the bullets zipped overhead. Johnny could hear Lieutenant Crandall yelling into his radio, "Red Leg 18, this is Zebra X-

Ray. Registration point 1, direction 1800, right 600, drop 400."
Crandall hollered, "Everybody blend into the bottom of your
hole, incoming!"

There was a second of silence and then with a scream and a
whoosh, artillery shells from the transports out in the dark
channel zoomed in and lit up the jungle fifty feet away. Fire lit the
night and Johnny popped his head up. He could see Japs running
around, their uniforms ablaze. He heard Crandall yelling again.
"Target, fifty right fire for effect."

Again the shells screamed over and hell broke the night open.
Johnny ducked back down. The impact of the explosions
knocked dirt down into the hole and onto their faces. Johnny
could hear Japs screaming. He looked over the edge of his hole
again and saw shadowy figures running, so he stuck his BAR out
and cut loose. The BAR jerked in his hands with its customary
heavy recoil, and the running figures went down. The red mist
rose in his eyes. "Yaaaaaah, run you Jap bastards! Run or die!" He
fired again and again.

"Johnny, Johnny, they're gone." Hands were pulling at him.

"What... what?"

Billy had a hold of him now. "They're gone. The barrage took
out the first wave, and you got the rest. Take it easy, Marine.
Easy, now."

Johnny rolled over and dropped back into the hole, his back
against the wall. "I love this, Billy, I love killing Japs. I love it."

"Yeah, I know, Johnny. I think maybe a little too much."

Johnny shook his head. "Bud asked me one time if I believed
in God. If there is a God who sends Japs straight to hell, then I'm
a believer. And I am become his strong right arm."

TOWARD MIDNIGHT SOMETHING STARTED IN THE WATERS
northwest of their perch on the ridge. From their observation

point they watched as flares lit the horizon above little Savo Island. Then the sound of heavy naval guns came rumbling up the hill through the rain, followed by huge flashes and explosions far out on the water. When the night quieted, Johnny felt a dampness coming in on a breeze from the ocean. A few drops of rain spattered down and then poured and then became a deluge. In a few minutes they were up to their waists in water in their hole, and the ground had turned to slimy mud. Achilles squad sat in miserable silence for the rest of the night.

WHEN DAWN CAME, THEY LOOKED OUT ACROSS TO CHANNEL TOWARD Savo Island. The channel should have been full of ships, their ships, but not one was in sight. Around 0800 hours a runner came up the hill. After a brief consultation peppered by some fervent cuss words, Lieutenant Crandall called his men together. "Well boys, the friggin' Navy is gone. The word is Admiral Fletcher heard the Japanese fleet was moving down from the big Japanese base at Rabaul. So he took his carriers, turned tail and ran."

Sergeant Shanks, squad leader for Hades squad, spoke up. "Fletcher? Isn't that the same jerk that turned around and left our boys at Wake Island? Said he didn't have enough gas?"

Crandall nodded. "Yep, 'No Gas' Fletcher, and when he left, Admiral Turner had to pull anchor on all the transports and bail out, too. A good thing, from what I hear. An hour after they sailed, the Japs came down Sealark Channel with heavy warships, snuck around little Savo Island and caught us dead in the water. It was over in fifteen minutes. Three cruisers went to the bottom, and that's where the rest of 2nd Division would be if Turner hadn't hightailed it."

Johnny spoke up. "But those transports had all the supplies.

We haven't unloaded them yet. And the rest of our guys—that was our backup."

"Where does that leave us, Lieutenant?" Zarate asked.

Crandall lit up a cigar. "We are friggin' marooned boys. Brass doesn't know when Fletcher or Turner will be back. So we'll just have to make do with what we got." He looked at his cigar and shrugged. "This may be my last cigar for a while."

Just then a short Marine in a field jacket walked up. Everyone saluted. Billy whispered to Johnny. "That's Red Mike."

"Edson?"

"Yeah."

Edson returned the salute and then pulled out a smoke. "How you boys doing?"

Lieutenant Crandall smiled. "Well, we licked'em good yesterday, Colonel."

"Sure appreciated you boys coming over. Saved our bacon. I'm asking the brass to assign you to my group. I need a few crazy Gyrenes where I'm going."

Sergeant Zarate asked a question. "Beggin' your pardon, Sir, but did you hear about the transports?"

Edson grimaced and spat. "Yeah, that a-hole Fletcher turned tail again. But that means nothing to us, so forget him. I hope a Jap bomb sends him to coward's hell. We have to stay focused— we got our work right here. When those chicken livers drop back in on the fight, we'll have this place all cleaned up for them. They can have a dress uniform dance for all I care."

"And what about supplies, Sir?"

Edson gave them a wicked grin. "Lots of supplies on Guadalcanal. The Japs have 'em. How about we go take them away?"

The men broke into grins, nodding their heads. Johnny felt his spirits lift. This was Red Mike Edson and where he went, the Japs always seemed to follow. Good. More Japs to kill.

HOLLYWOOD MARINES

BILLY MARTENS

M *y Diary Jack—Monday, August 17ᵗʰ, 1942 Tulagi*

OKAY, JACK, IT'S BILLY. I HAVEN'T TALKED TO YOU SINCE MY NEXT-to-last elk hunt, the week-long one in November '41. So, here's what's what: I'm in the South Pacific, I'm carrying a Model 1903, but I'm not after elk or a stag; America's at war with Japan, and I'm in the war—I've killed men, okay? It's been eating at me. Me, the good Mennonite boy who thought he should defend his country and all his Mennonite people who wouldn't defend themselves. So, I hung around the church parades yesterday, looking for answers. Any answers. Never really sat down, was just standing back of it all. I started with the Protestants. Chaplain Jackson was talking about a battle David fought. The faith he needed and the strength his faith gave him to endure and over-come and win. Not just the physical fight, but the fight in his head and the fight in his heart—the fight to overcome everything hard in his life. For himself, his family, his friends, his country, his God. His fights were the fights we all fight, not only against the

Japanese, but against all the difficulties we experience. When we came back home from the war, we would be better men because of what our faith had taught us about never giving up. Like David, who was close to God's own heart.

I drifted from him over to where Padre McKean and the Catholics were assembled. McKean was getting ready to serve Mass or whatever, had an altar set up on a table and had a pure white cloth draped over it—I guess he had that in his pack. He was finishing up what he called a homily and it was about the suffering of Christ, the Passion. About him taking wounds the same as our buddies had taken wounds. Nail holes like bullet holes. Raked across the skull where the crown of thorns had been pushed in. Hit in the side and bleeding out. Some of our buddies had died, just like Christ had died, and they'd died for their country, sure, but they'd also died for us, their friends, so we'd carry on with what had to be done and maybe even get home to our sweethearts and families again. Well, Christ had died for us too. He'd died so we could live again in our hearts and our souls. That was what Mass was all about. Christ had died to give us a second life. *Greater love hath no man than this, that a man lay down his life for his friends.* Our buddies had done that for us. Christ had done that for us, too. Mass was about realizing that, about realizing the sacrifice Christ had made for us, about making it real, taking it inside our heads and our spirits. Mass was about becoming a new man again because of what had happened on the Cross 2000 years ago. About being forgiven. About starting again. A brand-new man.

Being forgiven? Did I need to be forgiven, Jack? What had I done wrong? Killing? Was the killing my father and my church said was wrong, why I needed Mass? Did I need confession and absolution too? Did I need Rome and the Vatican and the Pope? Would that make everything right? McKean made it clear that Mass was only for *bona fide* Catholics. Maybe he saw me standing back there. He said it with a warm smile, but he meant it. Okay, I get it. So, I moved on.

I'd hung back on Saturday too, Sabbath, Shabbat, and watched Leon Levy pull some kind of prayer shawl out of his pocket and tug it over his shoulders, put a small round cap on his head, hold a prayer book in his hands, and rock back and forth. Rabbi Sol Davids had chanted and spoken in Hebrew and English. I liked the Hebrew, even though I did not understand what he was saying. But the English on its own was good too: "Blessed be the Lord, Master of the Universe who gives us the gift of life, the majesty of the heavens, who protects us, who is our shield, our high tower, our King." On Sunday, after I drifted away from the Mass, I found myself at his tent. Somehow, he had snagged some beer and was drinking it at room temperature. Or tropical temperature.

"Where would I get ice on Tulagi?" He laughed. "The Brits drink it warm, so I suppose I can do it too. But, *Adonai*, it is a different creature without a fridge." He gestured to a stool. "Rest your boots, Marine. I saw you yesterday. What's on your mind?" He pointed to a bucket near my feet. "Help yourself to *saki* or to a British beer. Tulagi temperature."

I didn't touch anything. Just said, "*Thou shalt not kill.*" Flat. Toneless. Like some kind of dead guy slumped in front of him.

Rabbi Davids took another swallow of beer. "Under the Law of Moses, the Mosaic Law, it was permitted to kill in self-defense. There was capital punishment—they executed men and women for crimes against the Lord and against other Jews. And there might be an accidental killing too. Which could be forgiven. Finally, soldiers could kill in warfare. This *thou shalt not kill* King James inflicted on the world, it's a lousy translation of the original Hebrew words that *Adonai* carved into the stone tablets."

"So, what isn't a lousy translation, rabbi?"

"Thou shalt not *murder* isn't a lousy translation, Marine." He swigged more warm beer. "Killing in warfare isn't considered a crime by the Master of the Universe. It isn't considered murder, no matter who tries to twist that verse for their cause. No, war is not ideal. It is not the best plan or the best path. But sometimes you have to fight. The alternatives are your own death or enslavement. *Adonai* knows all this. He is more understanding and rational about combat and more forgiving to the warrior than those who cry it is a sin to shed blood. Certainly, it isn't a great thing to shed blood. It isn't a great thing that a world should be at war as it is now. One day *Adonai* promises us it will end. Completely. All warfare. Forever. Until then, we live in an age when we must defend ourselves. It is not complicated. Only common sense. But humans, men, women, we like to complicate and bring shame where there is no shame. What did Jesus the Jew say? Greater love has no man than this, but that he lays down his life for his friends? So that is what we are doing here, Marine. Not so much are we fighting for America. Not so much are we fighting on Tulagi and Guadalcanal to keep the Empire of Japan from invading Australia. No. We are fighting for each other."

---

*Saturday, August 22**ND Tulagi*

So, Jack, scuttlebutt has it there was a big firefight on the Canal the other night. Now our top Marine, General Vandegrift, has pulled troops off Tulagi and is using them to reinforce the 1st Marine Division on Guadalcanal. I guess it was some big mess, and the Marines almost got flanked at some place the boys call Alligator Creek. They really had to hose the jungle and the creek bank. They're saying there's so many Jap bodies you can walk on them for a hundred yards or more and your boot will never touch the beach.

Of course, this drives my Mennonite buddy Johnny Strange crazy. (It sounds funny to call him Mennonite. Hell, it sounds funny to call me Mennonite. We've killed. We're at war. We carry guns and ammo. We hunt humans. I doubt our churches even pray for us anymore.) Johnny wants a battle every day. He wishes he could take on the Japs more than he wishes for decent chow (which we have little of). If he prays at all, he prays to kill. But we're stuck on Tulagi with those big damn land crabs. There ain't no Japs left anywhere on Tulagi or Gavutu or Tanambogo. You gotta go to Guadalcanal for those, Jack. But we ain't going to Guadalcanal.

THURSDAY, SEPTEMBER 3RD ON SHIP

We're going to Guadalcanal, Jack.

We're on this little boat and we're going to Guadalcanal.

What they call Cactus when they want to use the code word.

It's that Red Mike Edson's doing. It's just King Company from the 2/2. Him and Crandall and Rudebaker get along swell and he liked the way the company spearheaded the 2/2 fight on Hill 281. Picked us as reinforcements a few weeks back and now we're in. Wherever his Raiders are going we have to have his boys' backs.

As you can imagine, Johnny couldn't be happier. Me, I wouldn't mind a few more weeks of quiet on Tulagi. I'm pretty sure Cactus will be as noisy as heck, Jack.

FRIDAY, SEPTEMBER 11TH GUADALCANAL

I tell ya, Jack, we've been humping here and humping there. And all we get is shit from the 1st Marine Division. "Hollywood Marines, here come the Hollywood Marines, boys. Look, there's Clark Gable. Hey, it's Johnny Wayne and Jimmy Stewart. And isn't that Vivien Leigh? Hey, pack your bags, Marines. The Silver Screen is here. Turns out the war is just a movie with special effects and Jap actors, so we can all go home. Pearl Harbor happened on a Hollywood back lot." All because we trained in southern California.

The thing here is to protect the airfield on the Canal, this Henderson Field we captured from the Japs at the beginning of August and gave a Midway pilot's name. It's pretty clear Tokyo Joe wants it back, and the island is suddenly lousy with Japs. Word is a big attack is coming, but no one knows from where. General Vandegrift is convinced the Jap troops will come at Henderson from the shoreline from the coast. Red Mike and Colonel Thomas, Vandegrift's ops officers, they think the attack will come at Lunga Ridge, just by the Lunga River that runs by the airstrip. The Ridge allows the Japs to stay in the jungle and out of sight until the last moment where an approach from shore risks exposure. The upshot of it all was, Vandegrift let Edson and the Raiders and the Paramarines and any reinforcements tagged to Edson to have a rest break on the Ridge. I kid you not, Jack. We're bunkered down on the ridge for R and R. Johnny is livid. He thinks he will miss the big fight on the coast while we squat and play poker and smoke Lucky Strikes on the Ridge.

But that's not the half of it. Vandegrift split up King and said they needed the men elsewhere. He's into this coastal defense thing, like I said. The only piece of us that Edson has is Platoon X-Ray, about 38 guys now instead of fifty. He was cussing, but all that did was give the rest of us a more complex vocabulary to work with. So, all together there's a little over 800 of us on this Ridge. And X-Ray is strictly there to reinforce—we're 200 yards back of the line Edson is setting up, spreading his men among three knolls: Hill 80, Hill 123 and Hill No Name (what I call it). If there's a fight, and things get tough, Edson brings us in. Johnny is raging that there won't be any fight anywhere near the ridgeline.

Why only 38 of us now? Some were wounded or killed on Tulagi. But others caught malaria. Guys are getting the shakes and Bud has been run off his feet getting us to take Atabrine. It can turn your skin yellow and make you crap like a fire hose so the guys don't want it. And the Japs have been broadcasting that it makes you infertile. So, Bud has asked the chaplains to help him convince the boys it's safe to take and that Tokyo Joe is just messing with our heads. What helps the most is when a patrol overruns a Jap position and we get the food supplies and the *saki* and stores of actual quinine—the Japanese conquered the Dutch East Indies, that's where the world supplies of quinine are, and that's why the Marines and the US Army and our Allies don't have any of it. Once we find quinine when we capture Jap supplies, okay, the guys will take that without arguing. Making Bud's job easier. We also find cigarettes in the Jap camps. They're crap and we leave them to the centipedes and land crabs.

It's not just the platoon that's down in numbers. So's our squad, Achilles. Kramer we lost on Tulagi. McKeever is sidelined with malaria and it looks like Levy is coming down with it too. And Malena? No one knows what happened to Malena. But we figure a croc got him when he went swimming to wash the crud off his body. The other platoons have lost men that way, too. Those crocs are mean and strong, just grab you and roll you under till you drown and then chew you up. The assistant squad leader of Zeus, Corporal Crook, his whole crew saw the croc nail him. They were blasting away with their Garands and 1903s and the croc acted like they were tossing sand pebbles at him. Those uglies give me the creeps.

So, Jack, just to say we have eight healthy bodies in the squad plus Bud. Sergeant Zarate and Corporal Navarro have been crying to Crandall and Rudebaker for reinforcements, but there aren't reinforcements for anyone. Not since the Navy gutted out and left us holding the *saki*. Now and then we get some brave bluejackets who run their destroyers in and offload supplies by day, using the harbor at Tulagi. They bring in ammo and medical supplies. And chow. But the chow is usually those round cans of C-rations that taste like what dog dung smells like. We have no choice but to eat the slime. That's why guys are so eager to do patrols. If they find a Jap encampment and capture it they get first crack at the tins of fish and crab and bamboo shoots, or whatever the heck they eat for vegetables, and they can snag big bags of rice too that are easy to cook up for a platoon. We all figure the guys that find and take Jap positions and food stores ought to get the Navy Cross or the Medal of Honor.

I'm signing off. I got my hands on a round can without a label and when I opened it, crap, I'd lucked onto a B unit of rations. The M are the slime meals. In this B, I've got chocolate fudge, crackers, sugar tablets, and a tin of powdered lemon drink. I don't want anyone to see what I've got. I feel bad about not sharing it with Johnny. But not that bad. He wouldn't care. If I opened up my rations and had a ticket to a firefight with the Japanese that would excite him. But fudge? I love fudge, but he couldn't care less. He's over there smoking some Old Gold cigarettes he won off a bunch of Raiders in a poker game. They were sore losers, calling him a lousy Hollywood Marine. All the 1st Division guys call us 2nd Division guys that because we trained at Camp Elliott near Tinseltown. Just never heard Raiders call us that before. They saw us fight on Tulagi. Oh, what the heck. You play poker with Johnny, you lose your shirt, and you cry in your *saki*, unless he takes that too. 'Night, Jack.

BILLY SHARPENED HIS PENCIL WITH HIS BOWIE BEFORE TUCKING THE leather book and pencils in his pack. He'd been writing in the diary since he was 16 and had never missed writing entries every year. Usually about his hunts. Now he was writing about a different kind of hunt. They didn't want Marines taking diaries into the war zone in case the enemy got their hands on them. Billy thought that was crazy. Would Tokyo win the war because they found his mom's recipe for moose ribs on page eleven?

It was night. Jungle night. He brushed away a hovering

mosquito and adjusted netting over his face. "Bug off!" he snarled. He slept, cradling his rifle like a teddy bear he'd loved when he was four. Navarro shook him awake before dawn. Billy dug around in his pack and found another can without a label. He prayed and opened it. Right away, he could see it was dog meat. He groaned. But grabbed the spoon from his mess kit and made a big show of eating it with distaste. In-between, he sucked on his square of fudge, then his tablets of sugar, snuck a cracker into his mouth, and poured the powdered lemon drink into his canteen. Johnny wasn't even watching. Neither was anyone else. The sun rose and the jungle heat and sweat and day bugs were back.

Nothing happened. The day slugged past. Johnny kept listening for the sounds of gunfire from the beach and the sea, but except for the squawking of jungle birds their corner of the South Pacific was silent.

"We're gonna lose the war," Johnny griped, cleaning his BAR for the third time that day. "And do you friggin' know why?"

"Because you're up here instead of down there?" Billy offered.

"Yeah. That. Old Lady Vandy Grift has his men in the wrong places. We're screwed. The Japs will take the airfield, bring in their blasted Zeros and Bettys, slaughter us from the sky and win the fight for the Canal. It'll be another damn Bataan or Corregidor. Then they'll invade Australia and rule the Pacific. America will concede defeat and run back home and hide. Until the Japs land on the beaches of California and Oregon and Washington. And that, my Mennonite brother, will be that. *Saki*, rice, fish, noodles and bad cigarettes. That will be that. Shit."

AT 2130 HOURS, BILLY FELT HIS EYES HAD ADJUSTED TO THE darkness sufficiently to allow him to write a paragraph in his diary. Eyes close to the page, he penciled in the date: *Saturday night, September 12th*. Then he printed out a sentence, beginning with *All Quiet on the Pacific Front, a novel by William Jeremiah Martens...*

And then shells landed with a screech that, to Billy, was unholy. They ripped the night up with fire. He dove into his foxhole and Johnny dove into his. Blast after blast rocked the area around the Ridge. The ground shook and shattered. It wasn't land artillery. Billy was sure it was naval. The shriek reminded him of their own bombardment of Florida and Tulagi in early August. He heard Lt. Crandall bellow: "Get in your hole, Sharples! Get in your hole, Hot Kiss! Dammit! You crazy? You think they're firing rice balls?"

A Japanese searchlight blazed over the Ridge as the big guns continued to pummel the Marine lines. It was, thought Billy, like someone flicking a Zippo a half-inch from his eyes, it was so painful and so bright. He hunkered down further into his foxhole and screwed his eyes shut, his body jumping with every shell burst.

The explosions went on for 20 minutes. Billy checked his watch once the howling was over—2150 hours, ten to ten. Now the crack of rifle and machine gun fire was obvious. Marines were hollering. Grenades burst with loud thumps. The firing to the right was fierce. Navarro ran from hole to hole—"You guys okay? You guys okay?" Zarate was on his heels. "*Hombres*," he said, "*hombres*, we are in reserve. Don't go running out there just because you hear the shooting. The shooting is everywhere. We have to hang tight until Red Mike tells us where to go. We seal the gaps in the line. We fix the breaks. Stay put, *hombres*. Get back in your hole, Johnny. Our time will come."

"The blasted war will be over before our frigging time comes, Sarge!" snapped Johnny.

"Our time came on Tulagi. It will come here, too. Stay put, *hombre*."

"Fall back!" Billy and Johnny could hear the shouting off on the right flank. "Fall back! Get back to the Ridge! Go! Go!"

"That'll be the Raiders' C company!" hissed Johnny. "I played some of them in poker. They're positioned between the lagoon and the Lunga River below us. At least they were. Crap, Red Mike, come on, send us to save their butts. We'll show them what Hollywood Marines can do."

"FALL BACK, MARINES! FALL BACK!"

"Oh shit, Red Mike," seethed Johnny. "Come on, come on, come on! Send us in!"

Rifle fire rose to a crescendo on the right. Billy could distinguish the rapid shots of the bolt action Model 1903s from the semi-automatic fire of the M1 Garands. The chatter of the M1919A4, the 30-caliber machine gun, which Billy had heard from his sniper's perch on Tulagi, cut through the *bang bang bang* of the Garands. Now and then he was sure he could make out a Thompson submachine gun spewing its 45-caliber slugs. Shooting was going on from left to right, but it remained heaviest on the right flank.

Then it trickled out and stopped. Navarro ran along the line of foxholes of squad Achilles again. "Just stay tight. We don't know if the Japs will hit us again. The flyboys are coming in at first light to bomb and strafe the area south of us. That's where the Japs have been coming from. We will unleash our howitzers on them too."

"What happened on the right?" demanded Johnny.

Navarro arched eyebrows over marble black eyes. "You heard what we all heard. The Marines below the Ridge had to retreat. The skinny is one platoon was overrun. The others had to cut their way back to our lines."

"Why the hell didn't Red Mike order us in to help them?"

"Help them? Help them do what, Marine? Run? We're outnumbered and outgunned. Got that, Strange? We'll be lucky if half of us walk off this Ridge alive." Then Navarro flashed a blazing white grin. "But the damn Japs will be lucky if any of them walk off alive. We'll use our bare hands and stones if we have to, but we will hold. They're not getting that frigging airfield and the island. You with me, Marine?"

"Sir, yes, Sir!" snapped Johnny.

"Your time will come, Strange. Just make sure you're ready for it and not playing high stakes poker."

When Navarro had gone, Johnny looked at Billy. "Oh, I'm playing high stakes poker, all right. With the entire Empire of Japan. Just give me another day. Give me another day and night. Can you pray for that, Billy Mennonite? Can you get your God to give me that?"

18

TROY

THE CORPSMAN

I'd fallen asleep gripping a dying Marine's hand. I'd been asleep no more than three minutes—my watch had read 0700 hours, and now it read 0703. Red Mike patted me on the back: "Son, some other men still breathing need you." Then he tore the Red Cross armbands off my uniform and removed my helmet with its Red Cross in a white circle. He planted a plain green M1 tin pot on my head. "You're a Marine like the rest of us, Bud. No need for the damn decorations. We lost one of our corpsmen last night. He was all decked out in crosses too. Hard for the Japs to miss."

"I'm sorry, Sir."

"We need you alive. Understood?"

"Yes, Sir."

He nodded. "Good enough."

"Is it over, Sir?" I asked.

"Not by a long shot. They'll be back tonight. Let's get the wounded off the Ridge. Got enough morphine and plasma?"

"No, Sir."

"I'll get them to bring up more supplies."

I readied seven men for the stretcher bearers or body

snatchers to take down. Gave another five quinine we'd raided from Japanese camps and pointed them down off the Ridge too. They began to slowly make their way along a narrow path. So, we'd lost a bunch of men to bullets and another bunch to malaria.

I drank from my canteen. The water was warm and tasted like chlorine from the tablets I'd dropped in it. They didn't need a corpsman with dysentery any more than they needed one with a Jap gunshot wound to the head. I sat on the helmet Red Mike had given me, opened a can of C-rations, crushed a salt tablet into it, and spooned up the dog food without flinching. Back of the Ridge, I saw a line of bodies covered by their ponchos. Their heads were covered too, so that every man looked the same. I took another swig of the warm chlorinated water. *"I've drunk delight of battle with my peers, far on the ringing plains of windy Troy,"* I whispered.

I rubbed a hand over my face. Blood, and shattered bones, and screaming eyes, and mouths gone from Jap bullets, and hands grabbing me, desperate for more life. How many had I treated during the night battle? How many had I saved? How do you save someone who's been sawed in half by a Type 92 Nambu heavy machine gun firing 450 rounds a minute? Is this how I'd imagined it back in San Diego? Or Tonga?

Crandall sat down beside me. "Have you written that girl yet?"

"No, Sir."

"Have the exotic pleasures of Tulagi and Guadalcanal driven her from your sensitive Mennonite mind?"

"I think of her, Sir. But I have no idea what to say. My mind isn't full of romantic images anymore. I think about bags of plasma and gauze pads and sutures and guys bleeding out."

"You clearly need help."

"Yes, Sir."

"I have some ideas."

"I'm all ears, Sir."

"Tell Kalasia that her eyes glow like the Southern Cross."

"What?"

"A bit of a stretch, I'll admit. She may think it's corny. On the other hand, she may like it."

"She may."

"Tell her you've never gone one day without thinking about her."

"Well—"

"Just say it. That's an order."

"Aye, aye, Sir."

"Everything's an order. Writing the letter before you get shot is an order."

"Who's going to take the mail out? The Navy is off drinking coffee in Annapolis."

"You let me worry about that. I'll get some mail bags onto the next got-guts destroyer to dock at Tulagi. Okay?"

"Understood, Skipper."

"I'm going to take a powder. Either write the letter today and leave it with me or don't take a bullet tonight. Those are your choices."

"Got it, Sir. Thank you, Sir."

"Quit goldbricking and get out a pen and paper."

There was no writing done. I would just have to survive. I tried to put pen to paper but my mind was a blank, nothing more than a white wall. Red Mike climbed on a grenade box and gave a Hail Mary speech. He said he was proud of us and that we had the guts to hold the Ridge. I knew we didn't have enough ammo or grenades, I knew none of us had slept and that we were dragging our butts like zombies. But I also knew the 2nd Battalion, 5th Marines, 2/5, had been sent our way to reinforce and that a battery of 105mm howitzers were ready to zero in on the Japs at the orders of a forward artillery observer planted with us. And then I was dealing with medical supplies that were brought up to the Ridge, and all the corpsmen were making sure they had what they needed, and before long the sun was dropping into the sea. It was night. The sudden and quick South Pacific night. And with night came the Japanese, 3000 of them, and we were eight hundred.

The crack of rifle fire was immediate with the swift arrival of darkness. Muzzle flashes were pinpricks in the tropical night. *The lights begin to twinkle from the rocks, the long day wanes, the slow moon climbs, the deep moans round with many voices...* Except there was no moon. The sky was as black and impenetrable as cast iron.

Then suddenly it was the blast and ragged flames of grenades and the fall of naval shells cracking open the earth. The hammer of machine guns, our Brownings against their Nambus. Shouts in Japanese and yells in American. The *bang bang bang* of Garands and the *PING* as the stripper clips ejected after the eight rounds were gone and a new clip had to be inserted from the top. *Delight of battle on the ringing plains of windy Troy.* And then came my cry, my name, just like fresh gunfire: "Corpsman! Corpsman!"

I ran to the fallen Marine, dodging shellfire from what turned out to be Jap destroyers. Tulagi had been one thing. I'd had a bloody birth as a corpsman on Tulagi. But it had all happened in the daylight. That seemed to help. Everything that happened on the Ridge happened in darkness. You could not see except for the fast, vicious glare of bomb blasts and gun bursts. It was eerie, it was unknown, it was wicked and macabre. It was Dante in wretched skin and wretched blood.

"You're going to be all right, Marine," I said, bending over a Raider with a bad arm wound. "We'll stop the bleeding."

"My mom, tell my mom."

"You can tell her yourself. You'll be writing her a letter in the morning."

"Tell her I was brave. Tell her I never shirked my duty."

"I will. And so will you. Stretcher bearers! Get this man off the Ridge!"

The naval bombardment was over in minutes. But the fighting reached a fever pitch all around me. I saw men die as if they were under strobe lights—flash, flash, flash from guns and grenades—hit, crying out, falling, twisting, turning, arms gone, eyes gone, head gone, stomach gone—I ran through the fierce light show applying tourniquets, pressing gauze pads onto spurting wounds, giving injections of morphine, using rifles bayoneted into the earth to hang plasma, making sure the wounded had a few buddies with them and that stretcher bearers knew where to take them far away from the fighting and killing.

Red Mike had strung out his men about a mile along the Ridge, the left flank anchored at Hill 80, the center at Hill 128 (where he was stationed) and the right flank at a knoll that had no name. I kept answering cries for help that took me closer and closer to Hill 80. Suddenly I was aware of a surge against me, of Marines retreating back the way I had come. One captain grabbed me by the arm.

"They ordered us back to Hill 123, corpsman," he said. "The damn Japs shoved the Parachute Battalion off Hill 80 and Raider Company B was exposed and flanked. Red Mike wants us all in the center."

"How much time have I got left to find the wounded?"

"None."

It was crazy, but I pushed him away and I even felt a burst of anger. "I have a job to do. If retreating is yours, captain, get on with it."

He cussed me out, but all he got was my back. Raiders were helping their wounded buddies get away from the Japs and stretcher bearers were hauling out those who couldn't walk or limp. I scoured the area, saw Jap helmets and caps bobbing about two hundred yards away in the vivid bursts of rifle and machine gun fire, found two Raiders in a heap and knelt beside them. In moments, we were pretty much alone.

"I couldn't haul him anymore," one man gasped, his chest heaving. He only had one arm. The right one was gone. "I tried, ask God, but my strength isn't there."

"Never mind," I replied. "You did good." I pushed the largest compress I had left into his bloody shoulder socket. "Put your hand on this. Hard. Here." I had a square of fudge I'd been saving in my pocket from a B unit of C-rations I'd lucked out on. I pushed it between his lips. "Suck on that. Take your time."

"Doc..."

"I'll take care of your buddy. Don't worry."

"God knows I tried, Doc."

"He knows. God brought me here to help you out."

The other Raider stared at me with eyes like black marbles. Shrapnel had shredded his chest and lungs. I cut away his uniform jacket and wrapped his torso with gauze around and around. He bubbled a laugh, blood coming out of his mouth: "I'm the Mummy." I grinned back and gave him a syrette of morphine. Then I slapped him on the shoulder. "Let's go, Marine."

I hefted him up and did my first fireman's carry of the war. I told his buddy to follow us and I lit out running with the retreat. My legs were on fire by the time I reached a pit stop where a couple of corpsmen were triaging about a dozen wounded and stretcher bearers were standing by. I laid him down. His gauze was barely pink and he was breathing. "His bleeding's under control," I told them. I realized his buddy was not behind us. "I gotta go back."

"Hill 80 is lousy with Japs," one of them protested.

"I won't be long. Get this Raider off the Ridge. I gave him a syrette of morphine."

I took off. I think I ran a hundred yards and found my man face forward in the dirt. I scooped him up, dropping to one knee, and did my second fireman's carry, running back to the cluster of

corpsmen. They peeled him off my back and laid him on the
ground.

"He's dead." A corpsman twice my age looked into my face.

"No, he's not." I bent over the Raider and examined him.
There was no pulse.

"He bled out." The older corpsman closed the Raider's eyes.
"What the heck did you think was going to happen when his arm
was ripped right off like that?"

"I was going to suture him."

"Who the hell has time to suture a wound that size up here in
hell?" He put a lit cigarette between my lips. "You mean well, kid,
but you have a lot to learn. I hope you live long enough to learn
it." He lit another cigarette for himself. I saw they were Player's.
"Both flanks have caved. The Japs are coming at us like a bunch
of samurais. Red Mike is doing an Alamo at Hill 123. Who are you
attached to?"

I'd never smoked before. Why I didn't cough up a fit, I'll never
know. But my eyes were stinging and watering. "The 2/2."

"The 2/2's not in this fight."

"King Company. But Vandegrift only left one platoon
up here."

"Better hustle. I'm pretty sure all the reinforcing units are up.
We'll take care of these casualties and be at 123 in a shake."

I made my way to the center, that crazy first-time cigarette
dangling from my lips. Hill 123 was boiling with Marines going
every which way but straight. Some were howling, "WITH-
DRAW!" and heading off the ridge to the north, away from the
Japs. Others screamed that the Nips had poison gas. Scores were
abandoning the Ridge and heading to the rear. Red Mike bawled
like a bull and thundered like Thor: "FORM A LINE, MARINES!
GET YOUR BUTTS BACK HERE AND MAKE A FIGHT!
WHERE IN THE DAMN BLUE BLAZES OF HELL DO YOU
THINK YOU'RE GOING? THE WAR'S HERE ON THIS RIDGE!
GRAB SOME GUTS AND MAKE A FIGHT!"

The Japs screamed from behind and it felt like they were coming right up my spine. Suddenly my squad was all around me, firearms blasting into the dark. Strange was firing his BAR with one hand and grabbed me with the other, yanking me out of harm's way. Hernandez was right beside him, BAR pounding. Downtown Seattle Garowski was on one knee with his Garand, *bang bang bang bang PING*. And beside him were Jake Sharples, and Hot Kiss the Teacher, and Billy Sniper Martens, all slapping the bolts home on their Model 1903s and pouring fire into the attacking Japanese who were right on top of us.

And then, as if I were dreaming it, and not really experiencing it, someone yelled, "GRENADE!" I saw a Jap fragmentation grenade land and bounce right in front of us and Red Mike. I knew their fuses were short and that it would explode almost immediately. It was Sharples who moved, Jake Sharples of Ketchum, Idaho, and threw himself on the "Kiska" hand grenade, smothering the blast with his own skin and bone and soul. The explosion lifted him into the air and tore him in half. When he landed, he landed on his back, and his head was turned towards us. We all saw his brilliant green eyes. A shock wave swept through the whole front line. Then Red Mike was hollering again like Mars, like Ares, the god of war.

"MARINES! THIS LINE WILL HOLD! UNITED STATES MARINES! THIS LINE WILL HOLD TO THE LAST MAN!"

19

CIRCE'S BLOODY HILL

JOHNNY STRANGE

They came again. Like the tide moving inexorably upon a defiant beach, the Banzai wave crawled up the hill. For the first time Johnny Strange felt lost. The Japs were everywhere, screaming, coming, refusing to stop, even as Achilles squad and the men of X-ray platoon beside them poured a withering fire down the slope. For the first time he was afraid—afraid he was a coward, afraid he would let his buddies down, afraid he would run.

Then, just in that instant before he broke, there was a rushing sound of feet and the dirt at the back edge of the trench scattered as Lt. Crandall slid into the ditch.

"Don't do it, Strange."

"Do what, Sir?"

"Run. Don't run. If you run, you will die, so we might as well die here in our holes, right?"

Johnny settled.

He's right. There's nowhere to go but here.

"Look up there, Strange."

Johnny looked up the hill. There was Red Mike, standing erect in his command post. Johnny could see two fresh bullet holes in the loose tail of his shirt. Still, Edson stood defiantly, calmly directing the battle. "Look at him, Strange, and take heart. I'm more afraid of him than I am of the damn Japs, and you better be too. He's the last man on the hill. Behind him is Henderson field. If we don't stop them here, we're done, he's done and so is America."

Red Mike's arm was beckoning to men on both sides, and Johnny could hear him yelling. "Raiders, parachuters, engineers, artillerymen, I don't give a damn who you are. You're all Marines. Come up on this hill and fight!'"

Johnny pulled a deep breath. The whole exchange with Crandall had taken less than a half-minute and now Johnny felt something, courage, or hate, or the kill-lust flowing back into his body and his spirit.

Crandall grabbed Johnny's arm and pointed down the hill. "Down there, Strange, concentrate your fire at the head of that gully." He yelled at the rest of the squad. "Mark on Strange and concentrate fire."

The Japs were moving up a natural channel on the hill. As they came out in the open, they ran into a wall of steel death, blasting, tearing, smashing them to pieces. Johnny could hear Sniper's 1903 pinging in the familiar rhythm. Bam, bam, bam, bam—four Japs dead. He cut loose with his BAR and the front of the wave dissolved. On his left Julio's BAR fell into a rhythm with his and it was like a symphony of sound—the heavy barking of the automatics playing the bass line, the 1903s filling in the counterpoint and Crandall's Thompson ratcheting away like a crazed percussion section. And above it all the soprano rebel yells of the boys from 1st Division Raiders and Chutists up and down the line, like a demented aria.

Fifteen feet away from the trenches, the Jap wave broke, and they turned tail and ran down the hill. A wild yell, almost like an animal scream rose from the Marine trenches. Johnny's rifle was almost too hot to hold, but he kept firing, loading, firing, scream-

ing. Then he felt a hand on his shoulder. "Okay, Johnny, Okay.
Hold your fire. We held."

Johnny stopped. Lt. Crandall was with him, a rock, the heart
of Platoon X-ray and Achilles squad. He saw Bud moving
among the wounded and dying on the hillside. Billy slumped
against the back of the trench. Johnny looked over the edge of
his position. Down below he saw a movement, and then a Jap
soldier was dragging something into view. It was a wounded
Marine, a Raider from Company B. The Jap was an officer, the
red marks of his rank visible on his collar. He hauled the soldier
into view and forced him to his knees. His sword flashed red in
the light from flares above the field as he raised it high for the
beheading stroke. In the trench next to Johnny, a single shot
rang out and the Jap's head exploded into bloody pieces as he
flipped backwards down the hill. He looked over. Billy Martens
was looking down the barrel of his 1903, a grim smile on
his face.

"Don't mess with our boys, you son of a bitch," he muttered.

———

BY MIDNIGHT THE MARINES FROM COMPANY B BELOW THEM
crawled or scrambled or dragged themselves up the hill to the
relative safety of the knoll. The Raiders and "Chutes" formed a
new defensive line in the shape of a horseshoe with X-Ray
platoon in the center. Over to the right the 11th Special Weapons
Battery smoke wagons, the 105 mm guns commanded by Pedro de
Valle, kept up their firing from the top of the ridge, sometimes to
within 200 yards of the Marines' perimeter. Red Mike made his
way through the trenches, encouraging, uplifting and inspiring
his men.

He came by Achilles' position and took a knee. "How you
boys enjoying my R&R camp?"

There was a chuckle. A Gyrene in the dark over to the left

answered back. "Jeez, Colonel, if this is friggin' R&R, I don't wanna know what one of your fire-fights is like." More chuckles.

"You boys' been doing a hell of a job here. But don't rest on your laurels. Those animals are coming again, you can take that to the bank. I have just one more thing to ask of you. Hold out just one more night. I know we've been without sleep a long time. But we expect another attack from them soon, and they may come through here. I have every reason to believe we will have relief here for all of us in the morning."

More Jap flares lit the sky and at the bottom of the hill the surface of the Lunga River came into view, a ghastly red channel, like a river of blood. Johnny thought about what Red Mike had said.

Animals. That's right. Something turned us all into animals. This isn't how men behave, is it?

There was a rustle and then Bud crawled into the trench with him.

"Hey Johnny, wadda'ya know."

"Just got back from a Broadway show, Bud."

"Yeah, what a show. I'd like to meet the moron who wrote the book for this one."

"How ya doing, Bud?"

"Grim, Johnny. We got an aid station over there. I've been hauling C and B boys up the hill all night, so Colonel Edson ordered me to take a break. I have to go back soon. Lot of our guys are still alive down there. The Japs chopped and hacked some of them to death with bayonets and swords before we could get to them. Scum."

"Pigs."

"Yeah, it's like something turned them into pigs isn't it. Like the house of Circe."

"You still on that poem, Bud?"

"Well you must admit it's like somebody wrote us into it a

long time ago. Why else would General Price have given it to Billy? It's almost like a map."

"Well, I'm not so sure, Bud…"

"Look, Johnny, I know you walked away from God, but I have to tell you he hasn't walked away from you. He sends us signals, road maps, blazes on the trees of our life—this is the way, this is the path, walk this way."

"Yeah, well what's he telling us with this stinking poem?"

"He's telling us we have a long hard journey ahead of us. There are islands filled with danger and death waiting for us after Guad, just like they waited for Ulysses. But I believe Penelope and Telemachus are waiting for you at the end of this adventure."

"You mean Marjean and my baby."

"Gonna be a boy, Johnny."

"How the hell do you know?"

Bud smiled. "I got an inside track, Johnny boy, an inside track." Then he was gone.

* * *

THE NIGHT CREPT BY FOR THE MEN ON THE HILL. THEY COULD HEAR the screams of several Raiders being tortured at the bottom of the ridge. In the darkness Johnny turned to Crandall and asked if the fighting in Spain was as bad as this. Crandall shook his head. "The fascists under Franco were bullies, but they didn't have the guts these little shits do. This is the worst damn fighting I've ever seen."

At 0200, they saw a few flares hurtling skyward. Crandall shouted to his men, to the left and to the right.

"They're coming again, pass the word."

From the jungle below the bloodcurdling shouts of "Banzai" stabbed through the darkness.

There was a yell. "Left flank, left flank!"

Below their position, the Japanese hit the left flank. Captain

Harry Torgerson's Chutists met the onslaught and fought back with savage ferocity. Riflemen poured their fire into the assaulting enemy. Again and again the waves moved up the hill. Johnny pointed his BAR wherever the Japs massed the thickest. It was almost as if he could shoot two and there would be six more to take their place. He shot Japanese soldiers a half-dozen times or more before they fell. One enemy soldier, disemboweled by a shell, crawled right up to Johnny's position. Clutching his exposed intestines, he tried to pull out a grenade before Lt. Crandall put him out of his misery with a burst from the Thompson.

Then a Japanese mortar attack slammed shells into both sides of the ridge, severing the phone lines to the division CP.

Red Mike came down the hill. "Crandall, send one of your guys over to the 11th Marines FDC. Tell them to drop it five and walk it back and forth across the ridge."

Crandall saw the Teacher two holes away. "Hot Kiss, you're the fastest. Get over there and get Don Pedro to limber up his tubes, on the double. You heard the Colonel."

Teacher took off like a scared jackrabbit. In about three minutes the guns of the 11th Marines began belching round after round. Crisscrossing their shells from left to right and back again in front of the Marine perimeter, the gunners rained a curtain of steel down upon the assaulting enemy soldiers. The barrage cut general Kawaguchi's Imperial Army to pieces.

Johnny watched as the wave broke again and the Japs ran down the hill. At the bottom of the hill, he could see officers with swords screaming at their men and pointing back up the hill. A large detachment of Japanese soldiers came running up out of the jungle and joined the group that had retreated. They all turned and once more advanced up the hill. Red flares lit the night sky again, and the whole scene reminded Johnny of what he always thought hell might look like. The Japanese fired their sub-machine guns with great effect. Up and down the line Marines were going down.

The Japanese massed together and once more came right toward X-ray's position. Achilles and the rest of the 2nd Division boys responded with overwhelming fire, making every shot count. There was not a man alive that could stand in the face of such terrible firepower, and the Japanese soldiers were no exception. Once again they turned and ran down the hill, leaving over one hundred of their dead behind.

Just then Colonel Edson came along the lines. He was dirty and sweating and his uniform shirt looked like someone had cut it with a knife, but he was unharmed. He knelt down by Johnny's foxhole.

"We got into a little hand-to-hand down the line there," he said, "but we ran them off. The Japs aren't too eager to go one-on-one, not anymore, not after one of our boys, a kid named Reuben from Ohio, held off a whole platoon all by himself. When I got over to him there were twenty dead japs in the surrounding trenches, most of them with their brains bashed out. Kid was bayoneted and shot up pretty bad, but he held the line all by himself. If he lives, he'll get a CMH for sure. Damn!"

Edson was silent for a minute. Then he stood up and grinned at the squad. "You boys are doing a hell of a job up here. Keep up the great shooting. They can't take it but they'll still be coming back. You must hold here, boys." The colonel moved down the line to rally his men.

By 0400, the fighting exhausted Edson's men. And then the Marines on the ridge caught a break. Elements of the 2nd Battalion, 5th Marines filtered into the lines, relieving the weary Raiders and Parachutists. The battle for the ridge was winding down.

As the sun peaked over the horizon the pilots from Henderson Field put a head on it. They laced the jungle area around the ridge with 30- and 50-caliber machine-gun fire. The aircraft also unleashed torrents of 20mm cannon rounds, annihilating the retreating enemy troops. The Japanese General

Kawaguchi had no choice but to break off the attack and retreat.

Johnny looked down the hill. Jap corpses littered the blood-stained ridge. The twisted bodies of hundreds of men who had died for the Emperor lay in the grotesque attitudes of those who meet sudden and violent death. Heads and torsos contorted, their vacant eyes stared up the hill at the triumphant Marines.

Johnny slid his back down the wall of the trench until he was sitting, leaning up against the dirt. He pulled out one of the stinking Jap smokes.

Maybe Bud has an inside track after all.

JAP LOVER

BILLY MARTENS

B illy made his way off the Ridge after the battle along with
what was left of Platoon X-Ray—seven men instead of
twelve. Hot Kiss had picked up malaria and was shipped off to
sickbay, so that made them a half-dozen even. Billy was so tired
he didn't care if a croc was lurking underwater to snag a Jap or US
meal—he felt dirty, so he stripped and swam where a freshwater
creek emptied into the sea. Then he crawled back to the hole by
the coastline he shared with Johnny Strange and fell asleep.
Johnny was already snoring in his blankets beside the foxhole
with a sound like a whistling bomb, arms wrapped around his
BAR as if it were his girlfriend back in the States. The snoring
didn't bother Billy at all. But the other noises at night did.

First there was Louie the Louse, a Jap floatplane that dropped
four green flares over the beachhead, timing them to keep
breaking up the Marines' sleep. Billy cussed and pulled his blankets over his head, wondering why they never got the night
fighters Sunny Jim Vandegrift had requested again and again. But
even as he cussed Louie, night after stinking night, Billy knew
why they didn't get night fighters—for some brass, Guadalcanal
was a lost cause. Even MacArthur had doubted the wisdom of

landing troops there. And now that the Navy had lit out for better coffee, dames and sunsets elsewhere, leaving the Marines stranded, beached, abandoned and cut off, Roosevelt's Castaways, many had the Marines surrendering *en masse* by Halloween. All of which made Marines like Chesty Puller and Red Mike even more determined to stick it and prove everyone wrong, especially the here-today-gone-tomorrow Navy. Their stubbornness infected everyone on the Canal, including Billy Martens. He'd be darned if he'd let MacArthur, Tokyo, or the US Navy push him out of the Solomon Islands. He'd let a saltwater croc swallow him whole before he'd lay down his rifle and run like a sailor.

After Louie, there was Washing Machine Charlie, though Billy preferred to call him Maytag Charlie because Billy had played on a Little League team known as the Maytag Washers. It was probably a Betty with its engines deliberately out of sync so they'd make a loud and ugly whining sound. Maytag would drop bombs, too. Which made Johnny and Billy leap into their clammy foxhole as shrapnel sliced the humid night, banging skulls and cussing the other's hard head as much as they cussed Charlie.

"Hell of a way to fight a war," complained Johnny. "I'd rather be back on the Ridge pumping lead with my BAR."

"You can always volunteer to man a listening post some night," Billy replied.

"The hell with that, too."

The joke was on Billy. He drew the short stick of grass a week later and had to dig down into a jungle hole well ahead of the lines and listen all night, three nights in a row, for the sound of Japs trying to infiltrate Marine positions. The main defensive line, come October, was sandbagged and double-barb wired, and far beyond Billy's position heavily armed patrols were probing as far inland as the large, dark Matanikau River, about five miles. But he had no patrol to watch his back and no barbed wire or sandbags to hide behind, just centipedes and land crabs and palm trees and jungle rot. His dungarees smelled so bad he was sure a Jap could sniff him out a hundred yards away. But he was also sure the Jap would think the smell meant Billy was a disintegrating corpse and leave him to rot. Which worked for Billy.

Until the third night. He heard a *snicking* sound against one of his trip wires. This had happened on the first night too and had been four land crabs, a squad. He had let the crabs pass, convinced they were loyal to America. This time, he wasn't so sure. The *snick* was too loud and rough, as if it involved fabric, rather than the smooth shell of a crab. He waited a moment and heard more rough sliding sounds. Too many. He leaned out of his hole, trying to peer through the jungle dark. A slice of moonlight gleamed off a helmet.

"The Big Bam," he said in a low and clear voice and waited for the proper password in response.

It was silent for several seconds.

Then he heard a voice speak perfect American: "Apple pie."

The American was too perfect for a Marine.

He noticed the moonlit helmet had netting which few if any Marines wore on their pots.

To top it all off, the password was wrong. The response was supposed to be *Babe Ruth*.

Billy acted as coolly and efficiently as he might on a cougar hunt or a grizzly hunt, both of which were dangerous, whereas hunting a whitetail was not. He had already formulated a plan in his head. He tugged a grenade off his cartridge belt, pulled the pin, let the lever fly—he knew the *PING* would alert the Japs, but not soon enough—counted to three, and tossed. The explosion was almost instantaneous. It had burst in the air over the Japs. Screams cut through the night. Navarro had lent Billy his Thompson and Billy sprayed the dark with rapid submachine-gun fire.

"JAPS!" Billy screamed. "JAPS!"

In the glare of the grenade blast, he had quickly counted four helmets. He had no idea how large the Jap patrol was. He primed another grenade, didn't count to three, and threw it farther, praying a Mennonite prayer for divine protection that an alert samurai wouldn't have time to throw the grenade back. He heard a shouted exclamation and knew his grenade had landed amongst another group of soldiers. The WHAM lit up the night again. He saw two bodies without arms spinning upside down in the bomb blast. Then he slapped a fresh magazine into the Thompson and continued to fire. More screams. But now he heard Jap bullets zip past his head like wasps in a Montana August. He lowered his head, but kept blazing with Navarro's submachine gun.

Behind him, a Marine 30-caliber machine gun opened up, what old DI Butterworth had shrieked was a Browning M1919A4. Billy knew to dig even lower in his hole. Almost on top of the 30, a big Browning 50 began to thump crazy loud. Billy didn't want one of those cartridges to take off the back of his head, so now he vanished into whatever depth he could find. It seemed like every gunny who'd drawn listening post duty had carved out a little more space on his way to China. Billy made a note to do that for the next guy with his entrenching tool once show time was over at the zoo. For now, it was enough to hug wet dirt, roots, centipedes and worms as Jap slugs and American slugs chopped the air to pieces over his head.

A Jap jumped into his hole, landing on top of him—jumped or fell, Billy didn't think about it till later—and when he saw he was on a Marine, not a rock, he screeched, pulled a short knife, yelled "BANZAI!" and tried to saw Billy's head off his neck. The Jap was a cougar in Billy's mind, so his reaction was swift and required no thought. He plunged his Bowie into the Jap's soft belly and gutted him, slicing from left to right and then right to left, making an X that disemboweled the soldier. He collapsed on Billy, bleeding like a river as he gasped and choked on the blood welling up in his throat.

Billy pushed him off, but now was in an *All Quiet on the*

Western Front situation. He was forced to remain in the hole and watch the Jap pant and squirm and die, far more slowly than Billy had expected, just like the German soldier in the novel had to watch the Frenchman he had knifed pant and squirm and die. Finally, after five minutes of the Jap's death throes, Billy did what he'd have the mercy to do with a dying deer or horse or dog or calf. He thrust his Bowie into the man again, right through his heart. The man was dead in seconds. He clutched Billy's arm and gasped two words. Then the light went out of his eyes as if someone had yanked a lightbulb cord or flipped a switch. Billy had never seen that before, except in an animal. He heaved and sank back against the far wall of the hole, jerking off his helmet. He vomited again, but it was just bile and slime. His head drooped. *I'm tired, Lord God, I'm so tired.*

IN THE MORNING, BILLY TOLD CRANDALL WHAT HAD HAPPENED. Crandall knew some Japanese. So, Billy repeated the words the soldier had gasped at the end. Crandall squinted at him in a hard-core way and blew cigar smoke at his face.

"You shitting me, Martens?"

"No, Sir. I don't have Jap words I can just pull out of my head to impress you, Sir."

"You trying to make these devils human on me, Martens? Is that it? Is that how you Mennonites go about it in a war zone? Make everything God so loved the world shit?"

"No, Sir. It's just what he said. I have no idea what he said, Sir."

Crandall inhaled. "*Arigatou gozaimasu* means *thank you.* It's a very polite Nipponese way of saying thank you."

Billy did not reply.

"This is nuts. You shoot up a bunch of Japs and they come back at you with Tokyo etiquette and you take it? What else did

you do? Kiss their ass? You shit for brains Mennonite. We're here
to kill. To save America and kill. Not shoot a few and get a thank
you from the rest. What the frigging hell, Martens? Kill 'em all!
Frigging hurt them and kill them all so that the only thing they
have left to do is scream and die!"

Billy stared at the dirt.

"Dammit." Crandall blew more cigar smoke over Martens.
"Get out of here. Get lost. I don't want any more Mennonite crap
out of you today. *Arigatou gozaimasu!* What's next? They gonna
give you a lesson in Japanese origami next time you gut one?
Teach you how to fold your toilet paper into the stinking Bird of
Paradise?"

"Sir, I had no ide–"

"Shut up. Just get lost. A Jap officer decapitated a gunny from
Victor platoon an hour ago. I don't want to listen to your shit
about nice-guy Japs."

"He wasn't a nice guy, Lieutenant. He tried to skewer me so I
skewered him. I just wanted to put him out of his misery."

"Why? Let the damn creeps have some misery. Lord knows we
have enough of it on this rotten island."

"I didn't find it entertaining to watch him strangle on his
blood and guts, Sir."

"No? I would have frigging bought tickets." Crandall blew
more smoke. "Okay, Mennonite Martens. You got yourself a front
row seat to the next patrol to the Matanikau River. Maybe some
Japs will invite you to a tea ceremony while you're out there, a
chanoyu, you ought to love that."

"I don't care for tea, Sir."

"Well, I'm sure for your sake, since you love 'em so frigging
much, they'll offer you warm *saki* instead, Martens."

"Whatever you say, Sir."

"Damn right, it's whatever I say. This is a mixed-bag patrol,
guys from all four squads, so we have about twenty-five half-alive
bodies. You half-alive, Martens?"

"Half-dead, Sir."

"Yeah? I'm sure your Japanese buddies will help you out. Think a *geisha* would liven you up, Martens? Or do Mennonites even like to be cuddled by a woman?"

"Sir, I have no idea what a *geisha* is, Sir."

"You jerking my chain, Martens? I haven't been in the best of moods since Sharples got sliced and diced by a Nip grenade. I put him in for a Navy Cross. Which is more than I can say for you. You, I'm just putting in for a frigging Matanikau patrol."

"Thank you, Sir."

"You make no sense to me, Martens. You play footsies with a Nip in your foxhole. But his buddies you cut up with forty-five caliber slugs like some hitman in Chicago. Some of them you hate, some of them you love. Is that how it works with Mennonites?"

"I wasn't nice."

"Nice enough for him to shake your hand and bow his head."

Billy tried to hand back the Thompson. "I'm done with this, Sir."

Crandall shook his head. "Keep it, Mennonite boy."

"Sir, I'm a sniper, I use the–"

Crandall waved his cigar at Billy. "I don't need a sniper on this patrol, Menno Simons. I need firepower. Sergeant Zarate counted ten Nips you blew all to heck last night or sawed in half with the Thompson. Yet you cozied up to number eleven in your trench. Dammit, I just don't get it. But you killed the first ten, so the Thompson is yours to keep, Machine Gun Kelly."

"Sir, Corporal Navarro–"

"Corporal Navarro has another one now. Sergeant Shanks of Hades squad is down with the shakes. He won't be needing his Thompson for a while. Get used to killing with 45-caliber slugs, Mennonite. And I mean killing. Not pretty paper folding or looking for a bunch more polite thank-yous."

"Yes, Sir. Thank you, Sir."

"Stinking right it's thank you, Sir, Mister Menno Simons man.
Now get out of my damn sight. Patrol heads in-country at
0400 hours."

"Sir, I–"

"Shut the hell up, Mennonite boy. Go work on your Jap tea
time ceremony and make sure you have enough ammo for the
patrol. Three hundred rounds."

ANY PATROL ON THE CANAL, AS JOHNNY STRANGE GROWLED THE
next morning at 0401 hours, was a crapshoot. Who the hell knew
where Tokyo Joe was? Sergeant Brown of Titan squad ordered
him to take point, backed up by Private Menno Simons Martens.
Brown pronounced Billy's new nickname—that had swept the
battalion—with his infamous sneer and a crooked grin of brown-
black nicotine teeth, well-colored by years of chewing Red Man
Plug. He was carving off a fresh chunk with his Bowie, and
popping it in his mouth, when he spat a stream that landed
square on Billy's boondockers.

"Make sure y'all say *please* and *thank you* when we run into
the Japs today, Private Mennonite," laughed Brown, chewing
vigorously. "Make sure y'all kill 'em real polite, like, son." Then he
spat on Billy's boots again. "You're a sorry stinking excuse for a
Marine. Your boondockers look like you've been dancing the
jitterbug in the officers' latrine all frigging night. Clean 'em up
when we take our first break."

"What did you do?" Johnny asked Billy when they were far
ahead of the patrol and out of earshot. "Kiss the Jap before you
killed him?"

"All I did was kill him. The way I'd kill any dying animal. I put
him out of his pain."

"So, what's the deal with all the crap you're taking?"

"He said something to me in Japanese when I finished him.

Two words. Easy to remember. I asked Crandall to translate and
he turned it into Pearl Harbor. *Arigatou gozaimasu. Thank you.*"

"The way I heard it, the Nip said you were a good man and
that it was an honor to die for the Emperor at the hands of a good
Marine."

"Oh yeah, like hell, Johnny. As if I'd remember all the words it
would take him to say that."

"Well, now the guys are saying you're a no-good Nip lover."

"Let them say it to my face."

"Eventually someone will be all *saki'd* up and they will."
Johnny spat. "Forget about it, Billy. It'll blow over. Maytag Charlie
and malaria and this stinking hellhole island are getting to everyone. You're this week's scapegoat. If anything happens, it won't be
for another couple of weeks, when the boys are simmered up
even more than they are now. Because the Navy still won't have
shown up with the ammo, and the chow, and the bars of
bath soap."

IT HAPPENED SOONER THAN EITHER OF THEM EXPECTED. AT 0805
hours, with jungle sweat soaking their dungarees, Sergeant
Brown called for a ten-minute break. One gunny turned to Billy
and sneered like Sergeant Brown sneered, and said, "Hey, I guess
we haven't walked into the trap you and your Jap buddies have set
up for us yet, Mennonite boy. Maybe by 0900?" Even Johnny was
stunned by how hard and fast Billy used his fists. He decked the
Marine who had taunted him, knocking him cold, and when
another Marine tried to break it up, Billy punched his lights out
too. Finally, Corporal Navarro got involved, and ordered Billy to
back off, trying to pin his arms behind him, and Billy spun and
hit Navarro with a one-two, one-two, one-two-three combination
that sent the New Mexican flying. Sergeant Brown aimed his
Thompson at Billy.

"Okay, tough guy Mennonite," he snarled. "You just made it real easy for the platoon to get rid of you. Punching a non-commissioned officer in a time of war? Maybe we can do better than a court martial, Billy boy. Maybe we can line up a firing squad. You're under arrest, Jap lover. Strange, Hot Kiss, take his gun and rope his hands."

"Sergeant," Johnny protested.

"Do it! Or I'll throw you in the brig too!"

Billy didn't fight it. He let Hot Kiss take his Thompson and dropped his hands to his sides. Johnny wouldn't rope him so Hot Kiss the Teacher had to do it, pulling a coil from his pack and shaking it out, not happy with the world.

"I don't want to do this, Billy," he said, gently tugging Billy's hands together behind his back. "I wish I wasn't here. I wish I hadn't bucked the bug so quick."

"Not your fault, Hot Kiss," Billy replied. "Just don't do it too tight, okay?"

"I won't."

"The hell you say!" barked Brown. "Cut off his blood supply, Hot Kiss! Make sure his hands go white and fall off! Tourniquet him!"

"I can't do that, Sergeant."

"You can and you will. Cinch him up tight as the Nip-loving rice-hugger he is. That's an order."

A sudden spray of bullets cut Hot Kiss in two. The bullets would have snapped Billy as well, but Hot Kiss's body absorbed the entire burst. Hot Kiss fell hard against him and they both went down. A second burst killed two Marines from Brown's Titan squad and tore Brown's right shoulder open. It was a Nambu. Billy recognized the chatter of a Nambu. A third burst had everyone diving for cover, but Jimmy Mac McKeever, fresh off the malaria sick list. Still white as paper from his illness, looking dazed and blank-eyed by the sudden death that was erupting all around him, he stood rooted to the spot.

"Get down, Mac!" Billy shouted.

A fourth crash of firing from the Nambu took Mac's head off.

Billy cursed and pushed Hot Kiss to the side, grabbing for his Thompson that was lying in the grass.

"Where is he?" Billy demanded. "Where?"

"I don't know!" Julio Hernandez was blasting away at the jungle with his BAR, flat on his stomach. "I can't even spot the muzzle flashes!"

Johnny crawled up beside Billy. "The machine gun nest is by that big banana tree. The one with all the vines."

Billy stared. "Not much I can do from here with a Thompson."

"We can grab you a 1903 from someone."

The Nambu blazed again, a long hosing burst, probably too long for the machine gun's barrel, and they both watched three Marines get riddled by scores of bullets with nothing but tall grass to hide behind.

"No time," Billy replied. "We'd probably get hit as soon as we started crawling around."

"So, what are we gonna do? There aren't enough trees here. Nowhere to hide. They'll cut us to pieces."

"I tell you what, my Mennonite buddy. I've got nothing to lose. Brown will probably convince the brass I walked us into this trap and have me court-martialed, shot and hung upside down from a coconut tree. So, cover me."

Johnny stared at him. "Cover you? What the hell are you talking about?"

"You've got plenty of ammo for your BAR today, don't you?"

"Yeah. So what?"

"Use it."

When Billy was honest to God about it later, he knew when he jumped up and began to zig and zag through the grass towards the banana tree that his attack was pointless and suicidal, and that he didn't give a shit if it was, because he didn't care if he got killed. His body felt lousy and his soul felt lousy. He'd lost any sense of God or purpose or home. He didn't know what it meant to be a Marine, an American or a Christian anymore. So, he ran and expected to be gunned down any second.

But, as fate would have it, or God, or the angels that heaven had assigned to the Marine Corps, the Japs were switching out barrels when he began his run, and trying to get a new ammo belt started. BAR fire from Johnny and Julio Hernandez made the enemy keep their heads down as big heavy 30-caliber slugs whacked into the trunk of the banana tree they were using for cover. The Japs didn't spot Billy until he was about 50 feet away, and a lone charging Marine was the last thing they thought they'd see when they raised their eyes to shoot the Nambu again. He yelled in Mennonite German and raked them with his Thompson, killing the gunner, the feeder, and two others that were helping with the Nambu. Behind the nest, five Japs had just started setting up a second machine gun. Billy killed them too. An officer shrieked and came at him with a sword, and Billy emptied the rest of his Thompson into the officer's gut before slapping a fresh magazine into his gun. Wild-eyed, he swung his barrel in every direction, even behind him, looking for more targets. There weren't any. He stood dazed for a moment, not able to comprehend what he had just done. Then he saw the officer's samurai sword, the katana, picked it up and began to walk back to the platoon. The jungle birds cried out again as he walked.

He went straight to Sergeant Brown, who was being treated by Bud, the corpsman, and offered him the sword. Brown took it. Then Billy offered him his Thompson, smoke still curling like a line of cigarette smoke from its muzzle. Brown shook his head. He raised himself higher on his good arm.

"Now hear this!" Brown bellowed through clenched teeth, the pain from his wound digging hard lines into his face. "You did not see Private William Martens deck those two Marines. You did not see him deck Corporal Navarro. It never happened. Did it, corporal?"

Navarro had a crooked smile on his face, a smile made even more crooked by his torn and swollen lips. "No, sergeant."

"All you saw today was a hero. You will speak of nothing else, but how Private Martens took out two Jap machine-gun nests single-handed and saved your asses and mine. That is an order."

Brown stuffed a plug of Red Man in his mouth and shook his head at Billy. "You beat all. You do beat all, kid. The skinny is you carry medals from the Great War in your pockets."

"Yes, Sir." Billy saw that Brown was waiting on him, so he nestled the Thompson under the crook of his arm and brought out the medals.

Brown squinted. "A Purple Heart and a Silver Star."

"Yes, Sir."

"From your father's father. Chateau-Thierry."

"Yes, Sir."

"I reckon I'll put in for the Purple Heart. Might as well get something for being fool enough to stand and stare at a Jap machine gun. But you? No Purple Heart for you, son. You are as unscathed by bullets as the day you were born. No, for you, nothing else will do but a Silver Star. Then you'll have two of them in your pocket. Twice the luck."

"No, Sir, I don't think I–"

Brown held up his hand. "I started out with a court martial and a firing squad. Now I've bumped you up to a Silver Star. But push me and I'll get them to add another stripe to your sleeve. That seems right to me. Doesn't it to you, Corporal Martens?"

Billy stared at the sergeant, bewildered. "Aye, aye, Sir."

21

YEA, THOUGH I WALK

THE CORPSMAN

S ome guys have all the luck. Take Sniper for instance. One day the guy is a Jap-loving traitor, according to Crandall, and the next day he's a Silver Star Corporal and a hero. But that's the way it goes out here. One day we're climbing into Higgins boats, all spiffy and clean in our crisp new jungle uniforms, thinking patriotic thoughts and expecting to have this mess cleaned up in two days and the next day we're watching while the Navy sissies turn tail and run from a few Jap ships, leaving us stranded here on Guadalcanal. A month later none of us have an extra ounce of body fat, thirty percent are down with malaria or dysentery and all of us look like a bunch of pirates that came ashore hunting for buried treasure.

Like I say, some guys have all the luck. Some don't. Eddie Kramer blew his arm off the first day throwing a satchel and died in my arms. We think a croc ate Tony Malena, but only God knows. Sharpie fell on a grenade to save the rest of us and got blown in half. Teacher and McKeever both got it the same day Billy Martens ran through a hail of lead and chopped up those Jap machine-gun nests. They died, but Billy didn't get a scratch. How does that happen? Who knew five of our buddies would already draw the short straw on this stinking Island, and who decided? Sometimes it makes you think God is up there with a blindfold on, pulling names out of a hat. But here we are, and it is what it is. Achilles squad is down five guys. Vandegrift got replacements for the Company, but Rudy put them in Victor because they lost even more guys than us.

So the number of Marines on this dirt-pile is going down, down, down, and the number of Japs is going up. Scuttlebutt is that after Circe's Bloody Hill, the Japs sent the whole 17th army down here from Rabaul. I don't know if that's true, but I know there have been a lot more of the little slant-eyes around. When we heard the Jap General Hyakutake had landed a lot more troops west of the Matanikau River to reinforce the pieces of Kawaguchi's command that were left over after we kicked their butts at Bloody Hill, we tried to send our guys across the river, but they knocked us back twice.

Then we heard there was a bunch up at Aola Bay, which is miles from the defense perimeter, and they were landing more so the Brass sent Achilles and some guys from 1st Division up the coast to mess with them. We went there in Higgins boats that some Einstein had hooked together with cables behind two Yippie boats, like a sea-going freight train. It worked fine until we got up to the beach by Aola. The Higgins were usually stable, but the cable on the bow pulled the nose of the boat low in the water. Just short of the beach, one of them dipped under a big wave and the sea came in like a tiger on a goat. Eighteen Marines in the boat couldn't get their combat gear off and before you could blink an eye, the Higgins disappears under the water and those boys are dead.

Whenever stuff like this happens, I think of how we keep playing out the Ulysses theme. Everyone laughs at me or tells me to shut up except Billy. He's the one who got the poem from General Price, and he knows what it means. Sometimes I hear him muttering to himself, *"That which we are, we are; One equal temper of heroic hearts,"* and I know he puts a lot of stock in that poem. So when those guys got sucked under it makes me think of Charybdis, the whirlpool that sucked sailors down to their doom. But if you swung too wide to avoid Charybdis, Scylla, the seven-headed monster, was waiting in the rocks on the other shore to swoop down and snatch you right off the deck of your ship—and that's how it works here on Cactus—we're caught between the devil and a hard place.

Well that night, after those boys drowned, we're dug in the beach and everyone is in a foul mood. Maybe the other guys aren't putting it together, but I am. We have another trial coming. We are lying here on the beach between Scylla and Charybdis—death behind us, death out there in the trees. So I get busy. They say there are no atheists in foxholes and I'm a big believer in that, because I'm praying all the time. "Lord, keep me alive so I can keep some of these guys alive." I know that in the dark on both sides of me lots of other guys are praying, too. Catholics, Baptists, Jews, everybody is wondering if tomorrow is the end of the road, so they are putting in a word.

Morning comes early on October 10th. Crandall tells us our mission is to clean out the rest of the Japs we didn't kill at Tenaru River or Bloody Ridge. This end of the island is where all the Jap replacements come ashore and the ones we are after guide the landing craft in. If we can scatter them and destroy their head-quarters, it will make life a lot easier for our guys down on the defense perimeter. Crandall says there are two villages, Koilotu-maria and Garabusa, five miles up the beach where the Japs concentrate. So Achilles squad tosses down a few cans of dog food, forms up into our fire teams and we head over there—Cran-dall, Johnny, Billy, Zarate, Navarro, Julio, Garowski and Levy, all that's left of the snappy squad that climbed off the boat a month ago. The rest of the platoon spreads out around us, and we head into the jungle.

When we get to Koilotumaria, there's nobody around. Empty.

Then, over on the right there is a flurry of fire and some guys come around a hut dragging a dead Jap officer. Jody Timms, a guy from Zeus squad, is grinning. He's got a Jap sword, and he's waving it above his head. "Just didn't want to go to POW camp, I guess," he says. Then we hear fire from up the beach toward Garabusa. Crandall sends us on the run. In about ten minutes we are outside the village. We meet up with a Sergeant who tells us to get down. There's a busy little fire-fight going on. We see one guy down and I go check on him. He's dead, shot through the head. The Sergeant shrugs. "That's our company commander, Captain Stafford. He got it first thing. There are snipers up in those trees over there and we can't spot them."

Then I see a tall rangy guy stand up and move out into the lane between the trees.

The Sergeant does a double take. "That's Hooker, he's drawing their fire."

I watch as this guy walks unafraid. There's a snap and some-thing plucks at his shirt, a bullet from a tree down the lane. Quick as a flash the guy fires back, and a Jap pitches out of the tree. Our guy keeps walking. Snap! Another shot cuts by his face. Again he whips his gun up and takes the Jap out of his tree.

Billy's next to me and I hear him mutter, "Yea, though I walk through the valley of the shadow of death...."

More fire comes out of the trees and brush up ahead, and now our guys have the Japs spotted. We move in fast. And then we're in the middle of a real brawl. We've cornered the Japs and they know it. Bullets are flying everywhere, and it's every man for himself. I look around, but I can't see any of our guys. Some 1st Division boys are trying to work their way around behind the Japs, so I follow along. We get way over on the other side of the village and then we flush a bunch of Japs out of the jungle. They come at us like hyenas after a lion. One of the Japs throws a satchel and we all dive for cover. The bomb blows up right at the base of a tree next to me and another Marine while we are trying to burrow our way straight into the mud. I hear a loud snap and the tree crashes down and everything goes black.

———

WHEN I WAKE UP, I'M UNDER THE TREE AND IT'S NIGHT. THERE'S A moon out, and the jungle is lit up like a parade ground. The guy I was following is next to me. Remember how I said some guys have all the luck? Well, when that satchel went off I dove into a depression right next to that tree, so I'm lying under the tree without a scratch except for some superficial stuff, but when I try to move, I'm stuck. The guy next to me landed on top of a little rise and the tree smashed him flat. I can tell that the weight of the tree has burst his abdomen and his intestines have come out. He's still alive, but not for long. The tree branches are hiding both of us, and there's nobody else around. Except for the usual jungle bugs and night birds, the place is quiet. The guy next to me moans.

"Corpsman, corpsman..."

"I'm here, boy, take it easy."

"I can't feel anything in my body, corpsman."

"You got a tree lying on top of you and it smashed you. I'll do what I can."

"I'm gonna die, aren't I?"

"Bud. I'm Bud. And I don't know. I'll do the best I can, but the rest is in God's hands. What's your name?"

"Kenny. Kenny Nicholson. I'm from Dayton, Washington... Oh man, now I feel something. Aaahhh..."

"Take it easy, Kenny. I'll give you some morphine."

"No. No morphine. I'm dyin' and I don't want you to knock me out. I want to see it when it comes."

"Come on, Kenny. Hang in there. We'll get you home."

"Don't bullshit me, Bud, I'm dying."

Kenny lies there moaning for a minute and then he asks me a question. "You believe in God, Bud?"

"Yeah, Kenny, I do."

"Well, I don't. Had no use for him."

"Why's that?"

"I had a good life when I was a kid. We lived on a farm, and my mom and dad seemed happy. You know, like all the families in town. Then my mom ran off with a traveling salesman, and my dad became a drunk. He never got over mom leaving us, and it made him mean as hell. He used to beat me when he got likkered up. God never helped me... aaaahhh..."

"Sure you don't want a shot, Kenny?"

"No, Bud. I want my mind clear because I need to ask you something."

"Shoot."

"Why do you believe in God?"

Now, I'm a Christian and I've been one all my life. I know the Bible, I went to church, I heard the sermons, and I tried to keep all the rules. I figured if I did that was all I needed to be on good standing with God. But no-one ever asked me straight out why I believed in God. And then it occurred to me. I didn't know.

"Let me think about that, Kenny."

"Well, hurry it up, Bud. I haven't got long. I know it, and I need some answers."

So I explain to him, feeling my way as I go. "I believe in God because it's the only thing that makes any sense. See, being out here in this jungle and watching men turn into beasts has made it real clear that men aren't born good. We are all born with an evil inside us that doesn't take much to stir up. We think we're good guys, and then we find ourselves capable of the most horrible behavior. So where does that evil inside us all comes from?"

"Do you know, Bud?"

"The only answer I can come up with is that something happened to Adam way back in the garden that changed him from being a man who obeyed God... well something changed him into a man that decided he could live life without God's help, you know, because the serpent told him he could be just like God and that appealed to his pride."

"You believe all that Bible stuff, Bud?"

"Well, if the option is that a lightning bolt hit a puddle of mud and created some amoeba that changed into a man over a million years, I gotta tell you it's a lot easier to believe the Bible."

"That makes sense. But what happened to Adam, then?"

Now I'm treading easy, like walking through a minefield, but God is leading me and there is something important going on here that I don't want to screw up. "Well when Adam went his own way, the Bible says he died. But he lived for five hundred more years. So if he didn't die physically, he must have died spiritually. The only thing I can think is that when he disobeyed God and went his own way, God let Adam do what he wanted, like free will, you know. But God removed the spirit he put in Adam when he created him—the spirit that guided him and kept him from doing evil things."

"Yeah, I think I get what you're saying. Adam was kinda like a car with no gas."

"Yes, and without that spirit to guide him in the right things, Adam could do all the wrong things God didn't want him to do. And it changed him somehow, he got broken inside and he passed that brokenness down to all the rest of us."

Kenny moved beside me, just a little. "Aaahh... Oh God, that hurts..."

I found it interesting that Kenny the atheist was calling on God when the going got tough.

He took a breath. "So if we are all broken, Bud, how do we get fixed?"

Now I'm getting back on familiar ground. "Okay, Kenny, this is how it works. Adam died spiritually because God removed the spirit, the power that kept Adam alive. And when Adam died spiritually, that made him subject to physical death too. Look, I'm a corpsman, a medical man. I've studied the human body, and it's amazing. It heals itself all by itself. That means that somewhere inside us is something that would make us live forever if we had the power back inside us to make it all work. That power comes from God's spirit. Jesus was born with that Spirit in him, because, like Adam, God was his father. So when Jesus died on the cross because he had always had that spirit to guide him, he did nothing bad in his life. Because it's the bad things that make us guilty before God and the punishment for that is the same punishment Adam received. Death."

"You mean that's why we die, Bud?"

"Exactly. But the good news is that because Jesus wasn't guilty of any crime when he died, it meant that he paid the price for all our crimes. And when he rose from the dead, it meant that he had defeated death forever. And then he made that same spirit that had kept Adam alive available to us again. It's like we got a traffic ticket and the judge said fifty dollars of fifty days and you say you don't have fifty dollars, so you get the fifty days, but just as they are taking you away someone comes in and pays the fine for you and you go free."

I take a breath because that's a lot of talking. Kenny is quiet for a minute. "Did he die for me too, Bud?"

"He sure did, Kenny."

"So how do I get my ticket paid?"

Now I realize why I came all the way from Ritzville Washington and through all this madness and ended up in the jungle beside this dying Gyrene. "Just tell him you believe he paid the fine for you, Kenny, and that you believe he rose from the dead and that's your ticket out of death and into life."

"Can I do it now?"

"Sure, now would be a real good time."

And so I held the hand of a dying Marine in the fetid jungle of a stinking island no one ever heard of, and watched while he took the key to paradise in his hand ard went on a great journey. After he said what he now believed, there was silence.

"Kenny? Kenny?"

But Kenny's dead and I'm alone in the jungle trying to get out from under the tree and then I hear a bunch of voices but they're not speaking English and through the branches I see a Jap patrol walking straight toward me and I am in a world of trouble. Kenny's in heaven and I'm stuck here with a bunch of Japs.

Some guys have all the luck.

22

BAPTISM

JOHNNY STRANGE

"Have you seen Bud?"

Johnny Strange sat against a palm tree at the jumping off point at Aola Bay cleaning his BAR. Achilles squad was with the rest of the raiders waiting to get picked up for the trip back. Billy Martens was leaning on his rifle, looking around the camp. The moon was out over the Slot. Pam trees rustled in the breeze and except for the fact they knew they were on Guadalcanal, it could have been Tonga.

"No, I thought he was with you."

"I lost track of him in the firefight this morning and I haven't seen him since."

Two 1st Division guys ambled by and Johnny stood up. "Hey, you guys seen a 2nd Div corpsman? He got separated from our squad during the firefight this morning. He would have been with any wounded. You got any?"

One gyrene, a lanky Marine with a soft Texas drawl, shook his head. "We only lost two men. Captain Hughes, and another guy, Kenny Nicholson. He disappeared out there. Blown to bits, I guess. We sent a squad looking for wounded before we left, but they found no one. All present and accounted for, except Nicholson. You know how this damned jungle eats Marines."

Johnny looked at Billy. "Well if there is a wounded guy out there, that's where Bud would be."

Billy nodded.

Johnny picked up his BAR. "We gotta go back, Sniper. Bud's out there somewhere."

Just then Lieutenant Crandall walked by with Zarate and Navarro. Johnny called them over.

"Bud's missing. Have you guys seen him?"

They all shook their heads.

"Lieutenant, I think Bud got left behind. 1st Div has a missing guy and I'm betting Bud's with him."

Billy chimed in. "Yeah, Lieutenant, we gotta go back."

Zarate looked at the Lieutenant and then at Billy. "You want to wait until morning?"

Johnny shook his head. "No, Sarge, we have to go now. Bud's in trouble, I can feel it."

Crandall agreed. "Sergeant Zarate, take three men and head back. Find Bud."

Johnny stepped forward. "I'm going."

Navarro and Billy joined him. Crandall nodded. "You boys be careful. We drove the little bastards into the jungle this morning, but there's plenty more where they came from."

Just then Leon, Ricky and Julio walked up.

"What's up, fellas," asked Garowski.

"Bud didn't come back from the firefight. We going back to find him."

Leon slung his 1903 over his shoulder. "Not without us, you're not." Ricky and Julio nodded.

Crandall looked at the determined faces of his men. "You're right, Levy. That's an X-Ray Platoon boy out there. Sergeant, take these men and go find our Corpsman. I want Bud back here safe and sound or I'll know why."

"Yes, Sir. Let's go, Achilles. Grab your weapons and follow me."

Achilles squad headed north up the beach on a dead run.

AROUND 0200 HOURS, ACHILLES MOVED IN ON THE ABANDONED village of Garabusa. The night was quiet, the moon was almost full, and a pale light lit the jungle. Zarate asked a quick question.

"Where was the last place you saw him, Johnny?"

Johnny looked around. Over to the right he saw the hut where Captain Hughes had bought it. "That's where the 1st Div Captain died. Just when we got here, the Japs opened fire from over in those trees. We all scattered and I think Bud was with some of their guys. I saw them working their way around to the left, trying to get around behind. We were all watching the guy who was drawing fire, and I didn't pay attention after that."

Sergeant Zarate nodded and held up two fingers, dividing the squad in half. He took Julio, Leon and Ricky to the right of the lane of trees and Johnny, Billy, Leon and Corporal Navarro went left. Johnny pulled out his flashlight and keeping low to the ground, they worked their way around the lane of trees where the Jap snipers had hidden. The sniper bodies still lay where they had fallen, twisted grotesquely with that surprised look Johnny had often seen on the faces of men who come around a corner and meet death.

At the backside of the clearing they came to a fallen tree that looked like an explosion had blown it down. Johnny shined his flashlight down among the branches and jumped back. There was a dead Marine under the tree. Johnny pointed his flashlight toward the other side of the clearing and blinked it three times and then shut it off. In a few minutes the rest of the squad was beside them. They knelt down, pushed the branches aside, and checked the dead guy over.

Johnny shined the light on the man's arm patch.

"He's 1st Div all right. This is their missing guy."

Billy nudged Johnny and pointed to a depression to the left of the body back under the branches. Some medical supplies and a Syrette of Morphine lay in the mud.

Johnny crawled under and grabbed the supplies. The squad looked at what he had.

Zarate nodded. "Bud was here all right. That Gyrene wasn't carrying morphine, only a corpsman would."

Billy had walked around the tree to the other side, checking it out. He was looking at the branches and the ground.

"Hey fellas, look at this."

The squad moved around to the other side. Something had broken several of the branches off and pushed them aside, and there were two long furrows in the dirt coming out from under the tree. Johnny flashed his light. Opened-toed sandal prints covered the ground.

Billy wiped his forehead. "Shit, they got Bud."

Navarro edged in for a look. "Whadda'ya mean, Sniper?"

"I'm a hunter, Corporal. I read sign. Those two marks there—those are heel marks dragging through the mud. The sandal marks are Jap soldiers—must be about twelve of thirteen, a squad maybe." He pointed to a trail through the tall grass. "They came through there. The grass is all broken down where they walked. Bud must have been under the tree with the dead guy. The Japs came right up on him and someone saw him. They broke away the branches to get to him and dragged him out—not too long ago, because the mud's still wet where his feet dragged."

Billy looked around. "They went off down that trail, headed into the interior."

Johnny pulled his BAR off his shoulder. "How long ago, Billy?"

"Half an hour, maybe a little longer."

Johnny nodded to Zarate. "Sarge?"

"No doubt they took him to torture him. Let's go get him back before they do."

A FEW DRIFTING CLOUDS HAD FILTERED ACROSS THE INDIGO SKY, but not enough to block the moonlight. Achilles squad, with Billy on point and following the track, followed the Japs down a trail that led deeper into the jungle toward the south. The men moved fast, but silently through the jungle. After about an hour, Billy held up his hand. Everyone stopped. Billy pointed to some small mounds along the trail.

"Some of the Japs stopped here to take a dump. That's good. That means they don't know we are coming. As they get deeper in, they will get more relaxed. They'll camp somewhere up ahead."

Sergeant Zarate moved up beside Billy and looked down the trail. "There's a lot more Japs in that jungle than we can handle. We have to find these guys before they find the rest of their men. From the licking we gave them back at the village, I suspect that the main force is still on the move. Let's hope these guys don't have the same sense of urgency. Lead on Corporal."

Billy took point again with Johnny right beside him and the rest of the squad a few steps behind. Another half hour passed and then Billy stopped them again, this time with a signal for quiet. He pointed ahead. Through the jungle, the squad could see the light from a campfire. Zarate signaled Billy and Johnny and they crept forward. Billy made a downward motion, and they both went down on their bellies. Crawling forward through the trees, they came to the edge of a clearing. They saw the Japs gathered around a fire-pit in what looked like an abandoned village. There were three huts visible in a circle of trees. Johnny counted eight Japs around the fire. They were laughing and joking, passing a bottle of something from hand

to hand. It was clear they didn't think anyone had followed
them.

Johnny and Billy moved left and right through the under-
brush. Johnny spotted the first guard leaning against a tree
smoking a cigarette. He could see Billy around on the other side.
Billy held up his finger. One! A guard on the other side. They
slipped back to the squad. Johnny briefed. "Eight around the fire
—two on guard. That means two or three are sleeping in the huts,
and one of those is watching Bud."

Jesus Navarro pulled out his Bowie and grinned. Sergeant
Zarate laid down the plan.

"Julio, you're here with your BAR, Leon with you. Jesus and I
will take out the guards, left and right. Billy and Johnny will come
around behind the huts. When I take out my guard, I'll do the
night owl hoot. The Japs won't know the difference. Jesus will do
the same. The rest of you get into position quick. Give us five
minutes. When you hear the signal, Julio and Leon shoot the
guys around the fire. Spray them good. Jesus and I will cover the
flanks and direct our fire across and down. Johnny, you and Billy
get Bud."

The squad moved into position. Billy and Johnny circled
around the clearing until they were behind the huts. Then they
waited. The moon slid behind a cloud and then came out again.
Then there was a hooting sound that Johnny recognized as
Sergeant Zarate. One down. They waited. And waited. They
could hear the Japs laughing. The sake was getting to them. The
moon slid behind the clouds again, and then the second
hoot came.

Julio opened the dance with his BAR, the bam, bam, bam, of
Leon's 1903 beating a percussive echo. Johnny rushed around and
into the first hut while Billy took the second. Nothing! Johnny
heard the bam, bam of Billy's rifle in the hut next door. One more
hut. Johnny rushed out and piled into the third hut. The light
from the fire lit the interior and Johnny could see Bud lying on

the floor, his hands tied behind him. His shirt was open, and there were cuts and burn marks on his chest. He looked dead or unconscious. Outside there were screams and yells. Johnny could hear Julio's BAR booming. He knelt down by Bud and then Bud opened his eyes. "Johnny, look out!" Johnny twisted to the right and fell, and as he did, he felt a sharp pain in his shoulder. He looked up. The thirteenth Jap was standing over him with his rifle raised. The bayonet gleamed in the firelight, a dull red like there was blood already on it. Johnny's life flashed before his eyes. Marjean! My son! This was it. He would die like a rat on the floor of a dirty hut on Guadalcanal. Then Bud's leg lashed out, catching the Jap soldier just below the knees. The man went down in a heap as the bayonet went wide into the dirt.

"Kill him, Johnny, Kill the bastard!"

Johnny rolled over on top of the Jap and got two hands on the soldier's throat. The man struggled and tried to throw Johnny off, but Bud had rolled over and pinned the Jap's legs so he couldn't get any leverage. Johnny got a grip and squeezed. The man tried to pry Johnny's hands off, but Johnny was on him like white on an egg. The Jap's face turned red and then dark with blood. His eyes were bulging as he tried to dislodge Johnny. His struggles grew weaker. Johnny felt the Jap go limp. He grabbed the man's head and gave a hard twist. The neck snapped with a sharp crack and the man stopped moving. He was dead.

Johnny rolled over on his back, trying to catch his breath. His shoulder hurt. Outside, the gunfire stopped. Billy burst into the hut.

"Bud! Johnny!"

Bud smiled up from the floor. "What took you guys?"

Billy knelt down and cut Bud free. Zarate came into the tent. "Let's go. That gunfire will bring the whole Jap army down on us."

Johnny was still lying on the floor. Zarate knelt over him and lifted him up. His hand came away wet with blood. Johnny looked at Zarate's hand. "I think he stuck me, Sarge."

"Corpsman!"

Bud crawled over to Johnny and rolled him over. He took a quick look. "Yeah, the guy stuck him, but Johnny rolled and he took it high in the shoulder. He'll live, but we have to get him back." Bud opened Johnny's shirt, tore a piece off the dead Jap's coat and tied a wad of cloth around Johnny's shoulder. Johnny stood up.

Billy pulled Bud to his feet. "Can you walk?"

"Yeah. They only worked on my chest. They hadn't gotten to my feet yet."

Navarro and Leon rushed in. Zarate pointed to Johnny. "Get an arm around him and let's get the hell out of here."

Johnny looked at Bud. "You're a damn poor example of a pacifist, Corpsman. Thanks."

"It was him or you, Johnny, him or you. Couldn't let it be him."

Zarate grinned. "Good job, Johnny, Bud. Let's go, Marines."

And then the dark jungle swallowed up Achilles squad. Behind them lay a scattering of bodies and a pacifist's baptism.

2 3

TOKYO ROSE

BILLY MARTENS

M*y Diary Jack—Thursday, October 15th, 1942 Guadalcanal*

HEY, JACK, I WAS ON THE CHOW LINE TODAY, 1ST DIV GUYS RIBBED us and called us Hollywood Marines, as usual, only this time they were going after me too: "Hey, there's Captain Blood, there's Dive Bomber!" You know, from the Errol Flynn films. They got really loud, but I just ignored them. All I was interested in was the hot beans and pork. Chesty Puller himself pops up, asks his men what's the deal, they tell him I'm the guy that wiped out two Jap machine-gun nests by the Matanikau.

Chesty asks me if I really am that Marine. I didn't say anything, but Downtown Seattle Garowski was behind me and he goes, "He's your man, Lieutenant Colonel, Sir. Charged them guns blazing. So maybe he's more like Sheriff Wade Hatton in *Dodge City*, Sir" (another Errol Flynn movie, Jack).

Chesty gives me his Chesty look, a boyish gaze of bright, strong, eager eyes that go right through me. "Maybe so. Well done, son. The way I hear it, they're gonna pin a Navy Cross on you."

"Nothing like that, Sir. I did make corporal though."

"What's your name?"

"Billy Martens, Sir."

"Where from?"

"Montana, Sir."

"Montana, huh? The Japs pounded the snot out of Henderson Wednesday morning, corporal."

"Yes, Sir."

Well, Jack, everyone knew that. The Jap Navy must have fired a thousand rounds. No one got any sleep. The Nips blew Henderson to pieces. We heard that they ripped both airstrips up, almost all the aviation fuel was set on fire, more than half our Cactus Air Force planes were wrecked and they killed three or four dozen men, including a bunch of pilots. It was a mess. Scuttlebutt had the Japs going after Henderson again, and one Marine from 2nd Div swore he overheard Vandegrift griping that Tokyo was dropping off more troops and supplies every night. "There's gonna be another big attack," says Sunny Jim Vandegrift.

So, what Chesty tells me next is no big secret, all the gunnys are saying the same thing: "My gut is they'll go after the airfield with infantry."

"Yes, Sir," I reply, but crap, my beans are getting cold in my mess kit. So, I spoon them into my mouth while he talks.

"What company are you with, son?" asks Chesty.

"King, Sir. The 2/2."

"Huh. Rudy Rudebaker from Denver."

"Yes, Sir" (chew, swallow, chew, swallow).

"What platoon?"

"X-Ray. Lieutenant Crandall."

"Yeah, yeah. Spanish War Crandall. Red Mike says you guys fought like cougars on Tulagi and Bloody Ridge."

"Fought like Marines, Sir."

Chesty laughs and slaps me on the back. "X-Ray Platoon, King Company. I'll keep that in mind. We could use a gunner like you to reinforce us when the chips are down. Hey?"

A 1st Division guy says, "Yeah. Give us Captain Blood, colonel."

Another calls out: "Dive Bomber! Dive Bomber from Hollywood and we can't lose, Sir!"

A bunch of them begin to chant: "Dive Bomber! Dive Bomber! Dive Bomber!"

Chesty holds up a hand, grinning. "Go easy!" Then he turns to the server who's standing across from us over that big long table of grub. "Give the corporal another mess kit of beans on me." The server couldn't do anything else but follow orders. *Whap*. Another mound of baked beans and pork in my kit.

Thank you, God.

SUNDAY, OCTOBER 18TH

I hung at the back of Father McKean's Mass again this morning, Jack. He was all in white robes at his altar under the coconut trees. Afterwards, I didn't light out in time and he approached me. "What's up, Marine? You want to convert? You're always hovering around."

I shook my head, "No, Sir. Not convert. At least, not today."

"Then what's the deal?" he asks.

"I'm not sure what the deal is, Father. It kinda goes like this: Bible says, *Thou shalt not kill*. But I kill anyway. And I find out I'm good at it. In fact, I can play rough out there, Father. I can kill hard for a Mennonite boy. And I don't feel anything. Until it's over. Then I feel sick to my stomach and I... I want to jump off a cliff."

No one else is around. They've all gone for chow. The Padre

fires up a Players and gives it to me, then lights up another for himself with the USN Zippo he's got.

"You know that David, a man after God's own heart, fought battles against Israel's enemies," he says. "You should also know the verse you quoted, the Fifth Commandment, means, *Thou shalt not murder.*"

"I'd rather go to Tokyo, make some new buddies, and eat rice and fish with chopsticks, Sir."

"Hmm. I'd like that, too. But Tokyo wants to rule, Marine, and they don't care who or what they have to smash to achieve that end. I lost two missionary friends in China. Two priests. They were tortured and bayoneted a dozen times."

"Yes, Sir. I'm sorry, Sir. I know about China. What Japan has done in China is a sin."

He says, "They would do it in Australia too. If we let them. If you let them."

So, I reply, "God wouldn't let David build the Temple because he was a man who had shed blood. Solomon had to do it. David had fought too many wars."

"Okay, Marine. But it was still through David's bloodline we got Jesus Christ. David may not have been permitted to build the Temple in Jerusalem. But he sure helped build the Temple of redemption and sanctification that matters to the world. And I don't recall him being condemned for being a warrior either. It may have restricted what he could or could not do for God. Maybe this Pacific War will restrict what you and I can do when it's all over and we go home. But God never said, *David, don't fight.* Heck, if he'd been out fighting, and leading his troops like he should have been, he wouldn't have been standing on that rooftop in Jerusalem and seen Bathsheba pouring water over her naked body. Missing that view would have spared him and Israel a lot of pain, right?"

"Aye, aye, Sir."

"You want us to lose the battle for Guadalcanal, son? You

want to hear Tokyo Rose crow about the Death Marches of Sydney, and Brisbane, and Perth and Darwin after the Empire of Japan racks up the Aussies as their latest conquest? How about China? How many more Chinese would you like to see butchered, Marine?"

"None, Sir."

"Then what are you going to do about it?"

I didn't respond. What was there to say, Jack? Either you fight or you don't.

"Let me bless you. Let me pray for you." Father Erik puts a hand on my head. "The way I see it, you can pray, and sit, and wait for God to act without you. Or you can pray, and move, and watch God act with you. Let's go with the second choice."

"Yes, Sir."

It made more sense to me than sitting on my butt in Montana or making sure I took a wound so I could sit out the fight in the field hospital. I didn't think the priest's prayer would heal me though. Every time I took a life, I was sure I was still going to regret it afterwards. But if I didn't take Jap lives, the Japs would take my buddies' lives, Aussie lives, Chinese lives, hell, all kinds of lives, just like they'd been doing for years. It was a mess. Living a life in a world where conflict exists and forces you to make decisions you'd never make when there was peace, is a mess.

The choice my father had made haunted me every day—to never take a human life. And here was his first-born, carrying weapons on an island far away from Montana and America, doing that very thing. "I know it's harder for a Mennonite boy like you," Father Erik says as he finishes his prayer over me, "just like it's harder for Quaker boys or Hutterite boys or Adventist boys. But it's your cross to carry for Christ." My cross to carry for Christ? To kill? Jesus carried his Cross to save lives, and I carry my cross to take lives? *If any man will come after me, let him deny himself, and take up his cross, and follow me.* I don't get it, Jack, I still don't get it.

I drifted past the cemetery they'd set up at the edge of the jungle. It wasn't helmets on sticks anymore, and we couldn't waste 1903 bolt actions or M1 Garands on graves. They were placing wooden crosses and the crosses had the names painted on them. I found four of our guys in one row—Sharples, Hotchkiss, McKeever and Kramer. We never had a body for Malena, just some of the gear he left on shore, and at first there was no marker for him. Later on, Crandall ordered the graveyard detail to put up a cross and now I spotted it about a hundred feet from the others in the squad.

I had seen some gunnys cry over their buddies, but I couldn't do it. I'd never cried out in the open. I'd hardly even cried alone, except that one time on Tulagi after I'd killed men for the first time. I saluted the guys though. They deserved that. Especially Sharples, for saving us by diving on the Jap grenade. I even prayed the Lord's Prayer, but I didn't move my lips because other Marines were walking between the rows and they'd see that. I just did it in my head. Then I left.

———

TUESDAY, OCTOBER 20TH

Went to see Johnny in the hospital again—I've been there five or six times and no, he is not a good patient! —but they discharged him yesterday afternoon. So where did he wind up, Jack? Because he wasn't at our foxhole last night. Downtown Seattle Garowski said he'd bunkered down by the radio that was playing Tokyo Rose. I guess he was starved for a female voice, even an enemy female voice, and spent the night with her while I spent it with Maytag Charlie and Louie the Louse. So yeah, I found him at the radio that night with a bunch of other gunnys. Crandall had given him the day assignment of helping other Marines learn how to fire a BAR with half-decent accuracy—they were replacing the KIAs who'd handled the BAR. Johnny's

shoulder was sore as heck, but the doctors had declared him fit
for combat. I think even without arms or legs Johnny would be fit
for combat. He'd gnaw the Japs to death with his teeth.

So Rosey was getting kinda flirty about the time I showed up.
According to her, our girlfriends and wives had stopped waiting
months ago while we rotted on Guadalcanal and were with
other men now. What we needed to do was surrender, express to
the Japanese high command on Guadalcanal and Rabaul our
gratitude and good will for the way they'd treated us as prisoners
of war, and then ask to be shipped to Tokyo. There some lucky
Marines would get to broadcast with her. And beautiful
Japanese women would give us a very warm welcome. Was a
miserable island of snakes and crocodiles and malaria worth
losing our lives and lovers over? Capitulation to the Emperor,
followed by absorption into the superior Japanese culture,
consummated by marriage to a lovely Japanese girl would
change all our lives for the better. Did we know how amazing
geishas were? Hundreds of them were waiting to entertain a
rugged American Marine. Wouldn't that be wonderful, poor,
dear love-starved Marines? All we had to do was surrender and
make an oath to the Emperor. Then all would be well, oh, it
would be very well indeed.

Johnny was smoking Camels. He said he'd traded his K-
rations for them. He laughed as Tokyo Rose tried to seduce us
over the airwaves. "If the Japs could bring the gal I love here on a
boat, I might consider surrender. For a few hours, anyway."

Rose talked about the battles we had lost all over the Pacific
and on the Canal, to taunt us about our lack of reinforcements, to
ask if our C-rations were any tastier this week than they had been
last week and to commiserate with us over all the combat-ready
troops we had lost to the bite of the female mosquito. She item-
ized precisely how many aircraft their naval bombardment had
destroyed on October 14th, how many of our pilots had been
killed and what their names were, and how much aviation fuel

had gone up in flames. She said she knew we were being resupplied. This made her giggle.

"As soon as you have enough targets, our Navy will shell Henderson again and eliminate them. You know our Navy is better than yours. We did not abandon our troops to their fate as yours did. Where is your Navy? Hm? It's hiding in the shadows. Afraid to come out and face Japanese gunnery. We rule the seas. Especially at night. Oh, you poor, poor Marines. Why don't you surrender and end all this stupidity? You know we will win. You know we will sink your ships. You know we will shatter your airplanes. Pearl Harbor over and over—such a humiliation for America and her people. The island shall be under the flag of the Rising Sun before Christmas, Marine. Wouldn't you rather spend the holiday with me and my friends here in Tokyo than behind barbed wire on that ugly island? Consider, poor, hungry, love-starved Marines—nights with a perfect Japanese woman or nights with the crocodiles? Which would you rather have? Mmm? Ha ha ha. My poor, lonely American boys. You are losing the war and losing all chances at experiencing real love before you die."

WEDNESDAY, OCTOBER 21ST

Now this has been a wild day, Jack. It started with me daydreaming about a cool, crisp, sunny Montana elk hunt, 1903 in my hands instead of a Thompson (though I always have my 1903 on my back for sniping now too), continued with a jungle patrol I led to find out where the Japs are (answer: who knows?) and ended with Johnny and me coming back to a passel of green reinforcements. The US Navy had snuck in with troops they ought to have landed back in August, dropped them off and hightailed it. Rudebaker got the whole company in formation—there were only 121 of us—and parceled out raw meat gunnys to each

platoon as he saw fit... Fox, Victor, Mike and X-Ray. Then it's up to
the platoon leaders to stick these guys in their various squads. So,
Crandall assembled X-Ray to the side and gives Sergeant Garrity
of Zeus so many, Sergeant Brown of Titan and his mouth full of
Red Man Plug so many (his arm is deformed from the bullet
wound, but he was declared combat fit a week ago), Sergeant
Shanks of Hades so many (Sergeant Malaria, he's had it four
times), and then us, our squad, Achilles, and for us, Crandall has
a surprise.

"If King is the spear, and X-Ray the tip of the spear, then
Achilles is the pointy end of the tip of the spear." This image
made us all laugh. "Yuck it up, boys, but we ain't won this war by
a long shot, it's still ours to lose, and we can start by losing
Guadalcanal. I want us to be an almighty battering ram now that
we have reinforcements. I want us to smash the Japanese Army
into tiny little pieces. Achilles—recognize some of these faces
behind me, all pretty, and pink, and freshly shaved? Don't worry,
we'll get them looking like Ugly Jungle Marines soon enough.
Till then, do your best to make 'em feel at home and you can do
that by stealing their fags and K-rations as soon as possible."
More laughter. "Remember Frank Harte, our Captain America,
on the M1919A4 30-caliber machine gun, along with his partner
and ammo feeder and backup gunner, Sam Kane, Batman? And
on Ma Deuce, the M2 Browning 50-caliber Jap Buster, please
welcome back Tommy Earp, Not Related, our Superman.
Remember him? His ammo feeder and backup is Sid Greene,
Superman Too. Gentlemen, I finally convinced Battalion to make
us a heavy weapons platoon, and I'm putting the heavies in
Achilles, and Achilles is gonna take point, and our whole platoon
is going to personally wipe out the Japanese Empire in 1942, okay?
All squads are taking on an M2 mortar team too. Can I get
an *AMEN*?"

Johnny gave the loudest *AMEN*, most of the others cheered
and whistled and clapped, but *big bulls in the corn*, to quote DI

Butterworth, it did us all good to see Captain America and Superman heft those big puppies into our ranks, their backup men wrapped in bandoliers of machine gun ammo; hell, it was better than bacon and eggs and real coffee. So, they attached these gunners to us, which meant we still had a right to extra men to fill out our original 12, and Crandall dished those up, Jack. Lemme see if I can get their names straight (hope they live long enough to make memorizing them worthwhile):

Red O'Brien, Caldwell, Idaho, he comes with a shiny brand new M1 Garand,

Tom "Skillet" Baker, Caspar, Wyoming, M2 60mm mortar (2-man crew),

Paul Stoneroad, Santa Fe, New Mexico, M2 60mm mortar (2-man crew),

Brian "Over Easy" Mitton, Salt Lake City, Utah, M1 carbine semi-auto,

Nick "Big Band" Harrelson, Eugene, Oregon, M1 carbine semi-auto.

I have to say I liked the mortars being in all our squads as much as I liked the machine guns being in Achilles. Every Marine loves artillery, tanks, machine guns and flyboys. So, yeah, we are pretty much "in the mood" now. The rest of the company will expect us to kick butt with the firepower Lt. Crandall has saddled X-Ray with. So that puts me in my war spirit. Though it's true that after a fight I am not so thrilled, and I'm in my somber Lord's Prayer spirit. I hope I don't seesaw like this the whole war. It's confusing and exhausting.

THURSDAY, OCTOBER 22ND

Hey, Jack! Johnny and I have kinda taken Red O'Brien (he'd never heard of Red Mike) and Nick "Big Band" Harrelson under our wing. (They nicknamed him at Camp Elliott because he plays a very wicked trumpet.) Crandall wanted a platoon patrol today, more of a shakedown for the new guys, so he led us on a probe about three miles into the jungle, and we soon had the green guys sweating. One of them complained it was worse than Mississippi in July. I have to say I felt sorry for the machine gunners in our squad because the 30 is no lightweight piece of weaponry and the 50 is worse. The 50 gun and barrel is 84 pounds, the tripod 44 and one belt of 100 rounds of linked M2 ball ammo tips the scales at 35 pounds. And Sid, backup on the 50, was carrying more than one belt of cartridges as well as the tripod. So, Johnny and I started carting some of the ammo and the tripod and even the gun to give Sid Greene and Tommy Earp a break. Garowski and Levy were spelling Paul Stoneroad and Skillet Baker on the 60mm mortar and tripod as well as on the mortar rounds. Hernandez and Navarro were doing the same for Harte and Kane, Captain America and Batman, who had the 30, which is a 31-pound gun with a 14-pound tripod. Pretty soon Red, Over Easy Brian and Big Band Nick were pitching in too and giving a show of squad solidarity that pleased Crandall and Zarate.

Nothing happened on the patrol; we didn't even see a jungle bird up close, but the new guys were sodden rags by the time we returned to base. Their boots and puttees had been pristine before we set out, and now they looked appropriately scummed up. Not to mention how clean and tidy their green uniforms had been and how ship-shape their cartridge belts and pouches, how "in place" their canteen and grenades, until the patrol messed up their Hollywood Marine good looks. A nice tight battle would straighten them out... or kill them. Until then, the patrol had made them dirty, sweaty and disheveled, and Crandall nodded in satisfaction as he watched us trudge back the way we'd come. The fresh meat was looking a lot less like recruiting poster Marines than they had been when they came ashore and a bit more like The Bad Boys of Guadalcanal—a Garowski phrase he swore he'd sell to MGM for the next Errol Flynn movie.

Tokyo Rose knew reinforcements had arrived, she knew all the units, she knew how many men and she expressed regret that none of the new Marines would ever see beautiful Japan, or eat sushi, or climb Mount Fujiyama when the cherry blossoms were in bloom. They would all die on Guadalcanal, and the ravenous jungle would eventually reclaim their graves and their bodies become nests for the centipedes. "It's all a great pity for young men to waste away like this. Can't you see how terrible the Marines look who have been on that awful island since August? Do you want to look like them? Isn't it better to surrender, and make an oath to the Emperor, and come and live in Tokyo or Nagasaki and enjoy a glamorous Japanese wife?"

Garowski stuck his face in Red O'Brien's. "Do you want to look like me?"

"No," replied O'Brien. "Even when we were back in the States, I wouldn't have wanted to look like you."

We all roared.

"So, who do you want me to look like?" Garowski demanded.

O'Brien grinned. "Mae West."

STONEROAD AND SKILLET

THE CORPSMAN

The crap hit the fan again on Saturday. I swear, I had just started a letter to Kalasia, which Lt. Crandall had read the first paragraph of and made me add, "I remember your eyes being dark pools full of moonlight in the night," when a messenger comes tearing up to the field hospital in a jeep and starts hollering for the leader of Platoon X-Ray, King Company, 2nd Battalion, 2nd Regiment. Crandall goes over, real lazy-like, hears the kid out, and suddenly turns into a whirling dervish.

"Pack your kit, Bud!" he snaps. "We're getting back into the war!"

"What?" My fountain pen is still poised over the wrinkled sheet of paper on my knee. "I'm just getting started here."

"Save it for Halloween. The Japs are hitting Henderson again."

"They're always hitting Henderson, Sir, either with naval guns or patrols, what's the deal? We've got tons of gunnys up there."

Almost feverish with excitement, Crandall drew a Cuban cigar out of his chest pocket, bit off one end, crammed it in his mouth, lit it up, and exhaled a dark cloud into my face. "Not tons enough, Bud. The Nips hit us at the mouth of the Matanikau last night. So, the brass have sent the 2/7, 2nd Battalion, 7th Marines, to shore up the defenses there." He quickly read from a note the messenger had thrust at him. "Which leaves Chesty Puller short. They were helping him out and now he's on his own with just 700 men, the 1/7. That's all he's got to hold a 2500-yard line east of the Lunga River. Not enough, Bud, not nearly enough. He's requested the heavy weapons platoon X-Ray, King Company to reinforce. Rudy and Battalion say go. What have we got now, Bud? About 55 men or more with the machine gun crews and mortar teams? We can make a difference." He slammed his fist into his palm. "We'll show Chesty what Hollywood Marines can do. We'll turn this movie into the Marines in France during the Great War. We'll make it Belleau Wood and Chateau-Thierry and Mont Blanc Ridge all rolled into one. Errol Flynn and John Wayne and Clark Gable will get starring roles. I'll be Wayne. You can be Flynn. Johnny's pretty enough to be Rhett. Ha ha." Crandall slapped me on the back. "You can write all about it when we're done making chop suey. You can tell that sizzling Tongan beauty what a hero you are. The censors will probably black out the best stuff. No matter. You'll still be able to tell Kalasia how her eyes keep you awake at night. That line's sure to please."

He jumped into the jeep with the messenger driving. "One hour, Bud. They'll truck us up to the airfield and we'll deploy from there to the east of the Lunga. The more plasma and morphine you can hump, the better." The jeep roared off.

What the heck? Crandall was the one who had warned us war wasn't a John Wayne movie, and here he was acting like Joey Film Director, coming off like a John Ford or a Frank Capra or a Daryl F. Zanuck. But I got it. I knew for some guys that combat was a shot in the arm and that was Crandall—life was dull unless there was a fight. For other guys, combat meant bringing the whole mess one battle closer to the end, so they wanted to get on with it, kick the Japs off the island, win the war and go home. Still others did their duty and hoped they and their buddies would survive.

Me? I'd seen enough blood and guts to last a lifetime, heck, a hundred lifetimes. I'd be happy if the Japs just packed their bags and left the island to the land crabs and the Marines. That's what I prayed for. I also prayed none of the new guys would get killed. Our squad had already lost five of the original 12 men, and we'd seen Johnny wounded, so what was that, a 50% casualty rate? Crazy. Couldn't we have a casualty-free fight for once? I still had plenty of bad moments when my mind played back crap as if I were watching a grainy black and white newsreel in the cinema— Jake Sharples smothering the Jap grenade, Hot Kiss ripped in two by a burst from a Nambu machine gun, McKeever's head getting torn from his neck, me not being able to save Kramer no matter how much gauze and morphine and plasma I had. No more. Achilles needed a respite from sudden death. So yeah, I prayed my wild Mennonite prayer: *No more casualties for my squad, God, please.* But to me, that was like asking to breathe without oxygen, or to be planted on the moon without getting there in a rocket ship, or to never see anyone die again for the rest of my life. Such prayers could not be answered. They weren't going to happen on this earth.

So, I packed my bags and pushed my mind into "save a Marine, save a hero" mode. The trucks got us to the airstrip, we filed past the Cactus Air Force fighters lined up wingtip to wingtip, and disappeared among the coconut trees and their wide green fronds. It began to rain hammers and nails. We dug out our ponchos. A sergeant that Chesty had left as a guide led us over Bloody Ridge and down through a thick mess of jungle east of the Lunga. The battle line faced south and stretched west a mile and a half or more. It was pretty late in the day by then, still pouring. I'd read that the rainy season in the Solomons ran from November through April, so I guess the last week of October was soon enough for God to turn on the taps. Chesty came by, soaked, to talk with Crandall, and then vanished. Crandall told us, squad by squad, rain dripping off his helmet in big splashes, that patrols had encountered acres of Japs moving into position to attack. It was too late to redeploy and dig in again, the tropical night was coming on as fast as it always did, we had to sit tight and fight like we'd fought on the Ridge in September.

"All we ever do," complained Billy, "is fight over the same turf again and again. That's all the war is. A frigging barroom brawl over Henderson Airfield."

"They're all going to be like that," Crandall said quietly. "Every island we take will be so we can have another airfield. Every island we take will bring us closer to Japan. And every island we take will be taken by us, the Marines. Never mind the Navy and Air Force. The United States Marines will win or lose the war in the Pacific."

We finished digging in, though the rain made it sloppy work. The platoon had to cover a 300-yard gap. But now we had the big guns. Crandall placed the 50 in one place, the 30 in another, the two BARs somewhere else, the guys with the new M1 semi-auto carbines here and there mixed in with the Garands—only Levy and Billy had 1903s now, and Billy had his for sniping, the Thompson submachine gun for firefights. If this bugged Levy, he never let on. Just complained once that we would miss Tokyo Rose: "She's growing on me. How far is it from here to Tokyo?"

"You want a date?" growled Johnny.

"Maybe."

"She's not Jewish."

"You don't know that. She could eat kosher."

Johnny laughed, sighting along the line of his BAR as the sun set in purple and gold. "No Jap dame eats kosher. They're into lobster and crab and scallops and shrimp."

Levy did his shrug that lifted both shoulders, the left higher than the right. "She could be different. She could eat the good stuff. Like matzo ball soup and gefilte fish and lox and bagels."

Johnny laughed so loud Zarate warned him to pipe down.

"In your dreams, Leon," Johnny murmured, checking that his

magazine was full and that several others were laid out by his elbow. "In your ever-loving dreams."

The mortar teams in each of the squads were working to dig deeper holes just back of the line, but darkness hit too quickly. Stoneroad and Skillet had at least made sure they had plenty of mortar bombs, and all of us had helped hump those rounds in from Henderson. If they needed to shoot, they had the new M1 carbines. We had no idea how those carbines would perform. They were semi-auto with a 15-round mag so we were hoping they'd add a significant bite of firepower even if they didn't have the range of the Garand.

Garowski, Red, Over Easy Brian and Big Band Nick had our four Garands and were all next to each other, about twenty yards apart, where Zarate had situated them. He wanted them to fire in sequence, first Garowski and Red, then Over Easy and Big Band. The Japs had long ago figured out that the *PING* of an ejecting stripper clip meant a Marine's rifle was empty, and that's when they attacked. Zarate wanted them running right into a wall of fresh rifle fire from other Marines who had a full count of eight rounds ready to go.

New guy, Big Band Nick, he looked calm, but that didn't mean anything, Private Oregon Trail might just be a good actor. Over Easy Brian, on the other hand, was whispering too many funny stories to appear cool and collected to anybody. But the stories really were funny, and we enjoyed them, even Johnny was cracking up, the only problem was trying not to laugh out loud. Because if we did either Zarate or a Jap scout would kill us.

Red O'Brien just chewed gum and peered steadily into the rainy jungle dark in front of us as if he could actually see something. Maybe he could, maybe he was part owl. The mortar men, Stoneroad and Skillet, both chewed like Sergeant Brown of Titan squad chewed, Red Man Plug, and I wondered if the three would ever have the chance to meet up and have a spitting contest. Billy and Leon Levy, with their Model 1903s, were not supposed to be enormous firepower, but our surgeons, cutting out officers and non-coms and attack leaders. They were at opposite ends of our line. So were Zarate and Navarro.

The 50 and 30 were at the center of our squad, about a hundred yards apart. Frank Harte, Captain America, and Sam Kane, Batman, were still trying to deepen their 30's nest, but it was hard to use the shovels in the downpour without making the *clinking* and *splashing* sounds that would alert Jap point men. Tommy Earp, Not Related, aka Superman, and his gun buddy Sid Greene, Superman Too, had dug like gophers blitzed out on Atabrine—I'd already seen a few Marines go berserk on Atabrine's side effects—and had managed to build a deep machine gun nest from which Ma Deuce could greet the Empire of Japan. I sat back of all of them, and watched and waited, and prayed for every one of their souls. The rain let up at 2100 hours, nine o'clock. But it would come again. Along with the Japanese.

I dozed, thinking of lines that would help a Tongan woman, thousands of miles away, not to forget a Marine corpsman she had once been fond of. The more I saw of war, the more important she became to me. I realized I was erecting a kind of idol and making her into more than she was, but I couldn't help it. The first months on Guadalcanal, I hardly had time for her in my thoughts. Now I felt desperate for all that she was. If only Kalasia could touch me again, speak her warm words to me again, kiss me again with those sunset lips. It seemed to me that she was on the island, somewhere behind Japanese lines, hidden in the jungle, hoping I would get to her, save her, hold her and bury my face in her beautiful dark Polynesian hair while the tightness of her long brown arms put fresh strength and life into my war-battered spirit.

> *All times I have enjoy'd*
> *Greatly, have suffer'd greatly, both with those*
> *That loved me, and alone, on shore, and when*

Thro' scudding drifts the rainy Hyades
Vext the dim sea

I THOUGHT SOMEONE ELSE HAD SPOKEN THE WORDS TO ME. I WOKE up. But I'd been murmuring to myself. It was raining again. Then it stopped. I could see my squad grouped along the line like round smooth boulders in the dark. To be honest, I could only spot a few of them. The night was too thick with blackness and weather for me to see very far to my left or right. But I sensed their presence. I knew they were breathing, their hearts beating, their souls active. That's the way I wanted the world to remain.

But firing erupted far off on our right flank just after midnight. Rain was on again, off again, but the bright muzzle flashes, the crack of rifles, and the chatter of machine guns was obvious, cutting through the wet and the darkness. After a while, quiet returned, but the quiet after a storm is never the same as the quiet before, and the quiet that happens in the middle of a storm is really not a quiet at all. It was like the night had a strong heart and the jungle did too and I could hear both hearts beating together making the darkness thicker and more menacing.

Suddenly, as he told us later, Crandall played a hunch and fired one of his three flares into the blackness. The jungle lit up with a weird green color and the dangling, hissing flare made everything ghastly, like in a horror story. The faces of the Japanese troops that popped into view as they crept towards our lines were transformed into masks. None of us moved a muscle. The men crawling in our direction, bristling with rifles and bayonets and helmets slick with rain, looked unreal.

A Jap officer leaped to his feet, swung his katana in a wide arc, and screamed in English: "BANZAI! BANZAI! DIE FOR THE EMPEROR!" And at least a hundred soldiers jumped up with him and screamed and charged towards us, bayonets gleaming in the wet green light. They were only a hundred feet away. Still, no one in our platoon fired a shot.

It was Sergeant Brown, Red Man Plug Brown, ramrod of Titan squad, who broke the spell, bellowing: "HELP THEM DIE FOR THEIR EMPEROR! OPEN FIRE! FIRE! FIRE! FIRE!"

I jumped as our 50 opened up, blasting out long orange and yellow streams of light. I'd never been that close to one before, I was barely 20 feet away, and my whole body reacted to the loud crash and roar of its power. Then the 30 with its death chatter rocked the night. And suddenly our whole platoon was one sheet of flame—Garands, MI carbines, 1903s, Thompsons, they were all blazing, and I saw the Jap soldiers falling in clusters, five or six at a time.

Yet I knew they would still keep coming, and they did. Another mass of men joined them, and it looked as if our gunfire had had no effect. Instead of fewer soldiers, it looked to me as if they had multiplied to company strength, two hundred troops, and had the momentum to overwhelm our position, despite our big caliber machine guns and semi-automatic weapons. Marines yelled: "GRENADE!" and I saw at least five pineapples being tossed, but the explosions did not stop the attack. In 30 seconds, we would be going at the Japs face-to-face and hand-to-hand.

Then I heard loud explosive coughs to our right and left. And in front of me, the dwindling flare gleamed off the rain-wet tube of our 60mm mortar, which Stoneroad and Skillet had pointed in an almost vertical position at the night sky. *COUGH.* I did not spot a projectile leaving the pipe, but seconds later a huge blast ripped the dark apart into blistering yellow and crimson flame. All along the line, geysers of fire leaped up, taking Japanese bodies and lives and souls with them. Mortar bombs were bursting less than 50 yards from our position and the platoon ducked and fired, ducked and fired, while Stoneroad and Skillet, and other mortar crews, keep feeding their M2s and hurling a terrible death into the Japanese assault.

COUGH. COUGH. COUGH. WHAM. WHAM. WHAM. You'd think the Marine howitzers were dropping in rounds, except I knew the noise of that would be deafening, and the explosions far more massive. But for the Japanese, no matter how brave and aggressive they were, mortar shells were a sufficient reign of death and hell to stop them in their tracks. Mortar blast after mortar blast made the ground shake, and bullets from our 50 and 30 and BARs cut like the Japs' own razor-sharp katanas into their ranks. The flare was gone, but I could see all the killing and dying in the flashes of gunfire and furious explosions of grenades and mortar rounds. It fascinated and repelled me at the same time.

"CORPSMAN! CORPSMAN!"

The shouts came from the right of the platoon where Titan and Hades were positioned, and I took off at the run, crouching as Jap bullets continued to slice up the night from two or three dozen diehards. While I set up plasma transfusions and injected ampoules of morphine—Sergeant Red Man Plug Brown, who chewed and sat and grinned with his nicotine brown teeth, would get another Purple Heart—the firing sputtered out. But when I ran back to the platoon's left flank, responding to cries from Zeus squad, Hell's Kitchen was back in business. Another wave of Jap troops was assaulting the line and Captain America and Batman on the Browning 30, along with Superman and Superman Too on the Ma Deuce, were hosing down the ranks of samurais as they flung themselves at our squad.

I couldn't hear myself think. Truth be told though, I didn't need to because I didn't think. Treating the wounded had become automatic and instinctive. There was nothing to think about. I did what I knew how to do and what I knew needed to be done. I saved some and lost some. I wasn't God, and I didn't have a magic wand, so I didn't beat myself up over fatalities anymore. I did the best I could. That was all I could give my men and God.

PENELOPE AND TELEMACHUS

JOHNNY STRANGE

Johnny sat in a dugout next to the mail station, the letter from Idaho in his hands. It was from Marjean. His hands trembled as he stared at the address: Marjean Langston, 2235 School Road, Sandpoint, ID.

It's a real Dear John letter, I know it is.

He opened it part way and stopped.

I've been listening to that damned Tokyo Rose way too much. Don't be a coward, Strange—open the letter. It is what it is. Maybe it's not...

"Letter from home, Johnny?"

Johnny jerked like someone had shot him. "Damn it, Bud, don't sneak up on me like that."

Bud's lanky frame filled the doorway of the dugout. "Don't believe her, Johnny."

"Believe who, Bud."

"Tokyo Rosie. She's a liar, sent to do the devil's work."

Johnny shook his head and smiled. "How do you always get in my head like that, Bud? You some kind of psychic?"

"No, I told you. I got a direct line. If that's from Marjean, it's good news, Johnny. Open it up."

"Okay, but I bet she found some friggin' factory worker who's got an essential worker deferment. They're driving around Sandpoint in Marjean's little roadster, having a great—"

"Stop torturing yourself, Johnny boy. Shut up and open the letter."

Johnny sighed and finished tearing the letter open. Something dropped out on the floor, a square of white. Bud snatched it up before it could get muddy and turned it over. He smiled and handed the square to Johnny. "Telemachus."

"What?"

"Telemachus, Johnny, look."

Johnny looked down at the white square. It was a picture, a picture of Marjean and... a baby. Marjean was smiling, and Johnny could almost feel the love he saw in her eyes. He turned the picture over. Written in Marjean's neat handwriting were the words, "John Albert Strange. October 4, 1942." Johnny opened the letter with shaking hands.

Dearest Johnny,

Here is your son. He was born October 4. Daddy delivered him and everything went well. He weighed almost nine pounds, a very big baby, but I'm okay. I named him John Albert, for you and for Daddy. I hope you don't mind, but I couldn't keep calling him "Baby Boy."

I don't know how everything will work out, but I want you to know this. I am your girl forever, and I love you with all my heart. I know we don't know each other well yet, but I hope that when you come home, you will want me to be your wife and that would be fine with me. We might have gotten it the wrong way around, but I believe we can work it all out. Please be safe. I love you.

Marjean

Something inside Johnny Strange, something that had broken a long time ago, came roaring up from inside him like a submarine doing an emergency surface. It was as though the love of his girl and the picture of his baby son touched him with a burning brand and opened a half-healed wound in his heart that kept him from knowing who he was. He put his face in his hands and cried.

"I've got a son, Bud. I've got a son."

Johnny felt Bud's hand on his shoulder. "Yeah, I know. Told you, didn't I?"

"Yeah, you did, Bud, you did."

There was a long moment of silence. Then Johnny looked up and spoke. "Bud?"

"Yeah, Johnny?"

"I'm not sure I can handle this."

"What do you mean?"

"I don't want to love anyone this much. It gets in the damn way."

What are you talking about, Johnny?"

Johnny laid the picture down on his bunk and turned it over so he couldn't see it.

"I got this hate in me, see—hate for a slimy bastard who stole something from me, hate for my dad who wouldn't believe me, hate for a church full of a-holes who only want to make sure they look good. They didn't care what happened to me. And now this girl comes along and gives me love, and all I can do is hand her back the wrong end of the shit stick."

Bud looked at him with that sad look.

"Bud, don't you see? I finally got a reason to live. Killing Japs, that's what I live for. I don't want to live for Marjean or little Johnny. They're not real, Bud. They're somewhere far away, just a dream I had. Inside I still got this hate."

Johnny stood up. "I'm not gonna give it up, Bud!"

"But Johnny, don't you see? You have to let that hate go. It's killing you just as surely as if a Jap dropped a mortar right down your foxhole."

"Let me tell you something, Bud, and get this straight. Back in Idaho I was just John Strange, a pretty kid who never did anything and nobody ever cared about except some faggot who I should have killed when he touched me. But out here I'm Johnny Strange, Marine, BAR man, Jap killer, Tojo's Terror. Don't you see? I'm somebody out here. Back there I was nothin'. Jap killer is who I am, and that's what makes me a man. I don't have to worry about being a homo as long as I'm killing these little bastards. The hate makes it all real. Marjean and John, they're not real. They just mess me up. I don't need it." He turned away so Bud couldn't see the tears.

Bud was quiet for a long time. "Yeah, I can see that, Johnny. Hate is what gives you a reason to live. But it's stretching you so thin one day you'll just disappear. I'm asking you to think about something. Something new."

"What, Bud?"

"I know you have to kill, that's your job-—so kill for love."

"What do you mean?"

"Penelope and Telemachus are waiting for you at home. You have a long journey to get there, filled with a shitload of danger and lots of Japs—Japs who want to keep you from ever getting home. And those Japs don't want to just kill you; they want to kill Marjean, and little Johnny and everybody who doesn't kiss the ass of their emperor. We're here to do one thing—kill Japs. I get that. I know in a perfect world Jesus would have it otherwise, but you have to make sure you get home. The way home for you is over and through the bodies of the Japs. But don't think about Jenkins when you're killing them, that's death. Think about Marjean and John, that's life, and that's what will make you a real man in the long run. Kill the Japs, kill them good, but do it to keep your family safe. Now pack your gear, we got work to do."

"What are you talking about?"

"That's why I came to get you, Johnny. Chesty Puller needs help over on the Lunga line. He wants King Company right in the middle with our heavy weapons because every Jap between here and Rabaul is coming up that hill in about an hour."

———

KING COMPANY FILED INTO THE LINE IN A POURING RAIN, JUST before sundown. The downpour soaked Johnny to the skin as he slid into a foxhole next to Billy. Sniper glanced over at Johnny. "Hey, what's up Johnny?"

"I have a son, Billy, a little boy."

Billy grabbed Johnny's hand. "Oh, Johnny, that is great news. Great news. Praise the Lord." He stopped and then smiled. "Don't know where that came from."

Johnny looked down the sights of his BAR at something out in the jungle beyond the line. "That's okay, Billy. Praise the Lord and pass the ammunition."

They both laughed. Lieutenant Crandall came down the line in a crouch. The light was fading, and the rain pouring from the sky was like a vertical river. "We got a 300-yard gap to cover here, boys, but we've got a lot of firepower. I'm gratified that the brass saw fit to send us the heavy machine guns and Stoneroad and Skillet. We haven't had mortars before, and I'll tell you what—the Japs hate mortars. There's something hellish about that thunk, whump and scream a mortar makes when you fire it off that turns those Banzai heroes into little girls."

He moved on down the line. Over to the left, Johnny heard Levy complaining about missing Tokyo Rose's broadcast for the next few nights.

"She's growing on me. How far is it from here to Tokyo?"

"You want a date?" growled Johnny.

"Maybe."

"She's not Jewish."

"You don't know that. She could eat kosher."

Johnny laughed, sighting along the line of his BAR as the sun set. Darkness came with a thud. "Hey Levy. No Jap dame eats kosher. They're into lobster and crab and scallops and shrimp."

Levy shrugged. "She could be different. She could eat the good stuff. Like matzo ball soup and gefilte fish and lox and bagels."

Johnny laughed so loud Zarate warned him to pipe down.

"In your dreams, Leon," Johnny murmured, checking his magazine and laying out several more by his elbow. "In your ever-loving dreams."

They stared into the darkness, straining to see movement. The hours passed. Just beyond the lines, the jungle crouched, waiting like a beast ready to spring on any unwary traveler foolish enough to venture out into the Guadalcanal night. Then about midnight, Crandall fired a flare into the sky. There they were. The jungle was alive with Japs, crawling with them, like a stinking termite hive, each one with a purpose and a duty to their emperor—kill, kill, kill the Marines.

As the guns of Zebra Company cut loose, Bud ran by behind them.

"Remember, Johnny, kill for love, kill for love."

———

LATER, AS JOHNNY LOOKED BACK ON THAT FIGHT, HE REMEMBERED that the red-mist rage that had always risen, that kind of sick, killing joy from deep inside was not there that night. For the first time what Bud had said to him began to make a little sense. And so instead of the raw, lustful hate that usually filled his soul, where he imagined every Jap he blew apart was Harold Jenkins, something else rose up in him—a cold steel anger at these little arrogant pricks that thought they were so much better than everyone else that they could conquer countries with impunity, put people to the sword, rape the women and keep the men as slaves. His BAR barked into the darkness and he watched the Japs go down in rows as the heavy blows of the 30-caliber slugs knocked them into the hell reserved for tyrants and butchers. Every Jap that died that night was one less Jap that would make it to Australia or New Zealand or even America—one less son of a bitch whose hands would never touch an Australian girl or an American girl or kill another baby. Then in the heat of the fight he saw the face of his girl—his beautiful Marjean, holding their newborn son, and for the first time in a long time he prayed. "Dear Lord." Boom, boom, boom. "Help me make it through this fight." Boom, boom, boom-boom! "Let me get home to Marjean and little Johnny. Help me, Lord." Boom, boom, boom, boom.

Over to the right he heard the cry, "Corpsman, Corpsman," and he knew Bud was on the go. "Keep Bud safe Lord, and help as many of our guys make it through as you can."

He heard the ratcheting sound of Billy's Thompson break and then the higher pitched bam, bam, bam of the 1903 and he knew some Jap officer was on the way to his eternal reward. He heard the heavy 50s grinding away, and in their flashes he saw the Japs going down in rows. They were coming, they were coming, and then the greenhorns, Stoneroad and Skillet, entered the fray with a straight, up-and-down, steel, mortar-shell curtain that knocked the Nips on their butts. Death was in the air, raining down on the Japs like the water pouring from the heavens.

"Corpsman, corpsman!"

Another Marine down and Johnny could tell it was Sergeant Brown by the torrent of cusswords that cut through the dark. Up and down the line, the Marines poured death into the ranks of the Japanese and then Johnny Strange knew he would live—live another day, and maybe, if the winds were favorable and the course laid in straight, one day he would sail into the sheltered harbor of Ithaca and his queen and his son, the prince, would stand on the shore, hands lifted in greeting, with praises for a safe return rising to the gods. And as he killed Japs that night, the tears were running down his face.

DEAR MARJEAN

I can't tell you how proud I am of you and how happy I am to see my son in this world. I think of you every day and, yes, when I come home I want you to marry me. I guess this is my late proposal, and if I get some time off after we clean the Japs off this Island, I will get you a ring and make it official.

Something happened when I saw the picture you sent, Marjean. It was like getting washed clean in a cold Idaho river. My heart is changing from hatred to anger. Hate was easier, I think, because I could just go crazy and kill the enemy without needing a reason. Anger is about having to grow up and see the world in a new way, the way men with wisdom and courage see it. I still want to kill the enemy, but for a different reason. I don't want to just kill him because he's got yellow skin or because he's shooting at me. I want to keep him from going one step further in his conquest. He's had it easy up to now, but then he never had to fight American Marines. I want him to stop right here in his tracks, turn tail and run back to Tokyo. I want him to cry like a baby and warn everyone that the Marines are coming—inch-by-inch, step-by-step, island-by-island, we're coming.

I've made some good friends, Marjean. They are Mennonite boys like me. Billy Martens, we call him Sniper because he's a crack shot, and Bud Parmalee. He's the Hambo in our group, a conscientious objector, but I've never seen a braver guy. We look out for each other. Bud saved my life when we went to get him after the Japs captured him. He helped me kill the guy that almost killed me. Some pacifist, huh? And Bud has helped me to find out that maybe God isn't such a bad guy.

I have to go, but I want you to know this—to believe it and hold on to it even when it seems like the darkness will never leave and the sun will never shine again. We will win this war, and I swear to God I'm coming home. Home to you, home to our son, home to Idaho. I love you, Marjean, more than you will ever know.

Johnny

26

THE RIVER STYX

BILLY MARTENS

Billy had hoped to grab some shuteye the day after the night
attack, but waves of Japanese aircraft prevented that, their
bombs bursting on Henderson Airfield and all around it, hour
after hour. Henderson fighters, the Cactus Air Force, swarmed
into the air after them, like furious wasps, and the gunnys
cheered every time they flamed a Zero. To the bombs, the Japs
added naval shelling, so that by nightfall, the Marines were
calling it "Dugout Sunday." Billy noticed that Over Easy Brian
managed to sleep, despite the roar of explosions and aerial
combat, and did so with an inexplicable smile on his face. The
rest of the squad swapped jokes and tall tales while they were
bunkered down in their holes, and Johnny won a tin of K-rations
in a bet with Leon Levy about four in the afternoon. He made a
big show of eating it, especially the fudge.

Reinforcements filled gaps in the long line east of the Lunga
River, and ammo was brought up too—mortar bombs, 30-06
cartridges, the 35-pound belts of 50-caliber rounds, hand
grenades, boxes of 45-caliber for the 1911 pistols and Thompsons,
even a few satchel charges made their way to X-Ray Platoon.
Crandall rustled up a 37mm anti-tank gun he had towed to the

line. He got a couple of gunnys from Zeus squad to man it, explaining that he wanted them to fire directly into any assault waves and use the canister rounds he'd gotten his hands on: "They're messy and ugly and brutal, but war is hell and the Japs bought themselves front-row seats when they bombed Pearl Harbor."

Billy was amazed to be offered three drum magazines for his Thompson. Each held 50 rounds where the regular box magazine only had room for 20. He had taken to taping two 20 round mags together "jungle style," like other Marines, with the second mag ready to be flipped over and inserted once the first was empty. But the fighting side of him was intrigued with the idea of being able to fire 50 shots without reloading. Crandall's eyes gleamed through the smoke of his latest cigar as he watched Billy practice inserting the drum on his Thompson, which could only be done with the bolt retracted so that the submachine gun was ready to fire.

"Firepower, son of Montana, firepower," puffed Crandall. "That's how we win this war and get you back to your cattle ranch and lasso in time for the spring roundup."

The attacks began on their section of the line at 2000 hours, eight in the evening, and didn't let up till two. Billy emptied three drums in the first half-hour, the assaults were so fierce, and then had to wrestle one Jap soldier hand-to-hand and kill him with a knife, not having time to snap a 20-round box magazine into place. The anti-tank gun shredded the Jap ranks, killing with a terrible wanton slaughter as scores of metal balls sliced through the enemy soldiers' bodies. The mortar bombs and the big machine guns, the 30 and the 50, added to the destruction.

Still, the Japanese kept coming. They had guts and a ferocious devotion to their Emperor, whom they considered divine, and their island nation and Empire; Billy had to give them that. A lot of the guys called it fanaticism. But Billy reckoned it was Japanese patriotism, just like the Marines fought with their own ferocious brand of patriotism, no more, no less. So far as calling them fanatical went, Billy once asked the squad, when Johnny was off taking a leak during a lull in the fighting, if Johnny with his BAR wasn't as fanatical in combat as any Jap soldier running at them screaming, "*BANZAI.*" No one argued the point.

It wasn't as vicious a fight as Bloody Ridge, but it was no Sunday School picnic either. When the firing petered out, early Monday morning, the platoon's ammo supply was depleted and every Marine was exhausted. Billy watched Bud scoot about with his gauze and morphine and bags of plasma, and smoked through a pack of Player's. Achilles had cuts and scratches and plenty of dings, but no Purple Hearts and no KIAs, which Billy considered kind of miraculous, as if someone back home had been on their knees for the past six hours. Dawn showed Jap bodies twisted and chopped up and leering with the grotesque masks of the dead in the jungle in front of the platoon. Billy bowed his head as a wave of post-combat nausea swept over him. It was the same story—during a fight, he killed and felt nothing. Afterwards, he felt soiled.

They were kept on the line one more day and night. When patrols and scouts made it clear that Japanese forces had pulled back, X-Ray was ordered to rejoin its regiment for an assault on Japanese troops north of the Matanikau River. So, they humped east to the coast and turned north into the jungle, cussing as they lugged their machine guns and mortars in the toxic green heat and swampland humidity. Rejoining King Company and the 2nd Marines, Captain Rudy Rudebaker made sure X-Ray got chowed up and their ammo replenished, told them he was proud of how they had reinforced Chesty's thin line, and let them know the regiment was in reserve for a series of attacks against Japanese forces. Tagged as reserve, Rudy said it would give the Marines of X-Ray a chance to catch their breaths.

"Scuttlebutt has the Jap Army low on food and medical supplies," Johnny said one night, lying in the small tent he had set up using his poncho, rain slapping against its sides. "Someone got one lousy prisoner, and he was skin and bones and had sores all over his body. Bud says malnutrition."

"Yeah?" Billy answered, smoking a Player's. "They fight pretty hard for men that are bags of bones."

Johnny shrugged and lit up. He'd traded four packs of Lucky Strikes for two packs of Camels. "They don't have much choice, do they, except to fight? Nowhere to go but into the frigging sea. Same as us, really. Fight or swim. And I'm a lousy swimmer."

"We ever gonna get off this island, Johnny?"

"We are. Count on it, Sniper."

"How many more times are they gonna come after Henderson? How many more times are we gonna have to defend it?"

Johnny blew out a stream of smoke from his mouth and nostrils. "If they're smart, they'll keep coming. They won't want to lose this island. If they don't understand that, and we thrash them a few more times, they'll withdraw and leave us to rot. But that would be a mistake. Losing the Canal would be a mistake."

"I don't like being in reserve. I don't like not fighting if there's a fight going on close by. It gives me too much time to think about my mortality."

"There's a 20-dollar word. The trouble with you is, you don't have anything to think about except jungle and gunfire and a family that hates what you're doing down here. See the Southern Cross through that opening in the treetops? You need to look at it and think of a girl like I think about Marjean. She's so beautiful. As pretty as starlight. Dreaming about her gets me through many a night on this stinking island. Wherever they take us to rest up after the Solomons—because I swear on my BAR both of us are gonna get out of this cesspool alive—we gotta hook you up with a dame that makes your soul do back stands."

Billy laughed. "Hell, I can't even do back stands with my hands, let alone my heart and soul."

"We'll find her. You'll know. Just like I knew. And it'll be like a second life."

"Yeah?" Billy looked at the glowing tip of his cigarette under the roof of his poncho tent. "I could use a second life."

ON MONDAY, NOVEMBER 2ND, THEY WERE PULLED OUT OF RESERVE and put into the fight. They ordered Billy to take out the many snipers that were plaguing the advance and spent the day crouching behind tree after tree, mostly coconut palms, and hitting home with shot after shot. When a gunny from Mike Platoon asked him why he was so good at sniping snipers, Billy said it was because, after over a hundred days on the island, he'd become part jungle. Japs couldn't see him, he mostly looked like vines and high grass and banana trees and swamp. Another hundred days, and he'd be nothing more than roots and crocs and centipedes and palm fronds. He wouldn't be like jungle. He would be jungle.

He thought about this later as he dusted his feet with the powder he'd begged off Bud. Crud had got between his toes, thanks to day after day in wet socks—Johnny cussed that nothing ever dried out. Bud was going to declare Billy unfit for combat, but Billy practically broke down and wept at not being able to be there for his buddies during an offensive, so Bud relented and ordered him to use the powder morning and night—"If it gets to the point where you can't walk and keep up, you will get pulled, and it won't be me giving the order." Billy had begun to limp, his feet were so sore, but he wasn't the only one, and they needed every Marine that could move in a forward direction. He wasn't sure if the powder was helping or not. He applied it anyway, hoping it might help keep him upright and out of the field hospital.

Johnny borrowed the tin and used it too, grinning: "The thing is, we really are turning into jungle, Billy boy. I'm soon gonna be Frankenstein and you? You're already the Wolf Man."

"Are those our new nicknames?"

"So long as we're on this godforsaken island, yes."

"You really think it's godforsaken?"

"If you were Jesus, would you hang around to watch this slaughter?"

The next day, two of the company platoons, Victor and Fox, got into a brawl with Japs over a couple of well-concealed jungle bunkers. Bud was furious with how the fight had been handled and at the number of casualties, including five KIAs. The day after that, Mike platoon had a similar clash in jungle so dark with rain and treetops that Bud called it Stygian, a word many in the company had never heard in their lives.

"It's Greek mythology!" Bud snapped, impatient with everyone and everything in the heat and sweat and blood of the thick jungle that hugged the coastline. "The River Styx. Hades. The Underworld. The Place of the Dead. Get it?"

"No," Red O'Brien responded, chewing gum as he and other X-Ray Marines served as body snatchers, helping Bud move wounded Mike platoon gunnys to a Battalion Aid Station 200 yards back of the fight. "No one gets it, Doc."

Bud was exasperated at Red, grumbling under his breath as he bent over a wounded man and held up a bag of plasma. "You die and a boatman takes you across the River Styx to Hades. Charon is the boatman's name. Romans and Greeks used to put coins in the mouths of the dead to pay for the final boat ride of their loved ones. Stygian becomes Styx and means impenetrable and malevolent darkness. Where did you guys go to school?"

"Not in hell," replied Red, still chewing.

Orders came down for the 2nd Battalion, 2nd Marines, 2/2, to dig in soon after Mike platoon's bunker fight. They were a good hike from the coast and about 2000 yards west of the thumb-like peninsula of Point Cruz that Crandall showed his platoon on a torn and wrinkled map. "We're in thick jungle here, boys," he said. "The kind Japs love for hand-to-hand combat." Red had not stopped chewing the same stick of gum. "Yeah, we know, Skipper," he replied. "It's Stygian."

THEY SAT THERE FOR FIVE DAYS. THEN THEY WERE ORDERED forward again. The 2/2 met a wall of resistance from Japanese troops as they pushed towards their objective of Kokumbona. X-Ray platoon unlimbered their 30 and 50 machine guns, all the platoons cut loose with their 60mm mortars and King Company, taking point, was able to advance against heavy enemy firing and grenade attacks. But after a day of harsh fighting, Vandegrift ordered the Marines back to the east bank of the Matanikau River. Billy was as upset as the others at giving up the ground they'd already battled and bled over. The skinny was the Japs were trying to land over 10,000 troops to attack Henderson Field yet again, and the 2/2 needed to be there to shake Jap hands if enemy reinforcements landed. The truth of it hit home when the roar of naval battle made Billy jump awake early Friday morning, November 13th, the crash of firing and massive explosions out to sea yanking him from a dream about swimming in a sparkling turquoise mountain lake.

"What is it?' he yelled, startled. "What?"

"Easy." Johnny put a hand on Billy's arm. "We got ourselves a regular shootout between the US Navy and the Jap Navy again. I guess all that scuttlebutt about Tokyo wanting to land a boatload of reinforcements was true after all, Wolf Man."

"I was having a great dream, Frankenstein."

"Did it have a woman in it?"

"No."

"Then it couldn't have been that great."

They were close enough to the Pacific that they could see

some ships firing and two of them burning in sheets of orange flame. The shooting and explosions were silent until the sounds reached them several seconds afterwards—*thump, thump, thump.* The huge parabolas of red and yellow tracers gave out no sound the Marines could hear, but the vivid colors made their eyes widen and their pupils contract. No one in the squad had any smart comments to make, not Red, or Over Easy Brian, or Johnny. A few smoked. Most just watched the light show and listened to the distant thunder with their mouths partly open.

The night, they all agreed without humor, was Stygian. No moon, clouds as thick as death, a blackness like tar, or pitch, or a hopper of Pennsylvania coal. The gunfire sparkled against the dark as if were the Fourth of July. Now and then the Southern Cross came and went when the clouds parted. Billy had a weird sense of the presence of God that he could not shake or scoff away.

A FEW DAYS LATER, ON WEDNESDAY, NOVEMBER 18TH, THE 2ND Marines were ordered across the Matanikau again. Rudebaker told King Company the naval fight had been a mixed bag, the US had lost ships and men, the Japs had lost ships and men, but the big deal was the Japanese reinforcements could not land, there weren't another 10,000 diehard samurais to tangle with, and for that, they all had something to thank the USN for, for once. The Jap reinforcements, the brass was convinced, had been on their way to take Henderson Airfield.

"I told you," Billy grumbled. "The whole war is about fighting over Henderson Field."

"Well, Wolf Man, we're heading north again into Jap Land," Johnny reminded him.

"Yeah, sure, and we'll get pulled back again to defend Henderson, Frankenstein."

"Skinny has the Jap transports sunk and the soldiers in them drowned."

"They'll just land a bunch more. There's an unlimited number of Japanese troops. Marines, on the other hand, are in short supply."

"We have enough to finish the job, Wolf Man."

"Not if the Japs keep fighting to the last man, Frankenstein."

Johnny snorted. "Even if they keep fighting to the last man. Know the story about the Latin word *serviam*?"

"No," Billy replied as they trudged through the jungle.

"God asks the angels who will serve him in Heaven. And the devil, Lucifer, he goes, *not a chance. Non serviam—I won't serve.*"

"That's it? That's your story?"

"Hang onto your damn reins, cowboy. Michael the Archangel hears this and shouts, *Serviam! I will serve!*"

"So?"

"So, that's us, that's the frigging Marines. No matter who else quits, we don't know what that means. It's not in our vocabulary. We're with Michael, the warrior angel. We fight. We serve."

"*Serviam*," replied Billy.

Johnny nodded. "*Serviam*."

"Where'd you pick up a story like that?"

"Father McKean. I listened in on his Mass just before we moved up onto the line in October. You're not the only one who hovers around sky pilots."

"I saw he was up with the regiment on this one."

"Yeah. So are the rabbi and Ty Jackson."

Achilles squad took the point for X-Ray platoon, which took the point for King Company, which took the point for the 2nd Marines. Corporal Navarro led one fire team, with Hernandez on the BAR, Captain America and Batman on the 30, and Red, Over Easy Brian, Levy and Garowski the riflemen. The other fire team was headed up by Sergeant Zarate, with Johnny on the BAR, Superman and Superman Too on the Big 50, Stoneroad and

Skillet on the 60mm mortar, armed with M1 carbines, and Billy and Big Band Nick as the other riflemen—Corporal Billy, as always, serving as platoon sniper, as well as backup non-com for the squad.

A number of Japanese destroyers or cruisers might have been sunk. A number of Japanese soldiers might have been killed or drowned or never had the chance to debark from their troopships or transports. But it was clear to Billy and the other Marines, as they clawed their way back north through the jungle towards Kokumbona, that the fight had not gone out of the enemy, and progress was difficult, sometimes impossible, against their foe. Often enough, even with both of the squad's fire teams working side by side, the killing power of the 30-caliber and 50-caliber machine guns, along with the 60mm mortars, was still not enough to dislodge Japanese soldiers from their bunkers or their Nambu machine gun pits. Zarate had to order men to get danger-ously close and throw satchel charges that sometimes the defenders could toss out in time. It could take hours to get through a hundred yards of jungle infested with snipers, booby traps strung with grenades, machine-gun nests, bunkers and hidden trenches bristling with Jap riflemen.

By night, no Marine slept, always alert for an enemy marauder. By day, every rifle and machine gun was up and ready to fire, and Frank Harte, Captain America, took to carrying the 30 in his arms, ready to shoot: "Thirty pounds ain't much if it saves our skins." Even Tommy Earp didn't always bother to set Ma Deuce on her tripod when the jungle erupted in warfare. He just swung it down off his shoulder, braced it against his body, and had the muscle to fire the 84-pound gun from the hip, spewing one hundred rounds into bunker openings in long bursts of ten, killing every Jap inside stone dead.

But despite their fighting spirit, the Marines did not get far before Vandegrift ordered them to halt. On November 23rd, only five days after the renewal of the Matanikau offensive, even though they were convinced they could cut their way through Japanese opposition as tough and impenetrable as walls of jungle bamboo, the 2nd Marine Regiment was commanded to dig in and form a line a short distance west of Point Cruz.

It was while Billy had finished digging his hole, and was setting up his poncho like a tent to keep off the rain and sun, that he looked behind him the moment he recognized Father McKean's voice with its slight Irish-American accent. Bud and other corpsmen had made a spot for the wounded in a clearing under the coconut trees with their large wide fronds. Those that had a chance of making it were stretchered back to the Battalion Aid Station by the Matanikau. The others were being comforted until they passed—boys from Missoula, from LA, from Portland, Salt Lake City, Cody, Colorado Springs, Spokane. Ty Jackson and the rabbi were standing by respectfully while Father McKean knelt over one Marine, gently extending a crucifix to him while murmuring in what Billy knew was Latin. Sergeant Zarate was at Billy's shoulder.

"What's Father McKean doing?" Billy asked him.

Zarate was bareheaded. "The Last Rites. It's what a Catholic priest prays over you when you're dying."

Billy removed his helmet.

Zarate murmured in Spanish—*Santa María, Madre de Dios, ruega por nosotros pecadores, ahora y en la hora de nuestra muerte.* Then he lifted the crucifix that hung from a chain around his neck, kissed it, and made the sign of the cross over his chest.

"What did you just say, Sarge?" Billy asked.

Zarate continued to look at the dying Marine. "Holy Mary, Mother of God, pray for us sinners now and at the hour of our death."

27

THE CALLING—NOV. 1942

THE CORPSMAN

Dear Kalasia,

    I have started this letter ten times, but each time I did, the Japs decided otherwise. A lot of this will get marked out with a black pen, so I'll trust the censors to leave enough so you'll get an idea about what's going on here. Right now I'm back at a field hospital close to Henderson Field. One of our sergeants got wounded, and I brought him back here, and I'm waiting until I find out how he's doing. Our squad has been on the line for a week and faced some awful scraps. The Japs have a lot of nerve, and they don't give up. But they never fought Marines before. I think they believed we were a bunch of lazy, overfed sissy-boys who thought this whole war would be a walk in the park. Boy, were they surprised! I mean they are patriotic and devoted to their emperor and all, but there's something about fighting for a country that represents a different life—a country where everybody doesn't go around bowing and scraping and kissing one guy's heinie. It seems we're fighting for something bigger and better than that. Our boys have been putting up a harder fight than the Japs ever expected.

    Anyway, Lieutenant Crandall keeps telling me I need to write this letter and, I swear, Kalasia, I have tried many times. He even tried to get me to say how I remember your eyes being dark pools full of moon-

light in the night. That's true, but I don't need an officer to tell me how beautiful you are. I have plenty of my own words for that. Your beautiful eyes, your skin, your wonderful smile, like the sun coming up on a spring morning. The time we spent together is part of my dreams now and like I said before, it's the best part. I remember that moment when I was going back on board and you gave me something to make me never forget you. And so I can't. I can't ever forget you, and I haven't tried. Every soldier needs something to hang on to, so I'm hanging on to you, to us. I hope I live through this war so I can come back. I hope you're not married with a hundred kids when I do. Remember the poem —the one about Ulysses? "It may be we shall touch the Happy Isles, and see the great Achilles, whom we knew." I want to make Tonga my Happy Isles, Kalasia. I want to make it my heaven. After my "battle far on the ringing plains of windy Troy," I'll come see you. I want to take hold of the rudder and steer my ship home. Wait for me. I shouldn't be too long.

Bud

Whoever said war is hell never saw Guadalcanal. Hell is a picnic compared to this place. We've been on the line for weeks, sitting in stinking foxholes full of water up to our necks with rain pouring down. They say this is the rainy season on Cactus, but unless they went through Noah's flood, they do not understand what a rainy season is. The water turns the ground into quicksand. I heard one guy drove a tractor into a mud-hole over on the other side of Henderson and the tractor just disappeared. We also have vines, trees, snakes, but the biggest enemy, besides Japs, are the mosquitoes. Malaria is taking out as many of our guys out as bullets. We have so little quinine we have to take Atabrine. The guys don't want to take it because some fool started a rumor it makes you sterile. And it turns your skin yellow. I can tell which guys are taking it by looking at them. These guys are stubborn. They'd rather have the shakes than take this junk. I have to get them in line and watch while they take their pills, and still some guys hold it in their mouth and spit it out later.

If the Devil ever needed a perfect place to breed the Malaria-carrying Anopheline mosquito, it's Guadalcanal. There are shell craters, foxholes, and ruts all over the island collecting water and mud, and they give the mosquitoes a nice hole to lay their eggs. When they suck on a guy who already has malaria, they get the parasite and carry it to the next guy. So the disease spreads like wildfire.

The other problem we have is dysentery. There are rotting dead bodies everywhere, and everyone is getting sick from them. I mean the Marines leave no one behind and we try to bury all our guys, but the Japs are hiding in the jungle and we've been killing so many of them they can't carry the bodies away. At Bloody Ridge the Jap soldiers piled so deep in front of our line we had to bulldoze a trench and push them in. And stink. Man, this place stinks—from the rotting dead, the foul swamps, and the decaying mush under our feet—and so our guys get dysentery. Most of our guys have lost at least forty pounds and they think hitting the head every twenty minutes is standard operating procedure. Sergeant Zarate warned us that our undies would be stiff before we got back to the ships, and boy was he right!

Most of the guys have jungle rot between their toes, too, because the mud and rain keep their socks wet all the time. Billy's got it bad, but he keeps limping back to the lines. I give him as much powder as I can to keep it under control, but I don't even know if the stuff works. I hope he keeps his toes. He's a great guy, an incredible rifleman, and tough as nails. Any time there's a fight, he's right in the middle. He got recommended for a medal and moved up to acting corporal after taking out some Jap machine guns that mowed down two guys from our squad.

Billy's a funny guy. While the lead is flying, he's got nerves of steel. Dead accurate shot, takes the toughest jobs, but when the fight is over, he'll go off by himself and puke his guts up. This war is hard on guys that have grown up around God. See, for the ones who came with no previous knowledge, the atheists, the don't-care-one-way-or-the-other guys, killing Japs is just another thing they are doing. I don't mean it isn't like they are braver than the other guys, it just means no more to them than shooting a rabbit or taking a walk—just another day at the office if you know what I mean.

But the Christian kids, the ones that grew up in a pacifist church like the Mennonites and the Adventist boys, they heard about non-violence and 'thou shalt not kill' every day and night, and this killing business is a tough row to hoe. I know Billy's got his own war going on inside him, even though he's as gung ho as you get. He believes that American boys are the ones who will keep the yellow peril from steaming down to Australia, and then new Zealand, and maybe right on into America. He believes that with all his heart and that's why he's here. And yet, there's that little voice inside him, giving him a twitch every time he blows the head off some Jap officer, or cuts loose with that Thompson. It's something he needs to work out and it will either kill him or keep him alive.

And then there's Johnny Strange. Johnny's grown up a lot since he got here. When I met him at Elliot, he was a hater. He had a bad go back in Idaho and it twisted him up. But this God I serve sent him an angel at the last moment before he signed up— an angel named Marjean. I've said it before and I'll say it again, some guys have all the luck. Marjean is a dish, a real knockout. Betty Grable or Rita Hayworth are mud hens compared to Marjean. And that baby boy of Johnny's, he's the best-looking kid I ever saw. You know how a lot of kids look like lumps of clay that someone pushed their hand down right in the middle of their face? Well, not John Albert. That kid could be in the movies right now. And when Johnny saw the picture of his boy, he changed. He's growing up, and the hate is leaving his soul. I've never met Marjean, but somebody taught her that love is bigger than hate

and she gave that to Johnny as a going-away present. Not to say
losing the hate changed the way he fights. No, I think it made him
better. He's not so reckless, he thinks things through, like a man.
Johnny would make a good officer because he's a natural leader.
He's like the point on the spear, always right at the tip, always
sending those 30-caliber slugs right where they need to go.
Johnny will also figure out who God is before all this is over.

So my two Menno boys are growing up fast, and I get to
watch. When I think about all we've been through in the few
months we've been on Guadalcanal, I go back to the Ulysses
poem that Billy got from General Price. There's one line that says,
I will drink life to the lees. You might not know what lees are—
that's the wine at the bottom of a barrel, the last bit. I suppose
you could take that two different ways: we're either getting the
dregs of life, or we are living life to the fullest, we're seeing the
whole thing and getting everything it offers. I think it's both. You
couldn't find a place on earth that better shows the depths to
which men can sink. The Japs are the worst. They are stupid
about a lot of things, most of all about how to treat people when
they conquer them. Instead of making friends and winning the
people over, they rape the women, kill the men and strip the
country of everything valuable. In that way they are more like
beasts or a swarm of locusts than men. Our guys can be jerks too,
and I've seen bad situations. Men can either rise to sublime
heights or fall into the miry pit when everything is on the line.

But I don't think we are getting the dregs, I think we are living
life to the fullest on Guadalcanal; we are getting the whole
schamoley out here—life, death, friendship, hatred, God, the
devil... I mean people back home will go their whole lives
without ever feeling the intensity of living we experience in one
hour. There's another line in the poem that goes, *All times I have
enjoyed greatly, have suffered greatly, both with those that loved me,
and alone;* that says it too. Sometimes in battle we are all knit
together so tight it's like we share our internal organs—we feel

what the next guy feels, we see what he sees, we're thinking about how to keep the next guy alive... And then when we're alone, there is still that presence, that little voice deep inside that keeps speaking, calling, directing, guiding. "This is the way, walk ye in it."

I may get too philosophical here, but all of it makes me realize that like Ulysses, men need this kind of journey to become men. And I'm proud to play my part. Between the shakes and the runs and rotten feet, this is the sorriest, most raggedy-ass band of guys you have ever seen. But I'll tell you what. There has never been a better, braver, tougher bunch of men. There was a time you could only find men rising to nobility like this before the walls of Troy.

28

THE SUITOR—NOV. 1942

JOHNNY STRANGE

Marjean Langston looked out the big corner window of her room in her dad's house in Sandpoint, Idaho. Heavy snow was falling, and it covered the street that ran by the front of her house with a mantle of white. Occasionally a car went by, marring the deep soft blanket, but it was cold enough outside that the snow was sticking and even as she watched the invasive furrows filled again. From her window she had a panoramic view —the street, the side yard and the two-acre yard that led down to the Pend Oreille River just a few hundred feet behind the house.

Marjean loved this place. Before her dad and mom divorced, it had been a small girl's paradise. She spent her summers boating on the river or picnicking in the park-like setting of the expansive grounds. She remembered the parties her dad and mom had thrown—the large redwood deck by the shore lit up with tiki torches and the trees festooned with tiny white lights. Her dad loved big band music, and he often brought in a portable stage so he could invite the famous orchestras performing in Coeur d'Alene over to Sandpoint to give private performances for his wealthy friends. Ski trips to Sun Valley or White Pass in Washington State filled her winters, and her life had been that of a princess—Marjean Langston, the beautiful daughter of Albert and Geraldine Langston, pillars of a wealthy and cultured Idaho society.

Then her mom left her dad, and it was over. One day Marjean came home from school, and her mom was packing her clothes into suitcases. In three days they left Idaho and moved clear across the country to Rhode Island, where they lived with her grandfather in a run-down seaside home in Providence. Her mom had gone to work at an insurance company, and Marjean had taken up the lonely life of the girl who comes too late to a school to fit in anywhere. So Marjean had missed her dad, and she had missed her life as a princess. And then, a few years later, her mom got cancer and within a few months she died. Her grandfather moved into a home for World War I veterans and she had nowhere to go but back to Idaho. After the struggle of life on the East Coast, she was excited about taking up where she left off —parties, swimming, the cream of Sandpoint society's sons all begging for dates. And then she met Johnny Strange.

As soon as she got back to Idaho, word got around, and she got phone calls—all kinds of boys who remembered the golden-haired daughter of the wealthy Doctor Langston—and Gerald King was one of her most ardent suitors. That is why she had been at the King's lake-side cabin, waiting for Gerald and his family to arrive when Johnny Strange walked up out of the boathouse and her life changed forever. Her thoughts went back to that afternoon. When Johnny took her out in his boat, something had overwhelmed her—the wild freedom she felt with him, the wind whipping her face, the cold air stimulating her blood. When they got back to the boathouse, she was on fire with emotions she had suppressed after her mom died. And when Johnny stood before her, his dark eyes probing deep into her soul, she had surrendered to him in a way she never expected. Her passion had surprised her, for she had always been the ice queen, the girl everyone wanted to kiss but never could. And then in one moment Johnny Strange, a boy she had only known for one hour, claimed her heart. The problem was, she was still getting phone calls.

A cooing sound from the crib set against the wall broke her reverie. She turned and looked down at her baby boy. He saw his mother and waved his small hands and kicked; the cooing sounds turning to excited squeals.

"Do you want me to pick you up, John Albert?"

He waved some more and kicked again, and Marjean bent down and picked up her baby. He nestled into her arms and quieted. An enormous love engulfed her. This was her son, this was the fruit of her love for Johnny Strange, a love she would never understand but accepted, anyway.

There was a knock on the door and then Cecelia, their maid, peeked in.

"It's time for Johnny's breakfast, Marjean."

Marjean saw the bottle in Cecelia's hand and the little spit-up towel over her shoulder.

"Cecelia, shouldn't I be nursing him? I read that mother's milk is the best thing for a baby."

Marjean noted the look of surprise on Cecelia's face. "Well, Miss Langston, I don't know of any ladies of standing that nurse their children. They always have nurses and nannies taking care of those things."

Marjean laughed out loud. "Oh, Cecelia, don't be such a prude. I'm not a 'lady of standing'; I'm just a girl with a baby. Now, I know you know how it's done, because you have kids. So I want you to show me how."

Cecelia smiled and nodded. "Yes, Miss Marjean. I'll show you."

Before they could start, Marjean heard the phone ring downstairs and then her father's voice as he answered.

"Marjean?" Her dad's voice floated up the stairs.

"Yes, Dad."

"It's Gerald King."

Marjean frowned. "Oh, bother!" She handed Johnny to Cecelia. "Feed him this time, but remember, you said you will teach me."

"Yes, Miss Marjean."

Marjean went down the stairs and picked up the phone. "Hello?"

"Hi, Marjean. It's Gerald."

"Oh, hello, Gerald."

"Say, I'm just downtown and I got some new Glenn Miller records. I thought I'd come by and we could give them a listen."

"Well, I don't know, Gerald..."

Marjean's father walked into the hallway. "What does he want?" he whispered.

"Hold on, Gerald." She put her hand over the mouthpiece and whispered back, "He wants to come by with some new Glenn Miller records."

"Oh, let him, Marjean. It will do you good. You need a diversion."

Marjean hesitated, but her father nodded, urging her to answer Gerald. "All right, Gerald. See you soon."

———

TWENTY MINUTES LATER, MARJEAN HEARD GERALD DRIVE UP. SHE went to the hallway window and watched through the lace curtain. When he stepped out of his new Buick, Gerald looked the picture of a successful young businessman. His camelhair overcoat buttoned up tight, plaid winter scarf, the whole outfit gave a holiday touch to his jaunty appearance. Marjean watched as he made his way up the sidewalk, trying to stay out of the snow to avoid wetting his new leather shoes. A packet wrapped in brown paper was under his arm, and Marjean assumed it was the records. Gerald made his way up the steps and rang the doorbell. She put a smile on her face and opened the door.

"Marjean! How are you?"

"I'm doing well, Gerald, I'm well. Won't you come in?"

He stamped his feet on the doormat, and then stepped in. "Nice and warm—it's freezing outside."

"A little early for snow, isn't it, Gerald?"

"Oh, you never know about Idaho. Some winters, nothing, and the next one, Antarctica."

He laughed at his little comparison, but Marjean didn't find it amusing. In fact, despite his spiffy clothes, she found everything about Gerald plain and boring. Just then her dad walked into the hallway.

"Hello, Gerald, welcome."

"Hi, Doctor Langston. What's buzzin?"

"Pardon?"

Gerald smiled. "I mean, how are you?"

"Oh! Fine Gerald, just fine. Come on in and take off your coat. Can I get you anything? Coffee maybe?"

"Sure, Doctor, if you salt it with a little brandy."

Doctor Langston smiled. "Little early, isn't it?"

"Yeah, just kidding, Doctor. Some Joe would be fine."

"Good. I'll have Cecelia make some. You go on into the front room."

Marjean helped Gerald off with his coat and scarf and hung them on the coat rack. When she turned back, he looked her up and down. She did not like his expression.

"Boy, Marjean, you look killer diller."

"Why thank you, Gerald. Uh... how are things going at the mill?"

"Oh, just great, Marjean. Like my dad said, there's a big demand for paper products. The government is buying all the cups and plates we can make, and we're selling paper by the truckload. Great time to be in business."

They walked into the front room. Gerald put the package on the table and opened it. He took out the records and looked around. Marjean pointed to the Victrola in the corner. Gerald slipped the record on and stepped back. The smooth saxophone sound began, counterpointed by muted trumpets. "It's called Moonlight Serenade, and it's the gas."

Marjean looked at Gerald. Despite his suave appearance and cool exterior, he was just a high school kid all dressed up.

"Wanna dance?"

Marjean hesitated. "Aw, come on, Marjean. I won't bite."

She stepped over and he took her in his arms. Marjean didn't like it, but she liked the music so she moved with him. Then she found his arms tightening around her. "Gee, Marjean, you're so beautiful. You get me." She felt his hot breath on her neck.

Marjean broke away and pushed him from her. "Don't do that, Gerald."

"But Marjean, I thought…"

"Thought what, Gerald?"

"Well, we used to be close and…"

"What, you thought because I have a baby, now I'm a round heel?"

"No, Marjean, I…"

Just then a baby's cry came from upstairs. Marjean looked up. "Do you hear a baby crying, Gerald? That's my baby. And that's Johnny Strange's son. I love Johnny."

"But Marjean, you don't even know him. You were just with him one time…"

"How do you know?"

"Well I don't, but I assumed…"

Marjean felt the heat rising in her face. "You have no right to make assumptions about me or Johnny."

"Look Marjean, I'm sorry. I meant nothing by it. It's just that I'm crazy about you, always have been. And you don't know if

Johnny's ever coming back. And if he does, is he going to marry you?"

"That's none of your business."

"Well until he comes back and marries you, I will consider myself in the running. I want you to marry me. I'll give your son a name and I'll give you the life you're accustomed to."

"My son has a name, Gerald. It's John Albert Strange. And what makes you think I would marry a boy who's sitting at home, a slacker, making money and driving a fancy car while our boys, our men, are over in the jungle giving their lives to keep the Japs away from the women and children of this country. Do you think I would marry you so I could live in comfort while Johnny's over there fighting? You have another think coming."

Gerald's face turned red and then white. "Gee, Marjean... I..."

"Maybe you should go home and think about your life. Think about whether you earned the right to stay home while other boys are fighting this war. And maybe you'll find the courage to tell your dad you will join up too. Now, I think you should leave."

Gerald scowled and walked to the coatrack. "Okay, Marjean. I didn't mean to be such a dope. But I'll be back."

"When you're wearing a uniform, you can come back. Not until then."

The blast of cold air and the sound of the door slamming hit Doctor Langston as he came in with a tray. "Gone already? I thought he wanted to have some coffee."

"Oh, Dad. Gerald King is a fat head and a slacker. I sent him away. He thought I'd be easy because... because..."

Dr. Langston set the tray on the stand by the door and took his daughter in his arms. "It's okay, honey. Don't let it bother you. I understand." From upstairs the cry came again. "Now it seems something upset my grandson. Let's go see what we can do."

JOHNNY STRANGE WOKE FROM A DREAM, A WEIRD DREAM. HE HAD seen his mother, but his mother was dead, wasn't she? The plain blue dress, the little *kappe*, yeah, it was his mother all right. In his dream he was in his foxhole, out on the line, and he heard a rustle behind him. When he turned, there she was. She pointed her finger at him and spoke. "Stay alive, Johnny. Get home to Marjean; she needs you. You hear me, Boy."

Johnny sat up, rubbing his eyes. He was in a foxhole, out on the line. His mother wasn't there anymore—but her words rang in his head. "Stay alive, Johnny. Get home to Marjean."

The night was steaming hot, but a cold sweat ran down his back.

I hear you, Mama, I hear you...

29

THE NEW YEAR'S MOOSE

BILLY MARTENS

R oosevelt had changed the date for Thanksgiving from the last Thursday of November to the fourth Thursday. None of the Marines even thought about it because the change had come into law in late December 1941, when many of them had been scrambling to enlist, already training at Boot Camp, or enjoying their final Christmas at home. The fourth Thursday in 1942 was the last Thursday anyway, so no one noticed. And since everyone in Billy's regiment was digging in by Point Cruz on November 26th, their thoughts turned more towards surviving the Battle of Guadalcanal than roast turkey and cranberry sauce, though quite a few wished they could be back home and carving a big bird.

Billy remembered Thanksgiving, but volunteered to spend the night at a listening post, watching and waiting for Japanese infiltrators. None showed up. Maybe Tokyo kept Thanksgiving too, there were enough Japanese-Americans after all, and the samurais might be enjoying tuna and *yakisoba* noodles and *saki* in honor of their USA brothers and sisters. *Banzai*.

He didn't agree with the USA internment of the Japanese-Americans or *Nisei*. His family had roots in Europe and Germany.

Martens was a German name. Should all Mennonites with German backgrounds be placed behind walls of barbed wire too? His thinking turned toward letting able-bodied *Nisei* form regiments and prove their loyalty to America on the battlefield. Fighting spirit would always impress the American citizen.

Billy shrugged and popped a square of K-ration fudge he'd saved in his mouth—he doubted it would ever happen. FDR and Congress would never trust Japanese-Americans to fight against other Japanese in the Pacific War. Yet Congress trusted Americans of German background to fight the Germans and Nazis in Europe. He shrugged. Politics and politicians had never made sense to him or won his heart and loyalty, though he did like and respect President Roosevelt.

"Think of turkey all night?" Johnny asked him when Billy returned to his foxhole in the morning.

Billy shook his head. "Nah. We never did a bird. It was venison for Thanksgiving. And for Christmas? Elk."

"Yeah? What about New Year's?"

"Moose. I guess I like moose most of all."

"Huh. Never had that."

"Very rich. Very filling. Absolutely tender and full of flavor if you do it my mom's way."

Johnny groaned. "*Absolutely tender and full of flavor?* What are you? Some kind of damn radio ad? I got a stinking can of C-rations here and you're driving me crazy."

"After the war, you're coming to my ranch for Thanksgiving."

"Yeah, yeah, after the war. It will probably last a hundred frigging years the way the Japs fight and refuse to surrender. Them and their crazy code of *Bushido*."

Billy laughed. "A hundred years? Have a little faith, Johnny."

"In who? The Marines or God or the damn Empire of Japan?"

Billy laughed again and pulled off his boots. He hid his feet from his friend as he yanked off his socks because they were looking worse than they ever had, despite using Bud's "magic powder," sulfa, morning and night. Now that it was the rainy season, it never dried out between his toes. The pain was getting worse too. He thanked God they weren't pushing forward anymore and were digging in. He hoped they stayed in one place for at least a week.

Whether or not his hope had been a prayer, Billy could never say, but they stayed on the line at Point Cruz right through Christmas and New Year's and well into January 1943. There were jungle brawls on a small scale, infiltrators who were dispatched with Bowies and rifle butts and bare hands, patrols that reported lots of Japs dug into caves and ravines and hillsides and spoiling for a fight. But no push forward.

They'd heard the 1st Division was gone and had left the island to the US Army and the Hollywood Marines. They'd also heard the Army boys were having a hell of fight in the hills around the Matanikau on places called Sea Horse and Galloping Horse and the Gifu. Now and then the Marines could make out the *whump* and *crump* of distant explosions. The battles had been going on since December. The Marines wondered why they were still sitting on their cans while the Army was kicking butt. "*Ours not to reason why*," Bud quoted Tennyson, when the gunnys grumbled about it. "*Ours but to do and die.*" He went down the line handing out Atabrine in the never-ending fight against malaria. "You'll be back in action soon enough, men. And then you'll be swearing about that too."

"We just wanna get off this godforsaken island, Bud," someone would moan.

"Once the Japanese surrender, you'll be on your way to Tonga or Hawaii or Australia."

"They'll never surrender, Bud."

"So, we'll be here a bit longer than the 1st Div guys. Buck up. There are worse places to spend Christmas and Easter, Marine."

"Yeah, Doc? Where?"

"The North Pole." Bud would grin. "Only Santa and his rein-

deer like it there. Imagine if Tokyo Joe had invaded the
Arctic, hey?"

"At least we'd have Mrs. Claus to warm us up, Bud."

"Are you kidding, gunny? Mrs. Claus winters in Miami."

"Huh. Tain't funny, McGee."

Talk of Easter made everyone feel worse. How long was it
going to take to finish the brawl? Would they get pulled off like
the 1st Div and leave the island and the win to the Japs? That
stuck in every Marine's craw. None of them wanted to be on the
island. But now that they were in the fight, and buddies had died,
they wanted to see the Stars and Stripes snapping in the sea
breeze all over Guadalcanal, not the Rising Sun. To hell with the
Rising Sun. The Canal had to be an American victory. It had
to be.

"What about Easter, Billy?" Johnny asked the first week of
January. "You cowboys must've done a ham at Easter."

They were sitting in their holes under their ponchos in a
heavy rain. Two dead Japanese soldiers, that no one had dragged
away and buried because of snipers, were staring at them from 30
feet away. The thought of still fighting and dying in the jungle in
April was making everyone a little stir crazy: "Turn us loose to
finish the war or let us go home!" Dreaming about tables
groaning under roast pigs made Johnny feel a little better.

Billy was smoking his usual Player's underneath his poncho
as the rain banged and slapped against it. "Nah. Maybe that's
swell for some families, but we have bigger fish to fry in
Montana."

"Fish? What kinda fish?"

"Rainbow trout. Stuffed with corn flakes and bear and pan
fried in butter. Real butter. Not store-bought crap."

"Bear!"

"Bear's amazing, Johnny. You gotta stop living out of tins and
get some real food inside you. Nothing like bear fat to golden up
biscuits and breads and pie crusts. Mom won't use anything else.

And black bear steak with chives, and scallions, and wild mush-rooms, and wild garlic? Heaven! Two inches thick and drooling fat and flavor, Johnny!"

"Aw, shut up, will ya?"

"And the stuffed trout! The bear bacon, and corn flakes, and fat, and seasoning just comes together in your mouth like eternal life!"

"Shut up, I said! All I got is dog food in a can! Hell, even my dogs back home eat better than I do on Guadalcanal! Lousy C-rations!"

"You have an open invite to the Martens Ranch, Johnny."

"Yeah? You gonna teach me and Marjean and my kid to be cowboys?"

"You bet. Mennonite cowboys."

"Ha."

Billy described the ranch, the split rail fencing and Russell fencing—no barbed wire, which his father and grandfather hated—the horses, the beef cattle, the dairy cows, the rooster and the hens. Then he talked about the hills, and meadows, and high summer pastures for grazing. Then he went on and on about the Rockies, the snow-capped peaks, the purple flanks, the fall colors of the larch, the waterfalls, the frozen lakes in winter. Johnny didn't mind hearing about the wolf howl, the bull elk's bugle, the snort and *woof* of a grizzly, the wail of a loon. He didn't care if Billy talked all day and night about a world he'd never seen and maybe never would—it took him away from a battle that never seemed to end. Sure, he still wanted to fight, but it was coming on to six months in the same jungle and he wanted a change of scenery. If taking the rest of the Japs on single-handed could end it, Johnny was ready to lead the charge. He just needed the order to go. They all did.

Billy sensed the restlessness. It was there morning, noon and night. When he went out on patrols with the squad, it was running through the ranks, and when he returned, it was still simmering among the privates, and the non-coms, and among officers like Crandall and Rudebaker too. On the 10th or 11th of January, Bud came by at night and sat and watched until what he called the Menno Simons Marines swallowed their doses of Atabrine. Then he told Billy and Johnny the regiment would push forward sometime over the next couple of days. He'd been talking with Rudy, who had been talking with the new 2nd Div commander, Brigadier General DeCarre. It was no big deal letting the cat out of the bag since the news would be all over the division by morning. What the Menno Simons Marines wouldn't hear is there had been talk of relieving the 2nd Marine Regiment, the 2/2, before they got a chance to fire another shot on the Canal.

"What the hell is that all about?" demanded Johnny, suddenly aroused. "We've been slugging it out in the jungle since the beginning of October. We ain't been shirking our duty."

"That's the point. We've been on the front line for three months. About 100 days. It's too much. We've earned our spurs and then some."

"So, what are they going to do? Just shove us out to pasture?"

"No. They've decided the 2/2 will start the push inland while the 2/8 rolls up the Japs along the coast. It will mean using us as the Louisville Slugger for the first few days. But once we've broken the ice, they don't expect the Japs to last more than a week. That's the skinny. They must have some good info on Jap numbers and troop movements."

"Or not." Johnny had plunged into a bad mood boots first. "They'd better give us a frigging chance to do our part."

"We've done our part, Johnny. We've been on the line without a real break more than half the time the Marines have been on Guadalcanal."

"No. They gotta let us fire a parting shot."

"The 1st Div has already been relieved. You know that. They debarked weeks ago."

"I don't care about the Parris Island Rice Krispies boys. I care

about what folks think about us back home. I don't want the 2/2
to look like it's sneaking off the island dog tired and beat up. I
want us to fight, kick cans and bust Jap skulls. Then we can go.
Not before that."

"I told you. We're the Louisville Slugger for the final push.
We're the Big Bam. The Behemoth of Bust. The Sultan of Swat.
We're gonna break eggs, Johnny. Crack coconuts. Cut through the
green bamboo. We're it. The last tip of the last spear."

"Yeah? You'd better be right, Doc."

Bud made a face that Billy picked up as he struck a match to
light his cigarette. "I wish I was wrong. Maybe you want to make
war, Johnny. I just want to get you guys back home in one piece. I
don't want any more KIAs. I don't want to dump sulfa powder on
any more bullet or shrapnel wounds. I don't want to watch Father
McKean give any more Marines their Last Rites or hear Sergeant
Zarate whisper any more Hail Marys while a gunny from LA or
Spokane or Boise coughs up blood and guts and dies on me.
Okay? That's my prayer—over! I want it over! Fast. Now. Tomorrow. Be part of that for me, Johnny. Do that for your corpsman
and I'll buy you a cold beer in heaven."

Johnny smiled a small smile. "How about a cup of real coffee?
French roast?"

"Done. Just end the show. Send the Japs back to Rabaul or
Yokohama or Mount Fuji. Stop this crazy jungle war for me."

"Just give us the word, Ulysses," Johnny murmured, lighting
his own cigarette in a burst of fire that made his face a death
mask. "Just cut us loose."

On January 13th, a Wednesday, they did.

Crandall stood in front of X-Ray platoon, vigorously puffing
on one of his last three Cuban cigars.

"Finish it." A cloud of smoke and sparks. "We've been on his
hellhole since August. Now get us off it. But get the Japs off it first.
Finish it, men. Drop the curtain on this war. Run up the flag." He

smacked his fist into his palm. "Give them your own banzai. Run right over the enemy. Do it."

Billy, as sniper, took the point, eyes on the tops of the coconut trees. Johnny, BAR gunner, was right behind him.

The men of Nagasaki and Sapporo and Kyoto and Osaka were waiting.

30

MAS KIMORA

THE CORPSMAN

The fighting was already red hot by eight in the morning. It was that crazy Tulagi scramble again, the way we'd started in August, tons of ravines and caves and hills crawling with snipers and Nambu machine guns and—a new wrinkle for King Company—that ugly Jap knee mortar, the 50mm, with its distinctive *POP!* throwing bad news at us from 50 to 100 to 200 yards away. Garowski was down, peppered with mortar shrapnel, and Levy, and Over Easy Brian too, all within the first hour of combat as the boys rooted the enemy out of their holes yard by yard. They all lived, they all got Purple Hearts. But what an unholy mess. The combat intensity was insane. No wonder they wanted vets going in first before they brought up relief.

I didn't get any sleep the night before the Big Bam because I was rushing around with other corpsmen and getting all the meds organized. Gunnys were running meds to the front along with ammo and C-rations—sulfa powder, morphine, plasma, gauze, Mercurochrome, Atabrine, the kitchen sink. Now that the Navy was back, we had supplies galore. Once the shooting started, I didn't lack for syrettes or pressure bandages, I just needed another pair of hands. Fortunately, I had a lot of stretcher bearers at my disposal: "Get Brian back, get him back to the Battle Aid Station. Levy too. Double time. Then find me again. I'll need you in ten minutes. Probably less. Go. Go, go."

You have to know Johnny is everywhere, a holy terror, jamming his BAR into caves and emptying whole magazines of 30-caliber cartridges, lobbing grenades into ravines—he started a bush fire with one and the Japs ran out screaming, right into a wall of 50-caliber machine-gun bullets. He's giving cover to Stoneroad and Skillet too as they pump mortar bombs into spider holes and bunkers and chasms crammed with Japanese troops armed to the teeth. I'd heard Tokyo Joe was underfed and malnourished and dehydrated, sick as a tick, hardly able to lift his Arisaka 7.7x58mm and squeeze off the five rounds in its stripper clip. You could have fooled Achilles squad and X-Ray platoon—the men of Osaka and Yokohama were fighting like infuriated tigers, knocking our men down with killing fire second by second. I treated two Japs and sent them to the Battle Aid Station, even though my stretcher bearers grumbled about carrying them, and I have to say one was a bag of bones and open sores, yet still full of fight, while the other was as healthy as any of our gunnys. "You're going to be okay," I told Mister Fit, administering a shot of morphine, and squeezing his shoulder. He glared at me in fury: "Marine! Die! You die!"

Into the midst of this meat grinder, about 1330 hours, 1:30 in the afternoon, on the 13th, Johnny drags me out of earshot and gunshot of anyone else, hides us behind a huge banana tree dripping with jungle vines, lights a cigarette and says, "Bud, I got a Jap friend in Hawaii."

He could have shot me through the foot, the shock would have been about the same. "What?"

"I'm telling you straight, Doc. We were kids together, stateside. Then they up and moved to Hilo, on Big Island, you know, Hawaii."

"I know Hawaii, Johnny. Holy crap."

"We kept in touch. Last mail call, I got one from him. Didn't tell anyone. So, Hawaii didn't round up its Japanese. Hell, the Hilo side of Big Island is at least 80% Tokyo. Mas, that's his name, Mas Kimura, incredible guy, he says, *We Japanese-Americans are forming a military unit. Will know more in the new year. Maybe you and I can fight together.*"

I shook my head. "Not a chance, Johnny. It won't happen. FDR won't let our Japs fight Japanese Japs."

"We let our German and Italian boys fight Hitler and Mussolini's German and Italian boys in North Africa last fall."

"The Germans and Italians didn't bomb Pearl Harbor."

"Mas is a good guy, Bud, a really good guy. I don't mean good for a Jap, I mean just plain good, salt of the earth. We need guys like him to fight beside us—all the Japanese-Americans we can put in uniform, we gotta do it."

My head was spinning. "You don't make any sense to me, Johnny Mennonite Strange. One second you're gunning down Japs by the yard, the next you want them in X-Ray platoon, armed with Thompsons and helping us win the war in the Pacific."

"Our Japs, our Japanese, Bud, our Americans. Mas is a heck of a guy. If he vouches for the other American-born Japanese, then I know they're rock solid. They'd have to be."

"Johnny—"

"I can't tell the other guys about him, Bud. I can't. They'll say I'm a Jap lover. They won't trust me to have their backs anymore."

"I get that."

"And they'll never understand about Japanese-Americans fighting alongside us against the Japs from Japan. They'd never believe our Japs could be good American soldiers or Marines. Never. They'd think I was a traitor for spouting stuff like that. But I believe it, Bud. I know Mas is as much a patriot as I am. As much as Red Mike is, hell yes, or Chesty Puller."

"Why are you telling me all this now? Why are you telling me all this in the middle of a firefight?"

"In case... in case I buy it."

"What? When have you ever been worried about that?"

"It's the last go. The last battle. That's when the bullet can find you. The one with your name on it. Just before you make it home. You catch one in the gut."

"Johnny, look—"

"They're calling for a corpsman. You gotta go. And I have my own work to do. I just wanted you to know I'm not some Jap hater. I may act like it in combat, but I'm not, Bud. Sure, I'll tear my enemy to pieces. But not Mas. Not Japanese Americans like him. And he'd want me to fight. Just as rough as the Japanese fight. And he'd want me to win too. Because if he was fighting beside me today, he'd be fighting to win just as hard as I'm fighting to win. Maybe harder." Johnny laughed. "He really is the craziest guy, Bud. The most incredible guy. All American. As American as apple pie."

"I got it," I told him.

"Yeah?"

"For sure."

"And I'm okay, Bud? I'm not a bad Marine for sticking up for Mas and the others?"

I grinned. "No, you're not a bad Marine. You're a great Marine. And a great American." I slapped him on the arm. "So, go win the Battle of Guadalcanal and tell Mas Kimura all about what a hero you were."

I took off to help a couple of wounded Marines from Victor platoon on a hilltop. Johnny followed me, but not to give aid. He ran past, already firing from the hip, to link up with Billy, Julio Hernandez and his BAR, and Big Band Nick. They were pouring bullets into the black hole of a bunker.

I have to say I turned Johnny's conversation with me behind the banana tree over and over again throughout the day, wild and wooly as the day was. The battle was tough slugging, there were lots of casualties from the company, but no more from X-Ray.

Johnny didn't go down. Blood had worked itself under my skin until it looked like India ink. I stared at it and imagined Johnny shooting Japs with his Japanese American friend beside him also shooting Japs. The picture didn't fit, it didn't work.

But what if Johnny and Mas were right? What if we needed the troops and Congress gave the okay? What if they made Marines out of our Japanese Americans? What if the men from Hilo started knocking down the men from Osaka and Sapporo? What kind of war would that be? And what if Japanese Americans won the Medal of Honor? While family rotted behind barbed wire at internment camps on US soil? What did it all mean then?

This war is bigger than me, Lord, and it's a lot bigger than a war that's only about battlefields and killing. Where are we all going with this fight? Where are you going?

Some fighting went on after dark. The Japs loved night fighting and were convinced, for whatever reason, that we feared it. They were also convinced we disliked hand-to-hand combat, a form of fighting, samurais that they were, they felt they excelled at. Ours was a decadent culture, a prisoner told us, one of the few we ever got our hands on. Americans were soft and immoral and lazy, playboys and movie stars and gangsters. They had no principles, no code, no honor, nothing to fight for. I think Guadalcanal changed things around in their thinking. I'm pretty sure the Japanese felt differently about us in 1943 than they had in 1941 or '42. They certainly felt differently about us after that last drive to push them into the sea.

After almost six months of war, a part of me stopped thinking about what I was doing when I treated a wounded man. I knew what I was doing, yes, but a part of me stopped seeing what I saw, and a part of me stopped feeling what I felt. That's how I kept going. That's how the other Marines kept going too. They saw but did not see, they felt but did not feel. So, they could rise and kill again, day after day. And die. And take their wounds. And eat.

And sleep. And wake up to fight one more time. Just one
more time.

The battle sputtered to a stop about 0230 hours. The rain
clouds had cleared out and stars glittered bright and sharp like
the points of ten thousand knives. No one slept, or you'd sleep
forever—about a dozen from King Company were wounded
during the night. At sunrise, the bodies of 20 Jap infiltrators were
obvious and quickly buried before the heat and bugs got
to them.

Superman and Superman Too had been crouched by their 50
all night, one grabbing a few winks while the other watched. The
same went for Captain America and Batman on the 30, and
Stoneroad and Skillet on the 60mm mortar. We were down
Garowski, Leon Levy and Over Easy Brian, but we still had the
other new guys like Big Band Nick and Red O'Brien, so the squad
was strong. Worn and dirty, like a pair of good boots get worn and
dirty, but not finished. Not yet.

Johnny got me alone again, just as dawn was coloring the
jungle gold and red, something that should have been pretty, but
never was pretty on Guadalcanal. He was kind of obsessed about
what he'd told me, worried I'd tell someone else, worried he'd
spilled his guts beyond recovery, anxious about whether to write
Mas Kimura back, second guessing himself about whether
Japanese Americans should put on a uniform and fight for America. I gave him five minutes, all I had, because I needed to gear up
with fresh meds for the battle still ahead of us.

"Look, Johnny," I told him. "Everything you talked about
yesterday was good. I have no idea what Congress will do, but
there's no reason you can't write Mas back and say you believe in
him, you know, believe he's as much American as you or anyone
else that's a citizen of the United States, and that if they did let
him and his friends join a combat unit, you'd want it to be your
unit, the 2nd Battalion, 2nd Marines, your platoon, your squad.
Okay? Just do that. Keep in touch. You owe it to him. He opened

himself to you. Open up back. Tell him it's good, trying to get to a place where he can fight for the United States is good."

Johnny nodded. "I'll do that now. I'll write him and leave the letter with Father McKean to mail."

"Suit yourself. But I'm sure you'll be up to mailing it after this fracas is over."

He shrugged. "You never know, Bud. There'll be a lot of Jap bullets out there today."

I smiled. "Some things I do know, Johnny."

31

THE ENEMY WITHIN—NOV. 1942

JOHNNY STRANGE

Johnny Strange crouched down, his heart racing, and his insides stretched tight like the highest string on a piano. The dead Jap's leg still protruded into his foxhole, and Johnny took deep breaths to still the pounding in his chest as he wiped the man's blood from his Bowie onto his pants leg. The Jap had crawled up on him while he was answering a Nambu 92 that had somehow gotten into position to catch Achilles in a nasty crossfire. Johnny had just stopped firing to reload when he heard the padded rush of the Jap's feet coming. They said some guys developed a sixth sense in the jungle—the ability to step over the hidden trip wire, sense an incoming mortar shell, or step behind a tree just before that Jap sniper pulled the trigger, and in that instant Johnny knew it was true. He hadn't heard the Jap's soft sandaled steps coming; he knew he was coming.

Twisting to the right in his hole, he dropped his rifle. His mind told him to pull his knife, but to his surprise it was already in his hand and waiting. He looked up as the bayonet slid by him and jammed into the side of the hole right where he had been leaning to steady the BAR. The Jap, carried forward by the swiftness of his rush, slid forward over the edge of the hole and impaled himself on the upraised knife. Surprise twisted the man's features, and he tried to pull his own knife out, but Johnny ripped upward and then sideways, cutting through the man's intestines and up into his heart. The man's jaw worked and his eyes stared into Johnny's from inches away. "Maline, you... you..." and then he went limp, part of his intestines protruding from his split open uniform and blood flooding out of his open mouth.

Johnny gave a shove and threw the dead body off him, up and out of the hole. Then he slumped down and tried to collect himself. The last week had been hell, a gruesome montage of face-to-face encounters with Jap soldiers desperate to kill him. The Second Regiment had been dug in on a line west of the Matanikau River, supporting the Fifth Regiment from 1st Div. Then word came down that the Japs were landing troops on the eastern coast, and part of their force had hurried back to protect the approaches to Henderson field. To replace them the brass sent in the First Battalion of the 164th Army Regiment, and for the first time since Johnny had come over from Tulagi, gyrenes and doggies were fighting side-by-side. The Army guys were good fighters, tough, well-trained, and eager to show the Marines they weren't just Friday-night movie soldiers.

Sergeant Zarate had paid them a real compliment after the first few days of fighting. They had just flushed out a Jap patrol and one of the GIs had seen, not twenty feet away, three Japs and a nasty machine gun. The dog-face threw a grenade and wounded one of the Japs. Then he shot the second and dispensed with the third by running over and beating him over the head. As he headed back to their lines, Zarate had yelled out, "Where's the machine gun?" The guy had turned around, gone back into the jungle and pulled the gun from behind its log barrier, then hauled it back. Zarate looked at Johnny and grinned as they watched the guy trudge through the mud with the heavy 30-caliber slung over his shoulder.

"Shit, Johnny. Some of these guys could almost be Marines."

Since then, the fighting had disintegrated into a series of brutal confrontations. The Japs tried their best but for the first time since they sent their Imperial Army into the Solomon Islands they knew the bitter taste of being forced back step-by-step from ground they had claimed for the Emperor only a few months before. So Banzai charges and suicide attacks filled the first two weeks of November as the Japs tried to regain what the Marines had won from them at such great cost. Now Johnny sat in the foxhole, shaking. The hand-to-hand with the Jap soldier had brought home to him powerfully the razor edge he walked every day.

"Hey Strange, you okay?" It was Zarate, calling from the next hole down.

"Yeah, Sarge, okay. The Jap got close, but no cigar."

There was a muffled explosion, and then Zarate yelled again. "A guy from 1st just took out that machine gun and it looks like the rest of them have gone off to lick their wounds. Smoking lamp is lit."

Johnny looked down at his hands. They shook like leaves in a storm. *This is new, what's the deal?*

He reached for a Camel and found that the bayonet had torn away the button on his shirt.

Crap, I almost got stabbed again.

He pulled out a smoke and lit it up. What was so bad about killing this guy? And then he knew. The guy had looked just like Mas Kimura. The realization shook Johnny.

Man, I'm all mixed up. I can't worry about killing every yellow-skinned soldier because they remind me of Mas.

And then for the first time in a long time he heard the voice—the voice inside his head.

It's not the color of the skin that makes them your enemy, Johnny.

"What?" It surprised him. The voice had been so clear he answered it out loud. It came again.

It's not the color of the skin that makes them your enemy, Johnny.

"What are you talking about?"

It's what's in the heart that makes a man evil. For out of the heart come evil thoughts, murders, adulteries, fornications, thefts, false witness, slanders...

He remembered that verse. His dad used to quote it.

"What do I need to hear this stuff for?"

You need to understand that the battle is not with the Japs...

"What?"

None is righteous, no, not one; no one understands; no one seeks for God. All have turned aside; together they have become worthless; no one does good, not even one...

"So we're all evil, is that what you're saying?"

Yes!

"Hey Strange, who ya talking to?" It was Sergeant Zarate again.

"Nobody, Sarge, nobody. Just shaking it off over here."

––––––––––

Two hours later Bud came down the line, checking his boys. When Johnny saw him, he called out. "Hey, Bud!"

Bud dropped into the hole and pulled out a smoke. "What's up, Johnny boy?"

Johnny shook his head. "I'm not sure, Bud. Did you see the dead guy outside my hole?"

"Yeah. Dispatched to the great nothingness that all followers of the Emperor find when you spit them on the end of your Bowie."

"Yeah, that's fine, but this one shook me up."

"Whatta ya mean?"

"Remember, I told you about Mas Kimura?"

"Yeah, what of it?"

"The guy looked just like Mas. It set me back. I can't go

through the rest of this war thinking about Mas every time I blow one of these Gooks away."

"No, that would hinder your usefulness as a BAR man."

"But there's something else, Bud."

"What, Johnny."

"I heard the voice."

"The voice?"

"Yeah, you know, the inside one, the little one."

"Oh, that voice." Bud smiled. "So?"

"I haven't heard it for a long time… ever since Jenkins… well you know. I used to hear it all the time when I was a kid, but I haven't for a long time."

"What did it say, Johnny?"

"It said, '*It's not the color of the skin that makes them your enemy.*'"

Bud smiled again. "Ah-hah. God takes us to the woodshed on Guadalcanal."

Johnny scowled. "What are you talking about, Bud?"

"Don't you get it, Johnny? You thought about Mas Kimura for a reason. God set you up."

"Set me up?"

"Yeah. He's showing you something, something important."

"Why would God show me anything, Bud?"

"Because he wants you to go home to Marjean and little John, a different man. He wants you to bring something back from this war you can pass on to your son and he can pass it on to his son."

"What's that, Bud?"

"Look, Johnny. We're out here fighting these guys from Japan. They all have yellow skin and they all look the same, so it's easy to know who the enemy is. But what about your Buddy, Mas? He's not a Jap, he's an American."

"I don't get it, Bud."

"For us, a Jap isn't a guy with yellow skin, it's an idea—the idea that one country can subjugate another country, rape the women, kill the men and lord it over everybody. So anybody who carries that idea in their head and their heart in this part of the world is a Jap. And because they carry this idea in their heads and try to put it into action, they sent us out here to change their minds. But these guys have the idea so planted in them they can't get rid of it, so to prevent them from infecting the world, or imposing their idea on everyone else, we kill them, get it?

"Kind of. So you're saying that a Jap isn't a Jap because they have yellow skin, they're a Jap because of what they believe?"

"Right. Your buddy, Mas, is an American of Japanese ancestry, but he's no Jap. He's an American. And if they give him and his friends in Hawaii the chance, I'm betting they will prove that they are nowhere near being Japs."

"So we're not killing Japanese guys, we're killing Japs, Japs who are infecting the world with a disease?"

"Now, you're with me, Johnny boy. Think of it this way. A Jap, or a Hun, or a Mongol, or a Saracen, or a Roman, or Hitler... what's the difference? No difference, Johnny. They all had the same idea. And so guys like you and me, guys who believe men should live in peace, and treat each other with respect, and leave each other alone to live their own lives, guys like us, we sign up and put on a uniform and get a gun and we stand up to these bastards and tell them they can't pull their crap in the world anymore."

"So I came out here for the wrong reasons?"

"Yeah, in the beginning, but you've changed. I've watched you grow up."

"And when I got the picture from Marjean, it pushed me in the other direction?"

"That's right. And that's why you must live through this, Johnny. You will be a different man when you get home, a real man, a man who will help make this world a better place to live in."

Johnny sat without speaking for a long time. Then he looked

up at Bud, his face wet with tears. "That's good stuff, Bud, real good."

"Yeah and there's something else, Johnny."

"What's that, Bud."

"The little voice that's giving you the information? You know who that is, right?"

Johnny looked at Bud for a long time. "Yeah, Bud. I know who that is."

Just then, a series of explosions rocked the hole. Johnny heard Crandall yell, "Mortars!"

Then came the dreaded cry. "Corpsman! Corpsman!"

Bud smiled. "Gotta go, Johnny. Just think about it." Bud raised up to leave and then turned back. "And remember who you're killing and why. Lucky for us, they are easy to spot. When we get back home, it won't be so easy. That's why God's tuning us up out here."

And then Johnny was alone in the foxhole.

32

THE PURPLE HEART MARINES

BILLY MARTENS

It had just rained, and now the sun was coming back out. Sweat began rolling down his face instead of raindrops. Creeping from coconut tree to coconut tree, he winced every third or fourth step—Billy's feet were worse than they'd ever been. Still, he had a job to do and a duty to perform for his platoon. Bud still hadn't ordered him out of the combat zone, for which he was grateful, and now he had another chance to prove to the corpsman the decision had been the right one.

X-Ray was pinned down. Which meant King Company was pinned down. Which meant the Regiment couldn't advance. One sniper had done all this, and even after half an hour, Billy hadn't been able to spot him. Two men from Hades squad were KIA and one from Titan. Corporal Navarro and Julio Hernandez, the BAR gunner, were down and had been stretchered back. Gunnys were calling Achilles the Purple Heart Marines.

Billy felt responsible and didn't want anymore dead or wounded on his watch. So, he was making a wide circle through the jungle, hoping to pick up a muzzle flash from a different angle. He'd asked Johnny to give him ten minutes and then try to draw fire. He wasn't where he wanted to be when a sharp crack made him jump. The shooter was close. He scanned the treetops, but couldn't see anything, not a body and not a wisp of gun smoke. He prayed Johnny would do something else after realizing he hadn't heard the bark from Billy's 1903 that meant he'd taken out the sniper. Thirty or forty seconds went by.

Crack. Crack. Two shots, one on top of the other. Whatever Johnny had done had caught the sniper's attention. And had been the sniper's first mistake. Because Billy saw the flash of the second shot. And then he saw a boot. His eyes found the sniper high among coconut fronds. He edged closer, not taking his eyes off his enemy. The Jap's buddies had roped him right into the tree, wrapping him around his midsection five or six times. He'd never get free of that, and Billy knew he didn't intend to. He had made his choice to die holding off the Marines for the glory of the Emperor.

"Corpsman! Corpsman!"

The cry made Billy's body cringe. Had they had hit Johnny? The butt of his 1903 was tight into his shoulder. He exhaled, lined up his iron sights, ignored a fat drop of sweat that was rolling down his nose and itching like crazy, exhaled again, and squeezed. His body absorbed the recoil. The Jap's leg burst open.

Frantically, the sniper swung the barrel of his Arisaka where he thought Billy might be and fired. He missed by ten feet. Billy squeezed off another round. The sniper's body slumped, dangling from the rope tied around his body. His rifle fell into the jungle below. Billy kept his firearm on target. Once before, a Jap sniper had played dead and then tossed two grenades on the Marines as they crept past. Billy had no wish to repeat that experience. He aimed at the sniper's head and fired once more. And that was that. He lowered his bolt action.

"SNIPER'S OUT!" Billy yelled.

Later, he would remember that as the last shot he fired on Guadalcanal. He waited a few minutes, worried as hell that they had hit Johnny, but watching to see if any other Japs opened up on his squad as it moved forward. Nothing happened. And the squad didn't move forward either. Confused, he was planning to make his way back when the jungle moved with a crawling body. And a Marine helmet. And a familiar face.

"Johnny!" he hissed. "What the hell? Why isn't the platoon moving up?"

Johnny shook his head. "We're pulling out."

"What?"

"We're being relieved. All of 2/2."

"Why?"

"Shit, buddy, you heard Bud a few days ago. We've been on the line three months. Even I could use a hot bath and room service. Hey. I'm happy. We had our last boxing match with the Japs and did good. Come on. We're humping back a mile, and then the trucks will take us to the coast. We're done."

"I was worried you were hit."

"Nah. Not me. Zarate helped me draw fire and took one to the shoulder. Kinda just nicked him though, so he'll be okay. Purple Heart Marines, right?"

"Right."

<hr />

THE 2ND BATTALION 6TH MARINES REGIMENT, 2/6, WAS MARCHING up to the line as the 2/2 were being trucked out. Billy gave a few thumbs up to the gunnys. Then he slumped in his seat. He'd had no idea how tired he was until he gave himself permission to relax for the first time since the beginning of October. Now his whole body felt like it was falling apart. Even the ache in his feet couldn't keep him from letting his head droop down onto his chest and sway with the swings and swerves of the truck. At the beach, there was a hole for him already dug out by other Marines who'd slept there before heading inland, but he didn't crawl into it. Just laid down with his 1903 and his Thompson and slept.

The rain fell, and he didn't care. Let it. He didn't have anywhere to go. Crandall was saying how proud he was of the platoon, and Rudebaker was saying the same thing about the company. Billy smiled and slipped into a deeper sleep. He wanted to say, "Wake me up when we're back in Tonga," but his lips stopped working. Johnny told him later that he slept 36 hours straight.

They relieved the 2nd Marines on Thursday the 14th. When the came on line the 6th Marines found that the 2nd had broken the Japs wide open and the fresh men had no trouble driving the enemy back. The fighting ended on Sunday when they trapped their foe between themselves and the 8th Marines and the coast. They killed hundreds of Japanese troops. They captured only two.

The Army continued its battles in the hills around the Matanikau River. Johnny was smoking cigarettes and telling Billy the dogfaces were fighting hard and heavy, just like the Marines: "We ought to make them honorary gunnys." Billy had almost stopped speaking by then, a week after they had been relieved, because he didn't feel he had anything left to say on Guadalcanal —he just let Johnny do all the talking for the two of them. He could tell his friend was worried, but Billy didn't know how to explain what was going on inside his head. Johnny was conspicuously absent one evening when Father McKean showed up.

"How are you doing, corporal?" the padre asked, sitting down next to Billy and his foxhole.

It surprised Billy both to see him and to sense a kind of withdrawal from the chaplain growing inside himself. "I'm okay, Father."

"Want a Lucky Strike? I've got a tent full of them."

"Sure. Why not?"

Father McKean lit it for him with his USN Zippo. "I guess you'll be glad to get off Cactus."

Billy inhaled the smoke for several long seconds before exhaling. "Everyone's glad to get off Cactus. I'll bet the Japs don't even want to be here anymore."

"I'll bet not."

They sat together and smoked in silence. Marines moved back and forth all around them, but the two men were staring at the sunset and weren't distracted. Clouds were purple and gold while the sea itself was scarlet. Billy liked the colors. Not much else. He wished the chaplain would leave.

"Miss home, Billy?" asked McKean.

Billy groaned to himself. Now he was sure he'd been set up by Johnny or Crandall. He'd clammed up since the last Jap sniper he'd killed, and Johnny had bugged him more than once about being too quiet. Probably afraid Billy was cracking up. Billy knew he was fine... okay, maybe not fine, but far from feeling like going berserk. He was exhausted, that was all. Every part of him wanted to sleep for a million years.

"Billy?"

Billy shook his head. "Sorry, Father. No confessional for me tonight. You don't have to worry about me. I'm not heading out to sea and leaving my boat on shore. I have nothing to say. I've killed my last human being, at least, my last human being on Guadalcanal, and I'm more than okay about that."

"More than okay you killed him or more than okay he was the last one you're going to kill?"

"Oh, I'll kill more, padre. A lot more. Just on other islands. See, I know the strategy for this war, I figured it out for myself. We go from island to island and capture airfield after airfield. Pretty soon we're on top of Japan and bombing the crap out of the divine Emperor. Then we go ashore there too. None of them will ever surrender so none of us will ever stop killing them. Including me. Killer Billy. I and my rifle are insatiable. My father would be ashamed of me. Actually, he already is. If he knew how many men I'd shot to death in the past six months, he'd be even

more ashamed. He'd cut me out of the will. Hire the sheriff to bar
me from the ranch."

"Is that eating you?"

"Me? Nah. Maybe back on Tulagi. Or Bloody Ridge. But now?
I used to keep count of the souls I'd taken, and I lost count during
the last battle for Henderson Field. What my father thinks about
me isn't a big deal anymore. I've kind of gone blunt inside. My
conscience is clear."

"Is it?"

"Yes, Sir. Yours is. You're sending us all into the killing zone
with your blessing. If your conscience is clear, and God's too,
mine sure as hell should be."

"Scuttlebutt has us drying out in New Zealand."

"I heard Australia or Tasmania."

The padre shook his head. "The safe bet is New Zealand."

"Truth is, Sir, I never heard of the place until we met Kiwis
on Tonga."

"Well, I hope you got along with the Kiwis, Marine, because
I'm sure you'll be seeing a lot of them. Maybe even get yourself
a girl."

Billy laughed. "Hey. That felt good. I haven't laughed in
weeks. Maybe I need it more than I need sleep." He stubbed out
his cigarette on the side of his naked foot without flinching. "No
girls for me, Father. Don't need the heartache. I have no deSire
for friendship with the opposite sex. It would be much, much
better if I could just get out and hunt something that wasn't
human. Like a doe. Or a stag. Or a wild pig. Do they have wild
pigs in New Zealand?"

"I honestly don't know."

"Because that would be the ticket, Father. That would be the
train I'd hop on. And never get off. Hunting game in forests and
jungles for eternity. I wouldn't even have to catch them or shoot
them. I'd be happy just to track them. Only one rule—four legs.
They all have to have four legs."

McKean stood up. "Maybe you'll be offered that opportunity. I hope so. Sounds like you need it."

"It's all I need, padre. Food that isn't out of a tin of C-rations, some fresh air, clean water, and a thousand miles of wilderness. With no human beings anywhere nearby. That'll fix me. In case you were worried about how to fix me."

Johnny showed up when it was dark and raining. "Saw you with the priest."

"Yeah?"

"How'd that go?"

"Not anywhere he wanted it to go."

"What do you mean?"

"I mean he wants me to find God and a wife. And I'd rather lose myself in a jungle where there are no Japs to kill and just track deer and fry up venison over an open fire. Until next time he blesses me and sends me out to hunt humans and shoot them. Yes, Sir, until then, I just want to be left alone in the mountains. Does New Zealand have mountains, Johnny?"

"I don't know. I heard we're heading to Hawaii."

"McKean has us in Kiwi Land."

Johnny shrugged. "Wherever we dock is where we'll be. I just wish it was San Diego."

"I'll bet." Billy lit another cigarette from the pack the padre had left with him. "Hey, Johnny?"

"Yeah?"

"Don't ever send a sky pilot to hold my hand again."

33

THE LIGHT AT THE END OF THE TUNNEL—JANUARY 1943

THE CORPSMAN

"Sniper's out!"

I heard Billy yell from over on the left after the second bam from his 1903 echoed through the trees. Good, now I could go back to work. Over by the tree on my right, I hear Sergeant Zarate mumbling words in Basque. I think they are cuss words, but I'm not sure. I'd seen him go down when he and Johnny were drawing enemy fire so Billy could get to the guy who's had us pinned for half an hour. So once Billy cleared the tree, I got up and ran over.

"How ya doin', Sarge?"

Zarate looked up at me with a sheepish grin. "Damn it, Bud. I thought I would get off this Island in one piece."

There was blood on his shoulder so I popped open his shirt and looked. "Well, you can stop dreaming about going stateside, Sarge. This one might not even get you a purple."

"What about Navarro and Julio?"

"Well, they took one for the team but nothing serious. Julio got one in the fleshy part of his leg and he's bleeding like a stuck pig, but all the arteries are intact so he'll be up and around in a week. Navarro, I have to look at closer but not too close. He had turned around to tell Johnny something, and the Jap shot him right in the keister. Only thing I worry about is that Navarro is so thin it might have broken his butt bone."

Zarate tipped his head back and laughed. It was a satisfying sound because I hadn't heard my boys laughing in weeks. No, they had been a far different lot than the fun-loving boys who had splashed ashore in August. Worn down by the constant air attacks and the nightly shelling from the Jap ships out in the Slot, thin as scarecrows from the dysentery and malaria, these guys had shed their youth along with their pounds as they faced down a determined enemy in the stinking jungle and whipped him good. I was proud of my boys.

Things were different now on Cactus. The troopships that once came to Guadalcanal full of Marines now came empty and steamed away, filled with time-expireds. When we heard the First Division had left, we felt abandoned. That had been in December, and since then we had been mopping up. The problem with the Japs is that for every one we kill there always seems to be three more to take their place. It reminds me of a story I read about Cadmus, a guy in Greek mythology who killed a dragon and, on instructions from Athena, planted its teeth. From every tooth a soldier grew up, each one of them filled with hate and Cadmus had to kill all but one. That one he kept around to help build his new city. That's what the Japs are like. You can't capture them, you can't get them to surrender—I mean they will let their buddies tie them into a tree so they won't run away when the Marines come. I think they know their time is up on Cactus. You'd think they would just throw down their rifles and walk into Henderson with their hands up. But if that's what you think, you got another think coming.

The Marines in our squad fight like raiders, on the ground and in the bush. The Japs, in their split-toe sneakers, crawl through the trees, or come looking for any little hole in our line so they can sneak in and kill someone. I can't tell you how many times they have called me out to a listening post to find one of our guys with his throat cut. The heavy action stopped when Vandegrift pulled us back to a ridge just beyond the Matanikau. I guess they figured that the fight was over and there was no way the Japs would kick us off the island, and I appreciated that because it means fewer of my guys going home in body bags. I even hoped my guys could relax, but this is a different war with a different tension and it affects my guys in different ways.

Now that the Japs have retreated into the jungle, the Brass have been sending out seek-and-destroy patrols. Our guys go out every day and night. It's been like an Indian war fought out there in the dark rotten heart of Guadalcanal, in the black deadly nights—a war of sudden ambushes in which you might see the flash of the knife that's reaching out of the darkness to kill you or you might not. This is not a battle of Banzai charges anymore; it's one-on-one where a shot or the gurgle of blood or the soft padding of feet running away into the dark might follow the sudden rustle in the bushes. It strings our boys as tight as a cat in a room full of dogs.

Interesting thing though is that I always thought Billy was the stable one, and that Johnny was the one most likely to implode. But that's changed. Billy's different. Now he goes about his job with a grim determination, and he doesn't drop by the Sunday services anymore. He's short with me and he doesn't want to hear about Ulysses, or the journey, or about God. Billy goes off by himself when we are on break and cleans his gun. He keeps that rifle so clean you could suck spit off it. Hours and hours he's taking it apart and putting it back together, checking the sights, sighting it in. I'm worried about the kid.

Now Johnny, he seems to have found himself. When he came out here, he had a lot of hate in his heart. Hate for the guy who molested him, hate for the church that turned a blind eye, hate for his dad who took the guy's word above his own son's, and hate for the God who let it happen. But now he's different. I was talking to him one day about a week ago. He pulled out that picture and showed me again. I never tire of looking at it. And then I thought of something.

"Hey, Johnny, do you know how I know God loves you?" He looked at me and then said he didn't. I looked him in the eye. "He gave you Marjean and Little John."

Well, I saw the penny drop. Johnny stared at the picture. A sheepish grin came on his face and then he said, "Yeah, Bud, maybe you're right." Since then I've seen a little change. Oh, he still goes about his business, but it's like he's become a professional. We have a job to do, and he's doing it. I don't see that crazy recklessness he used to show where he wanted to get as close to Japs as he could so he could shoot them or stab them or just beat them to death with his fists. Now he stays cool under fire, always knows where the focus is, keeps his guys covered with that BAR and pays attention. I'm proud of the guy.

RIGHT AFTER OUR FIGHT TODAY, THE WORD CAME DOWN. THEY ARE pulling us out. Just like that, the fight is over for the 2/2. We're headed back to camp and the amazing thing is, it's twenty miles away. That's how far we pushed the perimeter.

I'M WATCHING THE GUYS STOW THEIR STUFF AND PACK THEIR seabags and looking around at the guys who made it through. Of the original squad there are only eight of us left—Sergeant Zarate, Jesus Navarro, Johnny Strange, Julio Hernandez, Ricky Garowski, Leon Levy, Billy Martens and me. We all look like crap —scarecrow thin and walking around like old men. We have cracked and furrowed skin and our eyes are a movie newsreel of all the horrible days and nights we survived. I got Billy to let me work on his feet now, since he can keep them dry. What a mess. I don't know how the guy took the pain, but that's what happened to these guys. When the Navy turned tail and ran the second day, we were on Cactus and left us to fend for ourselves, it put steel in our spines and sand in our guts. There isn't a guy here who would back down from anything. I'd hate to be a drug-store cowboy back in the States who tried to mess with these guys when they get home and become well.

The transports are waiting off the beach and the scuttlebutt is that our destination is Hawaii or New Zealand or even home. Me, I want to go back to Tonga. There's a certain someone who's waiting for me there, a beautiful brown-skinned girl who makes the stars dim in the sky when she smiles. I got a letter from her the other day.

Dear Bud,

Yesterday I visited the soldier hospital and helped the doctors there. They had a lot of men to take care of and I thought of you, my Corpsman. I've been thinking more about our deserted island—the one where we will sit in the warm sun and listen to the voice of Tané calling from beyond the reef. Where we will sit beneath the Southern Cross and watch our children grow up...

THAT'S WHERE I TOOK A BIG GULP. SHE WANTS TO BE WITH ME forever; she wants to have my kids. I'm torn because I always thought I'd get back home to Ritzville. But then I think about it. Ritzville is a little armpit town in the middle of the great rolling empty of the Inland Empire in Washington State. The only water is miles away, up by Spokane or over by the Tri-Cities. I mean, a lot of nothing. Yeah, I'd like to see my dad again, but then I think about that flashing brown body slipping by me in the warm tropical water, the soft lips that seared their way into my heart forever, the white sand and the blue water, and then I hear it.

Don't be a dope, Bud. Get your butt back to Tonga as fast as you can.

...TONIGHT THE STARS ARE CLEAR AND BRIGHT, BUD. THE RAINS CAME this afternoon with dark clouds, but then the clouds went away and it reminded me that sometimes I get afraid. I fear the enemy will hurt you or even kill you and my heart is dark, but then the sun or the moon comes back and I remember that there is always the dawn after the darkest night. Please come back.

Kalasia

I have to wonder, is Kalasia my Penelope, or is she my Calypso? So, I go to the only guy I know who's been around the quad. I find him at the mess hall getting some decent chow. I plop down beside him and pop it right out.

"Hey Johnny, how do you know if a girl is the one, I mean the right one?"

Johnny looks at me with a weird look, and then his face splits in a big grin.

"You're asking me?"

"Yeah, well, you're the guy with a real girl and a son and everything. I'm a little confused, being unencumbered with any previous knowledge on the subject of girls and love."

"Thought you had an inside track, Philo."

Now Johnny only calls me Philo when he wants to get under my skin. And he succeeds.

He grins again. "Kalasia?"

"Yeah, Kalasia."

"What do you want to know?"

"Kalasia wants me to come back to Tonga when I'm done with my tour and stay there—like marry her and raise a family."

"And how do you feel?"

"I don't know, I think the thought scares me. I mean, is she my girl or is she like the Siren that's calling from the rocks—like Calypso who kept Ulysses tied down for nine years when all he wanted was to get home to Penelope?"

"Close your eyes, Bud."

"What?"

"Close your eyes."

"Are you going to clobber me?"

"Naw, just close your eyes and think about Kalasia."

"Okay."

"What do you see?"

Well I saw the incredible paradise that was Tonga, and the blue sea, and the white sand and then her face—the face that, had it been in Troy, would have launched a thousand ships. I saw the lips raised for a kiss, I almost felt the smooth skin under my hand, I...

My eyes popped open. Johnny was looking at me. He grinned again.

"Don't be a dope, Bud."

Now where had I heard that before?

34

A BAG OF WINDS—JANUARY 1943

JOHNNY STRANGE

C *rack... zing!*
  "Sniper! Sniper!"
The sound of the shot echoed off the rocky wall of the ravine they had just emerged from. The brass had ordered a regimental push after 2/2 smashed the Japs in the Matanikau tussle, but they had bottlenecked in this narrow pass through the hills, and now the enemy had them pinned down. Johnny ducked behind a boulder and to his left Billy Martens huddled behind a banyan tree. The rest of X-ray hunkered down and spread out. The bottleneck locked Zebra Company in the ravine, unable to move.

Crack... zing!

Another shot whistled past Johnny's head.

Arisaka 99, heavier round...

They lay there trying to get a line on the sniper.

"Julio, can you see him!"

"No, dammit! He's up ahead and to the left I think!"

"Do you see him, Billy?"

"No, I can't eyeball him yet."

Johnny lay still, peering out from behind the rock.

Crack... zing!

Johnny jerked back and cursed as a splinter of rock drew blood from his cheek.

That was close!

Navarro was behind the same banyan as Billy. Johnny watched as he turned to say something to Billy.

Crack... zing!

Navarro was down, clutching his butt. "Corpsman, Corpsman!"

Crack... zing!

Another shot, another cry!

Johnny hissed at Billy. "We gotta do something, Billy. Our boys are going down."

"Okay, Johnny. You and Zarate put covering fire into that clump up ahead. See it? One hundred yards, sight left, a heavy tangle of brush in the trees."

"Yeah, I think so."

"I will work around to the left and see if I can get a flash or some smoke."

Crack... zing!

Johnny yelled at the rest of X-ray. "You guys make some noise over there. Give us some breathing room!"

The guns of X-ray opened fire. Sergeant Zarate looked at Johnny and nodded. Together they crawled to the banyan where Navarro lay.

"Jesus, you okay?"

"Yeah, I think so." There was a rustle in the grass behind them, and Bud's head appeared. He slithered forward. "C'mon, Buddy, let's get you out of here." He grabbed Jesus under the arms and dragged him away. Johnny and Zarate watched at Navarro's boots disappeared into the tall grass. Johnny pointed.

"Billy's gone left. He think's the guy is in those trees there, but I haven't seen a flash or any smoke."

Billy's voice floated back. "Cover!"

Zarate grinned. "Let's put the hammer down." He opened fire

with his Thompson, shedding the leaves in the clump ahead. Johnny got his BAR lined up and walked his shots across the face of the covert. BAM! BAM! BAM! BAM!

He still couldn't see anything, so he put his back against the tree and stood up. He peered around the tree.

Crack... zing!

Splinters flew and as Johnny spun away his pocket flew open and his wallet flew out.

Marjean!

Without thinking, he stepped forward to pick it up. Something hit him from behind and shoved him forward.

Crack... zing!

There was a muffled curse and Zarate hit the ground next to him. His shirtsleeve showed bright red blood.

"Damn!"

"Sarge!"

"Dumb move, Johnny. I thought you were smarter than that."

Johnny stared at Zarate.

That 58 had my name on it!

"Sarge! I..."

"Stow it, Strange. Just don't do it again."

"Corpsman! Corpsman!"

"I'm okay, Johnny just put some fire on that bastard."

Bud's voice came through the grass. "Who's hit?"

"Zarate!"

"Don't worry about me, Bud. It's a scratch."

"Okay. I got three down, Julio's one. I'll come get you when I can."

Billy again. "Hey, what's the hold up, guys!"

"Look after those guys them, Bud. Johnny and I gotta go to work."

Again the hammer of the Thompson and the heavier bark of the BAR cut through the jungle. They kept at it, moving their shots around to keep the Jap off balance. Johnny had an idea. He grabbed off his helmet and, using a stick that was lying nearby, pushed it out from behind the tree.

Crack... zing!

Crack... zing... peowwww!

The BAM... BAM... of the 1903 followed the sound of the slug ricocheting off the helmet. The jungle went quiet. Then, one more BAM!

"SNIPER'S OUT!"

Johnny rolled over. Zarate was cussing, an intriguing mix of English and Basque. Just then Bud crawled up. "Where's Billy?"

"Up there." Johnny nodded.

"Go, get him. We're pulling out."

"What?"

"We're time-expireds, Johnny; we're getting off Cactus."

THE TWENTY MILES BACK TO HENDERSON WAS A WALK IN THE PARK. Oh, yeah, they still had to watch out for Japs, but the guys were smiling and nodding at the Doggies heading in the direction the Gyrenes were coming from.

"Give'em hell, Doggies!"

The army boys were smiling and nodding, too.

"Hey, Gyrene, they sending you dumb bastards back to Hollywood?" But this time they gave us good-natured kidding, the kidding of men who have met the enemy together and shared the same trenches. Everybody knew what the 2/2 had done on Cactus.

"SARGE, YOU SAVED MY LIFE."

Zarate looked up from the cot where he was resting. "Yeah, well just don't make a dumb move like that again. How stupid would it have been for you to get killed the last day on this God-forsaken island?"

"I don't know what I was thinking. I dropped her picture and..."

"Well, maybe you should stow it in your gear and not carry it in the field. You're too good to lose, Strange."

"Thanks, Sarge I..."

"You owe me, Johnny."

JOHNNY HEADED OVER TO THE MESS TENT TO GET SOME CHOW. That's where Bud caught up with him. Johnny was expecting a lecture, but then he could see something troubled Bud. He laid a letter out on the table and looked at Johnny.

"Spit it out, Bud."

"Hey Johnny, how do you know if a girl is the one, I mean the right one?"

Johnny looked at Bud and grinned.

"You're asking me?"

"Yeah, well, you're the guy with a real girl and a son and everything. I am feeling a little confused being unencumbered with any previous knowledge of the subject of girls and love."

"Thought you had an inside track, Philo."

Johnny knew Bud didn't like being called Philo, and he could see it rankled him. So Johnny grinned again and explained the ways of women to Bud. After he got Bud on the right track, he asked him a question.

"What's the scuttlebutt? Where are we going?"

"I don't know, Johnny. Some say Hawaii, some say New Zealand, some say we might even go stateside. It all depends on the winds."

"Winds?"

Johnny knew he shouldn't have asked because Bud was an ear beater when he got going.

"Yeah, winds. See, Ulysses…"

"Not that guy again."

"Look Johnny, General Price gave that poem to Billy for a reason. For me, it's been like the north star."

"Okay, so what about the winds?"

"Well when Ulysses left the Island of Circe, he ended up on the Island of Aeolus, the god of the winds. Aeolus made Ulysses tell him the story of the Trojan War and was so entertained by it he promised Ulysses a fair wind to take him home to Ithaca. He also gave him a bag that had all the contrary winds in it. He made Ulysses promise he would guard the bag because if any of the contrary winds got out, it would blow Ulysses off course. So Ulysses tied up the bag and set out for home."

"What's that got to do with me?"

Bud smiled. "A lot. See, today you almost let the contrary winds out of the bag."

"Bud, what in the hell are you talking about?"

"Ulysses stayed awake for many days and nights, guarding the bag. The ship sailed on under the fair wind Aeolus had given. Just when they were in sight of Ithaca, Ulysses fell asleep. I mean, they could see home on the horizon."

Bud had Johnny's interest now. "So what happened?"

"Some of Ulysses' guys decided that maybe their captain had hidden treasure or something in the bag so they took a peek. When they opened the bag, a foul wind came out and blew them all the way back to Aeolus' Island. Well, it ticked Aeolus off and he wouldn't give Ulysses any more fair winds. So they spent the next ten years wandering around from island to island, going through many terrible times, trying to catch a fair wind home."

"Where do I fit in, Bud?"

"Well, I heard you almost bought it today by making a stupid mistake. Just like Ulysses' crew, you weren't thinking. Now, you've

changed a lot since we got here and you've gotten great at what
you do. When you came out here, you were crazy. Now you're just
a crazy good soldier. You're under a fair wind, Johnny. God is
blowing you home to Ithaca and Penelope and Telemachus.
Don't let the bad wind out of the bag."

Dear Marjean,

    *They have relieved us, and we're leaving Guadalcanal. I don't
know where they are sending us, but anywhere but here is fine with
me. Well, the best would be to be home with you and Little John, but I
don't know when that will be. I love you and miss you, and I thank
God that I lived through this. Marjean, I want to ask something. I
know when I left home, I was far away from God, but things have
changed and I think I know God loves me, because now I have you and
John Albert and I know you are a gift from Him. So I will start something new, something I haven't done for a long time—pray. I will pray
for you and John Albert and I will pray that God in his mercy will let
me live through all this so I can come home.*

    *I don't want to let the wrong wind out of the bag and I'll explain
that when I have time, but in the meantime will you pray for me too?
You know, I've never even asked where you stand with God, but I know
you love me and I can use all the help I can get out here. We're leaving
tomorrow and when I get where we are going, I'll let you know. In the
meantime, I love you and more than anything, I want to come home.*

                                            Johnny

    On January 31, 1943, the Marines of the Second Division,
Second Regiment, King Company, X-Ray Platoon, Achilles squad
boarded the transports that would take them away from the
living hell that had been Guadalcanal. Lieutenant Crandall
passed the word to his boys that their whole Division was up for a
Unit Citation.

Johnny Strange watched as his friends boarded the boats. He thought about the last months and he knew he had changed. They all had. Billy Martens was limping, but his feet were better since Bud had given him a real dog show and straightened his rotten feet out. But Billy was different inside, a lot more withdrawn. He had given Johnny an earful when Johnny tried to set him up with a chaplain.

"I'm okay, Johnny. I need to get out in the woods and shoot something that's not yellow."

Bud was quieter, calmer, his smartness turning into wisdom, but he could still flap his gums if you encouraged him. The rest of the squad was beat, dog-tired, skinny, and wasted. Relief had come just in time. Johnny picked up his rifle and his sea bag and climbed aboard the Higgins that was running them out to the transport. He thought of the boys they were leaving behind, and the guys that were lucky enough, or blessed enough, to be climbing up the net to the deck of the transport ship.

———

No one will ever know what we went through on Guadalcanal, and most of them won't care. But we know, and we care, and we will always remember. Maybe we'll walk into a bar somewhere after this and see one of these guys sitting alone having a beer. We'll walk up, sit down, order a Pabst and just say "Semper Fi, Mac." And that will be enough.

35

ROCK OF AGES

BILLY MARTENS

S everal days before they were set to debark from the Canal
and head out, Billy woke up and realized he didn't want to
take a Higgins boat off the island. He'd been dreaming about the
dead and was unhappy about leaving them behind. It wasn't
right. They should bring the bodies with them.

"Do the KIAs stay here?" he asked Johnny, who was trying to
shave, had nicked himself several times, and was in no mood.

"What?" Johnny snapped back. "Why the hell are you asking
me a dumb question like that?"

"I want to know."

"Buddy, last I heard, we had, I don't know, 5000 or 6000 KIAs
and war dead, and some are at the bottom of the sea. No, they're
not coming with us. This is the end of the line for them. Requi-
escat in pace. Rest in Peace. RIP. Coconut fronds. Ocean breezes.
Tropical sunsets. No Japs. Could be a lot worse. Could be a frozen
chunk of sod in Minnesota or North Dakota."

"It's not right."

"We can't cart 'em all back with us. Think about it, Sniper.
Half of them have rotted away by now. Others were blown to

pieces or cut in two. Hell, we never found McKeever's head, did we? They lived here, they fought here, they died here. With honor. Okay? So, they belong here."

"They belong with us."

"How many wars since Adam and Eve, Mister Mennonite? A million? Two million? Do you think all the bodies came home? Do you think all the dogfaces who died in North Africa last fall got their remains shipped back to mom and dad? We fought over this rock, Billy. It cost us. Our dead bled into this ground. That was the sacrifice. Let them stay with what they gave their lives for. This hallowed ground. Right? They made it holy. Let them stay like the dead stayed at Gettysburg."

Johnny made sense, but not sense enough. It still didn't sit well with Billy. The dead were talking to him. Awake and asleep. He didn't think it was crazy. He didn't think there was anything wrong with him. All men and women had souls. After they died, they were spirits. Released from the flesh. On their way back to God. Maybe they didn't want their bones left on some godforsaken island battlefield till the world ended. Joseph in the Bible didn't want his bones left behind either. His family carried the bones out of Egypt and buried them in Shechem in the Holy Land. Joseph had them promise they'd to do that, and it made perfect sense to the children of Israel.

When Billy lost one of his dogs on a hunt, his grandfather was going to bury Peak at the base of a pine. Billy wouldn't let him. He was only 14, but he packed his German Shepherd out on his back with all his camping gear and ammo. His grandfather saw the tears in Billy's eyes and the determination in his face and let him be. Billy couldn't stand the thought of his dog alone and cold on some faraway mountain the rest of Billy's life. Now he couldn't stand the thought of all these Americans alone and uncared for on an island far away from their loved ones. Who would tend their plots and crosses? Pray over them? Bring flowers? He said nothing to Johnny or anyone else because he knew they'd think he was nuts. He wasn't nuts. Human bones shouldn't just be left anywhere. They were sacred.

Of course, there was no plan he could come up with that put thousands of bodies on the ships. And he didn't know what the Japanese did with their KIAs or the ones who died of wounds or disease. He'd found bodies in the jungle, even skeletons in tattered Japanese uniforms, but never any graves. Did the Japanese ship out the dead when they shipped out the living?

These things walked through his daydreams and through his last nights on the island. He saw faces, and he saw lips moving. Not just Americans, not just Kramer or Malena or McKeever— the Jap he'd killed at the listening post, the one he'd plunged a knife into, wanting to spare him a prolonged death—he spoke with Billy too and there was no anger or rancor. A sniper he'd shot spent an hour with him as well, offering him a cup of warm *saki* while they worked things through. Billy smoked cigarettes with them and made his way down the chow line with them, all of them, Marines and Japanese both. But he couldn't answer their questions the way they wanted them answered, and he couldn't save their souls the way they wanted them saved.

There was a farewell service for the Marine dead. They placed coconut fronds over their graves. The chaplains spoke. A bugler played taps. It refused to rain when Billy thought it should rain. He prayed to God that thick clouds would cover the brightness of the sun and then that night, shroud the shine of the Southern Cross. His prayers were refused, just like the rain.

The bugler at the cemetery had been Big Band Nick, one of their rookies who had made it through and would ship back out with them. Later in the week, Nick was playing *In the Mood* with a couple of other musicians. They put on something of a concert that lasted over an hour. Marines crowded around. Billy drifted past, returned, listened a while to songs he'd never heard before,

then moved on again. Ty Jackson, the Protestant chaplain, was
holding a hymn sing not far off and Billy wound up there.

The men's loud voices drowned out any sound of trumpets
and trombones. But once more, Billy was listening to songs he'd
never heard. These were hymns his Mennonite church had never
sung. There were a few song sheets lying on the sand and he
picked one up, studying the words. One hymn struck home and
then suddenly the Marines sitting around him, men tough as
nails who had survived the worst the Empire of Japan could
throw at them, were bellowing it out as if they were at a church
service back in the States.

Rock of Ages, cleft for me
Let me hide myself in Thee
Let the water and the blood
From Thy riven side which flowed
Be of sin the double cure
Cleanse me from its guilt and power

Not the labor of my hands
Can fulfill Thy law's demands
Could my zeal no respite know
Could my tears forever flow
All for sin could not atone
Thou must save, and Thou alone

Nothing in my hand I bring
Simply to Thy cross I cling
Naked, come to Thee for dress
Helpless, look to Thee for grace
Foul, I to the fountain fly

Wash me, Savior, or I die

While I draw this fleeting breath
When mine eyes shall close in death
When I soar to worlds unknown
See Thee on Thy judgment throne

Rock of Ages, cleft for me
Let me hide myself in Thee

I WISH I COULD HIDE MYSELF SOMEWHERE, BILLY THOUGHT. *JUST LIKE* *this hymn says. If I could hide away in God for a few months, wouldn't that be something? Hey, for a few years. If God was that kind of God: A God who protected and defended and saved instead of one who judged and condemned and punished.*

If he looked at a girl twice, he was wrong. If he worked cattle, or split wood, or hunted, or fished on a Sunday, he was wrong. If he didn't fancy up for church, he was wrong. If he fought for his country, he was wrong. He was always wrong when it came to God. But if only this hymn was right. If only.

Billy folded the song sheet in half, and then in half again, and tucked it in his shirt pocket. The Marines were singing the last stanza like a burst of thunder. He took in the tune. Hummed it under his breath. Was sure he had it.

He stayed until the entire hymn sing was over. He heard all kinds of songs he liked. But none as much as *Rock of Ages*. The chaplain approached him, but Billy moved off, Model 1903 on his back, Thompson in his hands, helmet still on his head, even though most of the men were going around bareheaded. He didn't know where he was heading, he just knew he didn't want to talk, and he sure didn't want a sermon, not even a prayer. A rock to hide behind and save whatever was left of his soul? Yes.

His feet and head took him to the cemetery again. A few men

were walking between the rows of crosses and coconut fronds. Billy just stood back and let his eyes run over the names painted on the pieces of wood. He always found the names he knew, almost without trying: Hotchkiss, Malena, Sharples, McKeever, Kramer. And, as always, he didn't know what to say to them. Except that now he knew he couldn't bring them with him, even though he wanted to do that more than anything else in the world.

"There's nothing else I can do but leave," he whispered. "If they had killed me I could stay. Then there'd be no regrets."

Naked, come to Thee for dress
Helpless, look to Thee for grace

He saluted.
And walked away with his head down.
He did not return to the cemetery.

THE 2ND DIVISION DEBARKED ON SUNDAY JANUARY 31ST. A HIGGINS boat took all of those in X-Ray platoon who were still walking. No one looked back. Not even Billy. Everyone was staring at the big ships that would take them far away. Scuttlebutt had the Marines convinced it would be New Zealand or Australia. Billy stared at the water churning on the starboard side of the landing craft. No one had been shooting at them when they arrived at Guadalcanal. No one was shooting when they left.

It's a peaceful war now. It's always a peaceful war when the dead can't speak.

The war dead did not climb on board the ship with him. They did not sail when the ship sailed. Billy did not see them again. And for a long time, he forgot them just as if he had never dreamed and they had never been. The sky was a royal blue. The sea indigo. All the 2nd Division Marines remained on board a long time.

He attended every church parade they rigged on the fore-deck—Jewish, Catholic, Protestant. Heard *Rock of Ages* again. A few times he wondered what his father would preach if he were on the transport ship and talking to the Marines. Billy dismissed those thoughts. His father would hate what the Marines had done and what they would do next. He would be incapable of bringing any of the men comfort. He would not offer them a rock to protect their souls. He would just attack and harangue them.

Strangely enough, it was in that frame of mind that Billy wrote his first letter home to his father. He doubted the rough-edged Mennonite preacher-rancher would even open the envelope, let alone read it. But Billy felt compelled to write. At first, he was sure he was writing to justify his actions, to explain again why he had put on a uniform, why he had just walked through green jungles of hellfire for six months, lucky and blessed to emerge alive under a shining South Pacific sky. But that's not what came out of the pencil and his heart and ended up on the sheet of paper.

DAD

It is good to see the sun again. It's not as if there hasn't been one in the sky. But I sort of missed really seeing it for the past half-year.

I missed all of you too. Missed the meals and the laughter at the big oak table. Missed the kids. The horses, especially Buckeye. The fall roundup. Breathing in the bite of autumn leaves and wood smoke and the sting of the frost. The first fall of snow. The mountains in white. Elk tracks on the slopes. The storms when we made sure we were out every hour to uncover and spread the hay for the cows. Then indoors with the fire and lanterns and the crokinole board and the discs flying and the window panes steaming over with the heat, you happy and making huge pots of popcorn, always burning half of them, because that was the way I liked them.

We are so far apart in so many ways, Dad.

But there is one thing that is true.

I miss everyone and everything else in Montana.

But most of all I miss you.

Love, Your son, Billy

36

I AM BECOME A NAME

THE CORPSMAN

I don't think I realized what a big deal Guadalcanal had become back home until I had a chance to snag newspapers off the swabbies, papers that had come from New York, and Boston, and LA, and Seattle.

First of all, a war correspondent had written a book about the fighting called *Guadalcanal Diary*. It had come out on January 1st and was a bestseller. I saw a few copies floating around the ranks, but never got my mitts on one until we got off the ship. Hollywood had bought the movie rights for the book too.

Then there were all the newspaper columns and accolades and grainy photographs combat journalists had taken during the battles. Tributes were pouring in for the Corps. For once, most of the news wasn't about the war with Hitler. I saw a list of Medal of Honor winners and ones for the Navy Cross, Distinguished Service Cross and the Silver Star. I was sure I'd see Billy's name for his heroism in taking out those Jap machine guns nests on the Matanikau and saving the platoon, but he wasn't mentioned anywhere, not even for a Bronze Star.

And the news came in, scuttlebutt at first, but later on confirmed, that all the fighting on the Canal had ended and the last Japanese troops had been evacuated by the Jap Navy. The show was over. We'd only been at sea ten days when this came through. The chaplains held special services of thanksgiving that were well attended. I missed all of them because I was below decks helping to care for the wounded and our many cases of malaria, some of them severe.

My last hours on the island had been crazy. I had dozens of body snatchers running between the hospital and the Higgins boats, making sure all our 2nd Div boys ended up with us. Most of them anyways. Some couldn't be moved. And a lot of them would go stateside. They had their million-dollar wounds that meant a ticket home. Though, to tell the truth, about half of them wanted to stay with their buddies and see the war through.

The boys had always been glad to capture Jap stores and snag tins of crabmeat and squid and tuna and sacks of rice—not to mention bottles of *saki*—but nothing made me happier than lucking onto crates of quinine. It was so much better than Atabrine, and it didn't turn anyone yellow or nuts in the head. Johnny had led a patrol, his last one, that found a cave our guys had missed that was stacked with Jap cigarettes, canned fish, unprimed T99 grenades and quinine. They hoed into the fish, hated the tobacco, and ignored the grenades and medicine. Once I found out, I went back with another patrol to carry back all the boxes of quinine we could put our hands on. Some we left with the Army. The rest wound up on our transports. It helped. Thank you, Tokyo.

It was a long voyage, and eventually I had time to sit back and wonder how I'd made it out alive when gunfire and bombs and fury had been all around me. I wrote another letter to Kalasia, the most beautiful woman in the South Pacific, and wondered out loud to her too, scribbling my almost indecipherable words across thin sheets of paper. *They fell all around me, yet here I am. How does this happen? Is it prayer?*

But I tried not to write her that much. It was just too hard to think about her. It hurt to remember how far away she was and that the chances of my getting to Tonga again before the end of the war—which I was convinced would be years, not months— were zero times zero. Most of the time, I doubted we'd ever meet up. In my worst moods, I had her with another man she was not telling me about—I mean, how could she not be? A woman like her could be a star in Hollywood, and definitely a GI or Marine pinup, as well as nose art on a B17 Flying Fortress—*Lucky Lady*.

In my better moods, gazing up at the Southern Cross while I lay on my back on the foredeck, I saw us married and living back in the States, a passel of children on our knees, owning a house by the ocean. We had lots of trees and a big garden. Took up a whole pew in church on Sunday mornings. Went to the movies and ate popcorn and drank Pepsi-Cola. There were even grand-children in the daydreams.

I'd try to turn my mind off though. Kalasia was another life-time. Someone that existed before Guadalcanal. Before all the bloodshed and shattered bodies. Before I ever stuck a syrette of morphine into anyone, or dumped sulfa powder on their ugly wounds, or closed their eyes when I could not save them. Who was I now? I sure wasn't Bud from Tonga or even Bud from the USA. I couldn't be that guy anymore and I couldn't go back. I doubted she'd like who I'd turned into.

No, I hadn't killed. Or had any deSire to kill. But I was harder. It took a lot to make me flinch. I moved from body to body like a machine, not a man. I was used to blood. To screams. To eyes pleading with me, eyes I could not help. A lot of the time I felt nothing. Really, I couldn't let myself feel too much or I wouldn't be able to do my job. Kalasia would not want to be with some guy as cold-hearted as Bela Lugosi in *Dracula*. An hour with the corpsman and she'd gently pry herself free of my arms, thank me for the Pepsi-Cola and disappear into the tropical night for good.

Who was I kidding? She was class. Exotic. Paradise. And I was a poor Mennonite boy from Ritzville, Washington. I'd had my one lucky moment. Now the war had swallowed me up. What she'd liked, what had attracted her, was gone. The best parts of life were always too good to be true, weren't they? And there were never any second chances.

THE SHIP EXPLODED WITH EXCITEMENT WHEN WE SPOTTED LAND near the end of February. There it was, blue and purple on the horizon, too small to be Australia, everyone knew that much. We sailed around the whole thing before we realized there were two islands, so close, Crandall declared that *it looked as if they were kissing.* The word went through the Marines like wildfire—*New Zealand. We're docking at New Zealand. And not just for one or two nights either.* No one knew a thing about New Zealand, but the men were overjoyed. Bars, movies, dates with women, classy restaurants, *terra firma* where no one was shooting at you. Big Band Nick played a few licks from *In the Mood* on his trumpet and the Marines and swabbies laughed and applauded.

We saw the entire place from out at sea. Billy popped up at my elbow as I leaned against the taffrail, muscling others aside so that he could squeeze in.

"Whaddya think, Bud?" he asked me.

"Looks like the real McCoy, Billy. Another slice of paradise like Tonga."

He pointed. "Mountain peaks? Or is that this morning's apple juice at work?"

I laughed. "It was a little fermented, wasn't it? But no, corporal, those are mountains, for sure. Beautiful."

"There's no snow on them. Back home, there's plenty of snow on the peaks in February and March, even in April or May and sometimes June."

"Well, we're kinda upside down this far south. Their winter starts when we have summer up north. One of the docs told me they can get snow in June. So right now, it's like late summer or early fall."

"You're kidding."

"I'm not."

"Did the sawbones know anything about hunting?"

"I didn't ask. But I guess you'll find out soon enough. You can ask the locals as soon as you get your first pass."

"Wouldn't that be something? To get into real mountains again and suck that good air into my heart and gut. Track a deer. Light a fire on top of some crag."

It was good to see a bunch of life flowing back into Billy's face again. I'd been praying for him. He'd been a mess since the fighting for 2nd Div ended. Like a ghost drifting around camp. I hoped God and the brass would keep us in New Zealand for a while, at least two or three months, and give everyone a chance to feel like a human being once again. Not just Billy. Everyone. Crandall, Navarro, Hernandez, Zarate, Red O'Brien, Leon Levy, Garowski, Stoneroad and Skillet, Over Easy Mitton, Captain America and Batman, the whole crew. And Johnny. I needed him to stop with his Boris Karloff *Bride of Frankenstein* moments and just be a regular Marine, a regular American kid fighting for his country. Sure, he was a mixed-up Mennonite like Billy, but he didn't have to stay in his monster act. Maybe he could just be a man. Maybe he could just be a patriot.

As I was thinking about him, he shoved in next to Billy and offered him a Camel. They were both grinning, and I suddenly realized Johnny had popped some freckles right across the bridge of his nose. I laughed too. So now he was the All-American Boy, a defensive end right out of *Knute Rockne, All American*. "Hey, Johnny, win one for the Gipper." I put a stick of gum I'd been saving into my mouth. The transport was heading towards shore, and I could see a city nestled by the ocean. Rudebaker announced that it was Wellington and high time for all of us to get squared away. There was a scramble below decks as Marines got their packs together and straightened out their uniforms.

"I want you looking like parade-ground Marines!" Crandall bellowed. "Put on a show for the Kiwis! Make the ladies look twice! That's an order!"

A long voyage, a new shore, no Higgins boats, marching down a gangway shoulder-to-shoulder, rank after rank, everyone turned out as smart as they could make it, the streets lined with New Zealanders along our route to the railway station, men and women and children waving and cheering and clapping, block after city block of smiles—all we needed was ticker-tape floating over us like snow to complete the picture.

"You'd think we won the war," mumbled Johnny, marching perfectly in step at my side.

"We kinda did, Johnny," I said. "The Japs had plans for Henderson and bombing the life out of Australia and New Zealand. They had invasion on their minds. Now they've had to take one giant step backwards and people here can breathe easier. All because we captured Guadalcanal. So yeah, it's a big deal. It's okay to let it be a big deal, you know. We're heroes for now. Enjoy it, Marine."

"If you say so, Bud."

"You haven't had much of a chance to bask in the limelight during your eighteen years, Johnny. So, let it sink in."

"The fighting's not over. You know that, Bud."

"It is today. It is tomorrow. That's good enough for now."

The train would take us to our camp and to our barracks. We wouldn't be going anywhere that month, the month after that, or even the month after that. This was going to be a second home for a while. A long while. And that felt right to me. More than right. It felt holy.

Every smile, every cheer, every shout of thanks, made me feel like a new man, like someone who could take Kalasia in his arms again and tell her that he loved her, someone she could recognize, someone she would know was the man she had fallen for in Tonga. That if I'd changed, I hadn't changed beyond all recognition or possibility of redemption. I marched a little faster, drank in the good will a little more deeply, let the happy cries fall on my ears as if they were the thousands of drops of a sun shower.

> *I am become a name;*
> *For always roaming with a hungry heart*
> *Much have I seen and known; cities of men*
> *And manners, climates, councils, governments,*
> *Myself not least, but honor'd of them all;*
> *And drunk delight of battle with my peers,*
> *Far on the ringing plains of windy Troy.*
> *I am a part of all that I have met.*

"I am a part of all that I have met," I repeated. "Both the living and the dead."

AND IT WAS GOOD TO STILL BE AMONG THE LIVING.

ABOUT THE AUTHOR

Murray Andrew Pura was born in Winnipeg, Manitoba, Canada. He has twenty-five books published, was a contributor to the *Life With God Bible*, has been a finalist for The Paraclete Fiction Award, The Dartmouth Book Award, and The John Spencer Hill Literary Award, and has been shortlisted for the prestigious 2010 Kobzar Literary Award of Canada.

ABOUT THE AUTHOR

Patrick E. Craig is a lifelong writer and musician. After retiring
from the ministry in 2007 he concentrated on writing and
publishing fiction books. He has published six Amish novels, two
YA mystery books, one World War II historical novel and is about
to publish an Anthology of Amish stories. He lives in Idaho with
his wife Judy.

www.ingramcontent.com/pod-product-compliance
Lightning Source LLC
Chambersburg PA
CBHW071154100726
47908CB00002B/377